Pressed agai...
listened to Gerard's ...

The steady thump pounded louder, faster, and a low groan sounded deep in his throat. She smiled at how easily his body responded to her nearness.

Men thought themselves superior to women. Yet in the bedchamber, if a woman was of a mind, she could reduce a haughty baron to a mere male with the paltry weapon of a rightly placed hip.

Ardith was of a mind.

She looked up into Gerard's face, a smile threatening the corners of her mouth. "Mayhap women *should* be warriors."

Confusion showed in his eyes. "Ardith, are you feverish?"

Ardith had never learned women's wiles, didn't know if she could seduce. If she had any talent at all, now was the time to find out. She lowered her voice and half closed her eyes. "Aye, Gerard. I burn. Come ease my torment."

His reaction was *most* gratifying....

Dear Reader,

Author Shari Anton was first introduced during our 1997 March Madness promotion of new authors with her Civil War period romance, *Emily's Captain*. With this month's *By King's Decree*, Ms. Anton has turned her considerable talents toward the telling of a stirring medieval tale in which a Saxon woman must overcome corruption, jealousy and the shadow of barrenness, or be separated forever from the knight who holds her heart.

Devlin, by author Erin Yorke, is the story of an Irish rebel and an Englishwoman, who must battle distrust and betrayal before finding the happiness they both deserve. And Deborah Simmons returns this month with *The de Burgh Bride*, the sequel to her steamy adventure *Taming the Wolf.* This book features the scholarly de Burgh brother, Geoffrey, who has drawn the short straw and must marry the "wicked" daughter of a vanquished enemy, a woman who reportedly murdered her first husband in the marriage bed!

A city banker forced to spend a year recuperating in the country goes head-to-head with a practical country widow and learns that some of life's greatest pleasures are the simple ones in the next book in Theresa Michaels's new series, *The Merry Widows—Catherine*.

Whatever your tastes in reading, we hope you enjoy all four books this month. Keep an eye out for them, wherever Harlequin Historicals® are sold.

Sincerely,

Tracy Farrell
Senior Editor

BY KING'S DECREE

SHARI ANTON

Harlequin Books

TORONTO • NEW YORK • LONDON
AMSTERDAM • PARIS • SYDNEY • HAMBURG
STOCKHOLM • ATHENS • TOKYO • MILAN
MADRID • WARSAW • BUDAPEST • AUCKLAND

ISBN 0-373-29001-2

BY KING'S DECREE

Printed in U.S.A.

Books by Shari Anton

Harlequin Historicals

Emily's Captain #357
By King's Decree #401

SHARI ANTON

prefers to spend her free time at Civil War encampments, medieval fairs or pioneer cemeteries rather than doing housework. Her husband doesn't mind tagging along to any historical site she wants to visit—if they can take the Harleys to get there! She is also a member of RWA and Wisconsin Romance Writers of America (WisRWA).

The mother of two grown children and one grandchild, Shari lives in southeastern Wisconsin with her husband and a very spoiled golden retriever.

Shari would love to hear from you. You can write to her at: P.O. Box 510611, New Berlin, WI 53151-0611.

To my parents
Richard & Ramona Foley
Love ya!!

Prologue

England, 1101

'Tis not fair! Ardith pouted to herself, for there was no one else in the room to hear her complaint.

From her pallet in the sleeping chamber, she could hear the sounds of a feast coming from the common room, where her family and their guests celebrated the heroism of Corwin, Ardith's twelve-year-old twin brother. She didn't begrudge Corwin the tribute. After all, Corwin had saved her life.

For the past week she'd suffered the pain of her wound, lain on her pallet and sipped potions of mead and herbs. She longed for a meal of substance, craving a slice of the boar that had gored her before perishing under Corwin's sword.

Crossing an arm over the bandage wrapped around her middle, she ignored the pain of rising to her feet. She shuffled across the chamber to fetch a woolen mantle to cover her night rail. Thus clad she couldn't join the feast, but if she held to the shadows she might secretly hail Corwin to fetch her a piece of that beast.

Ardith stepped lightly over the earthen floor strewed with rushes, passed by the black-iron candle stand until she stood under the arch separating the two rooms of the manor. She hugged the timber wall as she crept between the arch and the tapestry that hung in the corner of the common room.

Safely in her hiding place, she peeked around the dusty tapestry, pinching her nose so she wouldn't sneeze. Serving wenches were clearing away the used bread trenchers. Soon they would remove the remains of the boar.

At the raised dais beyond the central fire pit, her father, Harold, lord of Lenvil, rose from his stool to signal the end of the feast. Beside Father stood Baron Everart, Lenvil's Norman liege lord, resplendent in robes of black wool trimmed with glittering gems. A pace apart from the baron stood a black-haired boy, similarly attired. Since the boy seemed near her own age, Ardith assumed he must be Stephen, the baron's younger son. She knew that somewhere in the crowd was the elder son, Gerard, Baron Everart's heir.

She supposed she owed the baron a word of thanks. If he hadn't shown favor to Corwin, and allowed her brother to spend most of the summer at Wilmont, where he'd learned to use a sword with skill, both she and Corwin might be dead now.

Two wenches reached for the meat platter. Ardith glanced about for Corwin, but she didn't see her brother. Intent on silently hailing the serving girls, Ardith took a step. But before she could sneak from behind the tapestry, she heard male voices that became louder as the men approached her hiding place. She scrunched down into the corner, hoping they would pass by quickly.

"I spoke with King William," Baron Everart said. "He questioned my decision but approved."

"You humble me with your offer, Baron," her father replied. "You could do better for your son than the fifth daughter of a Saxon vassal."

"So thought the king, but Ardith is my choice. What say you to a betrothal bargain, Harold?"

Father sighed. "I regret, my lord, that I must refuse. The chit has done herself an injury and is...damaged."

As the men passed out of hearing, Ardith shook with the realization that Baron Everart had offered a betrothal between herself and one of his sons. And Father refused!

Done myself an injury? Damaged?

She lightly touched her sore midsection. She would forever wear a scar across her belly. Did a scar make her damaged, lessen her value in marriage?

Suddenly, candle glow flooded the corner. A male hand had pushed aside the tapestry.

"And who have we here?" came a mellow voice, the English words laced with the fluid accent of Norman French.

Ardith looked up into green eyes, as green and bright as spring leaves. No longer a boy, but not quite a man, the Norman noble was strikingly handsome. His hair, in flaxen waves, hung to his shoulders in Saxon fashion, banded by a circlet of gold.

He stood tall and slender, his form adorned by a white linen sherte covered by a calf-length dalmatica of deep blue. Bands of vine-patterned red and gold embroidery trimmed the tuniclike garment's neckline and sleeves. A girdle of woven gold circled his trim waist.

Kind, she read his expression, and prayed her judgment sound. Norman nobles were often cruel to Saxon underlings—or so Elva, her father's sister, professed. This Norman must be Gerard, the heir to Wilmont.

"My lord," she said. Clutching night rail and mantle, she gingerly rose and attempted a curtsy. Dizziness assailed her as she bowed her head. Gerard's strong hands gripped her arms and saved her from falling.

He looked her over, from head to toe, and back again. His inspection ended at her face. He stared into her eyes.

"You must be Ardith, Corwin's twin. Your eyes are the same startling blue." He frowned. "I was told you were sore wounded and confined to your pallet. Why do you lurk behind the tapestry?''

Embarrassment crept on to her cheeks as she realized the foolishness of her actions. Father would be furious if he heard of the incident. Punishment would be swift and severe.

She tried to push away. Gerard's fingers tightened.

Holding back tears of frustration, she said, ''I wanted a hearty slice of that wretched boar.''

His expression softened. A smile played at the corner of his mouth. ''The boar that wounded you?'' he asked. At her nod, he said, ''I will order it so. Now come, back to your pallet with you.''

Deftly swept from her feet, firmly cradled in Gerard's arms, Ardith protested, ''I can walk, my lord.''

''Mayhap, my little lady, but you will not. Your strength begins to desert you.''

As he strode toward the sleeping chamber, Ardith couldn't help wonder if Gerard might, one day, have been her husband. He was so strong, so handsome, and the heir to a title—the fulfillment of every maiden's dreams. For which son had the baron asked for the betrothal bargain, Gerard or Stephen? Not that it mattered, now. Father considered her damaged somehow, unfit for either Norman lordling.

''Ardith, you little scamp! What have you been up to?'' Elva scolded, following them into the chamber. Hands on ample hips, Elva looked ready for battle. Unable to abide another humiliation, Ardith buried her face in Gerard's shoulder, praying that Elva would refrain from further scolding until Gerard left the chamber.

''Who is the Harpy?'' Gerard asked softly as he lowered her slowly, gently, onto her pallet.

''Elva, my father's sister.''

''And are you a scamp?''

Chagrined, she admitted, ''So I am told.''

He winked and flashed a beguiling smile at her before leaving the chamber, ignoring the glare Elva aimed at him.

After he was gone, Ardith asked, "Elva, did you know Father thought to wed me to one of the baron's sons?"

Elva spit out the word, "Aye. Harold thought to give you to the young lion. The Normans of Wilmont are vicious beasts, every one. Rejoice that you are spared the ordeal."

To the young lion.

To Gerard, Ardith realized, and her heart twisted at the loss. Gerard bore the coloring of a proud, regal lion, all tawny-gold hair and glittering green eyes. But she couldn't envision him as a vicious beast.

Gerard had such a nice smile.

Ardith rolled to her side and let the tears flow.

'Tis not fair!

Chapter One

Wilmont, 1106

Gerard rushed over the ice-crusted mud of the bailey surrounding the keep. An early-winter wind whipped at his cloak. The overcast sky suited his mood.

This morning's charade had been his idea. Having planned every detail of the mock funeral, Gerard hadn't expected his gullet to rebel as the empty coffin descended into the earth. Nor would his disquiet ease until he talked with his half brother, Richard, who could too easily lie within that coffin.

Leaping two steps at a time, Gerard climbed the outside stairs leading to the keep's second floor. He pushed open the heavy oak door and stepped into the great hall.

He merely glanced at the familiar tapestries hanging beside ancient weapons, hardly noticed the decorative marble carvings hewn into walls of expensive stone. Nor did he acknowledge the peasant women who scurried to prepare the feast he'd ordered to be served after the burial Mass.

The heavy door banged shut. Gerard glanced over his shoulder at Thomas, a young but trusted servant, one of the few people who knew of the ruse necessary to hide and protect Richard. Gerard shrugged out of his beaver cloak and tossed it toward Thomas.

"I will be with the monk. Bring ale," Gerard ordered, then bounded up the stairway leading to the family quarters.

At the end of the passageway he rapped twice on a door, paused, then rapped twice again. As expected, Corwin opened the door. Smiling ruefully, Corwin executed an exaggerated bow, saying, "At last, reinforcements. Do come in, my lord."

"Is Richard not behaving?" Gerard asked.

Corwin closed the door and slid the bolt. "As well as one could expect on the day of his own burial, I suppose."

"In a sullen mood, is he?"

"Peevish, my lord."

"Richard feels more himself, then."

"Aye," Corwin answered on a sigh.

From the bed, Richard grumbled, "You speak as though I am not in the room. Why not ask *me* how I feel?"

Gerard locked his arms behind his back and sauntered to the bedside. He looked into Richard's scowling face, a face so near a reflection of his own. The resemblance was striking, though they'd been born of different mothers—one a noble bride, one a peasant lover. Though Gerard claimed the advantage of height, when mounted and armored in chain mail and helm, he and Richard were nigh impossible to tell apart.

Because of the resemblance, Richard had almost died—the victim of an ambush meant to either kill or take as prisoner Gerard, the new baron of Wilmont. Basil of Northbryre and his mercenaries would soon pay dearly for their audacity.

"In this, Richard, your word is not reliable," Gerard finally responded. "You would have me believe you are ready for the practice yard."

"Mayhap not the practice yard, but able to get out of bed. Did you know that Corwin would not let me out of the chamber to use the garderobe, made me use a piss pot?''

"At my order."

"Did I not survive crossing the Channel?"

Confined to a pallet below decks, Richard had barely survived the boat trip home from Normandy, even though under the care of one of King Henry's physicians.

"You slept the whole time," Gerard countered.

"And I survived the wagon ride from Dover to Wilmont."

"By a gnat's breath."

"Surely I can survive a walk beyond this chamber."

Gerard crossed his arms and stated firmly, "Basil is sure to have a spy or two sniffing about. After all I've done to convince half the kingdom you are dead, you will not expose the ruse by roaming the keep!"

Corwin answered a signal tap on the door. Thomas entered with the ale. The beverage poured and served, Gerard dismissed Corwin and Thomas, bolting the door behind them.

Gerard lowered his relaxing body onto a chair. He stretched his legs toward the heat from the brazier, swirling the ale in his goblet.

"My burial went well?" Richard asked sarcastically.

"Father Dominic gave an impassioned plea for God's mercy on your soul. Stephen praised your bravery and loyalty to Wilmont. Half the wenches in the castle are overcome with grief. I would say you are well mourned."

A small smile graced Richard's face. "The wenches may cry for me, but they would wail for you."

Gerard raised an eyebrow. "Can they tell us apart in the dark, do you think?"

"One wonders. Since I am confined to bed anyway, mayhap I will call for one or two and find out."

Gerard wagged a warning finger. "You are in hiding and supposed to be an ailing monk. Call for a wench and I will confine you to this chamber for the entire winter!"

Richard squirmed at the notion, then said, "You cannot. You will need me at court. When do we leave?"

"You remain here until I send for you. Probably just before Christmas. Corwin and I leave in two days. He wishes to visit Lenvil before going on to Westminster."

Richard moaned. "You would leave me here with Stephen as my nursemaid. Have pity, Gerard. I will never be allowed out of this bed."

"Stephen will let you up when Father Dominic says you are healed, not before then."

Richard raised an eyebrow in surprise. "Father Dominic? You told him?"

"I thought telling the priest prudent, just in case."

"I will not need the final sacrament," Richard insisted. "Who all knows I still live?"

"Stephen, Thomas, Corwin, King Henry and his physicians." Gerard sighed. "I also found it necessary to inform Lady Ursula. I had hoped to avoid involving my mother, but she would plague Stephen with questions about the strange monk in a family bedchamber."

"I imagine my lying in this chamber instead of in that coffin, underground, vexes Lady Ursula to no end."

"No doubt, but she will not interfere with your care. Stephen will see to that."

"Your mother will prick him at every turn for his loyalty, try to turn him against you."

"He will hold fast. Sparring with Ursula will make a man of him, may even earn Stephen his knighthood." The brothers chuckled, then Gerard sobered. "You have certainly earned *your* knighthood, Richard. We will see to the formalities at court."

Gerard rose from his chair and headed for the door.

"Do you trust King Henry's promise?" Richard asked.

Gerard's hand gripped the bolt. "When Henry refused my demand for armed reprisal against Basil, he promised royal justice. I had no choice, at the time, but to obey."

"And if we do not get justice?"

Gerard flashed a feral smile. "Then heal well, Richard. I will need your sword arm when I seek revenge."

Richard returned the smile. "The mercenary captain, Edward Siefeld, is mine."

"As Basil of Northbryre is mine."

Sprawled across the bed on his stomach, an arm dangling over the edge, Gerard slowly opened one eye. The light hurt, piercing into a head too heavy to lift from the bolster.

"My lord," Thomas said softly, though urgently.

"By your life, lad, you best have good reason for waking me so early."

"I let you sleep as long as I dared, my lord. The household awaits you in the chapel. Father Dominic cannot begin Mass until you arrive."

Reluctantly, Gerard rolled over. Pieces of last night's drinking bout floated through his groggy memory. He'd tried to relieve his frustration with ale. A futile attempt.

He tossed back the furs and threw his legs over the edge of the bed. His head swam. Gerard drew deep breaths and compelled his body to function. Muscles rippled to his command as he stood, his warrior's body unaffected by the muddle in his head.

With a slight nod he approved the garments Thomas placed on the bed. Gerard donned the white soft-woolen sherte and the dalmatica of scarlet silk shot through with gold thread. He wrapped a girdle of gold around his waist. He would gladly have shunned the elegant clothing for less pretentious garb. But today, he must appear and act the baron.

He wasn't surprised that Lady Ursula stood at the front of the chapel, awaiting his arrival with tight-lipped censure. Within moments of the Mass's start, Gerard stifled a yawn. His mother glared. Stephen and Corwin exchanged knowing smiles. Father Dominic understood the suggestion and sped through the service.

After breaking fast on porridge and bread, Gerard ordered Lady Ursula and Walter, Wilmont's steward, to attend him in his chambers.

"As you can see, Baron Gerard, Wilmont fares well," Walter said, waving a hand at the scroll on the table in Gerard's bedchamber.

Gerard inspected the records of fees and goods due to Wilmont. Not for the first time, he was grateful for his father's unusual decision to educate his sons. Never would Gerard be at the mercy of clergy or steward to read messages or records, unlike most of his Norman peers.

He pointed to an empty space in the accounting and asked Walter, "What of these rents?"

"The coinage from Milhurst is overdue. Unfortunately, your father succumbed to the fever before he could visit Milhurst to collect."

Gerard's temper flashed. Basil of Northbryre, Gerard would wager, had somehow interfered with the delivery of Milhurst's rents—an easy task since Milhurst bordered Northbryre. He added the suspected crime to the list of grievances he would present to King Henry against Basil.

"Are other monies or goods overdue?"

Walter's bony finger pointed to another blank space on the parchment. "Aye, my lord, from this manor near Romsey, also in Hampshire. We are owed six sheep on the hoof every winter as tribute. The steward might yet bring them, though he is very late this year."

"Will you go to Hampshire to collect the tributes?" Lady Ursula interrupted.

The hope in her voice turned Gerard's head. Though almost forty, his mother had aged well. She studied him with eyes of silver gray, unfaded by time. Hair as black as a raven's wing framed her smooth face, pallid from countless hours spent praying in a dark chapel. Had Ursula prayed or mourned for Everart, only two months in his grave? Gerard doubted she'd shed a single tear over his father's death.

Gerard knew why she wanted him gone. She had suffered the commands of her husband; she would loathe taking orders from her son. Gerard couldn't summon sympathy.

"All in good time," he answered, then turned to Walter. "Have Frederick make ready to journey to Hampshire on the morrow. I have no interest in the sheep from Romsey, but I *must* know if Basil has moved against Milhurst. Tell Frederick I will give him instructions before he leaves."

Walter bowed his balding head. "As my lord wishes," he said and left the chamber.

Gerard leaned back in his chair and said to his mother, "You will no doubt be pleased to hear I leave on the morrow, not for Hampshire but for Lenvil, then Westminster."

Hands clasped tightly in her lap, she said, "Very well."

He almost laughed at the scheme so easily read on her face, but suppressed the impulse. Gerard leaned forward and rested his crossed arms on the table. He caught his mother's gaze and held it transfixed.

"Richard will remain at Wilmont. Stephen will oversee our brother's care with the help of Father Dominic. You will allow Richard to stay in the bedchamber in the family quarters until I send for him."

With each word, Lady Ursula's spine stiffened. Gerard braced for the inevitable tirade.

"You would shame me with *his* presence in the family quarters? Even your father did not insult me so, made the bastard sleep below stairs! Is it not enough I must tolerate him in my household without his being under my very nose?"

"I have done you the courtesy of explaining the need to hide Richard. After Corwin and I leave, only Stephen and Father Dominic, besides you, will know who rests in that chamber. Be aware, madam, that I will be *very* unhappy if the information spreads further."

Gerard reached across the table and grasped the jeweled silver cross that hung from his mother's neck. "Swear, by the cross you hold so dear, you will not interfere with Richard's care. Swear you will keep secret his whereabouts.''

Livid, his mother snatched the cross from his hand. "What blasphemy is this? *You* ask me to swear? You who were late for Mass and nearly slept through it? You would ask me to profane the Lord's teaching by allowing a by-blow, the proof of your father's sinful lust, to remain succored within these walls?"

Gerard barely held his temper. Ursula would never concede that Everart's decision to raise Richard as his own had gained Gerard a loyal brother instead of a bitter enemy. Gerard took pride in the loyalty of both Richard and Stephen, an odd but welcome relationship in a land where sons plotted against fathers, and brother fought brother over inheritance.

Like most noble marriages, the arranged union of Ursula and Everart had allied two noble families. No love, or even affection had developed between the pair. Ursula had endured her marriage, and for the most part tolerated her sons. But the middle child, born of Everart's peasant lover, Ursula hated passionately.

"Wilmont is Richard's home, by my father's wish and now mine. Your position is less secure."

Her eyes narrowed. "What are you saying?"

Gerard's glance flickered to the cross, to the jewels on her fingers, to her fine silken gown. "You are now a widow. Perhaps your God calls you to the religious life. Would that suit you, Mother? Life in an abbey?"

Ursula's mouth opened, then closed.

"Or perhaps you would prefer to marry again. I have no doubt that there is some male in this kingdom willing to have you to secure an alliance with Wilmont."

She paled. "You would not dare…"

"I would dare. Are you ready to swear your silence?"

She curled her fingers around the cross. Her voice shook as she said, "I swear." Then she dropped the cross as though it burned.

"So be it."

"Beware, Gerard," she warned as she rose from her chair. "You inherit not only your father's title and holdings, but his immorality as well. One day you, too, will face the Lord's judgment. May he have pity on your soul."

As the door slammed behind his mother, Gerard wondered why she still had the power to affect him. He should be immune to her curses, having heard throughout his life of how he would burn for eternity for one reason or another.

Then he brightened. With estate business resolved, he now had time to do what he'd ached to do since returning from Normandy—spend time with his son.

Gerard found Daymon in the hall, stacking pieces of wood as a nursemaid looked on. Gerard approached slowly, waiting for Daymon to sense his presence and make the first approach. Too often Gerard had returned from a long absence to sweep Daymon up, only to learn from his son's screams that young children possessed short memories.

When his son didn't look up, Gerard quietly asked the nursemaid, "How fares my boy?"

"Well, my lord, except he misses Baron Everart terribly. Daymon is too young to understand death. He only knows his favorite playmate no longer comes."

Gerard smiled sadly, feeling the same pang of loss.

"He seems healthy enough," he commented, noting chubby cheeks, bright eyes and a sure grip of fingers around wood.

Then Daymon turned to stare upward. Gerard saw the boy's mother in his face. If she'd lived through childbirth, he'd have given her a hut in the village, might even have found her a husband. Gerard hadn't loved the peasant girl, only found her winsome and responsive.

But he loved his son.

Gerard scrunched nearly to kneeling as Daymon continued to stare, yearning to reach out to the boy, but he waited.

Then a smile touched Daymon's mouth. Recognition lighted green eyes and little arms reached upward.

Scooping the boy from the floor, Gerard gave Daymon a hug. The boy clung, squeezing tight with both arms and legs. Daymon's obvious need stung Gerard's heart. The boy hadn't known his mother, had recently lost his grandfather, and now his father was about to leave again. Daymon had no one else, besides nursemaids, to whom he could turn for affection.

Gerard inwardly winced, facing the inevitable. He must marry. He should have married years ago, for both Daymon's sake and Wilmont's.

His father hadn't shirked his duty to find a bride for his eldest son. Gerard vaguely remembered talk of a marriage contract to the daughter of another baron, but the girl hadn't survived childhood. Several years later, Father had bargained for another maiden, but for some reason that betrothal hadn't come about.

Any number of females would vie for the honor of becoming mistress of Wilmont. The woman he settled on must be of good blood, and able to run a household. She needn't possess flawless beauty or a large dowry, though he wouldn't mind a comely wife or additional funds or land.

More important to him than wealth or beauty was that his wife be capable of affection. He most definitely wanted a mate who wouldn't balk at sharing the marriage bed and producing heirs. He didn't need love—the emotion having no place in a good marriage contract—merely the woman's acceptance of her place in his life.

Gerard raised Daymon to arm's length into the air and smiled at the boy's delighted squeal.

Acceptance. Was there a woman in all of England or Normandy who would willingly open her heart to Daymon, despite his bastard birth?

As Gerard lowered his son back into his arms, he saw Lady Ursula across the hall. Her glower set his resolve.

Such a woman *must* exist. He need only find her.

But first he would deal with Basil of Northbryre. Nothing must interfere with bringing that whoreson to his knees.

Chapter Two

Ardith knelt on the dirt floor of the sleeping chamber. In front of her swirled the most exquisite cloth she'd ever had the pleasure to pierce with a needle. As her sister Bronwyn turned in a slow circle, the emerald silk flowed past in soft, shimmering waves.

"Halt," Ardith ordered, then adjusted a holding stitch along the gown's hem.

"Oh, Ardith, Kester will be so pleased," Bronwyn stated with a breathless quality in her voice.

Ardith smiled. Bronwyn's husband, Kester, was besotted with his wife. Knowing how much new gowns pleased Bronwyn, he sought exotic fabrics as gifts. Kester had bought this rare silk from an Italian merchant, right off the ship.

Bronwyn had then rushed to Lenvil. Though she had servants to make her gowns, Bronwyn always returned home to Ardith when she wanted something special. According to Bronwyn, this gown would make its debut at Christmas.

"If you are pleased, Kester will be delighted. Now, turn once more." She again inspected her handiwork before declaring the session finished.

Ardith stood, flicking pieces of rushes and dirt from her brown, coarse-wool gown. Though she owned two lovely

gowns—a yellow wool for winter and a light green linen
for summer—she rarely wore them unless visitors were expected. For everyday chores, peasant-woven cloth served
best.

She pushed aside Bronwyn's honey-blond braid to undo
the lacing on the gown. "Now, you must finish your
story."

"Oh, I almost forgot. Well, as I said, King Henry sent
Kester to meet the pope's envoy. Kester met the ship at
Hastings and brought the priest to overnight at our holding
before going on to London." Bronwyn slipped out of the
emerald silk and donned a blue wool. She continued,
"From what I hear, Pope Paschal is *very* angry with King
Henry, to the point of threatening excommunication."

Ardith desperately wanted to hear more of the envoy and
the king. Having lived her entire ten and seven years at
Lenvil, she hungered for news of life beyond the manor.
But the jingle of tack and the thud of horses' hooves cut
short the conversation.

"Father has returned earlier than I expected," Ardith remarked. "No doubt his leg hurts and he cut his inspection
short. Would you fetch him a goblet of warm wine? The
brew usually eases his pain."

"How do you bear the grouch?" Bronwyn asked, placing a veil of sheer blue linen over her hair, securing it with
a silver circlet.

Ardith shrugged. "'Tis the change of season affecting
his mood. Once winter sets in and he stays off his leg,
Father's temper will improve."

"Why does he bother to inspect the fields once the harvest is in? Heavens, why would anyone want to look at
nothing but clots of dirt? *You* could tell him which fields
to plant next spring and which to leave fallow." Bronwyn
suddenly smiled. "Ah, I see. Father thinks he decides on
his own, does he?"

"Nor will I have him think otherwise," Ardith warned.

"As you wish, but do not leave me alone with him overlong. He *will* ramble on about oats and cabbages.'' With a sigh, Bronwyn turned and left the chamber.

Shaking her head in amusement, Ardith gathered up thread and needle and scraps of cloth, thinking of how different her life was from that of her sisters. One by one the girls had left home. Edith had entered the convent; the others had all married. By default, Ardith became the lady of the manor, if not in title, in practice. Someday, Corwin would marry and bring his bride to Lenvil. But since neither Harold nor Corwin appeared eager for that event, her place at Lenvil was secure for a while longer.

For forever, Ardith hoped, and to ensure her place she'd studied Elva's herb lore. She'd learned which herbs soothed a roiling stomach, which numbed an aching tooth, how to mix powders for headaches and salves for burns. She could poultice a wound and even act as midwife.

Surely Corwin would allow her to stay at Lenvil for those talents alone, as Harold had allowed his sister to remain near the manor. Had Elva not become outlandish with her heathen rituals—tossing animal bones and muttering pagan chants—Harold might have allowed Elva to live in the manor. But the day Elva had slit open a piglet to read the entrails was the day Harold had banished his sister to a hut in the village.

Though Ardith longed for a proper home of her own, she knew it folly to dream. She placed a hand over her belly, over the ugly scar marring her flesh, sealing her future. Elva had explained to a bewildered girl that though the wound wasn't deep enough to kill, the damage was severe.

Ardith could never marry because she could bear no man an heir.

Ardith shook her head. Why was she thinking of her barrenness now? Why did she let Bronwyn's visits, witnessing her sister's happiness, bring on these bouts of self-pity?

She could hear Bronwyn's light laughter and the sound of low, male voices coming from the hall. As she passed under the arch separating the two rooms of the manor, she saw not her father, but Corwin.

Her delight wiped away the dark mood. Without thinking, seeing only her beloved twin, Ardith squealed his name and ran across the room. Corwin barely had time to brace his feet before Ardith flung her arms around his neck.

From several yards away, Gerard watched Ardith gleefully sprint into Corwin's open arms. He recognized her at once, though he hadn't seen her for several years. There was no mistaking her deep auburn hair and vivid blue eyes.

Corwin lifted his sister and swung her around. Gerard barely heard the soft laughter of those around him as he watched the twins embrace. He was remembering the one time he had swept Ardith from her feet, held an adorable bundle of little girl in his arms.

Ardith had blossomed into a beautiful young woman.

She was gowned in coarse wool that hugged her ripe bosom and tiny waist before flaring over the curve of rounded hips.

Her smile alone could lift a man's spirits. Ardith's smile for Corwin caught not only her mouth and eyes, but lighted her entire face.

The tug in the area of his heart he attributed to envy. Of all the women in his life, from court ladies to peasant wenches, no woman had ever greeted him with such abandon.

Corwin put Ardith down. Her eyes narrowed slightly.

"Corwin, you inconsiderate beast, I could hit you," she said, and did, lightly on the shoulder.

"What have I done now?"

"What you have *not* done is answer my letters! Did you not teach me to read and write so we could exchange messages?"

Corwin smiled. "As I recall, I taught you the skill because someone *pleaded* with me to do so, not trusting old Father Hugh's eyesight."

"True, but did you not tell me to practice my writing by sending you messages, which you promised to answer? Fie on you, Corwin. How could you let me worry so?" Ardith backed away and looked him up and down. "You seem in one piece."

"Hale and hardy," Corwin affirmed. With a mocking bow, he added, "And most repentant. You must understand, however, that I had little time to take quill in hand. And believe me, Ardith, you would not wish to read of the war."

Gerard's envy increased as Ardith brushed a comforting hand along Corwin's arm.

"Was it horrible?" she asked.

"Aye. But I am home now, and in need of food and drink. Can you provide a keg of ale to help us celebrate?"

Ardith hesitated before answering, clearly dissatisfied with Corwin's short answer and change of subject. Then she nodded and smiled. "I believe I can. Tell me, how long can you stay?"

Corwin looked to Gerard.

Gerard answered, "For only a few days."

Ardith froze, though her cheeks grew hot. With her complete attention on greeting Corwin, she hadn't noticed the other people in the hall. Corwin hadn't made the trip from Wilmont alone. A goodly number of Wilmont soldiers mingled with Lenvil's men-at-arms and Bronwyn's escort.

And the niggling feeling grew that she knew that voice. Ardith prayed, a futile prayer, that the disembodied voice belonged to an unknown knight. She prayed that, just this once, the fates would be kind. But only one other man of her acquaintance could sound so much like Baron Everart. Gerard. Gathering her poise, she turned.

Her heart leaped as she beheld Gerard. Gerard—no longer the young man who'd carried her from hall to pallet and spoken comforting words to a distraught maiden, but a man full grown. The man whom, but for a cruel twist of fate, she might have married.

The young lion, Elva had christened the heir to Wilmont. The image had suited Gerard perfectly as a young man, but the cub had matured.

His eyes hadn't changed, but for the scant deepening of the lines in the corners. Green eyes, set wide of a noble nose, were still as bright as spring leaves. Over his eyes fanned thick lashes and heavy brows, matching his flaxen, shoulder-length hair.

The wavy lengths were damp and slightly matted against his head from the pressure of a recently worn helm. Her fingers itched to slide through the locks, to fluff his hair into a mane worthy to frame his high, proud forehead and square, tenacious jaw.

Over a simple black tunic he wore a hauberk of chain mail. His massive shoulders easily bore the weight of the armor as well as the baldric from which hung a scabbard and ponderous broadsword, tilted within easy reach of his right hand.

Gerard stood with regal ease. His very stance conveyed an aplomb that only a man sure of his position and power could attain.

He must have found her scrutiny amusing for he cocked his head and the corners of his mouth rose in a small smile.

"Greetings, Ardith. Had I known of your concern for Corwin, I would have ordered him to write, I assure you."

His words snapped Ardith from her trance. Blessed Mother! She was staring at Gerard as if he were a curiosity from a distant land. Controlling the tremble of her hands and knees, she dipped into a low curtsy. She closed her eyes as she lowered her head, striving for composure.

She mustn't allow Gerard to see the turmoil of her thoughts or the ache in her heart. He must never know how his kind words and thoughtful gesture had captured the fancy of a young maiden. He must never know how she cherished the memory in night dreams and unguarded lonely moments.

"Baron Gerard," she honored him, just above a whisper.

Gerard uncrossed his arms. The last time Ardith had curtsied to him, she'd tumbled forward, and for some perverse reason he was wishing she would do so again, just so he could catch her.

This time, however, Ardith had her body under control.

And her thoughts, he realized, as Ardith looked up and met his gaze squarely. Gone was the apprehension, the brief glint of anxiety he'd seen in her azure eyes.

He held out his hand. Ardith hesitated, then placed her fingers across his palm and rose as bidden. Her hand wasn't fragile, like Bronwyn's, but sturdy. No callus marred the pads nor redness blemished the palm, but neither was her grasp flaccid from idleness.

Gerard yielded to an impulse. He raised her fingers to his mouth, brushing his lips across blunt-cut nails. She didn't jerk away. Instead, she squeezed his hand.

He must have misread the anxiety he'd seen in her eyes. She assuredly didn't fear him, or shy from his touch, for which he felt inordinately grateful.

"Still the scamp, I see," he teased, nudging her memory of their first meeting.

She blinked in surprise, then blushed, a wonderful rose shade that complemented her unveiled auburn hair. "I am truly sorry, my lord, for not greeting you first as is proper. And you must think me a harridan for chastising Corwin in the presence of others."

"Shall we say you are spirited? Besides, I believe Corwin may deserve the rebuke."

She cast a guilty glance toward Corwin. "Actually, my lord, I always knew how Corwin fared. Baron Everart, God rest his soul, thought it important to keep my father aware of Corwin's whereabouts and health. Your steward, Walter, continued the practice."

Gerard nodded in approval. He must remember to commend Walter. Then her expression changed, and Gerard stood transfixed as she continued.

"I know my father will speak formally for Lenvil, but

until he does, I offer our condolences on the death of your father...and Richard. From what Corwin has told me, you were fond of them both.''

Ardith's genuine compassion tugged at his heart. He'd almost mistaken her words of sympathy for mere platitudes, but then the mistake would have been natural. Rarely did any of his acquaintances or peers show true emotion.

"My thanks," he said quietly. Stating how deeply her words touched him proved impossible. Nor would he do so before so many people.

"Ardith," Bronwyn prompted, "you *did* promise the men a keg of ale."

Ardith looked at Bronwyn, confused for a moment, then she blushed and pulled her hand from his grasp. "Of course. Bronwyn, would you see Baron Gerard seated? Corwin, come with me to carry the keg. By your leave, my lord?''

Walking across the short span of yard to the storage room attached to the kitchen, Ardith scolded Corwin. "You could have warned me the baron watched."

"Truth to tell, I forgot Gerard was standing there."

Ardith wondered how anyone could forget that a baron of Gerard's stature stood within the same room.

"You could have written from Normandy, let us know you were well," she stated as they entered the storage room.

"Come now, Ardith. If I had taken a fatal injury, you would have known."

Alone amid only sacks of grain and barrels of salted meat, Ardith felt safe to speak of the bond she shared with her twin. They had been warned by Elva, as children, to never speak of it lest someone declare them witches. "Do you truly believe so? Normandy is very far away."

Corwin put a hand on her shoulder. "What do you think?"

He sounded so sure and Ardith wanted to believe. "You may be right," she said, then turned to the task at hand.

"Now, I believe the brewer's finest is in that corner. Are you strong enough to heft the keg?"

"Chit," Corwin chided, hoisting the keg to his shoulder. "I could toss *you* over my shoulder and not feel the weight."

Ardith didn't challenge him. Corwin would feel compelled to prove his boast. Instead, she asked, "How many men are in the Wilmont company?"

"Twenty, besides Baron Gerard and myself."

She mentally sorted through available supplies. "I will inform the cook. Evening meal will be a test of her skills. There is little fresh meat to work with."

"The men will not care, so long as the food is hot and plentiful. You may want to send someone to the village to get help with the carting and serving, though."

Ardith nodded. "And for extra pallets for the Wilmont men-at-arms. The hall will be crowded tonight."

"You need not fret over sleeping space for Gerard, or most of Wilmont's men. Even now they raise the tents."

"Tents? In this cold?"

Corwin smiled. "These are true soldiers, Ardith, not pampered companions. Come, look at the field."

Ardith followed Corwin out of the storage room. In the field nearest the manor, Wilmont's men-at-arms erected small tents around a mammoth tent of scarlet and gold.

"Gerard likes his privacy," Corwin said. "Nor would he ask anything of his men that he is not willing to do himself. Granted, his tent is more opulent, but a tent nonetheless."

The scarlet tent appeared sturdy, capable of blocking chilly winds. Yet, why would Gerard forgo the comfort of a bed? With relief Ardith realized she wouldn't need to try to sleep in the same room with Gerard. Sleep would be hard enough to come by this night.

"Well, that solves that dilemma," she said. "Now all I must do is find someone to send to the village."

Corwin glanced around. "Ah, there is a lad who looks like he needs something to do. Thomas! Over here!"

A brown-haired lad crossed the yard at a brisk walk.

"Thomas, this is my sister Ardith. She has an errand for you. Be quick about it and she might feed you tonight."

"Corwin! What a cruel thing to say! Mayhap I will not feed *you* tonight."

Corwin shifted the keg and headed for the manor. "I have the ale. 'Tis all I need."

Ardith smiled and looked back at Thomas—just in time to see the uncertainty leave his eyes. And not, she realized, about being fed, but about her identity.

She couldn't blame the lad. Ardith knew she looked more peasant than lady in her coarse gown and uncovered hair. Which meant Gerard had probably noticed as well.

Ardith gave Thomas directions and instructions, then helped the cook until a group of women arrived from the village. When she finally returned to the manor, she found Harold had come home and, much to her chagrin, saw Elva seated in the shadowed corner near the tapestry.

Wary, Ardith approached her aunt. "I did not expect you to come up from the village."

Elva's gray, piercing eyes scanned the room and landed squarely on Gerard. Her thin mouth turned grim, and Ardith felt a twinge of panic. Elva's tongue had grown less cautious as she aged. Though she'd never voiced her hatred of Normans in front of Lenvil's liege lord, Ardith feared that, one day, Elva's restraint would dissolve and evoke punishment.

The old woman taunted, "Afraid I may anger Harold? Fret not, dear. He is too busy groveling before the Norman to notice me. Go, be about your duties."

Ardith shot a worried glance toward where Harold was relating an account of his day's ride, claiming Gerard's complete attention.

Well, not complete. Occasionally, as she oversaw the serving of the meal, she could feel Gerard watching. She firmly ignored the ripple in her midsection whenever their gaze happened to meet, or the flutter in her heart whenever his deep, rich voice drifted into her range of hearing.

After the meal, she waited until Harold had convinced Gerard and Corwin to hunt on the morrow before asking Corwin where he intended to sleep.

"Lay me a pallet in the sleeping chamber," he answered. "I have had enough of wet and cold. Gerard may prefer a tent, but not me."

"What? Sleep in a tent!" Harold blustered. "My lord, surely Ardith told you that you are welcome to the bed. If she did not, she neglects her duties. 'Tis your due!"

Ardith held her breath, fearing Gerard might agree to both sleeping in the bed and her neglect of duty.

"Nay, Harold, keep your bed," he said. Then Gerard looked straight into her eyes. "I will be quite comfortable...alone...on my pallet of furs."

Chapter Three

Gerard's spirits soared with the goshawk. The predator flew well within range of sight, her keen eyes searching the earth for whatever quarry the dogs might flush out.

Then she hovered against the pale, midafternoon sky.

"Another hare," Gerard said quietly, having spotted the hawk's intended prey.

Harold commented, "Never misses, does that one."

The hawk stooped silently, deadly, and made the kill. Gerard whistled the signal that Corwin had taught him earlier this morning. The hawk answered with a cry of triumph and flew to the padded leather on Gerard's outstretched arm. He fed her a reward of raw meat, noting how gently she took the tidbit from his fingers.

Accustomed to flying peregrine falcons, Gerard had selected the goshawk from the mews at Corwin's suggestion. She'd quickly displayed her strength in the field.

"Nary a mark on the bugger 'cept where the talons caught the head. That makes four clean kills, milord," the game bearer said, presenting the hare for inspection.

"Of course 'tis not marked," Corwin said. "Gwen never tears a pelt, so Ardith can use the fur for clothing."

"Gwen?" Gerard asked, eyeing the bird.

Harold snorted. "Aye, Ardith named her Gwen. 'Tis a

wonder the hawk hunts, for all the chit spoils the bird. I swear that hawk would heed Ardith's fist without the call."

"She does, at least in the mews and the yard," Corwin stated to Harold's disgust. "Ardith trained her, feeds her, never uses another bird when she hunts."

"Made a ruddy pet out of a hawk," Harold complained.

Gerard reacted privately, surprised and oddly proud that Ardith had trained the hawk. He knew ladies who liked to fly hawks, but none who would trouble to train her own bird.

"If Ardith likes the hunt, why did she not join us?"

Corwin answered. "Ardith said she wanted to finish stitching a gown that Bronwyn desires for court."

"About time the chit had a bit of work to do. Lord knows she has few duties about the manor," Harold huffed.

Corwin turned to hide a frown. Gerard managed to keep an indifferent expression. He'd noticed, yesterday noon and last evening, the efficiency of Lenvil's people. Ardith's gentle but firm hand had guided the manor's servants.

Bronwyn, dressed in fine clothing and delicate slippers, had played hostess. But Ardith, in coarse wool and leather boots, had assured a plentiful table laid, prompted a lad to keep the fire fed, kept ale and wine at the ready, and asked John, captain of Gerard's guards, if Wilmont's men-at-arms needed extra blankets.

He'd also noticed a decidedly independent side of her nature. She'd ignored his invitation to share his furs. She might have misunderstood, but Gerard didn't think so.

"Despite a preference for her mistress, the hawk flew well for me this day." Gerard deliberately kept his praise light. If he marveled overmuch at the bird, Harold would feel duty bound to offer Gwen as a gift. He didn't want the bird.

He wanted the bird's owner.

Harold shifted in the saddle. Gerard guessed the man's leg hurt, having noticed his limp yesterday. But Harold's dignity wouldn't allow him to complain before his liege lord.

"I suggest we return to the manor," Gerard said, halting the hunt. The party had bagged several hares and a few partridges and pheasants. Gerard supposed Harold's hunting forays were short and infrequent. Then who hunted fresh meat? Ardith? Perhaps. Gerard didn't doubt she could, not when flying so magnificent a bird as Gwen.

"Shall I take her, my lord?" the attendant offered.

Gerard looked at the hawk comfortably perched on his arm, grooming her feathers. Gerard wrapped the leather jesses around his arm.

"Nay, she is content and not heavy. I will carry her."

"As you wish, my lord," the attendant said, looking askance, but hurrying to take Harold's bird, then Corwin's.

"Are you content to ride with me, Gwen?" Gerard softly asked. The hawk simply continued her preening. Gerard chuckled and turned his horse in the direction of the manor.

Gerard looked around for Corwin, who'd been riding at his side. For some reason Corwin lagged a pace behind, studying a copse of trees to his right.

"My son remembers his triumph," Harold said with pride. He called out, "Proud of you, I was, Corwin. Never was there a finer meal than the boar you slew with your sword, and you a bit of a lad and new to weaponry."

Corwin rode up beside Gerard. "Killing the boar was no great feat, Father. 'Twas kill or be killed."

Addressing Gerard, Harold protested. "Corwin nearly separated the beast from his head. Cook had to piece the boar back together before impaling him on a spit. You should remember the feast, my lord. Baron Everart brought you and Richard to help us celebrate Corwin's bravery."

"'Twas Stephen who came, Father, not Richard."

"Are you sure? I seem to recall…"

"Quite sure. Richard was ill and could not come."

Harold stared at the horizon for a long moment, then

said, "Aye, 'twas Stephen. No matter. 'Twas a fine feast to honor Corwin's prowess."

Gerard remembered the feast. He'd been seated between Bronwyn and Edith, nodding at Bronwyn's endless chatter and wondering if Edith would ever end her prayer so he could eat. In his boredom his gaze had wandered the hall, finally resting on a head peeking from behind the corner tapestry.

After the meal, he'd circled the hall to investigate and found Ardith crouched in the corner. The discovery had been the one bright moment of an otherwise dreary day.

"Harold has the right of it, Corwin. You saved not only your life, but Ardith's. 'Twas a feat to warrant pride."

Gerard saw Corwin's pallor, but before he could remark on it, Corwin pulled ahead and grabbed the game bag from the bearer.

"If we are to feast on this meat tonight, I best get it back to the manor."

"Tell Ardith not to stew the hares," Harold ordered. "I want them roasted."

"Aye, Father." Corwin wheeled and rode off.

Ardith shooed a goat from the manor doorway. Since the weather had turned cold, the animals relentlessly sought the warmth of indoors. The peasants might share their huts with sheep and oxen, but Ardith was firm in herding the manor's animals toward their outdoor pens—except the hunting hounds, one of which loped past on his way to a spot by the fire.

She glanced beyond where Corwin now dismounted, looking for the rest of the hunting party. Gerard hadn't yet returned. She fought the disappointment, and lost.

Ardith had always known that someday she would again see Gerard. She hadn't known how much the meeting would hurt.

Last night, awake on her pallet, she'd relived their first meeting. She'd again felt Gerard's tender concern for an

injured maiden, heard those words he'd uttered to put her
at ease. But mostly she remembered the comfort of curling
in Gerard's arms as he'd carried her from hall to pallet.

Just before falling asleep in the wee hours before dawn,
she'd convinced herself she was glorifying a childhood
fancy. Then had come the dream, of the man Gerard, standing in the glen where the boar had attacked, his arms reaching out to her, beseeching. She'd tried to run to him, but
no matter how fast she ran she couldn't reach Gerard.

Forced to admit a continued enchantment with Gerard,
she resolved to stay as far away from him as possible.
Later, after Gerard left Lenvil, she would mourn the penalty
imposed by her wounding but once more, then put aside
for all time the folly of longing for a husband and children.

Corwin handed over the game bag. She almost dropped
the heavy pouch.

"A fine hunt," she commented, inspecting the contents.

"Father says—"

"He wants the hares roasted," she finished for him,
shaking her head. "He will risk his few remaining teeth for
the sake of his pride. Who took the hares?"

"Gerard and Gwen."

"She flew well for him, then?"

"Very."

By his clipped answers, Ardith knew some problem
chewed at Corwin's vitals. His next words confirmed her
belief.

"Ardith, could we speak in private?"

Ardith waylaid a servant as they entered the manor. She
gave him the game bag and instructions for the cook. After
filling two cups with mead, she sat on a stool across the
table from Corwin.

Corwin took a long pull of mead. His blue eyes locked
on her own, then he looked away, as though he'd glimpsed
her deepest thoughts and recoiled.

"Corwin?"

He leaned forward, his arms crossed on the table. "Ardith, are you happy here at Lenvil?"

The question was so unexpected it took her a moment to answer. "I am content," she said, keeping near to the truth. "I have duties to keep me occupied, people to talk to. My hawk. My horse."

Corwin's tone turned sarcastic. "And Father. He believes you waste away your days doing nothing. Were you to vanish for a time, he would realize who truly runs the manor. He thinks Mother trained the servants so well that they merely carried on with their duties after her death. God's wounds, he—"

"Corwin, stop," Ardith said firmly, putting a hand on his arm. "Father is as he has always been. He has never put any store by his daughters. He judges us all witless and useless. Watch tonight how he treats Bronwyn. Do you know he has not said a kind word to her since she came to visit?"

"Bronwyn has a home of her own to return to, a husband who treats her like a princess. But you, you must stay and bear his ill-treatment."

"You are kind to think of my feelings. But if you must know, I learned long ago to ignore Father's attitude. The more harsh and loud he grows with the onset of age, the more I close my ears."

"'Twas not just Father who ignored you, but Mother, right up to the day she died. Then *he* left you to the mercy of Elva, especially after..."

Corwin took a deep breath and closed his eyes.

Amazed by her brother's distress, she asked, "What happened to rile you so?"

Corwin cleared his throat. "Father complained about you to Gerard, and when we passed the glen where you were...hurt, Father started in again. Not once did he say he had almost lost a daughter that day, only bragged of how his son had provided meat for a feast. Then Gerard said...said I should be proud of how I saved you."

"Well, you should. Corwin, had you not killed the boar, he might have attacked me again. I could have died."

"Had I protected you as I should, you would not have been hurt. Had you not suffered the wound, you might have married and escaped Father's scorn."

Corwin's pained scowl and sharp words drove deep into Ardith's heart. Never had she imagined the horrible guilt he bore, and she knew that if she tried to ease that guilt now, he wouldn't listen.

Soon Harold would be home. If he found Corwin sulking, Father would surely find her at fault.

If Corwin refused comfort on events past, maybe she could ease his mind about the present and future.

"The past is past and cannot be undone no matter who claims fault. What matters is this day and the morrows to come. I am content, Corwin. I have a roof above my head and meat on my trencher. Someday Father will no longer be lord of Lenvil, you will. Then you will decide my place in the manor, judge if I still warrant sheltering."

Corwin looked horrified. "Ardith, I would *never* turn you out. You will always have a place at Lenvil."

Ardith smiled. "Then I have no regrets," she lied. There was but one regret, and his name was Gerard.

"I wish..." Corwin began, but didn't finish.

Ardith could hear the hunting party returning, ending her attempt to battle Corwin's demons. "Corwin, would you do me the favor of keeping Gerard out of the manor for a while?"

Distracted, Corwin's brow furrowed. "Why?"

"I have a hot compress prepared to ease the pain in Father's leg. If he does not use it, he will growl at everyone for the remainder of the day, and he will not use it if Gerard is anywhere in sight."

"How do you know his leg pains him?"

"It always does after he rides."

Corwin nodded as they pushed away from the table. Ardith turned toward the door. At the edge of her vision she caught movement. Little Kirk, just learning to walk, reached out a tiny hand toward the rocks encircling the central fire pit. Skirt and braid flying, Ardith sped toward the babe and reached him just as he put his hand on the hot stone.

The boy howled. Ardith bent and scooped him into her arms, oblivious to all but the anger pounding in her head. She quickly checked the boy's hand, found the fingertips lightly burned, and looked around for Belinda, Kirk's mother, who was nowhere in sight.

"Belinda!" she shouted.

"Cease your caterwauling, girl," Harold ordered as he entered, Gerard at his heels. "What vexes you this time?"

"Kirk burned his hand because Belinda left him on his own again," Ardith complained. "I swear, I will take a switch to the wench when I find her! If she chooses not to watch after her son, she should ask another to do so."

Ardith tenderly brushed away the large tears that streamed down the boy's cheeks as he sucked his fingers.

"Utter waste of time, worrying over the whelp of a whore," Harold murmured.

His words didn't surprise Ardith, but his next action mortared her feet to the floor. Harold plucked the tiny hand from the babe's mouth and examined the fingers. "I wager the brat has learned to beware the fire." Harold released Kirk's hand and limped toward the dais.

Harold had never shown the least interest in any child about the manor, save one—his son, Corwin. An utterly absurd notion struck and refused dismissal. Even while chastising herself for such foolishness, Ardith studied Kirk's face for likeness to Harold's. But Kirk favored Belinda, had no obvious feature from which to identify his sire.

Ardith gasped as a stream of warm water hit her backside, soaking her gown and hair, droplets flying forward onto her cheeks. She spun and saw Corwin put down a bucket.

"Blast you, Corwin! Have you lost your wits?"

"Would you rather I let you burn?"

She felt a tug on her plait. Gerard held up the end of her braid for her to see. She'd lost all but an inch of hair below the leather thong.

Gerard's tone was pensive as he fingered the singed braid. "Your hair must have brushed the flames when you reached for the child."

"Oh," was all she could say, watching Gerard's large hand twist and play with the burned strands. Had she known him better, she might have understood the odd look that crossed his face, then vanished.

Gerard reached for the babe and barked orders. "Corwin, find the boy's mother. Ardith, change your gown before you catch a chill. Bronwyn, help her."

"I will see to Ardith," Elva announced.

Ardith hadn't noticed Bronwyn and Elva enter the manor. Nor did she pay them much heed now, watching how easily Gerard handled Kirk, flipping the babe up and around to ride atop massive shoulders. Gerard didn't even seem to mind when Kirk grabbed fists full of golden locks to secure his perch.

Gerard gave Elva a chilling look. "Are you not Lenvil's herbswoman?"

Elva's glare was colder. "I am, my lord."

"Then be about your duties, woman. Harold needs care."

Before Elva could retort, Ardith intervened. "There is a hot compress in the cauldron," she told Elva, then turned to Gerard. "My lord, Father will refuse treatment if you remain in the hall."

Gerard stared at her for a moment, then said, "The lad and I will be in my tent until Corwin finds the mother."

He headed for the door, stopping only to grab a blanket from a servant's pallet to toss over Kirk.

"He misses Daymon," Corwin said in a low voice.

"Daymon?"

"Gerard's son is about a year older than Kirk."

Ardith's heart fell. "I did not know Gerard had wed."

"He has not wed. Daymon is his by-blow, but you would never know from Gerard's treatment of the boy." Corwin sighed. "I had best find Belinda. If Gerard has taken a liking to Kirk, I fear she is in for a scolding worse than you could hope to match."

Corwin strode off to find Belinda. Seething, Elva stomped toward the cauldron. With a sigh, Ardith walked toward the sleeping chamber. Bronwyn followed.

"Oh, dear," Bronwyn moaned, picking up the scissors.

"Be quick," Ardith said quietly.

With a few snips, Bronwyn trimmed the frazzled ends from Ardith's braid, hair never before touched by scissors.

"Your gown is scorched beyond repair. 'Tis a miracle you were not burned," Bronwyn said.

Ardith shook out her hair. "Since my hair is wet, I may as well wash it."

"You will catch your death," Bronwyn protested.

"I must dry it by the fire anyway."

Bronwyn fetched a bucket of warm water and bar of rose-scented soap. Together they washed Ardith's auburn tresses and wrapped her head in a length of linen.

Ardith changed into the dry clothing that Bronwyn had laid out—a chemise of ivory, and a wool gown of saffron yellow.

With bone combs in hand, they sought the heat of the fire and untangled the mass atop Ardith's head. She bemoaned the loss of hair as she combed. No longer did the tresses reach down over her rump. When properly plaited, the braid would only hang to her waist.

But what import had the loss of a few inches of hair when measured against the possible disaster to Kirk? She hoped Gerard would truly throw the fear of God into Belinda for neglecting the babe. If not, Ardith planned to take Belinda to task after the evening meal.

Duty demanded she speak with Belinda to ensure Kirk's

safety. And there was one particular question she needed
to ask of the woman. Belinda had never named Kirk's sire.
If Ardith's hunch was correct, if Kirk was indeed her half
brother, Belinda need never worry about the babe ever
again.

Ardith wondered if her father would object to the plans
forming in her head. Would Harold acknowledge a bastard
son? She could cite Gerard as an example—and Baron Everart. She could also praise the king's acknowledgment of
his bastard children. According to Bronwyn, at last count
the king had ten children, only two of them legitimate.

Would Belinda protest, refuse to relinquish the boy? No.
Not having to care for her son would leave Belinda free to
flit about as she chose.

The whore certainly had her place in the manor, keeping
Harold's few men-at-arms from molesting the village maid-
ens. But there were times when Belinda's chosen trade
grated on Ardith's nerves.

Like now, as Ardith wondered if the meeting in the tent
would end with Belinda offering her body to Gerard—and
Gerard accepting. Maybe, tonight, Gerard would have company in his tent, on his fur pallet.

Chapter Four

The cooking fire had died down to coals, so little light
eased through the shuttered windows of the kitchen. Standing within the meager light, Ardith confronted Belinda.

"I will take better care of Kirk, milady," Belinda said.

Ardith didn't doubt Belinda would, at least as long as
Gerard remained at Lenvil. According to Corwin, Gerard
had threatened to strap Belinda to the post the soldiers used
for spear practice should any harm come to Kirk.

Gerard's threat had jolted Belinda. All evening she'd
stayed close to Kirk, as if tethered to the babe. Even now
Kirk slept against Belinda's shoulder, wrapped within the
folds of his mother's mantle.

"I believe you will," Ardith said. "My concern for Kirk
goes beyond his safety, however. Belinda, could my father
be Kirk's father?"

"Nay, milady," Belinda said.

Disappointed, Ardith pressed, "Are you sure? Do you
know who Kirk's father is?"

"Quite sure 'bout lord Harold, milady. As a man grows
old his parts wither. Poor Harold has to work hard to get
his manroot stiff."

"Oh?" Ardith choked.

"Aye, his days of begettin' wee ones are over. You see
milady, for the seed to take root, a man has to plant deep

inside a woman. Harold just don't stay long enough or hard enough for the sowin' anymore.''

''I see.''

''Now you take a young, strappin' big man like the baron. Lay enough wenches beneath him and he could sire his own army, he could. Aye, he would furrow deep. Wager he could plant three or four babes before takin' a rest.''

Blessed Mother! How could Belinda so blithely speak of male private parts and the act that led to conception? Her *father's* male private parts...*Gerard's!*

Ardith knew how men and women coupled. One had only to walk into the hall at night to see men-at-arms and maids, servants and serfs, bouncing on pallets.

The sight and sounds had so disgusted her sister Edith that she'd fled to a nunnery. Not so her other sisters, who knew they would wed and were resigned to servicing their husbands. Though Bronwyn had never said as much, Ardith suspected her sister enjoyed the experience with Kester.

The one time Ardith had dared broach the subject, while learning midwife skills, Elva had dismissed the act as a needless waste of energy. '''Tis men who cannot resist the urge to fornicate,'' Elva declared. ''They measure their worth by the size of their rod. A woman need only lie still and hope he is quick about his business. Be glad you need never endure the demands of a male.''

Ardith had wanted to ask if Elva judged from firsthand knowledge but lacked the courage. She suspected not, because Elva had never married. Nor could Ardith quite believe Elva's statement. Too many maids smiled brightly on the morn after sharing a man's pallet. Belinda certainly didn't show any sign of suffering from male demands.

Had Belinda lain with Gerard? Was that how she knew his size and stamina? No, she hadn't. Belinda had used a wistful tone as though she would like to, but hadn't yet shared Gerard's furs.

Embarrassed, but fascinated, Ardith asked, ''How can you judge Baron Gerard's, or any man's...without...''

Ardith lost her courage, but Belinda understood.

"By his hands, milady. You take a look at the baron's fingers. They be long and thick, so his rod be long and thick. Aye, he would be a real handful, mayhap two, that one. Do you want me to describe him for you should he—"

"Nay!" Ardith took a deep breath and regained her composure. "My interest is not personal, you understand. My duties as healer bid me ask. I must know how things work if I am to treat ailments and the like properly."

"Of course, milady."

Ardith knew from the smile in Belinda's voice that she hadn't fooled the whore.

Gerard pushed aside his empty goblet.

The hall was quiet except for a low crackle from the fire pit and an occasional intruding snore. Corwin had succumbed, lay sprawled across a bench. Harold slept, facedown on his forearms crossed on the table. Men-at-arms and servants had taken to pallets scattered across the floor.

The manor's door opened and John entered on an icy gust of wind. "The watch is set, my lord," he said, picking his way among the pallets to reach the table.

Gerard's eyes narrowed as he waved John to a stool. "Why do you report instead of Lenvil's captain?"

John removed his helmet to reveal midnight-black hair and a full, though neatly trimmed beard.

"I may have overstepped my authority, my lord," John said with no apology in his voice, though he glanced at the sleeping Harold. "Since Lenvil has no defensive palisade or earthworks around the manor, I thought the most effective defense was to station extra sentries. I do not mind telling you, my lord, I feel naked in this place."

"'Tis within your authority to assign guards as you deem necessary."

"Aye, my lord, Wilmont's men. But if you walk the perimeter tonight, you will find a few of Lady Bronwyn's escort among the men of Wilmont and Lenvil. The lady's men asked for duty. They have been here for a fortnight and grow restless, as duty-conscious soldiers will.''

John lowered his voice to a near whisper. ''There is a lack of discipline among Lenvil's guard I find disturbing. The watch is haphazard. I had to rouse several of Lenvil's men for the night watch. They grumbled, expecting Wilmont soldiers to assume the duty.''

Gerard frowned. ''The guard grows soft.''

''I fear so. They have no regular weapon practice, no sport or heavy work to build muscle or strength. Should an enemy attack, I fear the manor would be overrun before a rider could reach Wilmont for aid. Lenvil is vulnerable.''

Gerard felt his anger pulse, at Harold for allowing his guard to become lax, at himself for not seeing the situation immediately. As baron, final responsibility for Lenvil's defense rested on Gerard's shoulders.

That any of his holdings could be vulnerable irked Gerard. That Lenvil was easy prey made him furious.

He'd found ease at Lenvil.

The war in Normandy had been long and harsh, the death of his father a bitter blow. Fury at Basil ate at his innards. Frustration at King Henry's order to deal with Basil in court grated against Gerard's warrior nature.

At Lenvil, he'd found a haven.

Near the arch separating the manor's two rooms, Gerard saw a flash of yellow. Why was Ardith awake and flitting about at this hour? Certainly not to speak with him. Ardith avoided him as though he were diseased.

He told John, ''Tomorrow we shall measure the seriousness of the problem. Arrange some sport to test their mettle.''

John's smile spread. ''Perhaps a ball game, my lord?''

Gerard's smile matched John's. ''You lead one team and I shall lead the other. Agreed?''

''With pleasure.''

''Good. Turn in, John. I will make the last round of the guard and ferret out our laggards.''

"Then I will see you next on the playing field, my lord. Prepare for a thrashing."

Gerard laughed lightly as John picked up his helmet and strode from the manor to seek his tent and bedroll. Gerard glanced toward the arch. Ardith remained hidden.

He sighed inwardly. This obsession of hers to avoid his company was annoying—and presented a challenge. In many ways, it was to Ardith's credit he felt content at Lenvil. Yet, it was also her fault he sometimes felt the leper, an outcast.

Ardith unbalanced his mind.

After his lecture to Belinda on the care of her son, Gerard had returned to the manor to see Ardith by the fire, her drying hair flowing about her shoulders. As she shook her head and combed her hair, the fire's light had danced off reddish strands, highlighting her auburn tresses.

She'd changed her gown. The saffron wool hugged her body like a sheath from shoulders to hips where the skirt flared to swirl about her ankles. His loins had stirred when she arched backward toward the fire, closing her eyes, reaching to run her fingers through her hair.

The sensuous pose had ignited his desire. His manroot urged him to close the distance, to press his growing need against the woman's place so enticingly presented. The thought of lifting her skirts and driving himself deep within her had made him shudder.

Then Ardith had opened her eyes and noticed him standing inside the doorway. She'd declared her hair dry and scurried off to the other chamber. She'd returned a short while later, her hair plaited and veiled, but she stayed as far away from him as was possible and still complete her duties.

And still she shunned him, hiding on the other side of the arch, unwilling to enter the hall while he was present. His patience snapped.

"Ardith, come out," he said brusquely.

Slowly, Ardith appeared from behind the timber. Though

she still wore the saffron gown, she'd dispensed with the veil. Her plait fell forward across her chest, snuggled into the valley between her breasts.

"Well, what brings you from your pallet, my lady?" he asked when she didn't move or speak.

"I came to fetch my father. He should sleep in his bed."

Ah yes, the dutiful daughter, concerned for Harold's needs. Harold—who spoke to Ardith only to complain, who noted her existence only when something disturbed his comfort. Such loyalty was commendable, but at the moment her devotion rubbed a raw spot on his temper.

"'Tis his own foolishness leaves him sprawled drunk across the table. Leave him sleep where he lies."

Ardith's chin came up. "'Tis you who bear blame for his drunkenness, my lord. He could not leave until you called a halt to the revelry and retired to your tent."

A valid accusation, one he ignored.

She'd called him "my lord" with a touch of censure in her voice. What would his given name sound like coming from her lips, in her sweet voice that chimed melodious when she smiled, or better, in a breathless whisper hovering on the fulfillment of passion?

He looked down at Harold. The old man was too far gone with drink to wake easily. If Ardith insisted that her father sleep in his bed, then Harold need be carried.

Gerard stood, too quickly. Lenvil's brewer made strong ale. He waited for the slight dizziness to fade, then commanded, "Take his feet."

As Ardith chose her path among the pallets, Gerard hooked his arms under Harold's, gripping him firmly about the chest. Ardith tugged at Harold's legs, dragging them from beneath the table. Then she turned around and bent over, hooking her hands under Harold's knees, presenting a prettily rounded bottom for Gerard to admire as she wiggled to secure her grip.

With a slight grunt, she straightened. "Ready, my lord?"

"Aye, my lady. Lead on."

None too steadily they moved, Ardith laboring with the weight, Gerard battling the effects of drink mixed with lust.

Gerard was sweating by the time they dumped Harold onto the bed. He plopped down to sit on the bed, elbows on knees, chin on an upraised fist. The chamber hadn't changed much over the years. Harold's bed dominated the room. Coals in a small brazier reduced the chill. Three pallets dotted the floor. Bronwyn slept on one, the other two remained empty; one meant for Corwin, the other Ardith's.

Ardith removed Harold's boots and stood them near the brazier. Gerard felt a tug on the blanket beneath his rump. He didn't move.

She came around to face him. "My lord, if you would stand a moment..." she said.

He reached out to capture her hand. She didn't pull away. "Do you dislike me, Ardith? Am I so loathsome you must keep your distance?"

"Nay, my lord. I meant no offense. But I have duties to perform and...you came to visit with my father, and Bronwyn is the one skilled in courtly ways and conversation and—"

"You lie badly, Ardith."

She bit her bottom lip and looked away. Gerard frowned and stood, slowly and carefully this time. He needed to get outside, into the cold air to banish the effect of the ale.

Still holding her hand, he felt the slight tremor that shook her. With his other hand he reached out and tilted her chin, forcing her gaze back to his face.

"Say my name, Ardith."

She hesitated, then said musically, "Gerard."

His fingertips moved from chin to cheek.

Harold stirred. "Ardith, a cup of water."

Ardith retreated a step.

Gerard knew he was on the brink of acting the tyrant, of

ordering Harold to get his own damned water, then hauling
Ardith off to the privacy of his tent.

"'Till the morrow, Ardith," he said, and left the chamber.

"Have they lost their wits?" Ardith exclaimed.

"Nay, Ardith, 'tis but a game," Bronwyn said, patting
the frosted grass beside her on the hillside. "Come sit and
watch. We should be safe at this distance."

Ardith wasn't so sure, though Bronwyn had chosen a
viewing site at least an arrow-shot away from the men on
the field.

"When Corwin said sport I thought he meant footraces,
or wrestling. I never imagined—" Ardith indicated the field
and tangle of men with a sweep of her hand "—this madness."

"Have you never seen a ball game?" Bronwyn asked.

Ardith shook her head, then watched in horror as a man
tossed a leather sphere to, she assumed, a teammate. Ball
in hand, the man went down under a barrage of opponents.
"They will kill each other."

"Oh, you may have a bit of bleeding to stop and a few
bones to straighten, but I doubt the blows will kill."

"When does the *sport* end?"

"When the team with the ball crosses the goal, in this
case the end of the field. Whichever team accomplishes the
feat, wins. Baron Gerard's team is getting close."

Though the day was cold, some men played barechested, among them Corwin and Gerard. From what she
could see, so far they had escaped injury. Others weren't
so fortunate. Blood ran from men's noses and from deep
scratches down their arms and across their chests. She tried
to assess injuries, but her gaze kept drifting back to Gerard.

When not buried under a pile of men, Gerard was easy
to pick out. He stood a head taller than the others, his
golden hair a beacon on the gray day.

Bits of mud clung to the hair on his muscled, sculptured

chest. His thighs bulged against his breeches, threatening to rip open the seams as he struggled. Black leather boots hugged his calves.

Where other men lumbered, Gerard moved with grace. Like a large cat, she thought. *The young lion.*

He reached down with splayed fingers and dug the ball out of the writhing mass at his feet. With a roar heard above the shouts and grunts of the other players, Gerard turned and tried to run. He bounded over one fallen man, but another caught his ankle, stopping his flight long enough for an opponent to leap on his back. Gerard dislodged the man with a shrug of his massive shoulders.

Gerard continued to shake off opponents. Caught up in the excitement of watching the display of raw strength, Ardith wanted to scream his name to cheer him onward. Then the tide turned.

Gerard's challengers kept rising and attacking until he finally succumbed. It took four men, hanging on him like leeches, to bring him down.

Ardith's stomach tightened as she watched for him to reappear. A clamor rose from the crowd. Whether the cheer was for Gerard's prowess, or because he'd managed to toss the ball to Corwin, Ardith wasn't sure.

She scanned the field. When she finally saw Gerard getting to his feet, she exhaled shakily and stood. "'Tis barbaric," she complained to Bronwyn. "I will return to the manor and ready water and bandages."

Bronwyn's gaze never left the field as she delicately lifted a shoulder. "As you wish."

Ardith tossed her hands in the air and turned toward the manor. Along the way she snared three serving girls, who protested having to leave the display of sweat-glistened male flesh.

"You will see their attributes up close shortly," she told them. "If this idiocy continues, they will drop from wounds and exhaustion and need tending. I fear we may not get water heated before they drag the first of the fallen back to the manor.''

Ardith's prediction proved true. As she cleaned scrapes and poulticed bruises, she noticed that Lenvil's men-at-arms had taken the worst beating. Nearly all had returned battered and bruised. From the men's talk, she knew the teams had been evenly divided, with men of all three loyalties on each side. Lenvil's soldiers had succumbed early and hard, leaving the men of Wilmont and Bronwyn's escort to play out the game.

As she glanced about the hall for another man to bandage, she saw Thomas standing in the doorway. He made a slight, beckoning hand motion. Thomas was dirty and a bit scratched, but otherwise seemed sound.

"My lady," he said quietly as she reached him, "when you have a spare moment, would you attend Baron Gerard?"

Ardith's apprehension blossomed. She pictured Gerard lying broken, bleeding profusely, dying on the playing field. "Where is he? How badly is he hurt?"

"In his tent, nursing a lump on his head."

"Why did he not come into the manor?"

Thomas looked sincerely shocked. "Oh, no, my lady, he could not. He would never show any weakness before the men."

Ardith looked around the hall. "Has the game ended?"

"Baron Gerard was the last man off the field."

She thought to ask who won, then decided she didn't care. She fetched a bowl and some rags, then gave the bowl to Thomas.

"The pond has frozen over. Go fetch ice and bring it to the baron's tent."

Chapter Five

Ardith pushed open the tent flap. Gerard sat on a stool near a small table, his booted feet spread for balance. With elbows on knees, he held his face in his hands.

"Did you get a cold rag?" he muttered.

"I sent Thomas for ice."

Gerard slowly raised his head. "What do you here?"

"Thomas said you need tending."

"I do not need tending. I need but a cold rag."

"Apparently Thomas thought someone should look at your head. Since I am here, may I?"

He hesitated, then nodded. The motion made him sway. Her bottom lip between her teeth, Ardith crossed the exotic rug spread as a floor for the tent. Her fingers trembled as she pushed aside his sweat-wetted hair. The lump was as large as a goose's egg and colored a nasty shade of blue.

Incredulous, she gasped, "You *walked* off the field?"

"Of course."

Ardith shook her head. "Men and their cursed pride. I thought my father the most stubborn man in England. Next you will try to persuade me you have no headache."

"Ardith, 'tis but a little bump on the head. I have survived much worse."

She swallowed the lump in her throat. She chose not to

ask how he'd come by the scar below his right ear, or what weapon had carved the jagged line across his left ribs.

Thomas burst into the tent and put the bowl of ice on the table. "Will you need aught else, my lady?"

"Nay," Ardith said, wrapping a chunk of ice in a rag. "Go into the manor and have those scratches cleansed."

The young man had almost made his exit when Gerard growled, "Thomas."

With a resigned sigh, Thomas turned. "My lord?"

Silence loomed as Gerard glared at the boy, silently expressing his displeasure. Then he said quietly, "Find John and Corwin and send them to me."

Thomas nodded and fled.

Ardith set the ice packet on the table and looked around for a heavy object with which to break the ice. Her gaze traveled quickly over Gerard's fur-piled pallet to a large oak trunk banded with black iron. Draped over the lid lay Gerard's chain mail, upon which rested a conical helmet of leather and iron with a gleaming nose guard.

His sword stood sheathed in the corner, the hilt jewel-encrusted and polished to brilliance. Ardith doubted she could lift the sword, much less use it to crush the ice.

Ardith picked up the packet and whacked it against the table. The ice cracked but didn't break.

"Ardith, put it down," Gerard wearily ordered.

She obeyed, then flinched when his fist hammered the packet, pummeling the ice into shards. He picked up the packet and put it to his head.

"You should lie down," Ardith said.

"Not yet," he replied, closing his eyes. "Mayhap after I speak with John and Corwin."

"You should don a sherte."

"Does my nakedness offend you?"

Ardith felt a blush rise. "Nay, my lord. I merely thought that given the cold air and the ice a sherte might provide some measure of comfort."

"In the trunk."

The helmet moved easily, but she struggled under the weight of the chain mail. From inside the trunk she drew an ivory linen sherte.

She held it out to him. "Brush the mud off first."

He raised an eyebrow. "Any other orders, scamp?"

Ardith couldn't resist. "Not as yet, my lord. Give me but a moment and I could surely think of another one or two."

He sighed, put the packet on the table and brushed the mud from the profusion of hair on his chest. Was the hair as silky as it looked, as fine textured as that on his head?

As he pulled the sherte on, John entered, followed by Corwin.

"Well?" Gerard asked of John.

"'Tis as we feared, my lord," John replied. He gave a sidelong glance at Corwin before continuing. "To almost a man, the Lenvil guards lack agility and stamina. Had they fought a battle, I fear most would have fallen within moments of attack. Of course, I have not seen them wield weapons."

Though John tried to soften the report, Ardith realized instantly the reason for this morning's game—a test of Lenvil's guard, and they'd failed.

"Last night, I found two Lenvil soldiers asleep at their posts," Gerard said. "Another did not hear me until I was close enough to slit his throat. Only one challenged my presence in time to raise an alarm."

"I will have their heads," Corwin said angrily.

Gerard smiled wryly. "They will need their heads, indeed all their wits, for what we are about to do to them. John, inform the men of arms practice tomorrow for both Wilmont and Lenvil. Bronwyn's men may join us if they wish.

"Corwin, inspect Lenvil's weapons. If needed, you may borrow arms from Wilmont stores. No man finds excuse to beg off due to lack of a weapon. And Corwin, 'tis my place to speak of Lenvil's weakness with Harold."

"Aye, my lord," Corwin said, but he wasn't pleased.

"Now, tell me about Lenvil's captain."

"Sedrick has captained the guard since before I was born. He is almost Father's age. 'Tis odd, I remember him as an unyielding taskmaster, whether in discipline or skills. You think to tell Father to replace him?"

"Nay!" Ardith protested. Three pairs of stunned eyes swiveled to stare. She knew she meddled in matters outside her realm of authority, but to take the captaincy from Sedrick was unthinkable. Still, she'd bandaged far too many bruises and cuts. Maybe, just maybe, they were right.

"We shall see," Gerard said. Again he addressed John. "I thought to leave in two days, but I will not leave until assured...Lenvil is well defended."

John slapped Corwin on the shoulder. "Come. Let us see how much work needs to be done."

During the ensuing silence, Ardith slowly walked over to the table, picked up the ice packet and gave it to Gerard. His fingers brushed her hand, arousing the warmth that surged through her whenever they touched. His hands, strong and callused and compelling, were larger than most men's.

By his hands, milady. You take a look at the baron's fingers. They be long and thick, so...

Ardith tore her gaze from Gerard's hand to look at his face. Bright green eyes had darkened to emerald. His mouth slashed a hard line across his rugged visage.

"I spoke without thinking," she said softly. "'Tis not by my say who captains the guard."

He dismissed her audacity with a wave of his hand, asking, "Ardith, how ill is Harold?"

"His leg pains him when he overuses the limb."

"There is more."

Somehow, Gerard knew of the more serious ailment, though at the moment Harold enjoyed a good spell. She briefly considered denying her father's affliction, but Gerard was Lenvil's liege lord, and she hadn't done as good a job of overseeing the manor as she'd thought.

"His memory suffers. Some mornings 'tis a victory for him to find his boots. He becomes better at remembering events of decades past than a happening of the day before."

"How long have you been overseeing Lenvil?"

"Nearly two years."

"Why did you not inform Corwin or my father?"

"The manor has not suffered, nor has the village or any of our people. We sow and harvest crops, earn enough in milling fees to pay our rents to Wilmont. I did not, however, notice the slackening of the guard. For that, I apologize."

Gerard shook his head. Ardith saw pain overshadow his anger.

"Gerard, please," she whispered. "You must lie down."

A smile tugged at the corner of his mouth. "You assume I can walk so far."

"Will you allow me to aid you?"

He held out an arm. Ardith grasped him around the waist. He smelled of leather and sweat, of linen stored within oak—and an essence wholly male, wholly Gerard.

She wanted to run from the tent as much as she wanted to stay snuggled under his arm. The few steps to his pallet took forever, yet were completed too soon.

He slid down onto his furs. "I will have your word, Ardith, to say nothing of what transpired in this tent, either about the guard or my head."

About the guard, she understood. About his head, she failed to comprehend. "Surely everyone already knows of the lump on your head. You *were* the last man off the field."

"Of necessity, because my men expect it, and because I could barely walk a straight line. Only you and Thomas know how big the lump is and how it affected me. Beyond sending you out here, Thomas will say naught to anyone else."

She'd protected her father's dignity and pride for so long that she could do no less for Gerard. "You have my pledge of silence, my lord," she said. He shifted the ice packet, reminding Ardith of his pain. "I have headache powders in the manor. I will mix one in a tankard of mead and send it out with Thomas."

"Ardith! Ardith!" Elva's shrill call interrupted.

Ardith smiled slightly. "If I am to keep your secret, my lord, I must waylay Elva."

"Interfering old buzzard."

She blamed Gerard's nasty words on his sore head. She slipped through the tent flap, almost bumping into Elva.

"Oh, Ardith." Elva sighed, nearly smothering Ardith with an embrace. "Be you all right? Did he hurt you?"

"Nay, Elva, be at ease," Ardith soothed, gently pushing away. "The baron has no reason to do me harm."

Elva grasped Ardith's arms. "You must have a care, Ardith. You must beware the beast. He will tear you apart."

The old woman's warning of physical danger at Gerard's hand baffled Ardith. She knew the only danger Gerard presented was to her heart, and the damage was already done.

"Come," she said, guiding Elva back to the manor, steeling her resolve against Gerard's prolonged visit. "Fret not. The beast cannot harm what he cannot catch."

Gerard looked on as Corwin bullied Lenvil's guards. After a week of drills, the guards showed progress. But Corwin was still angry. Having found his birthright endangered, he challenged the soldiers to match his mastery. Though he was only ten and seven, Corwin's skill with weapons had earned him the respect of even Wilmont's knights.

After a long talk with Sedrick, who'd admitted a problem with his eyesight, Gerard had reserved the right to choose a new captain. Now, having tested and talked to each Lenvil soldier, Gerard still hadn't chosen. To his mind, none was ready and he wouldn't entrust Lenvil's defense to a man not fully competent.

Gerard had realized, these past few days, it wasn't Lenvil he strove to protect. The holding was a fine one and Corwin's birthright. If the manor and village burned, the peasants and livestock scattered, the crops destroyed, the waste would raise his anger. His demand for justice would be swift against the knave who dared attack the holding.

But a manor could be rebuilt, people and cattle retrieved, crops replanted. Intolerable was the thought of Ardith's fate should the manor fall.

Visions of lovely Ardith hovered at the edge of his mind, ethereal and subtle, but always with him. He caught himself looking for her in the yard or in the manor, listening for the sound of her voice. His enchantment grew with each passing day—and night.

As did his hunger. He couldn't look upon Ardith without desire flooding his loins, hardening his manroot.

On the day she'd come to his tent to tend his head, he'd thought they reached an accord. But still she shunned him, as though she hadn't gently touched his forehead and stood so close that he could feel her warmth and smell her unique scent.

Had the desire to bed Ardith been the only source of his vexation, he might have ordered her to his bed. Often he'd thought of winding her plait in his fist, dragging her into his tent and flinging her naked body down onto his furs. None would gainsay him.

Odd, how he willingly abandoned that right in order to win her favor. Winsome and eager was how he wanted Ardith. Aye, he wanted her passion, but he also wanted her affection. From Ardith he wanted more than the mere joining of bodies. She *must* be kept safe, because after concluding his business with Basil, Gerard intended to take Ardith as his wife.

He needed royal consent to marry, but could think of no reason why King Henry should disapprove of Ardith.

Though not of noble blood, Ardith hailed from good stock. As fifth daughter she would have no dowry to speak of, but if Gerard didn't begrudge the lack, Henry shouldn't care. And she was Saxon, a happenstance likely to sway Henry to approve.

Gerard yearned to begin the delightful duty of siring a legal heir to Wilmont. Making babes with Ardith would be pure pleasure.

As for Daymon, Gerard was sure Ardith would lovingly accept his bastard son. Every child in the manor sought her out to soothe bumps and bandage scrapes. He strongly suspected her coddling eased their hurts more than the salves and strips of linen. She adored children, had threatened to whip Belinda over a bastard's care.

But hellfire, why did he so want the one woman in the entire kingdom who refused to respond to the desire that flared whenever their eyes met?

Gerard turned toward the sound of a horse thundering toward the manor, his hand automatically reaching for the hilt of his sword. Then he recognized the messenger who rode one of Wilmont's swiftest coursers. Foam frothed from the horse's mouth as the courier reined to a halt.

"Baron Gerard," the man said panting, holding out a rolled parchment. "From Walter. He bid me await your reply."

Gerard untied the ribbon and unrolled the parchment. Rage blinded him for a moment as he read.

"When?" he growled at the messenger.

"Yesterday, my lord."

Gerard crushed the message in a white-knuckled fist.

"What is amiss?" Corwin asked from beside him.

"Frederick has returned to Wilmont."

"Has Milhurst fallen to Basil?"

"Frederick could not say because he was dead, strapped across his horse like game from the hunt. Someone killed him and led the horse near enough to Wilmont for the horse to find its way home."

"Basil?"

"His minions, I suspect." Gerard exploded. "Devil take him! His audacity is beyond endurance. Tell John to have the men ready to march on the morn. We leave for Westminster."

Gerard stalked off to his tent. In quick, angry strokes he penned a message to Stephen, giving his brother permission to take whatever defensive measures he thought necessary.

After Richard's wounding, Gerard's first impulse had been to run a sword through Basil of Northbryre's gullet. But King Henry's staying hand had given Gerard time to realize that by seeking redress through the court he might gain title to Basil's holdings without putting men on the field of battle. And by doing so, Gerard could richly reward Stephen and Richard for their loyalty without giving up any Wilmont lands.

Gerard almost hoped Basil had been stupid enough to raid Milhurst. The mistake would add weight to Gerard's case. He shook his head at the notion. Leaving Milhurst open to attack, or not taking it back if Basil had succeeded with a raid, would be seen as weakness. Gerard added another order to Stephen's letter, to send two knights and ten men-at-arms to Milhurst.

His mind settled on the matter, Gerard turned his attention to leaving Lenvil. He had yet to choose a captain for Lenvil's guard. The ideal would be to leave Corwin here to handle the matter, but he needed Corwin at court.

And Ardith?

Gerard wondered what Ardith's reaction would be when informed she was making the trip to Westminster.

"Elva, Ardith needs your help. You must come up to the manor. We leave on the morn and there is much to be done."

"Then you help her, Bronwyn," Elva called to the closed door of her hovel. She shook out a square of black wool and covered the small table. On the cloth she placed a treasured Celtic cross, a gift from her long-dead mother. Beside the cloth she placed a thick, tallow candle.

"Ardith wants you to take charge of the manor while she is away. She is upset about this journey. Having you at the manor in her absence would ease her mind. Please, Elva. If you do not come, she will have to place another in charge."

Elva didn't answer, and soon heard Bronwyn's disgruntled huff and the shuffle of retreating footsteps.

She lit the candle. From the folds of her gown she retrieved a leather pouch and dumped the contents onto the cloth. She wished they were larger, these bones she'd managed to nab ahead of the dogs. The Norman, blast his hide, tossed his leavings *at* the dogs instead of flinging them over his shoulder into the rushes.

The bones weren't bleached. Slivers of meat and gristle still clung to the surface. She shook her head at the lack of time to prepare them properly. She gathered the bones in her hands.

Years ago, she'd misjudged the forces of fate. Thinking her precious girl safe, Elva hadn't bothered to augur the Norman's future. Now the beast was back and about to spirit Ardith away.

She'd saved Ardith from the clutches of Wilmont once. Could she do so again? She must.

Elva closed her eyes, mumbling the words she remembered as her mother's chant. She knew not the meaning, only remembered the pattern of sounds.

She tossed the bones onto the black cloth and read their dire message.

"Demon spawn," she hissed, and with a sweep of her hand, wiped the offensive prophecy out of her sight.

Chapter Six

All of Ardith's possessions fit into a small trunk. As she spread her yellow veil atop her good gown, she grumbled, "I still do not understand why I must go along."

"Ardith, when a baron invites a vassal on a journey, the vassal accepts," Bronwyn stated from her perch upon her own large trunk. Beside her trunk sat another, as large and as full. Bronwyn, sensibly, was taking advantage of traveling with the company about to depart Lenvil.

"Baron Gerard invited Father. My accompanying Father, as nursemaid, was an afterthought."

"Well, I surely cannot care for Father. He will not listen to me. Besides, I am glad you are coming. We can keep each other company on the road. Oh, Ardith, we will have such a merry time at court."

"Are you sure Kester will not mind our unexpected visit?"

"Not in the least. Kester's position as adviser to the king entitles him to lodgings at Westminster Palace. There is plenty of room for us all. Ardith, *do* cease looking for an excuse to beg off. All is ready. You are coming."

All was ready because Ardith had spent most of the night gathering provisions, with the help of John, whom Gerard had assigned to oversee Lenvil in Ardith's absence.

She still couldn't understand why Elva had refused to

take charge of the manor. She'd thought her aunt would enjoy the task, if only for the luxury of sleeping in the bed.

Ardith was of two minds about the journey.

Granted, Father hadn't been to court for many years to pay homage to the king. But Harold wasn't a well man, as Gerard knew. Why now? Why with such haste? Could they not have had more time than one night to prepare? And starting out on a journey under the threat of inclement weather was ill-advised.

Yet Ardith had never seen London, never traveled farther than the market at Bury Saint Edmunds, a mere two hours' ride to the west. Bronwyn made court sound exciting, full of interesting people and wondrous sights.

"You will need several new gowns," Bronwyn observed. "I have a few that might suit you with a bit of altering. If you do not care for them, I have stacks of cloth from which you can make your own."

"Surely, I will not need so many."

"Oh, three or four, at least. Ah, they have come for our trunks." Bronwyn slid off her perch to allow the men of her escort to lift the trunk. "Be careful, now. This one goes on the right of the cart. And make sure the tarp is secure. The sky looks ready to burst. You know how the snow sticks to the top and makes it hard to..." Bronwyn's voice trailed out of hearing as she followed the bearers out of the chamber.

Ardith looked about the room. All of her life she'd slept within Lenvil's walls, within this chamber.

"Ardith? Are you ready?" Corwin asked as he strode in.

Ardith tried to return the smile but found she couldn't.

"Why so glum, Ardith? Ah, I understand. 'Tis always hardest the first time, leaving home."

"Did your heart ache the first time you left Lenvil?"

Corwin shook his head. "I thought it a grand adventure, going off with Baron Everart to Wilmont. Of course, I had

Stephen for company. The two of us became fast friends on that journey. Where is your mantle? Here, put it on.''

Corwin held up Ardith's warmest mantle, lined with rabbit fur, and draped it over her shoulders. Ardith wrapped a long piece of wool about her head and neck.

Her brother grabbed her hand and pulled her out of the chamber. ''Come, Bronwyn is waiting for you in her litter. You two can gossip all the way to Westminster.''

Ardith scampered to match Corwin's stride. ''I thought to ride my horse.''

''Your palfrey carries provisions.''

Corwin didn't give her time for a last look about the manor; instead, he hustled her out of doors. ''What a grand procession we will make,'' he declared, waving a hand at the long line of men, animals and wagons.

At the head of the line stood Thomas, holding the reins of Gerard's destrier and Father's stallion. Behind them would march several of Wilmont's soldiers, followed by Bronwyn's litter and her escort. The remaining men-at-arms and the wagons and pack animals completed the company.

Ardith eyed Bronwyn's odd conveyance. The litter looked like the bottom half of a sawed-off wooden box attached to long poles, which fitted on to specially made harnesses on horses. A roof of canvas, held up by spindles at the corners, would keep off rain and snow. She thought it must be safe to ride in because Bronwyn would travel no other way.

''Come, Ardith. In you go or we shall leave you behind,'' Corwin teased as he handed her into the seat opposite Bronwyn.

Ardith smiled wanly. ''Promise?''

''Promise what?'' Gerard asked as he came up to the litter.

''Ardith is being difficult.'' Corwin sighed. ''It seems, my lord, she would rather not ride in such comfort. She would rather ride her palfrey, which we loaded down with food.''

Gerard looked at her strangely for a moment, then said, "Well, perhaps we can make other arrangements later. If everyone is ready, let us away."

By midday, Ardith was willing to walk to London. Somehow, Bronwyn had managed to fall asleep. So much for keeping each other company! Not that Ardith really minded her sister's desertion. This way Bronwyn wouldn't see and remark upon Ardith's distress.

Her stomach churned from the lurch and sway of the litter. The unnatural sensation of riding backward, seeing where she had *been* and not where she was going, added to her discomfort.

Her backside pained from bouncing on the thinly padded seat. Though she'd thought of pulling up the hem of her mantle to form extra cushioning, she couldn't do so while in motion. Her fingers had frozen into claws, gripping the sides of the litter. Corwin rode by often during the morning, waving as he passed. Ardith refused to loosen her hold, even to respond to her brother.

Finally, upon hearing Corwin's cry for the company to halt, she said a silent prayer of thanks to God—Father, Son, and Spirit—and every saint who came immediately to mind.

Bronwyn jolted awake as the litter came to a halt. "Goodness," she said, stretching delicately. "I have slept most of the morn away. I see the weather holds. Good, that means we can travel many miles yet before seeking shelter. Ah, Baron Gerard. How nice of you to assist us."

Gerard held the panel open. Bronwyn fairly bounded out of the litter, resting her fingertips briefly on Gerard's arm.

"How fare you, ladies?"

"Oh, quite nicely, my lord. I am, however, faint with hunger. Shall I bring you some cheese and bread, Ardith? Would you prefer wine or mead?"

"N-nothing, Bronwyn. I will eat later."

Bronwyn tilted her head. "Are you all right? You do look a bit peaked."

Ardith drew a calming breath. "I am fine. Do go and have your meal."

With a slight shrug of her shoulders, Bronwyn went in search of nourishment. Gerard stood at the opening, waiting.

"Have you ever ridden in one of these, my lord?"

"Nay," he said, inspecting the litter front to back. "From the way it moves, I would imagine the motion feels much the same as a ship in gentle seas."

"Gentle seas?"

"Aye."

"Have you traveled on many ships?"

"I have crossed the Channel several times between England and Normandy."

"And your opinion, my lord?"

Ardith gave him credit for trying to hide his smile. He *knew* she was stalling, unable to move.

"I would rather my feet on solid ground, or at least a good, steady horse beneath me."

Then he reached inside the litter, pushed her mantle aside and took a firm hold around her waist. His encircling hands were warm and reassuring.

"Come, Ardith. We shall walk a bit and you will feel better. Now, put your hands on my shoulders. Both hands, my lady. Very good. Move toward me a bit. A bit more."

"I feel such a dolt."

"Do you trust me, Ardith?"

"Aye, my lord."

"Then lean toward me and I will lift you out."

She did trust him, but as she leaned forward and Gerard tugged, Ardith flung her arms around Gerard's neck and clung. He grew very still, then his hands squeezed her waist. Ardith floated out of the litter, supported by strong arms and warm hands and her death grip on Gerard's neck.

She hung suspended for a moment before he lowered her

to the ground. Her feet on firm earth, Ardith loosened her hold to allow Gerard to stand upright. Expecting to see amusement, prepared to laugh at her own cowardice, Ardith looked up.

He smiled, but didn't mock. "Come, scamp," he said. "Let us see if you can walk."

Her hand tucked in the crook of his arm, they walked in silence up the road, past men and horses, until Ardith's legs no longer wobbled.

"I hope I need never board a ship," she stated firmly.

"'Tis not so bad once accustomed to the sway."

Her body and mind again in harmony, she thought to ask, "How fares my father?"

"Well enough." He stopped walking. "You worry over-much."

"Is that not why I came, to look after my father?"

"Partly."

Gerard realized his mistake as soon as the word passed his lips. Ardith withdrew her hand and faced him squarely.

"Then you must enlighten me, my lord. I heard of no other reason why I had to leave Lenvil."

Now wasn't the time to tell her the whole of his plans. Gerard wanted first to speak with King Henry, ensure no objection would come from royal quarters before bargaining with Harold on betrothal and marriage to Ardith.

But she was so damned adorable, her pert face tilted upward, her blue eyes flashing with irritation. Wasn't now a good time to hint at the joys to come?

He hadn't intended to kiss her, hadn't even intended to stray so far ahead of the rest of the company. But they were alone and the temptation was just too sweet.

He cupped her cheeks with his hands. "I wished you to come," he told her, then gently touched her mouth with his own.

Gerard felt her surprise in the slight tremble of her lips. He pressed through her hesitation, coaxed her honeyed mouth with featherlight brushes of lips. Finally, delightfully, she responded.

He cursed his chain mail, designed to deflect sword blows and spear points. He couldn't feel her hands where she placed them on his chest, twining her fingers in the metal rings. Nor could he feel the warmth of her body as he gathered her into his embrace.

The flash of her passionate nature, hidden under a thin veil of innocence, nearly shattered his resolve to be content with a kiss. With rigid control he kept his hand from straying to her breast, the gentle swell he longed to cup and fondle.

Knowing his limits, Gerard broke the kiss. Her eyes remained closed. Her lips, reddened and slightly swollen, stayed pursed for an instant, then relaxed.

When at last she opened her eyes, it was Gerard's turn to feel surprise. He saw sadness of unfathomable depth. A tear glistened in the corner of her eye.

"Oh, Gerard," she whispered. "Sometimes we may not have what we wish."

No, not right now, but soon. Gerard knew well the ways of seduction—a kiss here, a touch and sweet words there. When he was ready to claim her, she wouldn't deny him. Her response to his kiss told him as much. But why had the kiss brought on such sadness?

Before he could ask, Ardith pushed away, glancing back toward the company and the sound of an approaching horse.

"We have a problem, my lord," Corwin said as he reined in, his face all smiles. "We are being followed."

Gerard frowned. "By whom?"

"Elva."

"Elva?" Ardith exclaimed.

"Aye. I bade her return to Lenvil, but she refuses. She says that when Father banished her to the village, she became a peasant. Therefore, she claims the right of a freeman to go anywhere she damn well pleases."

"Where does she go?"

Corwin dismounted. "She follows you, Ardith. She says you will have need of her counsel at court."

Ardith crossed her arms, her expression stern. "I would wager she has read those blasted bones again. Every time she casts them, she sees some dire event."

"Superstitious nonsense," Gerard muttered, and began walking back to the main body of the company.

"Aye," Ardith agreed, falling into step. "But Elva believes in the old rites."

Corwin asked, "Do we let her join us? She is older than Father and the walk will be arduous."

Gerard shrugged the matter off as unimportant. Having one more person in the party made little difference. "Ardith?"

"If Bronwyn agrees, put Elva in the litter. I will walk."

Gerard waved Corwin off to tend to the old woman. "Why give up your seat?"

"I would give up my seat to anyone who would take it. I refuse to ride any farther in that device of torture."

Gerard's ire rose. No future mistress of Wilmont would trek the road like a common peasant.

"Thomas," he shouted. "Fetch my cloak."

Thomas dropped the destrier's reins and sprinted toward the cart bearing Gerard's tent and belongings. To Ardith's amazement, the warhorse stood still.

From the middle of the line came voices raised in argument. Harold lectured Elva on insolence. Elva shouted back from beside Bronwyn's litter.

"Oh, dear," Ardith said and took a step.

Gerard reached out and stopped her. "Leave them to their spat. Neither is helpless."

Thomas came running back, cloak in hand. Gerard whipped the beaver-lined mantle around his shoulders and fastened the gold brooch. He grabbed the reins, put his boot in the stirrup and in one fluid movement mounted the warhorse. He scowled down at Ardith. "Are you still determined to walk?"

"Aye, my lord."

He gave a long, resigned sigh, then held out his hands. "Come, Ardith. Ride with me."

The thought of riding on a warhorse gave her pause. Black as coal, sleek as silk, the destrier stood several hands taller than her palfrey. Warhorses were said to be mean as jackals, fierce fighters, protective of their masters.

"I thought 'twas bad luck for a destrier to carry a woman," she argued.

"Superstitious nonsense."

Ardith looked back. Everyone waited. Riding pillion was little better than riding in the litter. But if she refused Gerard's invitation, all would consider the rejection an insult to the baron.

She reached up. Gerard took a firm hold under her arms. She placed her foot on the toe of his boot. Expecting to swing up behind him, she said, "You should move your cloak, my lord, so I don't—"

With a jerk, Gerard pulled her up. With a thump, she landed sideways in his lap.

"—sit on it."

Ardith glared her displeasure.

"Are you really so unhappy with where you ride?" he asked.

No, she wasn't, but refused to admit aloud the comfort of the seat. Yet, she was uneasy. For more than a week she'd deliberately stayed away from Gerard. Now she found herself cradled between his thighs after an unexpected and unsettling kiss. Every inch of her flesh tingled in warning.

She felt the tug on her mantle as Gerard covered her legs. He pulled up his cowl, framing his blond hair with dark fur, then wrapped them both in beaver. Without glancing back, he gave a push with his knees and the horse moved forward.

Within the snug cocoon, Ardith felt the drowsiness she'd held at bay all morning. She turned her head from Gerard's chest and looked ahead at the road stretching endlessly through the countryside. One could see for miles from atop a warhorse.

She could hear the company behind them, the thud of soldiers' feet on the dirt road, the jangle of harnesses on the horses carrying the litter. She tried to sit up straighter, to peek over Gerard's shoulder at the parade behind.

"Why so curious, scamp? Must you ever be the mother hen, checking on her chicks?"

"Are you sure everyone was ready? How do you know one of the men was not back in the bushes and we leave him behind?"

"Then he must hike up his breeches and hurry to catch up. 'Tis one of the few privileges of rank I find amusing. I can leave without them—" he tossed his head back slightly "—but they cannot leave without me."

"And if my father's horse stumbled, or Bronwyn's litter came unharnessed, or a wagon's wheel broke?"

"Then Corwin would come tell me. 'Tis his duty to see the retinue moves without incident, to inform me of any problems. If I kept looking back to ensure the company intact, what need for Corwin to take his duty seriously?"

"You trust Corwin."

He nodded. "As I trust many others who serve me."

"John?"

"I am confident we left Lenvil in competent hands."

Ardith silently agreed. "Who else?"

"I trusted you, did I not, to hold a confidence?"

"You give your trust lightly, my lord."

"Nay, my lady. But once earned, 'tis rarely lost. So many questions. You look weary. You should sleep."

In this unseemly position? Cuddled close to Gerard? Atop a warhorse? Sleep?

"I think not, my lord."

"My lady is headstrong, a trait she will rue one day.

You have no work to do, no people to order about, no hurt needing your attention. In about three hours we will reach the abbey where we will partake of an evening meal and attend vespers. I will not suffer the embarrassment of one of my retinue falling asleep over her plate or during prayers."

"I would not!"

"Humph."

Chagrined, Ardith decided she was no longer speaking to Gerard. They could ride the rest of the way in silence.

She tugged her scarf forward to protect her cheek from the rings of his chain mail. The sway of the destrier's smooth gait and the warmth of the cozy nest Gerard had created lulled Ardith into closing her eyes. Through all the layers, she could hear the steady beat of Gerard's heart.

On the brink of slipping into the land of dreams, Ardith warmed to the brush of Gerard's lips on her forehead.

"Ah, my scamp. You have much to learn," he whispered. "You will come to realize that I always get what I wish."

Ardith woke to Gerard's lips on her forehead and warm breath on her cheek, luring her from sleep with gentle bait.

"We arrive," he said.

In a sweet haze, Ardith turned to look at the structure coming into view. The square bell tower stretched to the sky. The mammoth stone building sprawled over several hides of land. Monks, black-robed and tonsured, scurried to meet the approaching travelers.

Ardith wiggled to sit up.

"Ever been inside an abbey?" he asked.

"Never, though I saw the one in Bury Saint Edmunds. Are all the church's holdings so imposing?"

"Many are, and many of the abbots control as much land as some barons. A bishop who controls several abbeys oversees nearly as much wealth as in the royal treasury."

Ardith finally understood the king's reluctance to allow the church to appoint bishops.

Gerard pulled his destrier to a halt at the steps leading to the massive oak doors. The doors swung open and out stepped a slight man, no more finely garbed than the other monks, but of obvious authority.

"Abbot Cottingham," Gerard called in greeting. "We beg a night of your hospitality."

"Gladly given, Gerard of Wilmont. Welcome to our humble abbey. May you find peace within our walls."

"A place to spread my pallet and a chunk of the finest cheese in all England is what I crave."

A smile cracked the abbot's weathered face. "Would that all our noble guests were as easy to please." Then the smile faded. "Your father, may his soul rest in heaven with the Lord, was also easily pleased. I shall miss Everart's good company. But come, 'tis cold. A warm fire and tankard of mead await inside."

Ardith's stomach growled at the mention of cheese, reminding her of her missed nooning. Gerard had departed in such haste, not allowing time to eat after her stomach had settled. She didn't want to think about what had happened instead.

Gerard tossed the destrier's reins to Thomas, who'd appeared at the horse's head, then slid his hands under her mantle and around her ribs. "Ready, Ardith?"

Ardith looked down from the great height, wary. "Should we not wait for assistance? Mayhap Corwin—"

"I lifted you up here without aid, did I not?"

"Well, aye, but—"

"Then I can also get you down."

And he did, so effortlessly that no strain showed in his face. She shouldn't have been surprised. She'd seen him toss men aside during the game, and afterward had admired the sculpted bulk of his torso and arms.

Such wayward thoughts, she chided herself, *and in the presence of an abbot, no less.* Ardith turned toward that

august personage. He was looking at Gerard, his hand outstretched to indicate a monk who stood at his side.

"Friar Zachary will show the women to the ladies' court.
They will be provided with hot water and a meal."

"My thanks, my lord abbot," Ardith said.

Abbot Cottingham didn't answer, indeed seemed not to
hear.

"They have had a tiring day," Gerard said. "I am sure
they will appreciate any kindness."

The abbot nodded. "Then I will also grant dispensation
from vespers, so they may rest."

Gerard dismounted, and during those few moments when
his back was turned, the abbot looked her way. The brown
of his eyes had darkened with pure loathing, utter condem-
nation.

Chapter Seven

"Ardith, your imagination runs amok," Bronwyn stated.

"I imagine nothing," Ardith retorted. "Abbot Cottingham took a dislike to me, I am sure of it. Out in the yard, he would not answer when I spoke to him. He looked at me but once, as though I were dirt beneath his feet. And this meal we are served proves his sentiment. 'Tis hardly fit to eat! Would you serve such to guests?"

"Nay, but then neither am I a monk who must serve a wayfarer's portion to each of a large company."

Ardith looked down at the stale bread, a thick slice of cheese—which she had to admit was superb—and a cup of thinned mead.

She'd wager the abbot hadn't dared serve such to Gerard.

"And we are confined to the ladies' court," she continued her argument. "Did you see the look on Friar Zachary's face when he came for Elva to tend Father? *My* services were definitely not wanted. The abbot does not want me roaming about his precious abbey."

Having given up on eating several minutes before, Bronwyn sat on the edge of a cot, working a piece of embroidery. "I do not wonder," she said. "You are young, unmarried and quite beautiful—a temptation."

"To monks?"

"Think you a monk does not have lustful thoughts? Are

they not men? 'Tis not you the abbot dislikes, Ardith. He only protects his monks from the occasion of sin.'' Bronwyn looked up, smiling. ''You did present a fetching vision from atop Gerard's horse, surrounded in furs, half-asleep. A temptress if ever I saw one.''

Ardith took a bite of cheese to ease the growling in her stomach. A temptress, indeed. She'd looked half-asleep because she'd been half-asleep, having napped in Gerard's arms with the peace of a babe wrapped in swaddling. She blamed the imprudent lapse of self-control on her lack of rest the night before and the misery of riding in Bronwyn's litter.

''Oh, dear,'' Bronwyn muttered. ''Ardith?''

Ardith reached out to take the embroidery. The thread proved easier to unravel than the knot of turmoil caused by the memory of Gerard's kisses. She shouldn't have allowed his forward ways. But how could she have prevented either kiss?

The first kiss had caught her off guard. Who'd have guessed Gerard would take so bold an action while standing in the middle of the road, for anyone to see?

She should have pushed away, but a storm of emotion had hurtled through her defenses and had unleashed with heady fury. When wrapped in Gerard's embrace, she couldn't quiet the thunder of her racing heart or subdue the colors whirling in her head.

For the length of the kiss she'd belonged to Gerard, as though the long-ago betrothal had occurred, the resulting marriage celebrated. She'd reveled in the joy Gerard summoned from her heart, but as the kiss ended, the fantasy shattered.

The ensuing despair had nearly brought forth tears. He hadn't explained why he wanted her to make the journey, and Ardith hadn't cared right then for an explanation. Corwin's interruption and Elva's unexpected appearance had helped to push her upheaval aside.

Then Gerard had refused to allow her to walk. She

thought she remembered a slight brush of lips on her forehead before she had fallen asleep, and an arrogant statement that he always got what he wanted. The memory was vague, dreamlike. Not vague in the least had been waking from a deep sleep to Gerard's soft lips and warm breath on her cheek.

Bronwyn suddenly laughed. "Oh, Ardith. Now that I think on it, mayhap the abbot protects *you* from his monks. I would wager he thinks you belong to Gerard, as his leman."

Ardith gasped and nearly threw the straightened embroidery at Bronwyn. "Why would he think such a thing?"

"Why would he not? Look at your arrival at his abbey from the abbot's view. 'Twas beyond the ordinary, you must admit."

Stunned speechless, Ardith hid her blush with her hands.

Still chuckling, Bronwyn continued, "Let him think what he will. You will probably never see the abbot again." Then her laughter ceased. "Oh, Ardith. 'Tis such a pity you do not belong to some man. You would make such a fine wife."

"I do not want your pity," Ardith said harshly. "What is, is—and cannot be changed."

"I disagree. Not only can your lot change, but the sooner done, the better. Father has allowed an injustice, one that benefits him quite well. I have thought hard on the problem and believe I have a solution."

Ardith asked warily, "Solution to what problem?"

"Finding you a husband."

"Bronwyn..."

"Now hear me out, sister. Your inability to bear children is not the barrier to marriage you may believe. Granted, we must ignore the more eligible men in the kingdom. We must strike from our list any man who needs an heir."

"List?"

Bronwyn put aside her embroidery and counted on her fingers. "The man must already have his heir. He must be someone in need of a wife to warm his bed, serve as chatelaine for his manor and nursemaid for his children. I can think of several men who need such a woman. Of course, there is the problem of providing a dowry."

"Bronwyn, I have *no* dowry. Therefore, I have no prospects. This talk of marriage is foolish. Corwin has promised I shall always have a place at Lenvil. Why should I look for a husband?"

"Corwin may promise you shelter, but his wife may balk at the arrangement. Corwin must one day wed, and his bride may see you as a rival, not only for Corwin's affection but for control of Lenvil. The peasants and serfs are so accustomed to serving you that they may not welcome a new mistress. Do you not see how divided loyalty could cause misery?"

Aye, she could.

"But I have no dowry," Ardith protested.

"Remember when Agnes married, how Father nearly beggared Lenvil to give her a fitting dowry?" At Ardith's nod, Bronwyn continued, "When Elizabeth married, somehow Father managed to satisfy the contract through Lenvil's revenue. And Edith's entry into the convent did not come cheaply."

"You were not dowered."

"Nay, but I was fortunate that Kester wanted me for myself, and did not need lands or coin."

Ardith looked sharply at her sister. "You are saying that Father might be able to raise funds for a small dowry?"

"Possibly. You are the fifth daughter of a landed but not wealthy lord. No man who brings suit for your hand will expect much of a dowry. And I do expect you will have suitors. When properly gowned and trained in courtly manners, I suspect you will turn many noble heads. We shall have to turn hordes of males from our door."

"Really, Bronwyn!"

"You think I jest? You underestimate your beauty and grace, Ardith. Too, you will be a fresh face, an innocent in a court of jaded and conniving women. Make no mistake, sister dear, you *will* be pursued. As I said, we shall just be careful of who we allow to gain your favor.''

''Those men having an heir and not needing money.''

''Exactly.''

Ardith shook her head in disbelief. What man would want a barren wife who could bring him little added wealth? The idea was absurd, and yet...

What was she thinking? How could she possibly marry another man, feeling as she did about Gerard? But then affection was rarely a consideration when choosing a mate. Marriage contracts hinged on alliance and wealth. Fondness between husband and wife developed later, if at all.

She'd put aside the hope of marriage so many years ago. When the forsaken dream occasionally plagued her, she hadn't considered any man but Gerard as her husband.

Given time and distance, could she like, even love a man other than Gerard? Could some other man's kisses ignite the fire in her very core, muddle her thoughts, sap her strength? She knew only one man's kisses, the feel of one man's arms. Had she let her girlish fantasy of belonging to Gerard cloud her common sense?

Bronwyn said gently, ''You need not marry any man who does not appeal to you. If some special man does appeal, and Father balks at providing a dowry, we could petition Gerard for the funds.''

Ardith groaned at the suggestion. ''We will not petition Gerard for a dowry.''

''Why ever not? He is Lenvil's liege lord. 'Tis not uncommon for an overlord to dower a vassal's daughter.''

Ardith distrusted the merry spark that suddenly brightened Bronwyn's eyes.

''You must admit Gerard likes you, Ardith. He did show you marked favor today. Most knights would shudder at the thought of a female even *touching* their precious warhorses. Yet, Gerard invited you to ride.'' Bronwyn giggled.

"You should have seen the horrified look on Father's face."

The hinges on the door squealed as Elva entered the room. Relieved by the distraction, Ardith asked, "How is Father?"

"Same as always after too long a ride," Elva said. "His mood is surly and his leg pains. You would think, at his age, Harold would have more sense than to undertake such a journey."

"Elva, you are older than Father, yet you thought to walk the whole of the journey. Pray tell, who is the bigger fool?"

"The signs say I must stay close to you, that you will have need of me. I had little choice but to follow. Ah, compline," Elva said as the bells called the monks to prayer.

Soon, a chorus of male voices blended in song. The chant rose and fell, the Latin words muffled, the prayer haunting in the crisp night air.

"Think on it," Bronwyn whispered to Ardith. "We will talk more when we reach Westminster."

On the third day out of Lenvil, the weather ceased to cooperate. Ardith urged her palfrey through the dusting of snow. She didn't mind the snowfall, so long as the flakes fell soft and light without the company of a bitter wind.

Ardith found she was enjoying the journey. Gerard set a quick but not grueling pace. Corwin was attentive, stopping occasionally during one of his frequent trips up and down the line. When the road was wide enough, she rode beside the litter and conversed with Bronwyn and Elva.

Most of the time she rode ahead of the litter, behind several of Wilmont's men-at-arms. Over their heads she could watch Gerard and Father in the lead.

Never far from the surface of her thoughts was Bronwyn's wild suggestion of marriage, though Bronwyn hadn't mentioned the scheme again after that night in the abbey.

Corwin came up from behind. "After we stop at midday,

you are to ride at the head of the line. Gerard wishes you at his side when we ride through London.''

"Whatever for?"

"I did not question his order, but I believe he has your safety in mind.''

"How can I be less than safe when riding into the city behind a troop of men-at-arms?''

"I am sure he has his reasons. He always does.''

After a light nooning, the company assembled for the last leg of the journey. Ardith found her mare waiting at the front of the line. Gerard helped her mount.

"After we pass through the gates, stay close," he said, then swung up on his destrier. The warhorse pranced and snorted at the presence of a mare. With strong hands and powerful thighs Gerard brought the beast under control.

Through the afternoon she noticed changes in the countryside. The company passed through several villages. Throngs of people crowded the road, trudging through the mud to reach London's gates before nightfall.

Corwin called out for the company to close ranks. For the first time since leaving Lenvil, Gerard turned to look back. With a motion of his hand, he beckoned Ardith to pull up. She obeyed, urging the mare into the destrier's shadow.

The thick, stone wall surrounding London loomed nearly as high as treetop level. After passing through the open gate made of oak and iron, Ardith gaped at the city.

Wood houses lined the road, one butted against the other to form a solid line. Here and there a building of stone, usually a merchant's shop with residence on the upper floor, interrupted the row.

Wilmont's men-at-arms shouted warnings to clear the way. If someone didn't move fast enough, the soldiers enforced the command with a shove. Ardith had never seen so many people in so small an area. Mingling with the aroma of bakery and tannery, the sharp tang of refuse and body waste rose from slimy puddles in the muddy road.

Everywhere swarmed the beggars.

Ardith kept her eyes forward until they passed through the rabble. She noted churches with squared steeples and stone houses with three stories or more. Gerard slowed the pace as they rode past St. Paul's Cathedral, then Baynard's Castle, giving Ardith time to gawk at the massive structures. As they passed through the western gate, leaving London behind to continue on to Westminster, Gerard again spurred the company forward.

Ardith had little time to absorb the sights and sounds of London before they rode into Westminster. Where the Tyburn flowed into the Thames stood the imposing Westminster Hall, behind it the abbey, and off to the side the palace.

After entrusting her mare to a stable boy, Ardith looked back toward Bronwyn. Somehow Kester had learned of their arrival. Small of stature, but big of heart, Kester greeted Bronwyn with subdued but genuine affection.

Bronwyn immediately launched into an explanation of how her family now happened to be in Westminster.

Ardith looked around for the instigator of the hastily wrought plan. Gerard had disappeared, and with him, Corwin.

Later that evening, awaiting the evening meal, Ardith wondered how anyone could become indifferent to the splendor of the royal palace. Richly garbed nobles filtered into the hall from entrances guarded by soldiers from the royal garrison. Flickering light from torches and rings of candles brightened alcoves and reflected off pillars of marble.

A table sat on the dais that stretched the breadth of the hall, awaiting the king and the high nobility. Rows of tables extended down the length. Ardith sat on a bench toward the very end of one of these tables, as befitted her lack of rank.

"There you are. Would you like company?" Corwin asked.

"Aye, my thanks," Ardith said with relief. "Bronwyn told me to sit here, then went with Kester to take a higher place at the table. Can you stay with me for the meal?"

"Aye," Corwin replied. "Have you seen much of the palace yet?"

"Only Bronwyn's chambers and the passages leading here. Bronwyn promised to take me round tomorrow."

"I would take you myself, if I had the time. But the baron has some business to attend to and we won't be about much."

At the mention of the baron, Ardith looked to the high table. Gerard stood there, his weight shifted on to one hip, arms crossed, talking to another nobly attired man.

A woman walked up to Gerard, interrupting the discourse, laying a hand on Gerard's forearm. She was stunning. Gowned and veiled in a wispy fabric of pale blue, she gave Gerard a blinding smile. Twin plaits of silver-blond hair hung over her breasts, ribbons of blue interwoven in the braids. From this distance Ardith couldn't see the color of the woman's eyes, knew only they were light. The woman's lips, however, were so vibrant that Ardith wondered if she used berry juice to darken their natural color.

Ardith leaned toward Corwin. "Who speaks with Gerard?"

"That is Charles, the earl of Warwick. He is a staunch ally of Wilmont."

"I was referring to the woman."

"Lady Diane?"

"She is very beautiful," Ardith prompted.

"Very wealthy, too. Lady Diane is King Henry's ward."

Corwin proceeded to name and give a brief account of those who gathered in the upper reaches of the hall. Earls and barons mingled with knights and officers of the court. Though Ardith knew that tomorrow she wouldn't remember most of the names, she could fairly judge rank.

"Finally, we eat," Corwin commented.

"Do we not wait for the king and queen?"

Corwin shrugged. "The king must be eating elsewhere. As for the queen, she is not in residence. Several years ago she retired to Romsey Abbey and does not attend court often."

Ardith glanced at her father, who sat near to but below Bronwyn, and wondered what he thought of the placement.

Then a long line of servants carried platters of food into the hall, presenting the delicacies first to the high table. Ardith noted boar and mutton, pullets and dove, many of the same meats she served at Lenvil. There were loaves of brown bread, freshly baked. She thoroughly enjoyed a confection of raisins and almonds and rare fruits.

The hall was noisy and merry, the voices echoing off the high, vaulted ceiling. Ardith began to relax and enjoy the company of those around her. One young man, Robert of Bath, seemed determined to make her laugh.

"Corwin, have you finished?"

Ardith's fingers tightened on her goblet as she recognized Gerard's voice. The others around her stood, leaving her no choice but to acknowledge Gerard's presence.

Gerard's garb denied the pattern Ardith had worked out to distinguish rank. She recognized the simple gold circlet banding his tawny hair. He wore only two rings, both of gold and rubies, finely worked but not pretentious. His dalmatica of forest-green wool was girdled with woven strips of leather.

"Aye, my lord," Corwin answered. "May I escort Ardith to Bronwyn before we leave?"

Robert of Bath bowed slightly. "I would be happy to see Ardith to her sister if you are in a hurry."

Gerard looked Robert over as if assessing his worthiness. "If the lady will allow, I would seek the pleasure of doing so myself. Ardith?"

As Ardith opened her mouth to say she needed no escort, Gerard held out his hand and raised an eyebrow. As he had once before, he allowed her no option but to comply or give insult.

She placed her fingers across Gerard's palm. The contact caused a tingle that snaked up her arm and writhed down to her toes. Gerard tucked her hand in the crook of his arm and guided her through the crowd.

People moved aside, creating a path. Ardith noticed the deference only on the edge of awareness, her senses focused on Gerard. Not only did he look good, he smelled good. Bathed and shaved, Gerard no longer carried the odor of horse and leather. An elusive, wholly male aroma teased her nostrils, lured her to breathe deeper to savor the fragrance.

Gerard didn't linger to chat. He greeted Kester with a quick jerk of his head. Then he turned and strode away, leaving the hall at a swift pace, Corwin following.

Bronwyn frowned.

"Come now, dearest," Kester chided. "You must admit it neatly done. The tongues will wag for a week."

"Had he chosen anyone but Ardith, I would applaud."

"I doubt he has done your sister any harm."

Ardith crossed her arms. "Would one of you tell me what you are talking about?"

"Baron Gerard's motive for his unusual behavior," Bronwyn explained. "Never has he invited a woman to take his arm before the entire court. There are women in this hall who would give fortunes to be the object of the baron's regard."

Ardith immediately conjured the memory of the beautiful

blonde in wispy blue, a delicate hand poised on Gerard's forearm. She bit back the jealousy.

"Baron Gerard was performing a simple courtesy, Bronwyn. He came to the back of the hall to fetch Corwin, not me."

"That may be, but the court will speculate otherwise. Most will believe he has purposely rebuffed Lady Diane. Her advances tonight were quite blatant. Well, whatever Gerard's motives, we must make use of the moment. Come, I want you to meet Sir Percival."

Chapter Eight

Edward Siefeld's mind wandered as Basil of Northbryre restated his displeasure over the bungled assassination plot.

The events in Normandy were best forgotten. Edward had realized he'd waylaid the wrong man the instant the warrior had turned to fight. Out of the victim's mouth spewed, not the war-cry roar for which Gerard was renowned, but the pompous, taunting slurs of Richard.

With sword flashing, the bastard of Wilmont had dared to question Edward's parentage, to comment on the shape and whereabouts of his sex organ, to proclaim Wilmont's superiority over the chicken dung of the earth. Two of Edward's men had died. Others nursed wounds. But even Richard, with his enviable prowess, couldn't withstand the onslaught of ten men. Richard had fallen under Edward's own sword.

Basil paced between his bed and a table stacked with scrolls and the castle steward's accounts. Edward doubted Basil could read or tally. And since Basil's young wife had fled to Normandy with their son, the stack had grown. But as long as Basil paid well for the often illegal and usually bloody tasks assigned to the mercenaries, Edward didn't care how Basil kept his accounts.

Basil's ponderous frame finally halted in front of a ring of candles, blocking their light. Edward likened Basil to a black bear, gone old and to seed, but still dangerous. Silver-threaded, thinning hair topped Basil's head. With his hands clasped behind his back, Basil's paunch strained against the rich fabric of his robes, proclaiming his love of food and wine without benefit of exercise to keep his body fit.

But then Basil had no need to hone his body. With a garrison of men-at-arms to defend the keep, and mercenaries to command at will, Basil had never held a weapon in earnest.

"And now," Basil was saying, "Baron Gerard does not avenge his knight or strengthen his holding. He is a coward."

"Perhaps the baron does not know who killed Richard, or the knight we found snooping about."

"He knows, Siefeld." A smirk crossed Basil's face. "He knows and does naught. Everart would have mounted a company of knights and challenged me by now. His son sits in his keep and plays with himself."

Edward thought otherwise. He'd seen Gerard fight. The man was no coward. And having battled Richard, Edward wanted nothing to do with Gerard.

"Why is Milhurst so important to you, my lord?"

Basil of Northbryre wasn't in the habit of explaining his actions to inferiors. How could a mercenary understand the indignity borne by his family when, by the scratch of a clerk's quill, ownership of land had been transferred from Northbryre to Wilmont? Only by a quirk of fate had Wilmont held Milhurst at the time of the Domesday recording.

By all that was holy, the twenty hides of land, the manor and pasture and peasants, rightfully belonged to Northbryre. If he looked out from the north wall, he could *see* the edge of the demesne. A river flowed sluggishly through fields and forest, except in one spot where the banks narrowed and the water bubbled. At that churning bend stood a mill for grinding grain, an extremely valuable source of wealth.

Through the reign of three kings, the Barons of Northbryre had fought with both sword and petition to regain the

holding. Wilmont never yielded a single hide. The kings
ignored pleas for justice.

Edward's failure to dispose of Gerard infuriated Basil,
but now he deemed Gerard's murder unnecessary. If Gerard
wouldn't fight, Milhurst was vulnerable to seizure.

Basil watched the mercenary's eyes light in understanding as he answered, "One year's revenue from the mill
would keep your band fed, clothed and armed for ten years.
After the evening meal, we will discuss the best way to
take Milhurst."

Gerard closed the Domesday Book. For three days he
and Corwin had searched the pages and made lists of the
lands belonging to Wilmont or Northbryre. As he had
known all along, and had now confirmed, Wilmont rightfully owned Milhurst.

"I had not realized Basil so land-rich," Corwin said,
putting down the quill and flexing his fingers.

"Nor I," Gerard admitted.

"Do you have everything you need to present your
grievance to the king?"

"I want to know first if Basil has attacked Milhurst."

Corwin nodded his understanding. "Then you can claim
Basil broke the king's peace, as well as attempted to murder
a member of your family."

Gerard sanded the ink, then rolled the parchment. "Siefeld is the key. His shock at seeing Richard may rattle his
wits enough to confess all."

"What happens if Basil does not come to court? What
if he senses a trap?"

"Henry has summoned all the barons, demanding a
pledge of loyalty at Christmas. Any vassal not presenting
himself at court endangers his title and lands. Basil will be
here, and with him, Edward Siefeld. Basil does not step
foot from his castle without heavy guard." With a slow
smile, Gerard added, "If he does not appear, I will petition
Henry to let me be the king's punishing sword."

Corwin cocked his head. "I do believe you would prefer to pry Basil from his castle than to seek reprisal from Henry."

"An astute observation."

Corwin laughed, then stretched. "If we have finished, I think I will visit Ardith and find out what plagues her."

Gerard heard the note of concern in Corwin's voice, and became immediately anxious about Ardith. He and Corwin had worked long hours these past days, recording the official land grants, stopping only for the evening meal—Corwin always joining Ardith at the low end of the hall, Gerard forced to observe from the high table.

More and more he liked what he saw, was sure he'd chosen wisely. Bronwyn had taken Ardith in hand and gowned her in rich cloth, enhancing her natural beauty. She now looked more the noble heiress than Saxon peasant.

She showed respect to those of higher rank, but without subservience in her posture or expression. Her forthright manner might surprise some of his peers, but none could find fault or take offense. Those of her own rank actually vied for a place near her at table. Her sweet smile and genuine warmth drew people like iron to lodestone.

"All is not well with Ardith?"

Corwin shrugged. "She is upset about something. It could be no more than the strangeness of new surroundings. She is unaccustomed to the confinement of indoors."

Gerard could sympathize. "Do you think she would like a brisk ride through the countryside?"

"She would probably love it."

Gerard sincerely hoped so as they made their way through the palace. After depositing the lists in Wilmont's chambers, they discussed a route Ardith might enjoy. His plans vanished when Bronwyn answered the door of her chambers, crying.

"Oh, Corwin, I am so glad you are here." She sighed. "You too, Baron Gerard."

"Why the tears?" Corwin asked.

"'Tis Ardith. You must find her and bring her back. She is quite peeved and will not listen to reason. Elva went after her, but I fear Ardith is too swift for Elva's old legs."

"What has happened?"

"Sir Percival. I told Ardith he was coming to see her and that I was sure he was about to speak to Father. I thought she would be pleased! How was I to know she holds Percival in contempt? And now Percival is angry because Ardith was not here when he came, nor was Father. Then *he* left in a huff. Sir Baylor will be arriving any moment and I fear *he* will be angered. Oh, Corwin, this is such a muddle."

Gerard listened with growing confusion and alarm. "Bronwyn, where did Ardith go?"

Bronwyn tossed her arms in the air. "How am I to know?"

"I will find her. Corwin, stay here should Ardith return."

Gerard swept through the passages, setting torches to flickering in his wake. Servants scurried to get out of his way as he sought the elusive scamp. Not finding her in the great hall, he searched the kitchen, then the stable. He found her in a chapel. Much to his annoyance he also found Percival. Neither Ardith nor Percival heard him enter. They were much too involved in the chase.

Gerard leaned against the doorjamb, crossed his arms and smiled. Hellfire, Ardith was beautiful. Her eyes fairly sparked with anger. In a froth of pale green, from sheer veil to delicate slippers, Ardith resembled a picture he'd once seen of a sea nymph. She hiked up her skirts and dashed from behind a statue of Christ toward the marble altar.

Percival reached out to snare the fleeing nymph. He missed. Gerard snickered. An ox of a man, Percival lacked grace of footing, though on a battlefield one was glad of the man's skill with a sword. A berserker by nature, Percival used his sword to fell men as a farmer's scythe reaped wheat. But unlike the farmer who knows to stop at the end of the row, Percival would fight until overcome with exhaustion, even when the battle was won, unless someone managed to knock the man from his feet and let sense return to his head. Only once had Gerard attempted that task, and now bore a scar on his neck from the encounter.

If Percival's bloodlust had been running rampant, making coherent thought impossible, Gerard might have worried for Ardith's safety. But another lust had Percival in its grip, merely tilting his judgment.

They circled the altar once. Then Ardith, with a burst of speed, put the length of the marble slab between them.

"Come now, my dove," Percival cajoled. "You cannot elude me long. I only mean to have a taste of you before we wed."

"I am *not* your dove," Ardith shot back. "Nor would I accept you if you were the last man in England!"

Undaunted, Percival persisted. "But you do not have to accept me, my dove. Harold need only give his approval to the match. You should be friendly to me, Ardith."

"Father will not force me to marry a man I do not want!"

"Come, my sweet, let me show you how well we will deal together."

Percival lunged, landing atop the altar, sliding forward. Ardith cried out and stepped back, right into a pillar of marble.

"Touch one hair on Ardith's head, Percival, and you lose a hand." Gerard's voice rang menacingly through the chapel.

Ardith said a short prayer of thanks for Gerard's timely appearance.

Percival slid off the altar, his eyes narrowed. "Baron Gerard. What concern is this of yours?"

"As Ardith's liege lord, I have a say in whom she will marry. I fear, Percival, your suit is doomed to failure."

Percival frowned. "I was led to believe otherwise. Lady Bronwyn said—"

Gerard waved a dismissing hand. "Do not fault Bronwyn. She did not know my mind in this. She did not know I have other plans for Ardith."

What other plans? Before Ardith could ask, Percival appealed. "Can we not come to some bargain, Gerard? Surely my position is equal to anyone you may choose, and we would make glorious allies, you and I."

Ardith suddenly realized Gerard's reason for wanting her nearby. He had an alliance he wished to make and intended to use her as part of the bargain. Appalled, Ardith held her head high as she stepped toward the door.

Gerard grabbed her arm as she tried to brush past. "Where do you think you are going?"

She refused to look at Gerard, but knew she must answer. "I will return to Bronwyn's chambers."

"And deal with Baylor?"

Ardith's shoulders slumped a bit.

"I thought not," he commented. "Abide a moment while I rid us of Percival."

She didn't want to stay; she wanted to flee. But Gerard had this annoying habit of giving orders while other people were about.

Ardith turned to face Gerard. "As you wish, my lord."

His arrogant smile told her Gerard was pleased with her compliance. He released her arm.

"Ardith's future is decided, Percival," Gerard stated. "Further pursuit on your part wastes your time and taxes my goodwill."

"'Tis as you say, Gerard. But should your plans change, I would ask that you reconsider my suit."

Much to Ardith's dismay, Gerard nodded slightly.

Percival bowed to Gerard. "Then I bid you good day," he said, and quit the chapel.

Gerard placed a hand on her shoulder and with the other tilted her chin. His eyes were soft with concern.

"Did he hurt you?"

"Nay, my lord."

"But he frightened you. You are trembling."

Ardith let him believe his false assumption. She wouldn't tell Gerard that *his* touch caused the tremors. She tried very hard to remember that Gerard intended to give her to another man.

"Should we not return, my lord? Bronwyn will be worried."

The pad of his thumb rubbed across her cheekbone. Ardith stepped back and Gerard's hands fell away. He clasped his hands behind his back and his expression hardened.

"Bronwyn has been busy. Just how many suitors has she gathered for you?"

"Five."

"Five!" Gerard's surprise and displeasure echoed through the small chapel. "Who?"

Gerard paced as she rattled off the names. She wondered if any of the five was also Gerard's choice. She hoped not, though Gaylord wasn't a bad sort. At least Gaylord could make her laugh.

"All suitable men," Gerard commented.

"Bronwyn chose carefully."

"Has any of them sought out Harold to ask for you?"

"Not that I know of, my lord. Father is difficult to locate these days. He is so busy renewing old friendships that we rarely see him. We have not even had time to..."

Ardith bit down on her rambling tongue.

Gerard stopped pacing. "To what, Ardith?"

Sensing his likely censure, Ardith thought to evade the truth until later, until Bronwyn stood by her side to share the lecture. But Gerard's stern expression brooked no deceit. "To seek his approval for Bronwyn's scheme, ask if he could put forth a small dowry."

Gerard stood quietly for a moment. "You and Bronwyn set out to find a husband for you without consulting your father, without any male guidance?"

"Kester knows."

"Kester! Kester allows Bronwyn too much freedom. He

is an excellent knight, an intelligent adviser, but is much too lenient toward his wife!'' Gerard turned on his heel and headed out of the chapel. Ardith scampered to follow.

"Women arranging marriages," he grumbled, and shook his head in disbelief.

"And why not?" Ardith countered, nearly running to match his stride. "You just admitted that Bronwyn chose suitably. There would be more happy unions if women arranged marriages."

"Happy unions? You mean based on sentiment? Ardith, sentiment has no place in a good marriage contract."

"Well, maybe it should."

Gerard didn't answer.

Ardith suddenly realized they were in a section of the palace she'd never seen. "This is not the way to Bronwyn's chambers. Where are we going?"

"To the shoemaker. You need a new pair of boots."

Ardith didn't argue, indeed, couldn't argue. By the time they reached the shoemaker she was out of breath. Gerard ushered her inside and waved her to a stool.

The aroma of fresh hides in the small, dark shop was almost overpowering. All manner of footwear, from rugged leather boots to dainty cloth slippers, lay strewn on the bench and overflowed onto the floor.

While the shoemaker measured Ardith's foot, Gerard dug through a stack of leather. He tugged a piece from the stack and held it out.

"Do you like this?" he asked.

Ardith reached out and stroked the soft, supple piece of doeskin. Though she didn't understand his reason for the purchase, she knew arguing with Gerard over a pair of boots would be a waste of breath. Besides, these boots would be the most comfortable she'd ever owned.

"Aye, my lord," she answered honestly.

The shoemaker rose from his kneeling position, studying the outline of her foot drawn with a stylus on a wax tablet.

"A wise choice, milord," he commented. "The hide will keep your lady's feet warm and dry."

Gerard didn't disavow the relationship as he followed the shoemaker to the bench. In low tones and with slight hand gestures, Gerard gave instructions. The shoemaker grabbed a fresh slate and made a sketch.

"Will this do, milord?" he asked, presenting the design.

Gerard took the stylus and made another mark. "Like this," he said, and returned the slate.

"Very well, milord. They should be ready tomorrow eve."

Gerard spun on his heel and left the shop. Ardith's ire began to rise. The insufferable man hadn't even looked to see if she had her slipper back on, which she did, but still...

"Ardith!" Gerard bellowed.

She held her temper, thanked the shoemaker, then perversely took her time to obey the summons. She followed in Gerard's wake again, as he strode through unfamiliar passages and climbed stairs. Finally, he came to a door and pushed it open. He entered the chamber, crossing to a table stacked with scrolls and holding a pitcher and goblets. He poured a draft and guzzled it down.

Ardith warily followed, closing the door.

She marveled at the simplicity and comfort of Gerard's chambers. Within the sitting room stood an oak table and two high-backed chairs. She recognized the exotic rug on the floor as the rug from Gerard's tent. A large brazier, coals glowing, kept the chill at bay. An arch to the right of the room hinted at chambers beyond.

"Thomas?" Gerard called.

The lad appeared from under the arch. He looked first at Ardith, then at Gerard. "My lord?"

"Corwin is with Lady Bronwyn. Go tell them Ardith is with me and will remain here for the evening meal. Inform Corwin that he and Harold are to join us after they eat. Then make yourself scarce. I do not wish to see your face until you bring us our food."

Thomas quickly left.

Gerard refilled his goblet, then poured another and set it on the table. He plopped down in one chair, motioning at Ardith to take the other.

The wine was potent, the fire warm, but Ardith couldn't relax, not until she had some answers.

"You told Percival my future was decided. I should like to hear those plans, my lord."

"In due time. I will discuss my plans first with Harold."

She couldn't help chide. "You, too, have made plans without consulting my father?"

He smiled, set his goblet on the table. "Aye, but then, unlike Percival, I do not need Harold's consent or permission for any action I might decide upon, do I?"

Chagrined, Ardith silently conceded.

"Why were you in the chapel?" he suddenly asked.

"I sought a quiet place to think and pray for guidance."

"Did you find it?" he scoffed.

"Nay. Percival interrupted too quickly."

"You should not have been alone. Had I not found you when I did, Percival might have harmed you."

Ardith had already surmised as much.

Without another word, Gerard rose and left the room. He quickly returned, carrying a small, ornate chest. He nudged the scrolls aside and put the chest on the table. From inside he withdrew a dagger—a work of art in the form of a weapon.

Rubies and emeralds winked from the hilt of rope-twisted, gleaming silver. Inscribed runes ran the length of the tapered blade to its lethal point. Ardith nearly shuddered at the dagger's deadly beauty.

Gerard placed it on the table in front of her.

"Lion's Teeth," she whispered, remembering the name.

"You know of these daggers?"

"Corwin told me of them many years ago. They were given to the first Baron Wilmont by William the Conqueror." She glanced into the chest. Empty. "The other?"

Gerard reached down to the inside of his boot and flipped out a piece of leather. From an inner sheath he withdrew the mate to the dagger on the table.

He admired the blade, his expression somber. "I have carried this since I first learned to hold a weapon. This blade has often stood between me and death. As this one has served me well—" he pointed to the dagger on the table "—so shall the other serve you."

Chapter Nine

"My lord, you cannot give me this dagger," Ardith protested. "It should stay with its mate. 'Tis part of Wilmont's heritage."

He nodded. "And therefore mine to do with as I please."

"What if I lost it?"

"If the shoemaker follows my instructions correctly, your dagger will fit its sheath as securely as mine."

Ardith crossed her arms. "Then you can save the expense of the boots. I do not need a weapon."

"Since you choose to wander about unescorted, you will carry one. The next time someone intends you harm, you will be able to defend yourself."

"My lord, I know Percival was a bit overbearing, but you overreact to—"

"Overreact? Had I not intervened, Percival would have taken you on the chapel floor! Or did I misunderstand what he meant by showing you how well you would deal together?"

Ardith shifted slightly. "He intended to try."

"And would probably have succeeded."

"What if I promise not to venture out by myself again?"

"Wise, but changes nothing."

"I have no idea how to use a dagger."

"You will when we finish your training, beginning on the morrow, after you get your boots."

Gerard could be the most obstinate man. Couldn't he see she had no wish to carry the weapon, couldn't imagine pulling it out to threaten anyone, much less drawing blood? She mustered her last argument.

"My lord, I have spent my entire life learning to heal wounds, not inflict them. I daresay I would rather chase a bug from the room than squash it. I am no warrior."

He shoved his dagger into his boot, put the mate back into the open chest. "Some vermin warrant squashing."

Ardith stared at the dagger, resigned to the inevitable, but still puzzled over Gerard's stubbornness. He gripped the arms of her chair and leaned forward, looming much too close for coherent thought.

"Does your silence mean you yield?"

"You give me no choice, my lord."

"None. If it eases your mind, know that you may never need to use the dagger in earnest. Draw the Lion's Tooth and anyone of noble blood, or even not so noble, will know you are favored of Wilmont and have second thoughts of doing you harm."

She looked up into his eyes, the color of them heating from spring green to summer emerald.

"You are favored, Ardith," he said in a husky voice. "Surely you know as much." He brushed a fingertip across her cheek, the gentle caress astoundingly intense. "These suitors of yours, tell me, are you enamored of any?"

All of the men Bronwyn had presented as potential husbands paled when compared to Gerard. And she *had* compared, from color of hair to sincerity of smile, from sureness of stance to command of voice. Not one passed the tests that included, much to her embarrassment, the size of hand and length of fingers.

"Nay, my lord," she exhaled.

The last of her breath caught as he hushed further words. His lips were warm, tentative at first. Using just the right slant of lips, he achieved a tantalizing pressure, carving out and consuming yet another piece of her soul.

His tongue flicked along her lower lip until she opened to his prodding. He leisurely explored the rough edge of her teeth, then probed and circled, urging her to boldness with seductive rhythm.

Blessed Mother, the man could kiss! And just as she thought the pleasure too much to endure, he deepened the kiss and her body reacted.

Her hands slid up the long length of his arms, responding with a heart too full of love for Gerard to consider any other man as worthy of notice. Had she any doubts of her love for him before, they scattered as dry leaves to the wind.

Gerard delighted in Ardith's reaction to his prompt for more potent intimacy. He knew now that none of her suitors had tasted her honeyed mouth. He basked in her innocence, knowing she belonged to him alone. With growing urgency, he relished the idea of exploring her secret places and revealing the pleasures of coupling.

Without breaking the kiss, Gerard pulled Ardith to her feet. He struggled to be gentle as he drew her body close. Her form fitted perfectly against his warrior's frame, supple where he was solid, her curves melding against his angles.

His hand swept upward from the dip of her waist, grazed along her ribs, then halted at the swell of her breast. Through the layers of silk gown and linen chemise, a hardened nub welcomed his palm. Her breathing rattled in her chest as he kneaded the peaked mound. Then a small hum of surrender sounded deep in her throat.

Today, now, he would bed Ardith. He could wait no longer. For weeks he'd endured erotic visions of Ardith, sprawled in full splendor on his furs, a beckoning smile on her lips. He'd imagined her responding to his touch with reckless abandon, offering her virgin's blood without misgiving. He vowed to ease Ardith's initiation to the unique pleasures shared between male and female.

Ardith knew she was dying. Her legs weakened to the consistency of pudding, unable to support her weight. Her arms grew heavy, useless, held upright only by fingers twined into Gerard's dalmatica. She couldn't breathe. A fever gripped her body, coursing through her veins from a bubbling cauldron of heat buried deep within her core.

She would joyfully relinquish her spirit if only Gerard would hold and caress and kiss her until her final breath.

Ardith sighed when Gerard's lips moved from her mouth to her ear. She fought the dizziness, pressing her forehead into his brawny shoulder.

"Hellfire, how I want you. Yield to me, Ardith."

Her heart skipped a beat at the seductive tone, the near plea in his voice. She knew what he wanted, couldn't pretend ignorance, and she wanted Gerard with all the intensity his tone conveyed.

Yet, heart and mind battled over the wisdom of surrender.

Gerard sought to ease his lust, merely exercise his liege lord's seigneur rights. She'd be a fool to believe otherwise. If she judged his intent correctly, soon she would marry—a man of Gerard's choosing. 'Twas the way of things, and Ardith, though disinclined, accepted her fate.

But before submitting to another man's lust, she could know the joy of indulging Gerard, the way a wife indulges a husband, and store the memory away. Loving him as she did, she wouldn't shun this one chance to have him in the most intimate way possible.

"Willingly, my lord," she answered.

A smile of triumph spread across his handsome face. He bent, and with a swoop of his arm, swept her off her feet. Floating, cradled tight against Gerard's massive chest, Ardith threw her arms around his neck as he carried her to the lord's bedchamber.

Ardith gaped at the mammoth bed crowding the room, occupying the space of at least four pallets. Suspended from posts as thick as young trees, hangings of deep ruby en-

closed the bed on three sides, the fourth curtain tied back
by woven, tasseled cords. The mat was piled high with furs
of bear and wolf.

"Do not be frightened, Ardith."

Ardith shook away whatever expression had betrayed a
moment's hesitancy. "I fear many things, my lord, but not
you, not what we are about to do."

"Gerard," he said a bit impatiently. "Here I am not lord,
only a man." He swooped down for another kiss, then lowered her to the edge of the bed. She sank soundlessly into
the softness of feathers, not the straw she'd expected.

Then he knelt, removed her slippers and tossed them
over his shoulders. He gathered the hem of her skirts and
raised the cloth to just above her knees. With deft fingers
he untied the strings securing her hose. He took his time at
peeling away the hose, petting her calf and running a finger
along the crease at the back of her knee. By the time he
finished baring the second leg, Ardith's breath had gone
ragged again.

"Now your hair," he said, tugging at her hands, pulling
her to her feet. "I would have it loose."

Gerard quickly removed the veil and circlet, then un-
twisted Ardith's long plait. He slowly ran his fingers
through the strands, separated and fluffed until her auburn
hair flowed in shimmering waves around her shoulders and
down her back.

"Beautiful," he murmured, pushing the tresses aside,
kissing her neck, reaching for the gown's laces. He loosened them, then gathered up the cloth and pulled the gown
over her head.

Through the thin linen chemise he could see her lovely
body—her delicate shoulders, the gentle curve of her back
over a tiny waist, the rounded flare of hips over firm buttocks. His control slipped a notch, but his fingers didn't
tremble as he untied the string at the chemise's neckline.
The cloth parted, exposing the flesh of her upper back, begging his touch. Very gently he widened the opening.

Ardith's blue eyes had darkened and glazed. He gathered her in his arms, putting a hand on her buttocks to push her close against the bulge of his desire.

Gerard nearly groaned when she pressed against him. His patience wearing thin, he reached for the hem of her chemise. Ardith put a hand to her breast and flushed. He enjoyed the show of modesty, further proof of her innocence, but he wouldn't let her carry modesty too far.

"Nay, Ardith. Do not hide from me. I would see you."

She slowly removed her hand, her blush fading. Gerard quickly uncovered her body.

Hellfire, Ardith was lovely. She shook her hair forward in an attempt to cover her naked breasts, which only heightened their allure. Fingertips meshed, she covered the triangle of reddish curls at the juncture of her legs, deepening his curiosity.

Then slowly, with resolve in her eyes, her hands rose from shielding her woman's curls. She gathered her hair and pushed the tresses over her shoulders. Vulnerable but valiant, she stood stripped of clothes and pretense, his for the taking.

Hunger gnawing at his loins, he beheld the nymph who'd bedeviled his dreams. Her delicate beauty beckoned. Gerard gladly answered her siren's call.

Ardith held her breath as he caressed her breasts. His touch was firm, encompassing. As his palms grazed her nipples, they puckered and hardened. She leaned into the caress, seeking more of the delightful sensations. But she wasn't prepared for the feel of his warm, moist mouth when he bent and suckled a nipple.

The tug of his lips and rough texture of his tongue drove her wild with pleasure. She tangled her fingers in his hair, cradling his head until she could stand no more of the sweet torture. Ardith found his mouth and kissed him with ardor.

He smiled, picked her up, and tossed her onto the bed. Curling into a wolf's pelt, Ardith watched Gerard dispense with his leather shoes and cross-bound hose. He untied and

cast aside the girdle around his waist. Ardith's bravado fled
when he reached for the hem of the dalmatica. She closed
her eyes, heard Gerard's amused chuckle.

The bed sagged under his weight as he slid in beside her.
She opened her eyes to see him reach for the cord and close
the curtain. Enclosed in a private world of red-tinged light,
Ardith called forth her daring. He'd covered his male parts,
but not the rest of his warrior's body. Corded and muscled,
broad and trim, Gerard was magnificent and, if only for a
while, hers to savor.

Gerard claimed Ardith with arousing caresses, taking
care to move slowly. He started with her face, cradling her
chin, moving down to her neck. With a single finger he
traced her collarbone to the hollow of her throat. Then he
spread his fingers, foraging under the fur for her bosom.

The twin mounds were high, firm and like silk to touch.
Aching to behold her beauty, he drew back the fur and
gazed on perfection. "You are so beautiful, Ardith."

He gazed, and admired and fiercely vowed she would
soon be his in name as well as body.

Gerard reached down, tracing the long scar across her
belly.

"Gerard?"

He heard the uneasiness in her voice. "'Tis the mark of
your battle with the boar, is it not?"

"'Tis ugly."

Surprised at the bitterness, he assured, "Your scar was
nobly won. I know of no other woman who bears a mark
of such bravery." Then he bent and kissed her scar from
end to end.

Elva had said a woman need only lie still and endure,
an impossible feat under Gerard's ministrations. Did he
think her wanton for returning his kiss, for gliding her
hands over the breadth of his shoulders and the taut sinew
of his back? His soft moans had to mean he liked her touch,
enjoyed the nips on his neck. His nipples had even puck-

ered under her fingertip. Brazen? Maybe. But Gerard liked the caresses, she was sure.

Confident of the discovery, Ardith gently tugged and pushed until Gerard yielded to her wishes and rolled on to his back. With featherlight kisses she traced the scar on his neck, then the long, ragged battle wound across his ribs.

"You could have died from this wound," she said between kisses.

"I very nearly did."

"And was it nobly won?"

He hesitated, then said, "I stepped before a blow meant for my father. In the folly of my youth, I thought myself invincible, and learned otherwise."

Lower and lower the scar traveled. When she kissed his navel, his stomach quivered. Ardith smiled inwardly at the reaction, reveling in newfound power. She pushed the pelt down to find the end of the scar, and found more than she sought.

"Oh…my…lord," she breathed when her hand brushed his manhood, standing rigid from a thatch of curly, golden hair.

Eyes wide, she stared at the long, thick shaft. She'd seen male members, on small boys mostly, but also on men in unguarded moments. Lenvil's manor was much too small to guarantee anyone complete privacy. Never had she realized the proportions an aroused male could achieve.

Belinda had judged Gerard's size correctly. Ardith swallowed hard. The whore had said he would furrow deep, but hadn't commented on the depth or width required of a woman's field to accommodate such a plow.

"Touch me, Ardith," he said with a ragged voice, stroking her hair. "Fear no part of me."

"Gerard, I…"

"'Tis only flesh become hard to allow our joining. Touch me, Ardith."

His shaft twitched beneath her trembling fingers, then stood solidly proud. She stroked upward along the taut-

skinned underside, feeling his heat, realizing that by touching him her own desire increased.

One hand? Two hands? Ardith spread her fingers, but
before she could close around him, Gerard pulled away and
rolled her onto her back.

Gerard could barely control the need to seek release.
Knowing he must raise her need to match his own, he
nudged her thighs to part. She opened to him. His thumb
found the nub at the apex; his finger slid into her tight
sheath.

Ardith arched into his brazen caresses. Every nerve in
her body burst to life, every muscle craved to move to the
circle of his hand.

His mouth left her breast. "There may be pain," he said,
regret clear in his voice.

"I know. Gerard...please..."

He moved over her, cradled her hips in his hands and
raised her slightly. Slowly, inch by inch, his sword filled
her tight, hot scabbard. He paused, then plunged.

Ardith cried out as he severed the barrier, her nails dig-
ging into his arms. Gerard captured the last strains of her
cry with his kiss.

"Easy, sweet one. The pain will go away. Hold on to
me, and together we will see paradise."

Time proved him right. The pain receded. Just as she
began to relax, he moved, slowly at first, then faster and
deeper. She reached for she knew not what, until wave after
wave of ecstasy rippled through her body. Paradise. Heart
pounding hard against her ribs, Ardith embraced the heavens.

The pulsing of her pleasure drove Gerard over the edge.

Hellfire, Ardith pleased him, in both body and spirit.
Propped on his elbows, he planted kisses over Ardith's face
as breathing slowed and heartbeats returned to a normal
pace. Thrilled and replete, he rolled to relieve Ardith of his
weight. She followed, snuggled into his side—and yawned.

Gerard used the heel of his foot and his long reach to

retrieve a fur. He wrapped it around them to entrap the heat of their vigorous loving, then gazed into hazy, mesmerizing eyes of blue.

Ardith smiled and cupped his cheek, drawing him forward for a kiss. "You were right."

"Naturally," he answered, not quite sure which of the many things he'd told or shown her in the past hour she considered right, but it didn't matter.

She laughed lightly. "You are also rather arrogant, but then, it suits you." She yawned again. "Is coupling always so tiring?"

Gerard brushed back a handful of dampened hair from her face. "Only when very good."

"Were we good together, Gerard?" she asked, her eyelids fluttering closed.

"Oh, yea, scamp. Very, very good."

She fell asleep with a smile on her face. He pulled her closer, tucking her head into a comfortable niche on his shoulder. She slid an arm across his chest and a leg between his thighs.

Gerard played with her hair, knowing he'd never known a coupling so satisfying. Not only was his body sated, but his mind as well. Such contentment was a new feeling. No leman, no occasional wench had evoked such serenity, such peace. But Ardith had, with her innocence and abandon. Maybe that was why he—

He cut the thought short. Surely, the brilliance of their joining had scrambled his brain. He admitted a certain fondness for Ardith, but no deeper emotion. He'd wanted her with an obsession he'd never known with another woman. But that was only because he planned to take her to wife, was curious to know if she would please him in bed.

He had given no thought to pulling out at the last, a method he'd employed with others to withhold his seed to keep from siring a pack of bastard children. Instead, he'd wanted to stay buried deeply within Ardith's softness until long after the last tremor of his release. They would marry shortly, and the sooner she swelled with child, the better.

Gerard stroked Ardith's back and scattered feathery kisses on her forehead. Smiling, he conjured visions of ways he would let Ardith express her joy when she learned he planned to take her to wife.

Ardith burrowed deeper into the nest of down and fur. She didn't want to wake, but the low buzz of Gerard and Thomas speaking, pulled her from sleep. Then a door closed and all was quiet again.

The pelts and mat held the warm, rich aroma of Gerard's masculine scent, mingled with the heady odor of their loving. Awash with lingering contentment, Ardith propped herself on an elbow.

Gerard had tied back the bed curtain. Slivers of moonlight eased through narrow window slits and candles had burned to mere stubs. In amazement, she realized she'd slept the afternoon away.

Gerard padded into the chamber—sleepy-eyed, barechested, breeches molded to his lower body like a second skin. She ignored the brief tug on her heart, pushed aside the thought that never again would she see Gerard in all his virile glory, bathed in moonlight and drowsy from sleep. She knew she should feel embarrassment or shame for coupling with a man not her husband, for enjoying this stolen time, but she couldn't rouse regret for her decision. She'd joyfully surrendered to the man she loved, and would do so again.

A self-satisfied smile crossed his face as he sauntered toward the bed, scooping up her chemise from the floor without losing stride.

"I had hoped you still slept," he said, bouncing down onto the mat. "Since you are awake, ruining my plans for a gentle rousing, you must pay a forfeit—a kiss for each piece of clothing you wish returned."

"And if I do not wish to dress?"

"Then, scamp, I will collect the kisses anyway and our meal will get cold. Then Harold and Corwin will arrive and—"

"Oh dear, I forgot!" Ardith reached for her chemise but Gerard pulled it out of reach.

"My kiss first."

Ardith tried to satisfy the condition with a small peck on his cheek, but Gerard demanded forfeit in full measure, pulling her against him for a long, tender kiss.

"We will never get dressed if you persist," she breathed.

Gerard chuckled and handed over her chemise. Then he got up, flipped open a trunk and took out a square of white linen. "Here," he said, tossing the towel.

While his back was turned, Ardith wiped away the bloody proof of having become a woman in every way.

Gerard proved an adept lady's maid, deftly tying laces and plaiting her hair, though Ardith was glad for the veil to cover the uneven twists. After each service he performed, he collected a kiss, each kiss more potent than the one before.

Gerard ate with gusto. Ardith pushed small bits of meat around on her trencher but rarely put a morsel in her mouth.

"Do you find the food not to your liking?" he asked.

"The food is delicious."

"Then why are you not eating?"

Because she knew that when the meal was over, so was this special time with Gerard. Because she knew that Corwin would tell her father of Bronwyn's matchmaking and Harold would be angry. Because she knew that within a short while the entire direction of her life would change.

Within the hour, Gerard would name her groom and hand her over to another man.

Chapter Ten

"**W**ell, chit, I heard of your mischief," Harold said, lowering himself into the chair Ardith had given up. "Thought you had more sense. Can see now my mistake. Made up my mind. Sending you to the nunnery. Apologize for any trouble she caused, my lord."

Ardith cringed.

"Ardith is not entering a nunnery, Harold," Gerard stated. "She and Bronwyn should not have tried to arrange a marriage without your knowledge, but no real harm has been done."

"No harm?" Harold challenged. "We cannot let this go unpunished, my lord. What if other women took it into their flighty heads that they could choose their own husbands?" Harold visibly shuddered.

"Agreed. In this case, however, Ardith is not choosing a husband. I have already decided her future and she cannot fulfill my plans from inside a nunnery. As for trouble," Gerard continued with a shrug, "I find her company...pleasurable."

Ardith felt her cheeks glow red. She could feel Corwin's knowing stare, but refused to look at her brother.

"Planning to take her as leman, are you?" Harold asked.

"Father!" Ardith gasped.

Gerard smiled. "Nay, I plan to make her my wife."

His smile faded as he watched the reactions. Corwin stood with hands clasped behind his back, frowning. Harold braced his hands on his knees, shaking his head in disbelief.

Ardith's beautiful blue eyes glistened, her bottom lip trembled. "Oh, nay. Oh, Gerard," she whispered, then spun around and buried her face in her hands.

His confusion and frustration exploded. "What is this?" he roared. "I just offered to make Ardith my wife. One would think I had ordered her whipped!"

Harold looked up and cleared his throat. "Baron Everart once offered for Ardith...for you. Pained me to refuse."

"*You* rejected the offer?" Gerard asked, stunned. "Why?"

"Had to," Harold answered with a slight shrug. "Your father did not tell you?"

Gerard shook his head, a knot tightening in his gut.

Harold took a deep breath. "Baron Everart wanted to tie Lenvil closer to Wilmont, and to do so through marriage. I had other daughters to choose from, but he was decided on Ardith. Thought her most suited to your temperament. Told me to think on it while he asked royal permission. King William approved, though he felt Everart could do better by you. I did, too. Told him so."

"You refused because you thought Ardith inferior?"

Harold shook his head. "I refused because before I could agree, a boar ripped open her belly. Scrambled her innards. I could not give you damaged goods, my lord, now could I?"

Damaged! The word slammed into Gerard's vitals. "Damaged." He said the word aloud, trying to deny the meaning.

"The chit's barren. You need an heir, my lord. Ardith cannot give you one."

Gerard remembered tenderly kissing the scar that slashed pale and thin across Ardith's quivering belly. From end to end he'd paid homage to the mark of her courage.

Long fingers of defeat gripped Gerard's heart, squeezing

to an unbearable ache. Until now, whenever disappointment threatened, he'd found a way to thwart whatever obstacle stood in the way of victory. But neither wealth, nor influence, nor the strength of his sword arm could make Ardith whole.

Hellfire, he could *not* marry a barren woman. He couldn't marry Ardith. "Are you sure?" he asked, knowing the answer but protesting the unacceptable.

"Elva may be a ruddy nuisance with her muttering and bones and entrails, but she be good with ailments and such. There is no reason to doubt her judgment."

"I doubt," Corwin said softly.

Ardith turned, wiping away tears. She wasn't a weeper, but Gerard's bittersweet proposal had cut too deep. She'd listened to her father's explanation, relived the pain of the wound and the sorrow of her barrenness. She'd accepted Elva's word, as had her parents. That Corwin doubted was a surprise.

Harold sighed. "Have you trained for midwife now, son? What would you know of female innards?"

"No more than any other man, I suppose," Corwin admitted, turning from the fire. "But I do know Ardith. I *know* my twin."

"That foolishness again?"

"Call it what you will, Father, but Ardith and I know otherwise." Corwin crossed the chamber and put his hands on her shoulders. She looked up into bright blue eyes, eyes that could peer into her soul if the need was great. "Do you remember when I fell from the tree?"

"Of course I remember. You had climbed the oak. A limb broke and you fell. But Corwin, what has that—"

He shook her. "Just answer. Now, what did you do?"

"I ran to the manor, fetched two men-at-arms to help. I remember running behind them, shouting at them to be careful because—"

"Because you knew, without touching me, without asking if I was hurt, that I had broken my arm,'' Corwin finished.

"Poppycock," Harold injected.

Corwin ignored the outburst. "Who scolded me from here to heaven's gate when I damn near drowned in the river? Who was the one who came screaming through the wood, cutting through my fear so I could battle the current?"

Ardith remembered sensing Corwin's fear, his inability to breathe, and screeching his name as she ran.

"And who," he continued very softly, "has kept my most shameful secret these many years?"

"Nay, Corwin," Ardith whispered, putting her hand on his chest, begging him not to unburden his guilt before Harold and Gerard. Never, in all of the years since her wounding, had she or Corwin talked about what had really happened.

"I do not understand, Corwin," Gerard said.

Corwin backed away, the slump gone from his shoulders. "Ardith and I share a link, my lord," he said. "Though my father would wish it otherwise, the link exists. Elva warned us, as children, not to speak of it for fear of someone declaring us unnatural. But I swear, my lord, the link exists. Ardith knew my arm had broken because she could *feel* the break. She knew I was in danger when I floundered in the river because she could *sense* my distress."

Gerard's glance flicked from one twin to the other. "This link you speak of works both ways? You know what the other is doing, feeling?"

Corwin shook his head. "'Tis not constant, though when we are together, we can read the other's mood easily. Distance weakens the bond, yet if one of us were in mortal danger while far apart, I believe the other would know."

Harold slapped a palm on the table. "This bond you think you share with your sister is pure drivel and has naught to do with Ardith's infirmity."

"But it does," Corwin protested, looking not at Harold,

but Gerard. "The link flares hottest at times of great danger, or intense pain. Just as Ardith felt my arm break, so did I feel her pain when the boar slit her belly. Had not her pain stung me, pierced my panic, we might both have died that day."

Tension drained from Corwin. Gerard showed no reaction.

Harold's features twisted in pained denial. "You did not panic. No son of mine—"

"Father, I *froze*. I could not move from sheer terror. And because I panicked, Ardith nearly died. Would you have noticed, shed a single tear at her loss?"

"Corwin, please," Ardith pleaded for him to stop. Atop all else, she didn't want her father and brother to argue. Neither, apparently, did Gerard.

"What has this bond to do with the state of her...health?" Gerard asked.

Corwin ran a hand through his hair. "When I broke my arm, Elva straightened the bone and lashed on splints, which I grew heartily sick of wearing. One day, I decided to take them off. Ardith stopped me. She rubbed her own arm, told me the bone had not healed enough for me to remove the splints."

Gerard's eyes narrowed. "Then when Ardith was wounded, you also felt her heal."

"Not precisely, my lord," Corwin plunged on. "'Tis difficult to explain, harder yet to understand. 'Twas not the wound Ardith nearly died of, though she lost a lot of blood, but the fever that raged and refused to abate. Since that day, I have seen men wounded in battle survive deeper slashes, regain the use of limbs, become whole again. Your chest wound proves my point. Though split by a sword, the muscles healed and you regained the strength needed to wield a sword. Through both the link, and what I now know of wounds, I believe Ardith healed completely. I believe Ardith is whole, undamaged."

Ardith worried her bottom lip. Could Corwin be right?

The scar slashing across Gerard's ribs screamed of blood and severed muscle. Her own wound suddenly seemed a mere scratch.

"Why have you not told anyone before this if you are so sure?" Gerard prodded.

"Who would listen? Elva and my mother would have laughed. My father?"

Corwin glanced at Harold, seething in the chair, then looked back at Gerard. "The only one who might have believed was Ardith, and what good would the knowledge do her while at Lenvil? My lord, I beg of you, if you cannot bring yourself to risk marriage to Ardith, then allow her to choose from among the men Bronwyn thought suitable."

"Why would those men wish to take the risk?"

"Bronwyn presented only men who already have heirs, who need neither children nor coin. Or if she wishes, let Ardith return to Lenvil. But, please, my lord, do not allow my father to entomb her in a nunnery."

A quick rap on the door preceded Thomas, followed by two kitchen wenches. Thomas quickly sensed the tension in the room. "We can return, my lord," he said, and turned to usher the girls out.

"Nay," Gerard said. "Let them clear away the platters."

While the girls bustled about the table, Thomas pulled a scroll from beneath his tunic and handed it to Gerard. "A messenger has just arrived from Wilmont."

Gerard broke the wax seal and unrolled the parchment. He read, his face passive, then he handed the scroll to Corwin.

Corwin scanned the message. "You were right, my lord. What now?"

"Go down and find the courier. Send him back to Wilmont to tell Stephen to bring the monk to court. When you return, we will seek an audience with King Henry."

Corwin hesitated, glancing at Ardith.

"Later, I promise," Gerard said.

Ardith didn't understand, but obviously Corwin did be-

cause he immediately turned and fled the chamber. Close
behind, the kitchen wenches scurried out.

Gerard ran a hand across the back of his neck. He stood
but an arm's length away, easy enough to reach, yet too
far away to comfort. Nor was she sure he wanted her touch.

"You are dismissed, Harold," he said.

Her father stood. "May I remind the baron that he cannot
risk Wilmont on the whim of a brother who dotes on his
twin? I have never believed in this bond they claim to
share, nor should you, my lord."

"Good eve, Harold."

Casting an angry glance in Ardith's direction, Harold
bowed and strode out of the chamber.

With a wave of his hand Gerard dismissed Thomas, who
ducked under the archway leading to Gerard's bedchamber,
leaving her alone with Gerard in the sitting room.

Gerard paced. "Well, Ardith, you have been very quiet."

"I was not asked to speak."

"Which, I have noted, has never before stopped you
from offering an opinion." He stopped pacing. "Tell me,
does this bond really exist between you and Corwin? Can
you sense when the other is hurt or endangered?"

Ardith took a long, calming breath. She could hear Elva's
warnings never to speak of the link. *Unnatural. Witches.*

"If we are near to each other, aye. When Corwin was at
Wilmont, he took bruises and cuts I could not feel, but
when he was at Lenvil..."

Gerard cupped her face with his hands, tilted her chin
upward. She sensed his question before he asked and tears
welled her eyes again. Blast, she'd cried more this past hour
than in the past year.

"Then Corwin could be right? You could be...whole?"

Green eyes, filled with hope, begged the answer he
wanted to hear and Ardith longed to bestow. But she had
to be honest.

"I know not," she said. "Males and females are made
differently. We do not speak of an arm or leg. I want so

very badly to believe, but I would lie if I said I had no doubts.''

The hope left his eyes, but not the softness. ''Then tell me this—if given the choice, would you wed another or return to Lenvil?''

''No nunnery?'' Ardith choked.

The corner of his mouth twitched. ''I would not subject those good ladies to your sharp tongue and willfulness.''

''Then I would return to Lenvil, if Father will allow.''

Ardith melted against him as he pulled her close, enfolding her in a warm, tight embrace.

''Given a choice, would you marry me or return to Lenvil?''

How could he doubt? ''I would be proud and honored to be your wife.''

After an answering squeeze, he said, ''Your father poses a problem. I may not send you to a nunnery, but I believe Harold is angry enough to spirit you away before we can resolve this dilemma.''

Ardith frowned into Gerard's chest. ''Father may be a bit forgetful, Gerard, but he is not senseless. If you order him to desist, he would not dare disobey.''

''I will not take the chance,'' he said, loosening his hold but keeping her within the circle of his arms. ''Thomas!'' he called. The lad immediately rounded the arch. ''Give my greetings to Lady Bronwyn. Tell her to pack Ardith's clothing and have the trunk sent here.''

Ardith bit her bottom lip as she watched Thomas leave.

''Are you about to argue with me?'' Gerard asked.

Ardith shook her head.

Thomas returned, followed by two men carrying a large trunk, followed by Kester, Bronwyn and Elva.

''If you think to plead for Ardith's release—'' Gerard began, but Kester held up a stopping hand.

''Nay, Baron Gerard. Given Harold's anger, removing

Ardith from his reach is wise. Bronwyn and Elva are here to help Ardith settle."

"And you?"

"Merely to escort the women."

Something in Kester's tone alerted Gerard. After the others left the sitting room, he waved Kester into a chair. "Harold told you the whole of it?"

"He was rather blunt in his fury. I fear the entire palace will know the whole of it within the hour."

"I should have told him to keep his mouth shut."

"I asked him to, but…" Kester gave an eloquent shrug. "'Tis not Harold who concerns me now. Bronwyn, however, is most concerned about Ardith."

"Your wife is a meddler."

Kester smiled. "Aye, but she means well. In this case, I believe her reasoning sound. She wants to protect her sister as much as possible from the gossip spreading about court. You have never been one to pay heed to court intrigue, but I would advise you to pay heed now." Kester leaned forward. "Many here have taken a liking to Ardith. Given today's events, that will change. I fear Ardith will not understand."

Gerard conceded that Ardith's tender feelings might be hurt by the more vicious among the court's gossips. But tongues would wag. There was no way to stop them. They would accuse Ardith of becoming his leman, and for the time being, they would be right.

"There is one concession we would ask of you, Baron. Ardith will need someone to talk to, a sympathetic ear. We ask that you allow Elva to remain here with Ardith."

Gerard cringed.

"Granted," Kester answered Gerard's reluctance, "she is not the most pleasant of women, but she is family and also willing. In fact, she begged me to ask if she could attend her niece. She promises to cause you no trouble, or to speak against the arrangement."

Resigned, Gerard grumbled, "Should I hear one disparaging word fall from her lips, see one disapproving expression on her face, I will feed her to the fish in the Thames."

Kester stood. "There is another problem of which you should be aware. We did not think much of it until now, but some days ago, one of our servants told Bronwyn that Lady Diane's maid was asking questions about Ardith."

Gerard frowned. "Why is Diane curious about Ardith?"

"I fear you are one of the chosen."

"For what?"

Kester shook his head. "I cannot believe you have not heard. I swear, you must be the only man of worthy rank who is not fawning over Diane de Varley. She is not only beautiful, but rich as sin, and much pursued."

"She also has a tongue as sharp as my sword and the cunning of a fox."

"Which most men will overlook if granted her hand."

"Henry has finally decided Diane must marry?"

"He is allowing her to submit names of those she would have. You know how Henry indulges her. Gerard, if you are among those named, she may see Ardith as a rival, especially after you rebuffed Diane the other night in the hall."

"I did not rebuff her, precisely."

"Maybe not, but you showed a definite preference for Ardith's company. For that alone, Diane may try to win you over, just to prove she can. The woman has been known to act from spite, and if she has decided on you, she will not let a Saxon lass of no rank stand in her way."

"I will have to make my feelings clear to Diane."

"Then you had best do so quickly, before Diane presents your name to Henry. I can think of no one else Henry would rather see control those vast de Varley lands in Normandy."

"If there is aught else you require, my lady, you need only ask," Thomas offered.

"My thanks, Thomas," Ardith said.

"A flagon of wine and a basin of wash water would seem in order. Ardith will wish to refresh herself," Elva interjected.

Thomas looked to Ardith.

"Aye, that would be nice, if 'tis not too much trouble."

"None at all, my lady," Thomas replied, then ushered the trunk bearers out.

"One would think you had forgotten how to deal with servants," Bronwyn chided.

Ardith turned to look at her sister, who'd made herself comfortable, perched on the edge of the bed that dominated the third and last room within Wilmont's chamber. Fourpostered, with a feather mat, the bed looked like Gerard's, save for its smaller size and emerald curtains.

"Thomas is not my servant. I have no right to order him about."

"I would say Gerard gave you certain rights when he ordered you moved in here." Bronwyn looked about the room. "I have never liked this room. Lady Ursula always kept it so austere. It even smells of her."

Ardith walked over to the narrow window, and despite the cold winter air, opened the shutters. "Gerard's mother last used this room?"

"As mistress of Wilmont, Ursula is entitled to use it when in residence." Bronwyn cocked her head. "These chambers are held in reserve for Wilmont, have been since the first baron served the Conqueror. No one else is allowed their use, not even when the palace seams are strained with guests and no one of Wilmont is in attendance."

"Is Lady Ursula expected to attend court?"

"Nay. She stays at Wilmont. 'Tis said she is mourning Everart. I suspect the story false, but who can say? The woman has ever kept herself aloof."

"Ursula has her reasons," Elva said softly, moving to the corner by the window seat, where several religious statues, a prayer book and a crucifix sat on a small table. A prie-dieu awaited a supplicant.

"I did not know you knew Ursula," Ardith commented.

"I was still at Wilmont when Ursula married Everart." Elva fingered the crucifix. "Pitied the poor girl but could do naught to help her. I had problems of my own."

Elva, a young woman at the time of the Conquest, had served as Lenvil's Saxon hostage to the first baron of Wilmont, Gerard's grandfather, a Norman knight given land by William the Bastard, Norman conqueror of England. Something horrible had happened to Elva during that confinement to make her hate Normans so vehemently. Elva had never before admitted having been to Wilmont, much less told her story.

Before Ardith could ask the nature of Elva's problems, Bronwyn huffed. "Ursula's problem is her religion. There is no joy in the woman."

"One finds little joy under the thumb of Wilmont."

Bronwyn wagged a finger. "Elva, you promised. If Kester can convince Gerard to let you stay with Ardith, you *must* hold your tongue."

Ever since Gerard had reappeared at Lenvil, Elva's warnings to avoid men, the baron in particular, had increased. Here in Westminster, Elva had also complained about the suitors visiting Bronwyn's chambers, despite Ardith's assurances of indifference.

Ardith glanced at the door she didn't need to be told connected with Gerard's bedchamber. Having Elva underfoot would most definitely prove a hardship.

"Why would you wish to stay with me?" she asked, puzzled.

"I beg you, Ardith. The trial ahead will be difficult, and you will have need of someone who loves you."

"Kester and I agree," Bronwyn added. "Having Elva here may help stave off the worst of the gossip."

Ardith rubbed her forehead. By agreeing to stay in Wilmont's chambers, she'd silently agreed to more than merely avoiding her father until his temper cooled. Apparently, others realized it also, Bronwyn and Elva included.

"I doubt Gerard bargained on having Elva about. He may not let her stay," she said.

As though her thoughts had summoned him, Gerard entered the room, and after a swift glance about, he turned to Elva.

"Kester informs me you wish to serve Ardith," he said, his tone menacing. "I will allow it, with one condition."

Ardith felt her aunt stiffen, and braced for an argument.

"Ardith will suffer no harm while in my care," he continued. "Should you try to convince her otherwise, by word or deed, I will banish you from these chambers, return you to Harold and his mercy. There will be no pleas for a second chance. The first scowl or disparaging word seals your fate. Do you understand?"

To Ardith's amazement, Elva managed a small curtsy and said without hesitation or ire, "You have my word, my lord."

Gerard waved his hand toward the door. Elva stood still, but at a prod from Bronwyn, left the room without further protest. Bronwyn shut the door behind them.

Not until Gerard put a finger under her chin, closing her open mouth, did Ardith realize she gaped.

"I do not believe it," she whispered.

"I fear Elva's cooperation will be short-lived, but as long as she abides by the condition, she may stay." Then he caressed her cheek, his eyes following the path of his fingers, his tone softening. "I must leave for a while, to see the king. Will you miss me while I am away?"

Ardith laughed lightly. "I doubt you will be gone long enough for me to miss you. Besides, Bronwyn and Elva will keep me company while I set the room to rights."

His hand dropped and he glanced about, a spark of distaste lighting his eyes. "Make any changes in these chambers you wish. God's truth, I would prefer a change." Then he turned and left.

Ardith sighed, glad for permission to make changes. First, she would pack away Ursula's religious articles. Their presence would ever remind her that her relationship with Gerard violated church law.

Bronwyn and Elva returned with warm water and wine.

"Here, my dear, drink this," Elva said, offering a goblet of wine. "'Twill calm you."

Ardith drank, looking about the room, barely tasting the wine. "Ursula would be the first to consign me to the nether regions, would she not?"

"You are not to fret over Gerard's mother," Bronwyn said. "Gerard certainly does not. Ardith, some will think you honored, others will merely speculate. Then there are those who will judge harshly and censure. You must ignore them all."

"Dare I?"

"For your own peace of mind, sister, you had best learn to close your ears."

Chapter Eleven

Corwin at his side, Gerard stood before King Henry, who mulled over the grievances from the comfort of a thronelike chair in the royal bedchamber.

Behind Henry stood Kester. Leaning against a bedpost, Charles, earl of Warwick, frowned deeply. Gerard didn't mind the presence of either Warwick or Kester, called in to witness the proceedings. He respected and trusted both. Neither man would repeat a word of what he heard today.

King Henry I of England slouched in the chair, for all appearances bored with the audience. But Gerard knew better. Deep within Henry's eyes, a spark of ire had flashed when he was informed of the extent of Basil's treachery.

Yea, Henry was angry, but not because of any crime against Gerard of Wilmont. Henry possessed a mind capable of picking out the finest threads amid coils of thick rope. Henry knew, without Gerard uttering a word of warning, how Basil's boldness could affect the stability of the throne.

At present, Henry was at odds with most of the Norman barons over his attempt to administer justice with an even hand, treating baron and peasant alike. The English people took Henry to their hearts. The barons would consider any perceived weakness in the monarchy an excuse to unite in civil rebellion.

The king shifted slightly, betraying his discomfort. Still, his voice held no emotion. "We thank our baron for bringing these misdeeds to royal attention. We expect Basil of Northbryre to appear at court, and we will deal with these charges in an appropriate manner."

"Sire, I would be willing to ensure Basil's attendance," Gerard offered.

The corner of Henry's mouth quirked. "We believe our summons sufficient guarantee of his attendance. Have you sent for your witness, Gerard?"

Gerard swallowed his disappointment. "Health permitting, Richard should arrive any day now. With your permission, sire, I would like to grant Richard his knighthood. I feel he deserves the honor, as well as a reward."

Henry's eyebrow rose. "You plan to settle land on Richard? Pray tell, which of Wilmont's estates are you willing to part with?"

Gerard smiled. "Not Wilmont land, sire." Gerard held out a scroll—the list of Basil's holdings in England. "I know my king will be generous when he bestows restitution."

Henry straightened as he took the scroll and scanned the list. Gerard hoped to receive half of the lands. Henry would undoubtedly keep the rest.

The king rolled the scroll and dismissed the formal portion of the audience with the command "Now, tell me about Ardith. I hear that you have taken her into your protection."

Gerard smiled slightly at the term, but grew uneasy at the king's sudden shift of subject.

Warwick suddenly asked, "Ardith? Is she not the girl your father sought to betroth you to many years ago?"

"My father spoke to you of the betrothal to Ardith?" Gerard asked, surprised.

Warwick chuckled. "Aye. One would have thought him enamored of the girl. He described Ardith as possessing the face of an angel, the spirit of a hawk and the soul of a knight. Unusual praise for a female, but then Everart considered Ardith the perfect mate for you. He was quite disappointed when his plans did not work out.''

''As well he should,'' Corwin mumbled. Gerard silently agreed, but shot Corwin a warning glance, still wary of the king's purpose.

Henry leaned forward. ''Kester informed me of what transpired today. This girl has no lands to bring you, no coin. A midwife has declared her barren. Why would you still consider taking Ardith to wife?''

''Sire, my father was correct in his judgment of Ardith—she *is* lovely and spirited. She is also well versed in the running of a household. As to her barrenness, Ardith is an untried maid, and there is some doubt as to the midwife's pronouncement.''

Gerard ended with the argument he knew would likely sway Henry. ''She is also Saxon, and we both know of your wish for more blended marriages.''

Henry firmly believed it crucial to the kingdom's future to fuse Normans and Saxons into one people—English. To the chagrin of the Norman nobility and the pleasure of the common folk, Henry had set the example by marrying a Saxon princess.

Queen Matilda hadn't retired to an abbey in Romsey for lack of feeling for Henry. She'd simply been unable to bear the viciousness of the court. Gerard also knew that, although he and Matilda lived apart, his queen held a special place in Henry's affection.

Henry's expression softened, though he tapped the scroll on his knee. ''I applaud your reasoning, Gerard, but I had hoped to reward you in a different manner. As you know, Lady Diane needs a husband, and I would welcome a loyal, strong baron to oversee the de Varley lands in Normandy.''

Gerard checked a visible cringe, though inwardly his vitals twisted. Henry's planned reward wasn't to his liking, but an honor nonetheless. Diane de Varley as wife…hellfire, he could barely stomach the woman. Gerard glanced at Kester, who flashed an I-tried-to-warn-you smile.

Henry voiced his musings aloud. "I can understand, however, why you might not consider my bequest as a reward. And you say there is some doubt of Ardith's barren state?"

"Aye, sire," he answered.

The king rose from his chair, adjusted his royal robes and proclaimed, "Then we decree Baron Gerard of Wilmont, our loyal and trusted vassal, betrothed to Ardith of Lenvil for the length of a year. If within the year the lady proves fruitful, they may marry. But should the lady prove barren, we declare the betrothal void, and Gerard must wed Diane de Varley and accept custody of the Normandy lands that come with her. What say you, Baron Gerard of Wilmont?"

Stunned, Gerard protested, "What of Lady Diane, sire? Did you not give her the freedom to wed where she will?"

"She has chosen—you—and with our approval. Diane will abide by the conditions of the decree. Will you?"

Gerard uttered the only possible answer. "You are most generous, sire."

The king motioned to Kester. "See to the proper papers. Warwick will act as witness."

Both nobles voiced appropriate responses, or so Gerard thought. He was hearing another voice, one feminine and sweet-toned, acceding to the decree, then dragging him off to bed to begin the delightful task of proving fruitful.

As they left the audience chamber, Corwin said with a slight smile, "I am glad the task falls to you to tell Ardith. I would wager she will object."

The pleasant vision dissolved. Ardith might certainly object, with reason. The custom of betrothal, bedding, then wedding upon conception wasn't unknown, indeed was common practice—among the peasants.

Sitting across from Ardith in the sitting room of Wilmont chambers, Gerard watched various reactions flash across

her face as he divulged the relevant portion of his audience
with Henry—the betrothal decree. When her features stilled
into thoughtful repose, he relaxed, settled back in his chair,
taking her silence as acceptance.

The silence lasted overlong.

"You are very quiet, Ardith," he finally commented.

"I merely consider my choices, my lord."

His eyes narrowed. "What choices?"

"Well, I could obey my father's wishes and hie myself
off to a nunnery. Or I could merely go back to Lenvil. By
the time Father returns he will have forgotten what angered
him and life will go on as before. Or," she continued on a
sigh, "I could marry Gaylord."

"Gaylord!"

"Of all the suitors he alone can make me laugh."

All of her *choices* didn't include betrothal to him. Gerard
reined in his temper and leaned toward Ardith. "A nunnery?" he countered. "You are quite unsuited to a life of
prayer. You would be miserable. Go back to Lenvil? Your
father may be forgetful, but I doubt his anger over your
and Bronwyn's venture will soon fade. As for Gaylord,
when he hears of the decree, he will take his suit elsewhere."

"I feared as much." She grew thoughtful again. "Mayhap I could go to one of my sisters. Agnes might have me."

He resisted the urge to reach across the table and shake
her. Instead, crossing his arms on the table, he asked,
"What of our betrothal? How do we fulfill the conditions
if we are not together?"

She showed genuine surprise. "Surely you do not intend
to play out this farce?"

The hell he didn't.

"Did you not tell me you would be proud and honored
to be my wife? Does not a betrothal usually precede a wedding?"

Her tone sharpened. "Aye. But we both know there will

be no wedding. This *betrothal* does no more than make me your whore for a year.''

''Come now, Ardith. As my betrothed, no one would *dare* call you whore.''

''Mayhap not to my face, my lord, but you cannot control people's thoughts. What matter if they call me *lady*, if behind their hands they whisper *slut?*''

''You knew when you moved into my chambers, did you not, that we would share a bed?''

Her lips pursed, eyes averted, she answered softly, ''Aye. And for a week or two, until I went home, I thought I could close my ears. But for a year...''

''Ardith, a betrothal is as binding as marriage. It proclaims you belong to me, grants me the rights of husband as well as overlord. Who is to gainsay us?''

Azure blue eyes, moist with unshed tears, met his gaze squarely. ''Mayhap, in the eyes of man we commit no wrong, but not in the judgment of God and the church. The clergy will censure not only us, but the king, for this decree.''

Bile rose to his throat, his body tensed, and the words slipped out before he could check them. ''The opinion of the clergy be damned! What care I for pious posturing when the bishops—''

A gentle hand on his arm, a plea in Ardith's eyes halted his tirade. ''Do not blaspheme, Gerard. It serves no purpose.''

He shook off her hand, snatched up the goblet she'd pushed aside and took a hefty swallow. The wine tasted bitter, as though soured. ''Where did this come from? 'Tis foul.''

''Elva gave it to me. I have no idea from where it came,'' she answered softly.

Gerard got up and tossed the remains into the brazier. In control of his anger again, Gerard turned back toward Ardith.

''The clergy can rant if they wish,'' he finally answered.

"Marriage among nobles is an affair of state. The king himself set our betrothal. If the bishops wish to object, they may take their complaint to Henry."

Ardith had hoped Gerard would heed the possibility of church censure, though his callousness shouldn't surprise her, not since she'd heard of Lady Ursula's warped piety.

"What about Lady Diane? Has she agreed to the terms?"

"Henry, I believe, is overconfident that Diane will agree. She is not a patient woman. More likely she will turn her attentions to another man and ask for release."

"And if she does not, if she decides to wait, will you marry her?"

"If I must." He waved a dismissing hand. "Hellfire, Ardith, why do we speak of failure when we have not yet made an attempt at winning?"

Bronwyn had warned her to brace for gossip, for the wry glances of those who wondered if she shared Gerard's bed. No longer would they merely wonder. Now they would speculate on Gerard's stamina as he labored to infuse life into a dead womb.

The king had bound her to Gerard, more closely than vassal to overlord, for a year. She was to live with him and try to conceive a child, and only if the impossible happened could they marry.

As much as she loved Gerard, how could she spend a full year living as his wife, then relinquish him to another woman? The heartache would be unbearable.

"What of me, Gerard?" Ardith said softly. "If we cannot marry, what happens to me? My father may not let me return to Lenvil. After this...test, no man will have me as wife."

"Ardith, I am your liege lord. You must know I would take care of you. I have any number of manors that could use a good chatelaine, or healer. As for a husband..." He shook his head. "I would have to give the matter some thought. There might be someone who..." He tossed his hands in the air. "Why are we even discussing this? I want you as my wife. You want me as your husband. Ardith, if we do not take advantage of this betrothal decree, we have no chance whatever at marriage.''

Ardith conceded. All her life she'd dreamed of a life with Gerard. If she turned coward now, she would never know for certain if she'd tossed aside her fondest dream for naught. The dream, the life she wanted with Gerard, was worth the risk, though she wouldn't admit as much to Gerard. He would scoff if she capitulated out of love, for the chance to fulfill a fantasy.

Gerard didn't love her, and as he'd stated in the chapel after hearing of Bronwyn's matchmaking, sentiment had no import when making a marriage contract.

''These manors you speak of,'' she said, drawing a surprised look. ''If this betrothal does not lead to our marriage, you would be willing to place one in a woman's care, my care?''

''Aye. You have done well at Lenvil. A small manor would not be beyond your capabilities.''

''Then I suppose, my lord, we are betrothed.''

Gerard watched her leave the room, satisfied with the result of this most uncommon conversation with a woman. He'd planned to dig deep into his coffers, placate Ardith with jewels or rich garments, the usual trinkets women found appealing. He smiled. His Ardith wasn't typical of her sex. She cared naught for baubles, wore her newly acquired clothing with indifference.

Fearing an uncertain future, Ardith craved a holding, a home, a gift of permanence and real worth. Her wishes had surprised him, until he realized the wisdom of her request.

His smile soon turned to a frown. He'd granted Ardith's unusual petition. Then why, he wondered, was Ardith not happy?

Readying for the night ahead, Ardith sat on a stool and allowed Elva to comb through now unplaited auburn hair.

A night rail of pale yellow hung in wispy folds from Ardith's shoulders, the hem puddling around her bare feet.

She handed a goblet of wine back to Elva. "This wine tastes odd."

Elva took a sniff. "Merely poor quality. You have become used to the fine wines from Kester's stock. Drink," her aunt instructed, giving Ardith back the goblet. "'Twill calm you for the night ahead."

"Is my nervousness so evident?"

"Aye. You tremble. Drink."

Ardith took a deep breath to quiet her body, but her inner turmoil continued. She was as nerve-wrought as a bride awaiting her groom. But there the similarity ended. There had been no ceremony on the church stairs, no presentation of the dowry, no feast—none of the rituals practiced since beyond memory when two people joined in wedlock. She glanced at the door that connected the bedchambers.

"Mayhap Gerard will not come tonight," Ardith said softly.

"He will come," Elva huffed. "You know, dearie, I was right proud of you for demanding a reward—and such a rich reward."

Ardith had wondered how to tell Elva of the betrothal, to soften the blow so Elva wouldn't screech her disapproval and kindle Gerard's temper. At the moment, she couldn't see a hint of the smoldering hatred Elva had always professed toward Wilmont. Elva accepted the news well—too well.

"You overheard us speaking in the sitting room."

"Aye. I could not help overhear. The baron's voice travels great distances when he speaks."

"And you are not angry?"

"For your sake, I will hold my tongue. I will not risk banishment. You still have need of me, so the bones say."

"Do the bones also say whether I can get with child?"

"Watch your tongue, girl. Do not slander what you do

not understand. Besides, we both know you cannot conceive.''

Ardith looked away, the words too painful to hear.

''And even if you could,'' Elva continued, ''who is to say a year is enough time? Look to your sisters. Agnes and Elizabeth breed with ease. Both had babes during the first year of marriage. But Bronwyn, nearly two years wed, is childless.''

The connecting door opened. Elva put the comb on the table, picked up the partially finished goblet of wine and quietly left the chamber.

Chapter Twelve

The heat in Gerard's emerald gaze lured Ardith into his arms, as a moth drawn to flame, ignorant of the danger.

But she knew the danger of playing with fire, knew the folly of succumbing to temptation. She firmly pushed the awareness aside. She'd made her decision, accepted her fate. For as long as she could have him, be it for a year or for life, with or without the decree, she belonged to Gerard.

If she couldn't give him a child, she would give him her love, and if not the marriage he sought, then a liaison he'd never forget.

So we begin.

Pressed against him, she listened to his heartbeat. The steady thump pounded louder, faster. Ardith smiled at how easily Gerard responded to her nearness.

Men thought themselves superior to women, took pride in their warriors' prowess and control. Yet in the bedchamber, if a woman was of a mind, she could reduce a haughty baron to mere male with the paltry weapon of a rightly placed hip.

Ardith was of a mind.

She looked up into Gerard's face, a smile threatening the corners of her mouth. "Mayhap women *should* be warriors."

His confusion showed in his eyes and voice. "Ardith, are you feverish?"

Ardith had never learned women's wiles, didn't know if she could seduce. If she had any talent at all, now was the time to find out. She lowered her voice and half closed her eyes. "Aye, Gerard. I burn. Come ease my torment."

His reaction was most gratifying.

Gerard moved with the grace of a young lion. He bent his golden-maned head, delving for a stunning kiss as he swooped her into his arms and carried her to the bed. Ardith floated within the snare of his embrace, hearing the promise of sweet pleasure that he vowed with silent, mobile lips.

Her night rail melted away under his practiced hands. Gloriously naked, Ardith slid into bed as Gerard disposed of his garments. This time, watching him disrobe, she didn't close her eyes as he whipped his sherte over his head, exposing a body of sculpted perfection.

Over the wide plane of his chest, from nearly shoulder to shoulder, from prominent collarbone to taut stomach, glistened whorls of golden hair. A thumb-width scar slashed through the coils to below his navel, where the hair thickened into a thatch surrounding his male parts. Her female places quickened, responding to the urgency of his growing desire.

"Is aught amiss?" he asked, his voice rumbling low with a note of unease.

What could possibly be amiss? Surely, Gerard knew his body was magnificent.

"I wished only to admire, Gerard. I am sorry if I offended."

His smile widened as he joined her, pulling her into his arms. Ardith pressed close to his warmth and raised her lips. He responded as a man with a terrible thirst, drinking long and deep.

"You did not offend," he said at long last. "If you enjoy the sight of my body, you may admire all you wish. In truth, the mere thought of your eyes upon me heats my loins.''

His callused hands brushed her soft cheeks. His fingers played with her hair, twirling the strands as he explained, ''I only wanted to know if you still feared my size.''

Ardith remembered her earlier apprehension upon learning the size of his member. Hot upon the memory burst another, of how Gerard wielded his mighty sword, of the ecstasy spawned when sword entered scabbard. Her searching fingers eased along his side, skimming his trim waist, then hip. He hissed when her hand closed around that part of his body now as hard as iron covered with silk.

''How could I fear that which gives me so much pleasure?''

Relieved at her words and willingness to touch him, but unable to withstand the sweet torture, Gerard eased from the cocoon of her hand. Her touch, like no other woman's, threatened his control.

Maybe, someday, he would teach Ardith how to enjoy pleasure without joining their bodies. But until she swelled with his babe, he wouldn't veer from the method needed to get her with child. Nor, he ruefully admitted, did he want to, for sliding into Ardith's depths had proved addictive.

The silken skin of dark-peaked, rounded mounds met his hand, rising and falling with her breath. Gerard rolled to his back, bringing Ardith belly to belly. Her hair swirled in a fan of auburn, then fell into a veil around her face and down her back. An enticing scent, delicate yet hardy as a field of wildflowers, invaded his nostrils. He closed his eyes and breathed deeply. He couldn't hold back a chuckle at the sudden thought that no warrior had ever smelled quite so good.

''What made you say women should be warriors?'' he asked.

Smiling slightly, she wiggled, nudging his member's memory of the task at hand. ''Because males are so easily subdued.''

"Hmm. Was this how you intended to subdue Percival?"

"Gerard!"

The horrified look on her face set him chuckling again, then he grew serious, remembering Percival's pursuit. "Did the shoemaker deliver your boots?"

"Aye, while you met with the king." Her eyes held a wary look. "Must I learn to use that dagger?"

In this he would brook no argument. He would guard her well during their betrothal, but someday…the thought of Ardith alone, out of reach, rankled.

"Pray you never have need to use a weapon against an enemy, but you *will* learn. Have a care for your safety, Ardith. Remember you belong to me now."

"I carry value to you?"

Her tone teased, but Gerard saw the uncertainty. How could Ardith doubt? Wasn't she the mate of his choosing?

He ventured a teasing smile. "Aye, you hold value, Ardith. I might even hold you equal to my destrier."

"Your horse, my lord? How flattering!"

But Ardith didn't really take offense. If Gerard deemed her as valuable as his indispensable warhorse, her value was high indeed.

Gerard rolled, flinging her to her back, pressing her into the mattress. "I *might*," he said huskily. "Are you a good mount, Ardith, equal to the demands of my ride?"

Ardith's breath caught in her throat. Gerard hovered above her, his eyes dark, his body tense. She could picture him riding the huge warhorse. Regally, skillfully, Gerard could guide the destrier with a slight suggestion from his knees, a firm hand on the reins.

"A mount's performance depends much on the rider. Are you a skillful rider, Gerard?"

"What is this? A challenge, my lady?"

Ardith stroked the plane of his chest and raked her nails through the golden whorls. As her fingertips brushed pebbled nipples, he swallowed hard.

"Nay, not a challenge, for then one must be the victor,

the other vanquished. I would have us both prevail. Is that possible?''

"More than possible. In truth, I would say probable.''

Gerard quieted any further rejoinders with a kiss, long and hungry. Ardith fed his soaring passion with matching fervor. He noted the lack of surrender on her part. She leaped into the fray as an equal, taking and giving in full measure.

He struggled for control, even attempted to slow the pace. But Ardith would have none of it. Her insistence for the coupling strained his flimsy grasp on sanity.

Unable to do otherwise, Gerard answered her silent plea and slipped inside her welcoming warmth. Breathing hard, he lay quietly atop her, man joined to woman, flesh within flesh. Then she squirmed, and he was lost.

With long, smooth thrusts he stroked her velvety woman's place, riding high on the tide of passion. Ardith crested on an upthrust, crying out as ripple after ripple lapped at the dwindling sands of his control.

Joyfully, Gerard joined Ardith in a sea of oblivion. His member pounded in completion, emptying wave after wave of life-giving fluid into her depths.

He kissed her sweat-sheened forehead. "You drain me dry, scamp," he whispered. "How can we not succeed? Bear me a child, Ardith. Male or female, I care not which.''

Her arms tightened around his trunk. "I fear you wish for the impossible, Gerard. You may be unwise to expect success.''

"Mayhap, but neither will I accept failure, not without a fight. And I fight to win, Ardith, always.''

Ardith could feel the stares. Seated at evening meal beside Corwin, her skin prickled beneath the flagrant curiosity of the court. She concentrated on the morsels of meat and bits of bread she put in her mouth. They went down hard, hitting her stomach with a thud.

Voices buzzed around her, too low to hear words clearly.

Surely not everyone gossiped about the unusual betrothal, but some did, and the knowledge nudged Ardith's anger. She wanted to scream a defense, tell everyone to stare at King Henry or Gerard. The king had declared the betrothal and Gerard agreed to the terms. She was merely a pawn, innocent.

Except she wasn't innocent. She'd protested but then yielded, not to the decree, but to a man, Gerard. Body, heart and soul, she'd yielded.

And Gerard had well and truly claimed the offered prize, again and again, with tenderness, passion and reassurance. Her body still ached from last night's vigorous comfort.

"As bad as all that?" Corwin asked softly.

The question brought Ardith up sharply, until realizing Corwin didn't feel her aches, was only reacting to her mood.

"I will survive," she said, amazed at the conviction in her voice.

"Now that Gerard has sent Father back to Lenvil, mayhap the talk will die a swift death. I knew Father would not like the decree, but to vent his spleen before anyone who would listen...well, Gerard would not tolerate it. Too bad Gerard cannot send Lady Diane away as well. Her tongue is quieter, but just as angry."

An understatement. Lady Diane de Varley's opinion of the decree had spilled out of the audience chamber, flowed down passageways and now whirlpooled in the hall. Ardith almost felt sorry for the noblewoman. How galling it must be for Diane, to be told she must bide her time while the man she'd asked for in marriage tarried with another woman for a year.

Ardith glanced toward Lady Diane's place at table, and for the briefest second their gazes locked. Diane's seething anger, bright in her eyes, sent a chill up Ardith's spine.

I will not cower. With purpose, Ardith took a deep breath, raised her chin and looked about for friendlier faces. She found Gerard's.

Sitting at the high table, Gerard chuckled at some comment of King Henry's. Though he was less grandly attired, Gerard's bearing commanded an esteem rivaling the royal personage at his side. That Gerard held the king's favor was evident, that Gerard liked his monarch was unmistakable.

Then Gerard turned away from his king. He looked down the long row of tables to where she sat. He held her gaze entrapped for a long moment, then a small smile graced his face. He winked—*winked!*—then turned back to listen to Henry's next comment.

"I hate to leave you on your own like this, but I have duties to attend," Corwin said. "Will you be all right for a few moments until Gerard comes to fetch you?"

"Could I come with you?"

"You could, but Gerard will look for you here when he is ready to leave. Best you stay put. Gerard has had a trying few days and I would not cause him undue worry."

Ardith lowered her voice to a whisper. "The audience with the king yesterday—more was discussed than the betrothal, was it not?"

Corwin smiled and leaned toward her ear. "Aye." With that cryptic affirmation, he left.

Ardith forced herself to finish her meal, then looked about for Gerard, more than ready to seek the privacy of Wilmont's chambers.

"They say Gerard is bewitched," a woman behind her accused. Ardith turned on the bench to face the female whose voice dripped with venom. Lady Diane's gray eyes smoldered with fury. A catlike smile graced her full, sensual mouth. The deep blue of her gown and veil emphasized the silver-blond of her hair and flawless texture of her creamy skin. Diane stood stiff, lovely—and dangerous.

Ardith stood, dipped into a curtsy and chose her words carefully.

"I assure you, my lady, I have neither the desire nor

power to affect any man's mind, much less a man of such strength of will as Baron Gerard."

Diane's laugh rang wicked. "He does have a habit of doing what he wishes when the whim strikes him, does he not? The trait heightens his appeal."

Ardith withstood Diane's appraising gaze. Feature for feature the lady compared. As anger melted from Diane's face, Ardith knew she'd been judged wanting and unworthy. With a dismissing sniff, Diane looked to the high table where Gerard took leave of King Henry.

"And Gerard could not resist the challenge Henry presented in this betrothal. Ah, men. They will play their games."

A game? Was that how Gerard viewed the betrothal? Ardith didn't think so. Gerard was quite earnest about marriage. But if Diane wished to believe otherwise, why argue?

Diane spun back, her eyes narrowed. "Can Gerard win?"

Wanting badly to say aye, to tell the other woman not to plan a future as Gerard's wife, Ardith answered, "Time will tell, my lady."

"A bit lower, Ardith."

"Gerard, I cannot—"

"You can. Now, tighten your hold. There...ah...very good."

Ardith wet her lips and tried to concentrate. Only to please Gerard would she suffer this lesson.

"Let it slide in your fingers, mold to your palm. Feel the warmth, the power," he whispered urgently.

To her chagrin, she did. The beautiful, lethal dagger became an extension of her hand. No wonder males liked hefting blades, testing their prowess on the practice field or in the heat of battle. The false sense of immortality could prove addictive, and deadly.

"Can we halt now?" she pleaded.

He stood within her reach, feet spread, his hands motioning her forward. "Not yet. Lunge at me."

She gasped. "But you have no shield or armor!"

"Pretend I am Percival, come to ravish you. Remember the cur's leering gaze, his outstretched hand. Smite him with your blade, Ardith. Teach him not to trifle with a woman belonging to another man."

Ardith basked in his deepening scowl. She tried not to smile, but her mouth twitched. Gerard straightened, put his hands on his hips.

"The thought of Percival's hands on your body is amusing?"

"Nay, Gerard. 'Tis your attempt to goad me with a dullard such as Percival. *You* wish to run him through, not I."

He pondered for a moment. His scowl eased. "True," he admitted. With a wry smile, he observed, "'Tis Lady Diane *you* wish to run through."

Ardith's humor faded. "I have no wish to run anyone through."

"You had words with Diane," he continued. "Words not to your liking. What did she say to you, Ardith?"

Her hand tightened on the hilt of the dagger. "She seems to think I bewitched you somehow. I assured her I had not the power, nor is your will subject to beguilement."

"A serious charge."

Ardith shook her head. "I think not. She merely wonders why you would have me over her, as does the rest of the court." Ardith put the dagger on the table. "As do I. Diane can bring you so much more."

"Only land in Normandy I am not sure I want. 'Tis the devil's own temptation, I will admit, but defending holdings in lands so far apart spreads men and supplies too thin and stretches loyalties to breaking. I would rather any lands I may gain be here in England."

"Then why me, Gerard? I bring you nothing," she said, the words slipping out before she thought better of asking.

He crossed his arms, tilted his head. "I could give you

many reasons for choosing you, if you like, but looking back, I think I decided on you the day you burned your hair rescuing Kirk. I knew then you possessed that rare quality I hoped to find in a wife but feared I would not—the ability to defend and care for a child not her own, a child of low birth.''

Ardith remembered snatching Kirk away from the fire and her anger at Belinda, then being doused with a bucket of water and the pungent smell of singed hair. She suddenly understood the odd look on Gerard's face when he'd fingered her damaged plait. She'd surprised him by rescuing the whore's child, a bastard. And with that understanding came the memory of Corwin's revelation about Gerard's bastard son, Daymon.

"I have such a son," he continued, running a hand through his hair. "I had hoped to find a wife who would not reject him based on the circumstances of his birth. I was raised in a household where my mother barely tolerated her sons and was physically and verbally cruel to the bastard my father recognized and raised as his own. I intend to bring up Daymon as I would any legitimate child, but I would have less strife in his life than what Richard endured from my mother." He smiled. "Then I saw you, holding Kirk, spitting fury at a whore for neglecting a bastard child. Heedless of injury to yourself, you saved that child from serious hurt. I knew then I could trust you with my son."

Ardith hesitated, not sure if she wanted to know about other women who'd shared intimacy with Gerard. "What of Daymon's mother?"

"Died in childbirth. Now, if you are finished stalling, pick up that dagger and we will continue with this lesson."

She picked up the dagger, still mulling his bizarre but rather endearing reasoning. "You want your wife to be a mother to Daymon?"

"If she chose. I ask only for acceptance of his place in my household."

"You continually surprise me, Gerard. I know of no

other man who would turn aside wealth merely to gain a
nursemaid for his son.''

"I want you for myself too, Ardith. Never doubt that.
Besides, within a few days, if all goes as planned, I will
gain lands near as rich as Diane's without having to marry
a shrew in the bargain. Now, place your feet as I showed
you.''

His seemingly offhanded statement about gaining lands
confirmed Ardith's suspicions. She'd sensed for days that
something was afoot, and Corwin had all but verified it.
Would Gerard tell her what was going on if she asked? He
might, but something in his stance and expression said he'd
not put this silly lesson off any longer.

She ran her thumb over the dagger's razor-sharp edge,
set her feet. "Of all your strange notions, Gerard, this is
the oddest. I know of no other man who wants a warrior
for wife.''

He crouched. "Not a warrior, Ardith, just a wife able to
defend herself. Now, whenever you are ready…''

Ardith adjusted her grip on the dagger. The metal
warmed to her palm. A heady feeling of power surged to
her head.

As Ardith lunged, Gerard stepped aside and reached out.
A mere twisting of her wrist sent the dagger skittering
across the floor. A tug on the same wrist threw her off
balance and brought her body up hard against his.

She could feel his restrained laughter.

"Before you attacked, you closed your eyes. One cannot
hit a target one cannot see.''

"I have no liking for this, Gerard.''

"'Tis because you have no skill as yet. Try again.''

As the lesson wore on, Gerard pondered the wisdom of
giving Ardith the dagger. She did all he asked. She held
the weapon with a natural grip, easily learned the proper
flex of wrist and moved with supple grace. He acknowledged her talent but mourned her lack of fervor.

"Enough for now,'' he relented.

She slumped with relief.

"Ardith," he said gravely, putting his hands on her shoulders. "You must swear me an oath. Never, no matter the provocation, draw the dagger against an enemy unless you are prepared to spill blood."

Her head tilted, azure-blue eyes widened in question.

"Your distaste for the weapon shows in your face, a fault you must either overcome or learn to mask. Any hesitancy on your part to put the blade to proper use gives an enemy the advantage. Now swear."

"Have no fear on *that* score. I do most heartily swear," she stated firmly, thrusting the blade into her boot sheath.

Chapter Thirteen

Ardith put the last of Ursula's religious statues in the crate. Thomas would take them away; Ardith cared not to where.

Now that she was done, she would need some new task to fill her hours, to allow her to remain in Wilmont's chambers, away from the prying eyes that stared at her whenever she ventured out. Christmas was only a week away. Each day more people milled about the palace. Nobles from the farthest reaches of the kingdom were arriving at court to swear oaths of fealty to King Henry. Where they gathered, they talked, and watched. Some even dared to look pointedly at her belly, revealing ignorance as well as lack of delicacy.

Well, the watchers would be disappointed a while longer. Her flow had begun this morning.

Boisterous voices from the sitting room disturbed the peace. Ardith smiled, knowing Gerard must have returned.

A shrill scream rent the air. Elva ran into the chamber and bolted the door.

"We must hide," Elva said, her eyes wide with fear. "Nay, we must flee. Quickly, gather your possessions. Nay, we will leave without them."

"Calm yourself, Elva. What has frightened you so?"

"'Tis the devil's work, I tell you. Did I not warn you of Wilmont's evil? He is dead, but he walks, he speaks."

Ardith's heart slammed into her throat. Something had happened to Gerard. But even as she panicked, she heard hearty laughter echoing down the passage. Had evil befallen Gerard, the sounds would be quite different.

"Elva, you do not make sense."

"The bastard, Ardith. Oh, heaven protect us, the bastard has come back from the dead!"

Ignoring Elva's protest, Ardith answered the knock at the door, throwing back the bolt to admit Thomas.

"My lady, we have guests. My lord Gerard wishes your attendance."

Elva's eyes bulged. Gnarled fingers clamped Ardith's arm. "Nay! Dear one, my only child, I beg you not to venture out."

Elva's terror and Thomas's amusement pricked Ardith's curiosity. Thomas certainly wasn't afraid of whoever Elva declared a spirit. Ardith pried Elva's fingers loose.

"You may remain here, if you wish," Ardith said. "But I cannot disobey Gerard's summons."

"If you will not listen to reason, then I must protect you." Elva waddled over to her bag, rummaged about and pulled out a small sack attached to a string. "Put this around your neck so the spirit cannot draw your soul from your body."

"My lady, no spirit haunts these chambers," Thomas said.

His statement bolstered Ardith's decision to refuse the charm. "I have no need of your charm, Elva. Come, Thomas, we have kept the baron waiting."

As she neared the sitting room, Ardith recognized Gerard's voice. An answering voice sounded familiar.

Passing under the arch, she smiled at Stephen, Gerard's younger brother. Stephen had matured since she'd last seen him. His shoulders seemed wider. He stood taller than she remembered. His raven-black hair, in stark contrast to Gerard's, gleamed nearly blue in the candlelight. Only in the color of Stephen's green eyes and the square set of his jaw did the relationship to Gerard manifest.

Strong and fit, Stephen was certainly no spirit, and as he turned to greet her, she told him so. He laughed, but with little humor.

"Nay, Ardith. 'Tis not I who sends Elva screaming," he commented, then moved aside to allow Ardith to see the last man in the room. "'Tis Richard who put the old woman to flight. His ugly visage would frighten the most stouthearted knight."

Richard? But Richard had...died, struck down in Normandy! Yet before her stood a man of height and breadth to rival Gerard. His hair was the same color of spun gold and his eyes the same bright green...

Ardith felt herself pale.

"Pray, do not faint, my lady," Richard said, holding out a hand. "I am no spirit, though Stephen has wished me into the netherworld more than once these past weeks."

Hesitantly, Ardith touched Richard's hand, finding it warm and strong. Ardith looked to Gerard for an explanation.

"We contrived Richard's demise for good purpose, Ardith, and his robust health must remain secret a while longer."

She heard the command and though she didn't understand the need, with a mere glance Ardith gave Gerard a pledge of silence.

Stephen made a mocking bow. "Having delivered this insufferable monk to your hands, Gerard, I take my leave. I intend to find Corwin, then an agreeable wench or two, and get blindingly drunk."

Gerard's brow furrowed, but before he could speak, Richard put a cautioning hand on Gerard's forearm. The half brothers stared at each other for a moment, then Gerard nodded his head in permission. Stephen strode hurriedly out of the chambers.

"He may blather while in his cups," Gerard commented.

"I think not," Richard countered. "Stephen may be young, and angry, but he is not foolish. And he well deserves to raise some hell."

Gerard lifted a questioning eyebrow. "My mother?"

"Lady Ursula tried hard to sway Stephen's loyalty. They fought often, sometimes viciously. Stephen bent, but did not break." Then Richard frowned and scratched his chest. "God's bones. This robe eats at a man's flesh."

"You tire of monk's trappings?"

"I am weary of this robe and hiding my face with this infernal cowl. How much longer must we continue this charade?"

"Only a few days. My informants tell me Basil is expected on the morrow, or the day after."

Still scratching, Richard let out a satisfied grunt.

Gerard motioned to Thomas. "Go into my trunks and find something for Richard to wear before he rubs his hide raw."

Richard needed no urging to follow Thomas. Ardith watched Gerard's half brother disappear into the lord's bedchamber, still a bit awed by his resemblance to Gerard, and that for mysterious reasons, Gerard had gone so far as to feign Richard's death.

Gerard watched the questions flicker in Ardith's eyes and decided to tell her enough of the story to ease her mind.

He began with Richard's wounding in Normandy, told her of his desire to strike against the man responsible, then of Henry's command to settle the score at court. Within the space of a few minutes, the story poured out. Gerard wondered at his candor. He hadn't planned to tell her the whole. Men didn't unburden ordeals to women.

But it felt good, the telling. The great weight on his mind had eased, and Ardith not only understood his plans, but seemed to approve.

With a sigh, Ardith rose from her chair. "I should go to Elva, assure her Richard is not a specter." Then she tilted her head, an endearing little habit of hers when she meant to argue or question. "I assume your brothers will sleep here. Must we arrange for pallets?"

"I doubt we will see Stephen again tonight. Richard can have my bed. I will share yours."

Ardith flushed. How did one tell a baron he must find another place to sleep? He misunderstood the reddened cheeks.

"My brothers know of our betrothal, Ardith. Neither will be surprised nor care if I sleep in your bed."

"'Tis not your brothers' opinions that concern me, Gerard. There is another...I cannot...oh, dear."

"Cannot what?"

Ardith's words came forth weakly. "You should not share my bed tonight. My woman's time..."

"Ah," he uttered, a wealth of disappointment in the tone. Whether because they couldn't share intimacy, or because the bleeding meant no babe abode within her body, Ardith didn't ask, only accepted the comfort of his open arms.

"Then we will lie quietly, keep each other warm. I have grown used to having you near when I sleep."

The confession eased her qualms. After a light pat on her rump, he withdrew, saying, "I must see to Richard."

"And I to Elva."

He frowned slightly. "I trust you, Ardith, but not Elva. Order her to remain in these chambers until I say otherwise."

Thomas burst through the doorway into the sitting room, panting, "Basil is here, my lord."

Gerard exchanged a brief glance with Richard before asking, "Is Edward Siefeld with him?"

"Aye. Stephen said to tell you Basil looks harried. No doubt riding through the storm taxed him."

Gerard tamped down the blood rush that prepared his

body and mind for battle. He resisted the urge to grab his sword and reduce Basil's body to a bloodied corpse.

Henry wanted to pass judgment, inflict punishment. Given Henry's penchant for devising gruesome penalties, killing Basil outright might equal a show of mercy.

"Irked by a bit of snow, is he? Well, we shall soon make him forget his cold fingers and damp garments," Gerard promised dryly. "Inform Kester we are ready for our audience with King Henry."

Thomas obeyed swiftly.

"I suppose this means I must again don monk's robes," Richard grumbled.

"Not for a while yet, and then only for a short time."

"So long as it is the *last* time," Richard remarked as the door opened again.

Stephen entered, picked up a goblet and filled it with wine. "The last time for what, Richard?"

"For subjecting my body to the torture of haircloth. Where is Basil?"

Stephen warmed his wine with a hot poker from the fire, took a sip, then turned to face his brothers. "We may have a problem, Gerard. The palace seneschal refused Basil rooms in Westminster."

Basil's rank entitled him to space within the palace. By rights, the seneschal should evict a lesser noble to make room if need be. Only by direct order from the king would the seneschal dare the insult.

"How did Basil react to the affront?"

"He threatened the seneschal with dismemberment. The seneschal calmly told Basil to take his complaint to the king, then assigned Basil to a commandeered merchant's residence."

"So now Basil knows he is not in Henry's good graces," Gerard growled.

Richard voiced the question nagging at Gerard. "Will Basil heed the insult as a warning and leave?"

"I think not," Gerard mused. "Basil must know he

should stay to soothe Henry's ire, whatever the cause. But we must guard against the possibility of Basil's sudden departure. Stephen, assign a few men—''

''Done. Corwin and two others watch the house. I told Corwin to keep to the shadows.''

Gerard lifted his goblet in salute. ''Well done, lad.''

But Stephen didn't return the salute. His hand tightened on his goblet. ''I am no longer a lad, Gerard.''

Since arriving in London, Stephen had spent little time in Wilmont chambers. He and Corwin had caroused, drinking and wenching into the wee hours of the morn. Gerard had no idea where the two slept or even *if* they slept, nor did he care as long as they minded their duties.

Gerard suddenly felt older than his six and twenty years. That his *little* brother had become a man irked. Damnation, how would he feel when his son, a mere toddler now, stood tall and sure, proclaiming his manhood? How he missed the tyke!

''You are right, Stephen. I will try to remember.''

King Henry had decided to make an example of Basil of Northbryre by judging Wilmont's case before the entire assembly of nobles. Ardith and Bronwyn watched the proceedings among the crowd in Westminster Hall. Garbed in holiday finery, the nobles of England gathered for the formal ceremony of placing their hands between King Henry's palms and swearing to serve crown and kingdom.

Gerard had been among the first to utter the oath. Now he stood near Kester, a few steps to the right and a bit behind the throne. Ardith could feel Gerard's tension, though he strove to appear relaxed.

Richard leaned against the wall in a dark corner, the cowl of his monk's robe pulled forward to hide his face. Ardith tried to find Stephen and Corwin, but couldn't.

Finally, Basil of Northbryre waddled toward the throne and knelt before the king, presenting his prayer-folded hands. By rote, Basil mumbled the oath.

"Liar!" Gerard's voice tore through the chamber. Noble heads snapped around to the sharp outburst. Shocked gasps punctuated the charge, then faded into silence.

Ardith wished she could see the accused's face, assess his reaction, but could see nothing of Basil save the back of his head. King Henry released Basil's hands and slumped back into his throne.

"What is Gerard about?" Bronwyn whispered.

"Hush," Ardith said impatiently.

"A serious accusation, Baron Gerard," the king commented.

"And totally without foundation," Basil stated, struggling to gain his feet.

In two strides, Gerard reached Basil and pushed him down. "Stay on your knees, the better to beg the king's mercy."

"I have no need of mercy!" Basil flung out an entreating hand. "Sire, Wilmont's audacity is an affront to the crown. I demand an apology for this outrage."

Henry smiled indulgently. "Do let the man rise, Gerard."

Gerard stepped back. Basil scrambled to stand. Ardith frowned. Did Henry sympathize with Basil?

"Oh, dear," Bronwyn said softly. "Basil is in deep trouble, is he not?" To Ardith's questioning look, Bronwyn continued, "'Tis generally agreed one must beware the danger hidden by the veil of Henry's smile. I have seen this smile of Henry's but once before, just before he ordered two children blinded and dragged through the castle moat, as punishment for an offense by the mother."

Ardith fought to keep her voice hushed. "How cruel!"

"Cruel indeed, for the little girls are his grandchildren, by one of his bastard daughters."

Blessed Mother.

With an upraised hand, the king silenced the low murmurs buzzing among the nobles. "This man is our sworn

vassal, Gerard. You charge he lies. Have you proof of dis-
loyalty?"

Gerard stated his grievances, which Basil countered with
ready defense.

Basil flatly denied stealing rents from Milhurst bound for
Wilmont. Why would he steal from Baron Everart? Why
risk Everart's wrath for so paltry a sum?

Covet Milhurst? Never.

Lay siege to Milhurst with intent to overrun? Nonsense.

"Sire, I really must protest," Basil told King Henry. "I
had heard the manor had been victim to raiders. I sent my
men to observe. I merely wished to protect Wilmont interests until Baron Gerard could stir himself to reclaim his
lands."

"Your men did not *observe*," Gerard snorted. "They
laid siege for two days, then attacked."

"An unfortunate incident," Basil claimed. "When we
discovered our mistake, we withdrew."

"You were driven off!"

"Sire, obviously Baron Gerard does not believe I acted
only with the best intentions. No words of mine will change
his mind. I appeal to your superior judgment."

Gerard drew himself up to his full height. Hands that
could so gently touch Ardith's body to soothe or arouse,
clenched into white-knuckled fists. Eyes that could spark
with laughter or smolder with passion, narrowed to menacing slits. Gerard looked—lethal.

Ardith feared Gerard would reach out and snap Basil's
head off. Instead, Gerard turned toward the doors and
sharply nodded at the guards. Two liveried soldiers opened
the doors. In strode a man, dressed all in black, followed
by Stephen and Corwin, who sheathed their swords as they
entered.

The veneer of Basil's composure cracked. "Once again,
Wilmont violates the sanctity of the ceremony. He brings
a mercenary into our midst! By all that is holy, I demand
an accounting for this unpardonable insult."

Gerard ignored Basil, motioning the newly arrived trio forward. The man in black didn't move, until Stephen reached out and gave him a shove.

"Sire, this mercenary captain is Edward Siefeld," Gerard said. "You may remember him from Normandy. He and his band served knights' duty for Basil of Northbryre."

Edward Siefeld bent a low bow to the monarch. Out of the corner of her eye, Ardith caught movement—Richard, moving from his shadowy corner.

"And fought with distinction, I am told," Basil said.

"Aye, he and his band fought well," Gerard conceded. "Had he confined his fighting to battles, I would have no quarrel with Siefeld. But he also chose to follow your orders Basil, orders given him before he left England's shores."

Ardith moved to get a better view. Hands clasped behind his back, feet slightly spread, Siefeld stood stoic, as though uninvolved in this quarrel between barons. For the benefit of the attending nobles, Ardith supposed, Gerard chronicled the events leading to Richard's wounding in Normandy. He then formally accused Siefeld of attempting outright murder on a member of the nobility, at Basil of Northbryre's command.

"Oh, come now, Gerard," Basil censured. "Your bastard brother was wounded in battle and died of those wounds."

"Did he?" Gerard said, a feral grin spreading.

Siefeld shifted his weight, then looked hard at Basil.

"All England knows he died!" Basil said, waving his arms in exasperation. "You made a spectacle of bringing the man home and burying him at Wilmont. Sire, I demand atonement for enduring this outrage! Gerard seeks to slander my name with charges he cannot prove."

Gerard gave another hand signal. Richard stepped forward and pushed back his cowl.

Bronwyn screeched—then promptly fainted. Ardith quickly caught her collapsing sister.

Bedlam reigned.

Gerard ignored the gasps of disbelief, the flurry of hands making swift crosses over chests, the paling of faces and the women who succumbed. Basil stared at Richard, unable to speak. Much to Gerard's delight, Edward Siefeld reacted to Richard as hoped.

Siefeld uttered his thoughts aloud. "Nay. 'Tis not possible. You are dead, damn you. You are dead!"

"A much exaggerated notion," Richard answered flatly, then addressed the king. "Sire, 'twas Edward Siefeld who thought he made the killing blow. Indeed I might have died had it not been for the good care of your physicians."

Basil recovered from the shock. He cleared his throat and dusted his robes, as though wiping away the taint of any wrongdoing associated with his person. "Since no murder was done, I see no point in continuing this bit of drama. The bastard was only wounded, therefore—"

Gerard took a step forward and planted his fist squarely in Basil's face. Blood spurted from a broken nose as the man crumpled to the stone floor. "My apologies, sire, for spilling blood. I will gladly pay to have the floor cleaned."

Henry smiled wryly. "Aye, you will." Then he shouted, "Basil of Northbryre stands accused of crimes against Wilmont and the crown. Will any man in this assembly stand witness for his character?"

Not a soul breathed a word.

Henry summoned guards, instructing them to haul the prisoners off to White Tower. "We will let them contemplate their deeds and punishment from the dank hole of the subcrypt."

Henry stretched an arm toward Kester, who placed a scroll, tied in red ribbon, in the king's hand. The king, in turn, gave it to Gerard. "We suspect you will be pleased."

Gerard bowed. He knew this scroll listed the Northbryre lands the king bestowed as restitution. Though eager to read the list, Gerard resisted the impulse. "My thanks, sire."

The king stood. The room became quiet. "Richard, come

forward. Baron Gerard feels you worthy of knighthood, and we agree. Before this assembly we will bestow the honor.''

With pride and a sense of completion, Gerard looked on as Richard knelt before Henry and, with strong voice, took the vow to serve crown and country. The ritual completed, Gerard shoved the scroll into Stephen's hand. ''Guard this well. Within is your future.''

Chapter Fourteen

"More wine!" Gerard bellowed as another group of nobles pushed into the sitting room. Finding herself in the awkward position of playing hostess, Ardith hoped the procession would end soon. At least the fates had proved kind. The nobles all but ignored her in favor of Gerard and his brothers.

For the greater part of the day, Gerard had wallowed in the accolades of earls and barons, minor nobles and courtiers—anyone who cared to cross the threshold of Wilmont's chambers.

That many came to gape at Richard bothered Gerard not one whit. Nor did the curiosity vex Richard, who chatted with all as if it were common to have risen from the dead. Stephen told a spirited tale to all who cared to listen, and many did, of how he'd found Richard after the attack and borne him to the safety of camp and into the care of the king's physicians. Corwin stood by, adding facts Stephen missed in the telling.

Gerard received the praise for a show of power and favor rarely displayed in court.

"I wish you luck in trying to control that man," Bronwyn said tightly. Ardith smiled. Poor Bronwyn. Fainting at the sight of Richard had embarrassed her sorely.

Control Gerard? The idea had never entered Ardith's

head. She might voice her opinion, but Gerard did exactly as he pleased with a tenacity that could be terrifying.

Like now. Gerard chose to celebrate. His spirits high with victory, he called for wine and food, slapped peer and inferior alike on the back, accepted praise from the sincere and the fawning with equal aplomb.

Low murmurs suddenly replaced boisterous laughter. Ardith turned toward the door to see the cause.

Lady Diane de Varley stood in the entry and, as though the woman possessed the power of Moses to part the Red Sea, the crowd shifted, clearing her path to Gerard.

Ardith's firm sense of duty quickly squashed the personal wish to avoid the woman. Grabbing a goblet of wine, she faced Diane at midchamber.

"You honor us, milady," Ardith said, holding out the goblet. "Wine? Or mayhap you would prefer mead."

Diane's ice-gray eyes narrowed. "You overreach your rank here. Get yourself gone from my sight."

Startled, Ardith lowered the goblet. "My lady, I—" She stopped at the feel of Gerard's hand wrapping around the back of her neck.

"Greetings, Diane," he said in a low voice.

Diane blinked, and in the space of it, ice gray melted to sultry smoke. "My lord Gerard," she purred, dipping into a curtsy. "Your performance this morning was quite splendid. My compliments."

Gerard nodded an acknowledgment.

Diane waved a delicate hand at the roomful of people. "And so many attend you. I just now heard of the gathering, or I would have come sooner. You should have sent for me, Gerard... But I am here now, and will set everything to rights."

"I had not realized anything amiss."

Diane smiled sweetly. "Of course not. You are so rarely at court you are not expected to know all the proprieties to be observed. And after what you did to Basil this morning, no one would dare snub you for the lack of a few niceties, those a lady would provide to save her lord embarrassment."

Ardith bristled at the woman's audacity, knowing that every propriety had been observed—with help from Bronwyn.

Gerard's hand tightened on her neck. "My guests and I have no cause for complaint. Ardith has seen to everyone's needs in timely and gracious fashion."

Ardith had never seen anyone blush quite so prettily as Diane managed to blush. She then placed her fingertips on Gerard's arm and said in a conspiratorial whisper, "That may be. But my lord, one does not allow his leman to hold sway over guests of such noble rank. That is why I came so quickly when I heard."

"If you came to displace Ardith, you came for naught. She is not my leman, she is my betrothed, and as such will greet my guests."

"My lord, all know this betrothal doomed. And when it ends, you and I will wed. My place is here at your side, Gerard." Diane's fingers moved over Gerard's arm in a slight but definite caress. "Truth be told, if you were to end this game you play, quit the challenge of filling her barren womb, I would gladly undertake the task of giving you the heir you seek."

Ardith's hand tightened on the goblet. She fought hard to keep from tossing the wine in the woman's face.

"A generous offer," Gerard said.

Diane smiled brightly.

Ardith thought to toss the wine in *his* face until he continued, "But I have no desire to marry you, much less share your bed. I will if Henry insists, but will do my utmost to avoid so distasteful a marriage. Stay if you wish, but your presence here is neither needed nor particularly wanted."

Gerard's rejection hit Diane like a slap across the face. Her smile disappeared. Her features twisted into confusion, then seething fury. Diane's hand flew from Gerard's arm as though she'd suddenly discovered him fatally diseased.

"One day, Gerard of Wilmont, you will sorely regret having spoken to me so," she vowed, and with the bearing of a royal princess, turned and quit the chamber.

Ardith sighed with relief at Diane's departure, but the sincerity of Diane's parting words kept complete relief at bay. As a ward of King Henry's, Diane held some power. Enough to truly harm Gerard?

"You have made an enemy, Gerard."

He carelessly shrugged. "Pay her no heed, Ardith. Come, I want you to meet someone," he said, dismissing the entire affair.

For the remainder of the afternoon, Gerard kept her by his side, despite her wish to again fade into obscurity. Not until after the last of the well-wishers left did he allow her a measure of space when he hoisted his bulk up onto a table and waved Stephen and Richard into chairs. Legs swinging, smiling smugly, Gerard reached out a hand to Stephen. Stephen handed over a scroll.

Gerard made a great show of untying, unrolling and reading it. He then took out his dagger and cut a strip from the top of the scroll.

"Henry kept less of Northbryre's lands than I thought he would." Gerard waved the strip of parchment. "This is mine."

"Basil's castle in Hampshire," Richard guessed.

"Very astute of you, Richard." Gerard cut the remaining sheet in half and held the pieces out to Richard. "Choose."

Richard balked. "Stephen should choose. He is full brother."

"An accident of birth we ignore. Besides, you outrank Stephen. Rank does have its privileges."

"Were it not for Stephen, I would not have lived to rise to knighthood. Stephen should have first—"

"God's wounds, Richard!" Stephen broke into the argument. "Choose and be done."

Richard relented. Gerard handed the remaining list to Stephen. "You hold these lands in vassalage to Wilmont.

We will negotiate rent and knight service on the morrow. This bequest should satisfy our pact."

Ardith knew nothing of the pact now satisfied, knew only that Gerard, amazingly, was dividing the bulk of the holdings between Stephen and Richard. The contentment of the brothers signified a promise made, and now fulfilled.

"After we come to terms and the recording of land transfers are made," Gerard continued, "notice of the change of ownership will go out to the holdings under the king's seal."

Stephen suddenly looked up from the intent study of his newly acquired wealth. "Might I deliver the notices?"

"All of them?"

"Aye." Stephen pressed on. "We should take advantage of this opportunity, Gerard. If one of us delivers the notices, affirms Wilmont authority from the outset, the fewer problems later. I can detect rebellion and squash the trouble before it can breed."

"Besides, you want a look at your holdings."

Stephen smiled crookedly. "Well, that too, but I still believe my idea a good one."

"Stephen makes a good case," Richard said thoughtfully. "If he visits each holding, we will get a truthful accounting."

As though preparing a major campaign, the three fell into a discussion of men and mounts and provisions. Gerard fetched a map and they outlined a route.

"Mayhap I should go along," Richard suggested, obviously fancying the rigors of the road after so long a confinement.

Gerard pointed a forefinger at Richard, an unrelenting look on his face. "You are returning to Wilmont. I will not have you wandering about until you regain full strength. Besides, someone must take the deeds to Walter. He should be told of the new holdings."

"You are not returning to Wilmont after court?"

"I have other plans."

The announcement came as a complete but not unwelcome surprise. Ardith had assumed Gerard would want to winter at Wilmont. She knew he missed his son, and winter was the season when lords planned crop plantings and livestock needs for the warmer months. She hadn't looked forward to meeting Lady Ursula. Ardith gave thanks for the reprieve.

Richard seemed to follow the drift of her thoughts. "Lady Ursula will not be pleased when she learns how you favor us, Gerard, especially me. She will wail and screech until no one dare cross her path."

Gerard smiled wryly. "Will you hide?"

"I intend to sleep in the armory and take my meals at the low end of the table."

"Coward."

"Give me a blade and an enemy to face and I will fight till my dying breath to defend Wilmont, but Gerard, facing your harridan parent fills my heart with dread."

"She is only a woman. You are a knight. Tell her to remember her position."

"*You* tell Lady Ursula. I believe part of her problem is that she has *no* position and well knows it."

Oblivious to—or ignoring—his brothers' bantering, Stephen studied Gerard's map. "Mayhap I should take Corwin with me. He might enjoy the adventure."

"I wish you would not." Ardith put fingertips to lips. Again she'd interfered, drawing the sharp attention of three pairs of eyes, eyebrows raised in surprise.

"You worry over Corwin?" Gerard finally asked.

"Nay, not Corwin. I hoped Corwin could go back to Lenvil to care for Father. He should not be alone."

Gerard wondered why Ardith should care. Hellfire, Harold gave Ardith naught but grief, treated her little better than a serf. Yet he would ease her mind. "Before Harold left for Lenvil, the physicians poked and prodded till he refused to cooperate. Save for his leg, his body is sound for his age. As for his uncertain memory—'' Gerard shrugged a shoulder ''— John is aware of the problem.''

Ardith bit her bottom lip. Gerard recognized the gesture. His lady wanted to protest, but apparently thought better of doing so in front of Stephen and Richard.

Richard rose from his chair, yawned and stretched. ''If you have no further need of me, I am for bed. Mass on the morn will be early, and a pompous affair. I intend, however, to enjoy the festivities now that I am alive again.''

''I am off to find Corwin,'' Stephen announced.

His brothers gone, Gerard gathered Ardith in his arms, anticipating festivities in the privacy of her chamber.

''Gerard, where are we going if not to Wilmont?''

''To a small manor near Romsey. The rents are late. Now seems as good a time as any to find out why.''

''Romsey?'' Ardith's pert mouth pursed in concentration. So very kissable, that mouth. ''The name sounds familiar, but I know not why.''

''Queen Matilda retired to a convent there some years ago,'' he said, dipping for a kiss, once, twice. ''Mayhap you heard the name in connection with her.''

''Hmm.'' She breathed against his mouth, laying her arms on his shoulders, her hands against his neck. ''You may be right.''

His loins beginning to burn with familiar, pleasant fire, Gerard lost the thread of the conversation.

Never, in her entire ten and seven years, could Ardith remember being so cold. Despite protection from frigid winds by the heavy canvas walls of the tent, despite the heat from glowing coals in the brazier, her body refused to warm.

The weather didn't affect Elva's ability to sleep. Snoring softly, she huddled on a pallet near the brazier.

With a sigh Ardith burrowed deeper into the furs and pulled the cover over her nose, wishing Gerard less impulsive but knowing he wouldn't change.

Gerard's patience knew definite limits.

Nearly a fortnight had passed since King Henry's banishment of Basil of Northbryre and Edward Siefeld to the Tower's subcrypt, where they still languished. Gerard, knowing he couldn't rush Henry or influence the harshness of Basil's sentence, had decided to leave. As at Lenvil, he issued orders one day for departure on the next, throwing men-at-arms and maids into a frenzy of packing.

Ardith didn't argue against his impetuous decision, for she was eager to leave. No longer need she endure Lady Diane's cutting remarks or the whispers of the court.

Nor did she wish to witness whatever punishment Henry saw fit to inflict on Basil. Bronwyn had told her of people who'd suffered Henry's tortures—including his own grandchildren—each tale more gruesome and each punishment more cruel than the last.

So this morning the company had assembled and left Westminster at dawn, pressing on until nearly nightfall when Gerard pulled off the road and ordered the tents pitched. After a light meal of bread and cheese, Ardith had sought Gerard's tent and the comfort of a pallet, gratefully accepting the warm, spiced wine Elva had prepared.

A brisk breeze stirred the fur of her coverings as the tent flap opened. Ardith buried the rest of her face. She could hear Thomas and Gerard rustling about but had no desire to peek out.

Naked as the day he was born, Gerard crawled onto the pallet. He uncovered her face.

"There you are. I knew you must be in here somewhere."

Ardith reached out, putting an icy hand on his chest. He sucked in his breath, then yelped and shuddered when her feet curled around his calves.

"Hellfire! Why did you not tell me you had frozen?"

She sighed, relieved she still had toes. She could feel them now. "I had thought you as vulnerable to cold as the rest of us mere mortals. I was wrong. You are so very warm.''

Gerard pulled Ardith's body close, noting she'd stripped down to her chemise, no further. She pressed hard against his body. The soft purr from her throat scolded him more sharply than a Harpy's shriek.

He'd pushed the company hard without thought for Ardith's comfort. The men-at-arms hadn't complained—but they would never admit so unmanly a discomfort as cold toes. Elva had huddled in a wagon in a deep nest of furs. Thomas, young and full of high spirits, thought the ride a grand adventure.

Only Ardith suffered. Her rabbit mantle and soft boots hadn't kept her warm. He gathered her hands. How had she held on to the reins with such stiff fingers? Thank the Lord her palfrey was gentle, easily guided.

He would wrap Ardith in his beaver cloak for the remainder of the journey. They should reach the manor tomorrow, within a few hours of breaking camp.

Tonight he would share his heat. Nay, tonight he would *create* heat. He reached for the hem of her chemise. Ardith slapped at his hand.

''Gerard, you cannot mean to want this now,'' she whispered.

''Can you think of a more pleasant way to drive the chill from your body?''

Her lips were against his chest. He felt her smile. ''Nay. But we are not private.''

''Thomas and Elva sleep. Unless you scream when your body convulses with pleasure, they will remain ignorant of our labors under the furs.''

She was quiet for a moment, then lightly scolded, ''Labors? 'Tis such demanding work, then, making love to me?''

He embarked on an assault of her senses with hands and mouth. '''Tis a grueling task. I sweat. I breathe heavily. My body strains with the anguish of testing my endurance." He pulled her hand downward. "I ache to complete the chore that leaves me too weak for aught else but sleep."

"My poor baron," she teased softly, her now warming hand sliding in delightful torture over the hub of his need.

From near the brazier, Ardith thought she heard a noise. She glanced toward Elva. No movement. No sound. Without further concern, Ardith gave in to Gerard's pleasing and successful method of warming her body.

Gerard signaled the company to halt at a rise overlooking the Romsey holding.

"The manor looks abandoned," Ardith observed.

He silently agreed. No peasants bustled about the timber building, tending chores. No smoke curled upward from the hole in the center of the manor's thatched roof. The silence nudged his warrior's instincts.

He dismounted and drew his sword. "Thomas, I will take two men. Tell the others to guard the women and wagons."

"You should don your mail," Ardith said softly from atop her palfrey.

He looked up sharply into her troubled azure eyes.

"Ardith, I grant you, something is amiss, but no grave threat awaits."

Ardith slid from the saddle, faced him squarely. "Yet you call for two men and draw your sword." Boldly, she placed a quieting finger on his opening mouth. "When you least expect it fate can wave a brutal fist. Have a care, Gerard, for if fate proves unkind, I would miss you dreadfully."

She tugged at the palfrey's reins, taking only a few steps before he called her name. She turned.

"Have Thomas fetch my hauberk."

"At once, my lord."

Gerard shook his head over the foolishness of donning armor. If his men thought his overcaution disturbing, so be it, for at the small concession, Ardith had smiled. He would concede far more to ease her mind, to elicit the smile that gladdened his heart.

She would miss him—*dreadfully*. What would she miss? The laughter, or spats, or loving? How long would she grieve? A fortnight? A month?

Hellfire, he had sunk to degrading depths, all because of a slip of a woman with a blinding smile.

Hauberk donned, he checked to see Ardith surrounded by soldiers who knew their lives forfeit should they fail at their duty. Flanked by two men-at-arms, Gerard cautiously approached the manor.

"Hail in the manor!" he shouted, oddly expecting an answer.

The door opened, creaking on weather-brittled hinges. A young man, lean and tall, eased from behind the doorway, brandishing a shepherd's crook as though it was a weapon. The fright in his eyes disputed his scowl and bold stance. Gerard admired the peasant's pluck. Though faced by three men, one an armored knight, the man's knees didn't quake.

"Your name," Gerard ordered, sliding his sword back into the scabbard.

"I be Pip," came the answer in a thin voice. Then, to Gerard's surprise, Pip challenged, "Who might you be, milord?"

Gerard raised an eyebrow. "Your liege lord, Baron Gerard of Wilmont."

"Everart be baron."

"No longer, Pip. My father died several months ago." Gerard raised a beckoning arm toward Ardith and the remaining guard on the hill. "Are you the steward? I will have an accounting for the sorry state of this manor."

"'Tis old Biddle you be lookin' for. He lies yonder."

The grave wasn't fresh.

"Curled up his toes nigh on a year ago, milord," Pip offered. "Ate his victuals, went out to do the necessary and *pop*—" Pip snapped his fingers "—over he goes."

"Then who cares for the manor?"

"The tenants, milord. We take our turns stayin' in the manor, keepin' things right and tight. We knew the overlord would come nosin' around someday, wantin' his rents."

Gerard briefly wondered why his father had let this manor decline to such pitiful condition, ripe for raiding, but had little time to ponder as the rest of the company pulled into the yard. He helped Ardith from the saddle.

"Ardith, meet Pip. 'Tis his day to guard the manor."

"A pleasure, milady," Pip said with a slight bow. "Would you be wantin' to come inside, now, out of the cold?"

Gerard ushered Ardith ahead, following Pip into the manor. Gerard squinted, sniffing. Beside him Ardith coughed and covered her nose against the stench.

Sheep. A dozen of the woolly creatures milled about the single room of the manor. Gerard's eyes watered.

"Yer rents, milord," Pip said proudly.

"Pitch the tents!" Gerard bellowed out the door.

Two days later, Ardith put a trencher of mutton and gravy on the trestle table before the scowling lord of the manor. "Come, Gerard," she chided. "'Tis not so bad, now. I think we could even sleep in here tonight."

Gerard's nose scrunched. "Not I."

"The women have worked hard to make the manor habitable for their overlord."

"As the men have worked hard to build a stable for the horses and a pen for the damned sheep. I have consented to take my meals in here, Ardith. Push no further."

Ardith was too weary to argue. The tenant wives had given up two full days from their own chores to scrub and sweep—and shovel—transforming the makeshift animal pen into a manor worthy to house the baron.

They'd chattered while they worked, tripping over one another's stories to give Ardith the history of the manor. She now knew how old Biddle had gone about his duties, which women possessed which talents, who grew crops and who grazed sheep.

The manor claimed no village. Freeman tenants held farms scattered over the area, raising oats, wheat and barley. Some kept flocks of sheep, others ran pigs in the nearby woodlands. For goods the tenants couldn't raise or make, they bartered in nearby Romsey.

From Ardith, the women had sought reassurance about their new liege lord. She told them Gerard would be strict but fair. As a warrior unequaled, he would safeguard the farms and their livelihood from raid.

Not wanting the peasants to misunderstand her position, Ardith also told them of the betrothal decree.

Meg, a young woman heavy with child, confessed, "Well, now me and me Pip ain't wed yet either. If a priest happens through and we got the time, we'll say the vows. If not..." She shrugged and smiled.

Relieved at the lack of censure, Ardith had directed the work as though she really were the lady of the manor.

Gerard pushed aside his trencher, rubbed a hand over his eyes. His weariness matched her own.

"How long do we stay here?" Ardith asked.

"For a while yet. I must appoint a steward and provide some defense for these people."

"The women think guards unnecessary. They feel safe, being so close to the city—and the abbey. Meg told me that last summer some bandits thought to cause mischief but the queen's soldiers drove them away."

"So the men told me. But the soldiers fight only to shield the queen from possible harm, not the tenants."

"This manor cannot support many guards."

"Another failing I must change. I think we will winter here. Mayhap I will send for Daymon and spend a quiet season."

Daymon—Gerard's son. Thoughts of the tenants fled as she fought the twinge of panic at meeting the boy. She loved children. A tyke who resembled Gerard would be

impossible to resist. She would fall hard for the motherless
son of the man she loved. If Gerard sent for Daymon, if
they lived here as a family, 'twould make the eventual parting more painful.

"That might be unwise."

"You do not wish to spend the winter?" Gerard asked,
surprised at Ardith's reluctance. He had thought her content.

She picked up the used trencher. "I meant sending for
Daymon. 'Tis very cold for so young a child to make such
a long journey."

"He is a healthy lad. If properly cared for—"

"Gerard," she interrupted, "children, especially little
ones, tend to illness. You should not risk his health. If you
wish to see him, go to Wilmont for a spell."

He noticed she meant to send him off to Wilmont, alone.
She frowned slightly, her gaze slid away.

Until now, whenever Ardith questioned his decisions, she
faced him squarely and stated her opinion. He wondered at
this odd change.

Did she object to Daymon's coming because of the
weather, or because she didn't want his bastard child underfoot?

Gerard banished the unwelcome thought that Ardith
might spurn Daymon. Ardith would love any child under
her care, baseborn or not, her own child or another
woman's. He remembered her cold hands and icy feet.
Surely, she only wanted to spare Daymon.

"Ardith?"

Her gaze slid back. Fatigue marred her eyes. He smiled
with relief. His little warrior was simply tired, too weary
to spar in her usual forthright manner.

He took the trencher from her hand, pulled her down
onto his lap. She wrapped her arms around him, buried her
face in his neck.

"You may be right," he yielded, not without reservation

but with respect for Ardith's common sense. "The weather may yet be too harsh for Daymon to make a long journey."

Her body relaxed. "A wise decision," she said against the side of his neck, her warm breath puffing near his ear. "Will you go to Wilmont?"

"Will you come with me?"

"Would I have a choice?"

"Nay." He ran a hand along her ribs, fondled a breast covered by the thick, coarse wool of the gown she wore while cleaning. "We have a child of our own to create, remember? Where I go, you go. Where you are, I will be."

Ardith squirmed, pressing into his caressing hand, then abruptly drew back. "Shall we retire to the tent?"

"Why? We are alone."

"We are?" Ardith sat up straight, looking around. Gerard's men-at-arms had finished eating and left, choosing not to linger over ale. Meg no longer knelt by the tub, scrubbing pots. Even Elva and Thomas were nowhere to be seen. "Where did they go? Gerard, did you order everyone out?"

"Did you hear me give an order to clear the room?"

"'Tis mightily strange that everyone should vanish without taking our leave."

"You find that disturbing?"

"Nay," she admitted, then added, "just...odd."

Chapter Fifteen

"My lord, if you have no further need of me, I would like to see how the work progresses," Thomas said, hanging a mended bridle on a wooden peg.

Gerard nodded his permission, running a hand over his destrier's flank, half noting the pounding of hammers from where his men-at-arms were building an armory.

"I, too, milord. By your leave, o'course," Pip said.

Gerard glanced at Pip, approving of the man's interest in the eruption of improvements currently taking place. Given some tutoring in numbers and letters, Pip might make a good steward. And Meg would do well as his helpmate. From the hut where the couple lived, Meg accompanied Pip to the manor each morning. While Pip worked in the stable or helped with the carpentry, Meg helped Ardith in the manor.

At a wave of Gerard's hand, Pip scurried from the stable, bowing briefly at Ardith, who stood in the doorway. Even at this distance, several stalls from the opening, Gerard could see the dejection on her face.

"If you are not too busy, Gerard, I should like a word with you." She tugged up the hem of the overlong beaver cloak he insisted she wear whenever venturing outside, wandered over toward an overturned crate and sat down.

Arms crossed, he leaned against one of the posts that

supported the roof. "What has happened?" he asked, silently vowing to throttle whoever had caused her distress.

She waved a hand, indicating the stable. "Look about you. What do you see?"

Confused, he answered, "A stable. Horses, hay, leather. What of it?"

"But no people. As soon as I appeared in the doorway, Thomas and Pip scurried out like hares pursued by hawks."

"Their leaving had naught to do with you. They finished their chores and wished to watch the men work on the armory."

"Ah, the armory. Your men cannot abide sleeping in the manor. They must build a place of their own."

"They are used to wintering in the armory at Wilmont. If they wish to expend the energy to build one here, I see no reason to deny the request."

She shook her head. "They wish a place of their own to escape me, Gerard. Your men do not like me."

He nearly laughed at the absurd notion, but the tear forming in the corner of her eye stopped him cold. "Not like you?" he asked gently. "Those men would lay down their lives to protect you."

Her lip trembled. "Only because I belong to you."

Gerard knew his soldiers extended allegiance to Ardith from affection as well. Why, the dolts went to great lengths to win her approval.

"When you expressed a wish for a long table and benches, did they not make them?"

"They tired of eating while sitting among the rushes."

His men had eaten under conditions that would have horrified Ardith. Sitting cross-legged on the floor of a warm manor, balancing trenchers on knees while eating hearty, tasty meals could be termed luxury. On the night Ardith made a passing comment about the need for a bigger table, the men had drawn lots, vying for the honor of fulfilling her wishes.

Nor had the fawning stopped with the completion of the

table and benches. They hung on her every word for some hint of how to serve Ardith. No task was too arduous, no chore too menial. Her feet were cold? They chopped and split extra wood for the pit. She needed a bucket of water? They hauled four from the stream. There was a draft from a corner? They mixed mud and straw and plugged the timbers. She'd turned his soldiers into drudges, and they minded not one whit.

"Shall I line them up and let them grovel at your feet?" he teased.

Ardith looked horrified. "Nay! They would do so out of loyalty to you, Gerard. And 'tis not only the soldiers, but the peasants who shun me. What have I done to offend them?"

"Surely, you jest!"

"Not so," she countered, shaking her head, the tear finally falling down her cheek.

The peasants were as infatuated as the soldiers, mayhap more so. The farmer tenants, their wives, the children— they adored Ardith. Gerard could stand no more. He squatted before Ardith, enfolded her hands. "What brought this on, Ardith?"

"Meg refused my invitation to stay for evening meal."

There had to be more. "And?"

"Do you not see, Gerard? At Lenvil, people lingered long after mealtimes, sharing food and drink and talk. Here, no one will stay about the manor for long, not even Meg or Pip. Meg prefers to return to her hut when her chores are done. Even Elva leaves, goes home with Meg."

A blessing, Gerard thought of the old woman's absence. "Elva stays with Pip and Meg because it is so near Meg's time. Once the babe is born, Elva will return."

Ardith shrugged a melancholy shoulder. "Mayhap, but what of the others, Gerard? Will they ever come to accept me? I had thought..."

Gerard completed her thought silently. Ardith would make this manor her home. He'd watched her strive to make the manor more comfortable, to become friendly with the peasants. He'd even thought to interfere. This wasn't the manor he intended for Ardith, should settling her in some manor become necessary. This holding was too distant from Wilmont.

She continued, a bit of anger creeping into her tone, "The women do not come unless they bear gifts, as though I am some ogre who must be appeased. Then they hustle off with barely a word. I have tried to get them to sit for a while, to talk over a cup of ale, but they will not. The only days I can tempt anyone to linger are the days you go hunting."

"Then mayhap 'tis my fault the peasants avoid the manor," Gerard said thoughtfully. "Thomas and my men know I like my privacy. They may have made comment to the tenants, who took it as warning to stay away."

"Nay, 'tis *me* the tenants dislike. You should hear how they praise their new liege lord. These people love you."

"And I have heard them praise you. I wonder—" Gerard broke off, not daring to voice the outrageous explanation that flickered through his head. He had to test it first. He stood up and pulled Ardith to her feet.

"Come. Let us inspect the armory."

Within moments of their arrival the hammers fell silent. Gerard walked about the inner walls, inspecting, showing Ardith points of competent construction. The men had done a good job. They had also vanished.

"Do you see what I mean, Gerard? All I need do is walk into the soldiers' midst and they leave."

Gerard shook his head. "Nay, not you. Us." He put his hands on her shoulders, saying, "One more test. Go into the manor. I will follow in a moment."

She looked at him quizzically, then obeyed.

Gerard waited silently. Soon, the soldiers returned, hauling logs they wouldn't need for several hours. He smiled, more sure of his conjecture. As he reached the manor, the tattoo of hammer on nail again split the air.

In the manor, Ardith thanked a tenant's wife for a round of yellow cheese. Meg pulled loaves of brown bread from the fire. Elva carded wool sheared from a sheep butchered for meat. Gerard had no more than fetched a cup of ale and sat down at the table when silence loomed, only he and Ardith remaining.

He broke off a chunk of hot bread as she sat. He tried not to smile, but failed. "Ardith, did you tell the women of the betrothal decree?"

"Aye." She sighed. "I fear they stay away because they disapprove."

He chuckled. "Nay. They vanish because they wish us success. I swear, Ardith, I believe I could fling up your skirts and have you anywhere, anytime I pleased, and we would not be disturbed. Beware the next time you come looking for me in the stable. Henceforth, I will keep a stall in readiness, empty of horse but strewn with fresh hay."

A rosy blush crept up her neck and bloomed on her cheeks. "Gerard, you cannot mean...they would not...they give us privacy to...Blessed Mother," she groaned, burying her face in her hands.

His laughter burst out. "The tenants and soldiers conspire, Ardith. They give me opportunity to indulge my lusty whims whenever it suits my mood. How can I not approve?"

The dagger flew true, the tip burrowing deep into the mound of hay, slicing a turnip neatly in half. Ignoring Gerard's pleased smile, Ardith unstuck the dagger, brushed bits of hay and dirt from the turnip, and tossed the vegetable into the soup pot with the afternoon's other targets.

"You improve, Ardith."

"I should hope I show progress. You insist on the practice often enough."

"Why do you still grumble?"

"Because I see no point in the lessons. I cannot get past your guard. You disarm me with ease."

"Because I know how you will thrust, the extent of your reach. A stranger will not know your style. And you will have surprise in your favor. A foe will not suspect a woman of carrying a blade more lethal than an eating knife, much less knowing how to use the weapon." He pointed at the dagger. "You can also hit a target. You need not even get close to your enemy to do mayhem."

Ardith wiped the blade on her skirt. "So long as I need only draw turnip juice and not blood I am content. Nor, might I remind you, does a turnip move."

As though he hadn't heard a word, Gerard continued the lesson. "Your grip is firm, your thrust steady and well aimed. But to defend yourself properly, you also must learn to control your emotions. Show an enemy only what you wish him to see. Learning how to bury fear or anger under calm reasoning is as vital as the speed and angle of your lunge."

Ardith slipped the dagger into her boot with a sigh. As always, the manor had cleared of people as soon as Gerard appeared, leaving the two of them alone. Often they used the privacy as the peasants intended, dallying for hours among the furs of their drape-encircled pallet. At other times they merely shared a quiet repast. Occasionally, too often for Ardith's comfort, Gerard insisted on these lessons.

Ardith half listened as Gerard droned on about watching an enemy's eyes, how to use body leverage and choosing the right moment to draw the dagger from her boot.

Aye, she could draw the dagger, might even be able to threaten. But to kill, to stick the lethal blade into someone? Never. The mere thought turned her stomach.

"Ardith? Did you hear one word I said?"

"Of course, Gerard."

He shook his head. "Your eyes told me differently. What were you thinking of?"

Ardith seized the chance to switch to a more pleasant, and possibly profitable, subject.

"Sheep."

"Sheep?"

Ardith smiled at his scrunched nose. "I know you think of sheep as smelly, annoying beasts. To the peasants, however, the sheep represent a good portion of their livelihood."

"There do seem to be a great many around. What of it?"

"I know you inspected the holding." When he nodded, she continued, "Then you know that much of the land cannot be put to plow because of the hills. The tenants raise some crops, enough to feed their families. They rely on the sheep, actually the fleece, for the coin to buy cloth or tools or other goods." She cocked her head. "Why does Wilmont take rent in the form of a whole animal? Meg said old Biddle drove six sheep to Wilmont every year. Would it not be easier to take the rent in fleece, or in coin from the sale of the fleece?"

"Possibly. I would have to ask Walter. Mayhap my father wanted the meat rather than the coin. You are leading up to something, Ardith. What?"

"You should buy more sheep."

"Ugh."

She laughed lightly. "I am not asking you to live with them, Gerard, merely purchase them, begin a flock to support the needs of the manor and pay the rents to Wilmont."

He looked skeptical.

"This land could support twice the number of sheep now grazed in the hills. Romsey is becoming a major trading center for fleece. More merchants attend the market fair every year and the price rises. If we increase the flock now, within a short time this manor could show a nice profit."

We? Gerard folded his arms across his chest. "Since you have never been to the market fair at Romsey, I assume you learned the way of traders from the tenants."

"From Meg, mostly. She says the tenants let Pip haggle with the fleece merchants. He always gets a good price."

Her smile widened. "If we do increase the flock, I think Pip would be a good choice as master shepherd."

"I have other plans for Pip."

Her smile faded. "Oh?"

"Pip is a smart young man. He knows the land and the tenants. With a few lessons in letters and numbers, I believe Pip would make a good steward here."

Understanding washed across her face. "I see," she said quietly.

"Your idea holds merit. I will discuss it with Pip."

The meager praise was all he would offer in recompense for refusing her the stewardship. He felt no remorse for crushing her hopes. Ardith should be planning what she could accomplish as mistress of Wilmont, not as the steward of this remote manor.

As though knowing his name had been bandied about, Pip cautiously entered the manor. Looking relieved at seeing his lord and lady in the center of the room, fully clothed, he addressed Ardith.

"Milady...'tis Meg. Her pains begin."

Ardith shot up from the stool. "Where is she?"

"In the yard, milady. We had begun walking back to our hut when—"

"Well, bring her in here! Gerard, we will need a pallet near the fire. Is there water in those buckets? Now, where did I put my scissors?"

"I suppose this means I must sleep in the armory this night," he grumbled.

"Depends on the babe," Ardith said absently. "Some birthings go swiftly. Many do not, especially a woman's first."

Meg entered the manor, supported by Pip on one side and Elva on the other. Pip looked almost as pale as Meg. A pain struck the laboring peasant woman as she lowered herself to the newly furnished pallet. She groaned.

Gerard hefted a full keg of ale onto his shoulder and swatted Pip between the shoulder blades.

"This is no place for a man," Gerard announced, shoved cups into Pip's hands, then pushed him toward the door. "Let us find a warm corner to sit and await the birth."

Gerard decided to hold vigil in the armory. Of his soldiers, three men stood early watch, another three slept. The others hunkered over a game of dice. Gerard sat on a pallet and opened the keg.

After the fourth cup of ale, Pip wiped the foam from his mouth with his sleeve. "I know Meg has the harder job, but the waiting is not easy."

Gerard couldn't sympathize. He hadn't kept vigil for Daymon's birth. No one had told him of the impending birth until it was over, placing his new son safely in his arms, saying the mother had succumbed to birth fever.

Would Meg succumb?

Would Ardith? The thought chilled Gerard to the bone.

Evening dragged into night. No news came from the manor. Gerard sent a soldier for another keg of ale.

When Pip passed out, Gerard lay back on the pallet and closed his eyes. He couldn't get comfortable, couldn't sleep.

How unknightly to so crave the softness of fur and the nearness of a woman's body that sleep hovered beyond his grasp. And how senseless to worry over that same woman's death in childbirth when Ardith showed no sign of being with child.

As dawn's rays brightened the sky, the woman of his musings cautiously stuck her head into the armory. Gerard scrambled to his feet and went outside.

She smiled up at him. "A boy, Gerard. Mother and babe are well and sleeping."

"As is the father—" Gerard laughed "—well, actually, the father is sotted. We saluted the babe's coming, Meg's health and Pip's virility until Pip could no longer speak lucidly. Shall I wake him?"

"Let him sleep. 'Twill be the last uninterrupted night's

rest he will get for a while." Ardith's fingertips brushed the shadow under his eye. "You did not sleep well."

"Nor did you."

"I was otherwise occupied."

"So was I."

He put an arm across her shoulder, guiding her back to the manor. Now they could both get some much needed rest.

"Meg wants to name the babe for the new overlord. Would that please you, Gerard?"

Gerard thought he did an admirable job of hiding the pride swelling his chest. "A common enough practice. Look how many males were named for Henry after he became king, and there are enough Williams about to form their own army."

She put fingers to her lips, telling him to keep quiet as they entered the manor. All was peaceful. Meg slept on the pallet near the fire, her son bundled in blankets tucked against her side.

Gerard looked down at the child's rose-blotched face.

"'Twas difficult, this birthing, for both mother and child," Ardith explained. "The boy fought hard to stay within his mother. We nearly sent to the abbey for Sister Bernadette."

"For a nun?"

"Aye. She is a midwife of some repute, or so I hear from the women."

Gerard tucked that piece of information away, relieved that he knew of someone, besides Elva, who could attend Ardith should the necessity arise.

Ardith felt his sigh, wondered why he hadn't slept. Surely Gerard wouldn't worry over the birth of Meg's child. He had little at stake in the outcome. Yet his features had softened when looking down at the boy who now shared his name.

Gerard tended to bury the softer side of his nature beneath a brusque demeanor. Few men would ever know of

the gentle heart beating within the breast of the *young lion.*
His mate, mayhap, or his cub…

His cub. Daymon. Gerard must have looked on Meg's
babe and remembered his son's birth, bringing forth the
tender smile. Guilt bubbled. She'd thought only of her own
feelings when convincing Gerard not to send for Daymon.
By what right did she dare try to separate a father from his
son?

"Gerard? Mayhap I was wrong. Mayhap you should
send for Daymon."

A grin spread across his face, not the smile of relief she
expected, but a grin of victory.

Chapter Sixteen

The following morning, Ardith watched a cart rumble into the yard, wondering if Gerard had ignored her earlier protest and had sent for his son anyway. The child seated next to the cart's driver could only be Daymon. The resemblance to Gerard, and Richard, who rode beside the cart with a mounted guard of five—all armored—was too striking for the little one to be other than Gerard's son.

Unless the fur-cloaked child belonged to Richard.

The notion died when Gerard shouted a greeting to Richard, sprinted across the yard from the stable and held up his arms to the child. The little one hesitated, then squealed and lurched forward. Gerard caught him easily in a hearty hug.

Ardith slowly approached the pair, comparing tot to man. Against her will, her heart skipped a beat and began to melt. She hadn't wanted to lay eyes on Gerard's son, but now she couldn't wait to hold him.

Daymon rested his head on his father's shoulder, a thumb stuck in his puckered mouth. He watched her come closer through unblinking green eyes. She halted a pace away and wiggled her fingers in greeting. Daymon stopped sucking.

Richard dismounted and waved away the men-at-arms and the cart. Ardith paid scant heed, her attention firmly focused on Daymon. With a gentle touch, moving slowly,

Ardith ran a finger across the boy's downy, pudgy cheek, brushing away a smudge of dirt. Her eyes misted when he smiled around his thumb, the only clean finger on the little fist.

Becoming bolder, Ardith nudged aside the fur to circle Daymon's ear, then tickled lightly under the lobe. He scrunched his neck and giggled, a heart-tugging, merry sound.

"Friends already?" Gerard murmured. His eyes flashed with humor; his mouth curved upward in delight.

"Not yet, but soon. Greetings, Richard."

"Ardith," Richard acknowledged.

Content with the progress in befriending Daymon, Ardith tucked the fur back under his chin. "We should take our guests inside, Gerard, where there is warmth and food. They are surely weary from the journey."

"In a moment," Gerard said and, unexpectedly, held out Daymon. Without hesitation, Ardith took the child. She could feel Daymon's tension. He held his body stiff, but didn't wiggle to be put down. She gave him a gentle squeeze, hoping to convey reassurance.

"Well?" Gerard asked of Richard, in that tone of voice that demanded an immediate response.

"I returned to Wilmont and delivered the land deeds to your steward, as you ordered me to do. I was right about your mother, Gerard. She is most displeased with your decision to gift Stephen and I so richly, though she is less disturbed with the gift to Stephen than to me. As soon as I felt strong enough to sit a horse for several hours without falling off, I left, as I am sure you knew I would."

Gerard shrugged. "Aye, but I thought you would hie off to find Stephen and Corwin. Why come here? Why bring Daymon?"

Richard tilted his head in a questioning pose. "When you did not return to Wilmont, the thought occurred to me that you were planning to winter here. Are you?"

Gerard nodded.

Richard half smiled and reached out to ruffle the fur covering Daymon's head. "Good. Then we shall all enjoy some peace for a few months."

Ardith bit her bottom lip to keep from saying something she ought not against Gerard's mother. Gerard had told her of what Richard had suffered from Ursula because of his bastardy. The suspicion that the little boy in her arms had been subjected to the same treatment tugged at Ardith's heart so hard that tears threatened.

Then Richard turned his half smile on her, and the look of sympathy—nay, pity—in his eyes told her that she, too, had been included in his *all*.

Gerard crossed his arms. "What happened, Richard?"

"Nothing that should surprise you. Ursula also knows of the betrothal decree. Her ire over the land gifts is nothing compared to her fury over your agreeing to the betrothal. She has made it known to all and sundry that she will not sanction your immorality, that she would not allow your...Ardith into her presence. It might be best if you do not take Ardith to Wilmont until the decree is satisfied."

Richard had been about to repeat Ursula's exact words, Ardith realized.

Your whore.

The memories of every lewd glance, every deliberately turned head, every vulgar word that she'd endured at court came flooding back. She'd felt welcome here in this small manor, with these accepting peasants. She'd done as Bronwyn had advised—closed her eyes and ears to those who would condemn her. Now, because she had shut out the rest of the world so well, had brushed aside the consequences of her selfishness, Richard was advising Gerard to stay away from his own home.

Whore. The word echoed in her head as Ardith turned on her heel and strode to the manor, scorning Gerard's harsh command to halt. She fought to keep down the bile rising in her throat, blanked her mind in the only way she knew how—work.

"Pip, we have guests. The cart needs unloading. Bring their belongings into the manor," she announced sharply.

She whipped the fur from around Daymon, letting it fall to the rushes. "Elva, this child needs a bath. Heat water."

Elva looked askance, but she, too, obeyed.

Ardith refused to think beyond the next task. She would close her mind to all but the immediate need to act the chatelaine seeing to her visitors' comfort, close her heart to the pain that would overcome her composure if she pondered Richard's revelation.

She unfastened her beaver cloak, letting it fall atop Daymon's discarded fur. Daymon squirmed, staring at Meg and little Gerard. Knowing the distraction would keep him occupied for a short time, Ardith plopped Daymon down next to Meg.

"Meg, this is Daymon, Gerard's son."

Elva gasped. Ardith ignored her aunt's reaction, the note of censure.

Keep moving! Keep busy!

Ardith dragged the wooden tub near the fire. The water in the cauldron was barely warm enough for bathing. She dumped the water into the tub. Sensing the next step, Daymon sprang to his feet and ran, but Ardith was faster. After a short dispute over possession of his tunic, Daymon soon sat in the tub, splashing merrily.

She tossed Daymon's patched tunic of rough wool and the hole-riddled hose into the fire. Gerard would be incensed if he saw them. Flames consumed the filthy garments, clothing unsuitable for the son of a baron, even a bastard son. Who'd dressed the child so? Ursula? Nay, not Ursula. The woman would never touch a bastard child, not even the child of her eldest son. Surely Richard, or some servant, had packed a chest full of spare garments for the boy.

Kneeling beside the tub, she watched Daymon play, letting him soak before plying rag and soap.

The manor door banged open, an almost impossible feat

given the size and weight of the oak panels. Gerard. He looked like a storm cloud about to burst. The waves of his anger rippled through the manor.

Only once had she seen Gerard this angry, the day he swung a meaty fist into Basil of Northbryre's face. Today he was angry at her impertinence in the yard, for defying an order. Mayhap he had cause. She *had* carried off his son, a grubby little urchin who looked better by the minute, without permission.

Though Gerard's fists were clenched, she felt no fear. Deep within she knew that no matter how enraged, Gerard would never harm her.

Gerard still stood in the doorway, ready to roar.

"Close the door, my lord. Your son will take a chill," Ardith ordered, knowing fair well she shouldn't goad Gerard. How calm she sounded while her insides churned!

"Don your cloak, Ardith," he snarled.

"I am busy, my lord. Surely, you can see—"

With long strides, Gerard covered the distance between them, scooping up the cloak without altering his step. He snapped it open and settled it around her shoulders.

"Come."

"Gerard," she began to protest, but never finished. He picked her up, high up. She landed on her stomach, flung over his shoulder like a sack of grain.

"Elva, care for Daymon," he barked, then announced to the others, "Ardith and I will be away for a while." He spun and headed for the door.

"Where...are we...going?" she asked between bounces.

"Out."

"Gerard..."

"Keep still, Ardith."

As he strode across the yard, he called out, "Richard, I am taking your horse."

She nearly swooned when Gerard swung up into the destrier's saddle. He settled, then pulled her down across his lap. With a slap of heels on horse, they were off.

The ride was wild, a furious race on a monstrous horse. Gerard never slowed, not for sheep, or boulder, or rough terrain. If the obstacle didn't move out of his way, he guided the well-trained warhorse around, or over or through.

Gerard would kill them both, she was sure, but Ardith couldn't shut her eyes as they whipped over the land like the winter wind. It was frightening. It was exhilarating. And quickly finished. Gerard pulled the destrier to a halt at an abandoned crofter's hut.

The horse's sides heaved like a blacksmith's bellows. He snorted, blowing out a white cloud of breath. Did Gerard notice the beast's labored breathing? Nay. He was too intent on dragging her into the hut.

Had there been a door, he would have slammed it, but he settled for shoving a stool aside with his foot. His anger had diminished but not vanished. Ardith drew her cloak tighter and waited for the inevitable roar.

"Why?" he finally asked in a shout less severe than she expected.

"Your son was cold and in grave need of washing so I—"

"Liar. I know why you ran. I want to know why you did not stop when ordered."

The need to lash out took control of her tongue. "What more do you want of me? I have been obedient! Too obedient! For too long!"

Hellfire, Ardith was beautiful when her temper flared. Azure-blue eyes darkened to flashing sapphire. Wisps of auburn hair had tugged loose from her braid and fallen across her face and into her mouth. With an angry brush of her hand she pushed them out of the way, so as not to interfere with her tirade.

He'd brought her out here to make clear that while he tolerated much, he wouldn't allow disobedience. Her safety, someday, could depend on immediate compliance.

But first he must quell her anger. He took a step toward Ardith.

"Stay where you are, Gerard," she warned.

"Then come to me, Ardith."

"Nay! You think to soothe me. Well, I will not be soothed. I do not want you to touch me."

Never again touch Ardith, or kiss her lush mouth, or feel her body pressed close? She demanded the impossible.

"I want quit of this betrothal," she said. "I will send a missive to Henry petitioning release, for permission to return to Lenvil."

She didn't, couldn't, mean what she said. The thought that Ardith might be serious prodded his ire.

"Return to Lenvil? I think not. I will not allow you to go back to slave for Harold."

"Being slave to my father can be no worse than staying with a man I do not like much right now. I could hate you, Gerard!"

"You could never hate me. You love me!"

She gasped and held her breath. He recognized her terror, her vulnerability. His heart pounded against his ribs, drummed a warning against the folly he was about to commit.

"You love me, Ardith," he said fiercely. "That is what you hate. You hate the weakness of will leaving you open to hurt, to so much pain you can barely breathe."

He put his fist to his chest. "You hate having your heart in my keeping, afraid I will squeeze the lifeblood from your body, leave you to rot and die. You fear I will take your soul, stomp on it, fling it into the pit of hell."

"Gerard, please," she whispered, quivering.

"And there are times when you think your heart will burst with joy, when a touch flings open the gates of heaven, when a whiff of scent sends you reeling among the stars. When we are apart you long for the sound of my voice, for the sight of my face. When we are together you ache for my touch, for a kind word, for a smile."

She sat down on the stool and closed her eyes. Her shoulders slumped in dismay. He took no pleasure in her raw sorrow at having her secret revealed, but neither was he repentant.

He knelt in the dirt at her feet, like a supplicant begging favor. Where was his pride? Gone, vanished with his reason and judgment.

Gerard grasped her hands, clutched them to his chest. "Ardith, sweet Ardith. How do you think I know your joy and sorrow? Feel how my heart pounds. Do you not know? Can you not guess? Look at me, love."

Ardith opened her eyes, blinking back tears.

"I fought hard, but I lost the battle," he admitted. "My heart is as much yours as your heart is mine. Be gentle, little warrior. I am not accustomed to defeat."

His fierce visage, so beloved and dear, affirmed his feelings. He'd succumbed to a gentle emotion, to love, and hated his weakness. Gerard might love her, but he found no joy in the loving, for reasons very different from her own.

Ardith smiled, a sad smile. "So proud, my young lion."

"Hellfire, woman, I kneel at your feet, my gut in knots, my heart bleeding. Where is the pride in that?"

"You lost a battle, yet you intend to win the war. Gerard, I beg you, if you love me let me go. Let us part while there are fond memories and no bitterness."

"Nay."

She hadn't really expected any other answer. Gerard considered her as his and he would keep her, and to hell with her wishes. He would keep fighting despite all odds, against all reason, no matter what anyone else advised. Yet she had to try.

"Gerard, no matter that we love each other, the day will come when you must marry—another."

"We have had this talk before, love, and my feelings remain the same. No woman before you has brought me such joy and peace. No woman after you could please me as you do. Whatever the future brings, you will always be the wife of my heart.''

She sighed. ''Oh, Gerard. What am I to do with you? What can I say to make you see the folly of remaining together?''

''You cannot convince me of any folly. So tell me you love me and never again speak of parting.''

''Another command, my lord?''

''One I fully expect you to obey.''

She put her hand on his cheek. ''I do love you, Gerard. I suspect I always have, and always will.''

All thought of lecturing Ardith on disobedience fled. She normally yielded to a command without argument. And sometimes she anticipated his wishes before he voiced a request. Nor could he fault Ardith for running. Richard's news had pushed Ardith beyond endurance.

He had no wish to argue with her further. His heart was too full, his spirits too high. With Ardith pliant and warm in his arms, he had other notions of how to spend the afternoon.

He laid a long, warm kiss on her neck, nibbled at her earlobe. She shivered. The crofter's hut was cold. He would keep her warm.

''I need you, Ardith. Love me.''

''I do love you, Gerard.''

Using the cloak as a pallet, her gown askew but not removed, Ardith reveled in Gerard's ferocious loving. With gentle words and warm body he bestowed his love, that precious gift Ardith had never hoped to receive. His eager mouth worshiped her face, her breasts; his skilled fingers stroked her womanhood to near bliss.

And she loved him back. Heart and body he belonged to her, and she declared undeniable ownership of both.

Then he entered, rigid and near bursting.

''Ah, my love, my love,'' he whispered harshly.

Ardith soared higher than ever before. The pulsating rapture went on and on.

Gerard collapsed beside Ardith, panting, drained, but oh so satisfied. And he'd felt Ardith vibrate and throb, so hard, so long. Did the admission of love push sex to a higher level of pleasure? Could a man die of ecstasy?

Then he would die young, but happy. He pulled her close and prayed for the first time in many years.

This time, God, please. I need her.

When had she bled last? Three weeks ago, in Westminster. Another week or so, and they would know.

"Gerard?"

"Hmm?"

"These other women you spoke of. Just how many did you attempt to find joy with?"

He smiled sleepily. He thought to tease, to tell her that hundreds of women could attest to his virility, then thought better of goading her temper.

"Not so many as you might think."

"None still hold an interest for you?"

What was wrong with the woman? Hadn't he just told her, and shown her, that she was the only woman he would ever want, ever need? He found her doubts a little annoying, but the hint of jealousy in her questions was fairly endearing.

"After being with you, I could not hope to find joy in another woman's bed. I have neither bedded every female I have cast my eye upon, nor do I intend to. Does that ease your mind?"

"Somewhat. But, my love, be warned. Should you ever play me false, I will separate you from your man parts."

He started to chuckle at the savage threat, then stopped, brought up short by the feel of cold iron on his warm inner thigh. Her dagger. She had slipped past his guard.

Hellfire.

"Surprise," she said softly, immense satisfaction dripping from the single word.

Chapter Seventeen

Gerard lay motionless. The point of the dagger rested uncomfortably close to the flesh she threatened to maim. "Well done, Ardith. Now put the blade away." He paused, then added, "Take care."

"Aye, my lord." Slowly, she slid the flat of the blade down his leg before slipping the dagger into her boot.

He let go his breath in a relieved rush. She chuckled. He flipped her onto her back, pinning her hands above her head.

"Savage little minx. I should beat you for impudence."

"Make love to me instead."

"Hah! You dare threaten castration, then ask for the pleasure my staff can give you? Nay, scamp." He denied her request with a shake of his head. He tried to look fierce, "First you must repent."

"I vexed my lover but I pleased my weapons master, did I not? Shall I seek forgiveness for learning my lessons well?"

Damn, she had learned well. But he'd warned her about drawing the blade unless in earnest. Then again, she *had* drawn the blade without his having to order her to do so. Maybe she'd rid herself of the revulsion, a sign that she accepted the weapon as her own.

"Your weapons master may praise you, but your lord

seeks amends. Think you can pull a blade on a baron and hope to escape punishment? If one of my men pulled a weapon on me, he would forfeit his life.''

Her self-satisfied smile faded. ''Gerard, you must know I meant no malice.''

''Despite your intention, the crime is committed and you must suffer punishment.''

She squirmed. ''Such as?''

He kissed the worry creases forming around her eyes. ''Mayhap I will sentence you to a week of lying naked on a pallet, your legs spread, ever ready to welcome the staff you threatened to sever.''

She blushed. '''Tis futile to threaten ravishment, my lord.''

He kissed her brow, her cheek, then nuzzled in her neck. ''But if I did not come to you, if I took my imperiled man parts elsewhere for pleasure?''

''You just said you would not, and I trust your word.''

Gerard shifted his grip on her wrists, freeing one of his hands to roam Ardith's body. Her bodice had shifted upward during the previous tussle, covering her breasts. He caressed a mound, feeling the nub harden through the layers of cloth.

'''Twould be apt punishment, methinks, to let you lie alone, waiting for my touch, wanting the joining so much you ache.''

She moaned softly and closed her eyes when his mouth found the hollow of her throat. She tugged to free her hands. He held them fast.

''Would you be so cruel?'' she whispered.

The stirring in his loins intensified. He tugged the hem of her gown upward, sought the curls of downy hair at the juncture of her thighs. She arched into his hand, her fire ignited, fueling his desire.

''Would you suffer, my love?'' he asked, stroking the moist passage of pleasure, fanning the flames.

''As much as you would suffer.''

She knew him too well. By denying Ardith, he denied himself. Damn her for knowing. Damn himself for giving her the power to shred his heart should she choose. He moved over her, flesh sliding against flesh, seeking the fulfillment Ardith's straining body promised.

"Aye, I would suffer. And so would I suffer if you came to some harm. I would have your oath, Ardith, that henceforth you will obey my commands, willingly, without argument."

"Is an oath given under torture valid, my lord?"

"Your word, Ardith."

Her eyes flashed with indignation, her spirited nature rebelling. Then they softened. "You are the only man I would trust not to use my pledge against me. If you require an oath of obedience, then I swear it to you."

An unwelcome sound pierced the passion-ignited roar in his head. Hoofbeats. Heavy and nearing the hut.

Gerard looked down at Ardith, her face reflecting the same surprise and irritation he felt at the interruption.

"Richard comes. We will finish this later," he promised, rolling away.

Ardith gritted her teeth and tugged at her clothing. "How do you know the intruder is Richard?"

Gerard struggled to his feet, tucked his bulging parts into breeches. "Only a destrier pounds the earth so hard. Since I stole Richard's horse, doubtless he now searches for it with mine."

He smiled at Ardith's grumbles as he left the hut.

Richard dismounted and tossed the destrier's reins to Gerard. After a quick perusal of Gerard's disheveled state, a knowing smile lit his face. "Did I interrupt aught of import? Saints above, Gerard, I thought I gave you sufficient time to subdue the wench."

"Have a care, brother. I am in no mood for your taunts."

"Oh, ho! Gave you fits, did she? Do not scowl, Gerard. I came only to retrieve my weary horse, not to prod your temper. You might, however, wish to end your tryst quickly and return to the manor. You left it in an uproar.''

''How so?''

Richard swung up into the saddle of his destrier. ''Daymon is crying for his father. Meg cannot silence her babe who wails at the tot's cries. Elva is wringing her hands and preparing salves.''

''Salves? For what?''

''Ardith's bruises.''

In the ensuing silence, the brothers stared at each other. Gerard felt Ardith's hand on his sleeve.

''Elva has always warned me of you, Gerard,'' she said. ''My aunt is sure you will one day beat me.''

''I would not—''

''I know, but Elva does not.''

Gerard looked down into trusting blue eyes. Did Ardith also know he would lop off the hand of anyone who dared raise a fist to her? She did. He'd threatened as much to Percival in the chapel at Westminster. Had he loved Ardith even then? Probably.

Richard cleared his throat. ''Shall I reassure Elva that Ardith is unharmed?''

''Nay. She will see for herself when Ardith returns.''

With a brisk nod, Richard rode off.

Ardith shrugged a little deeper into her beaver cloak and watched the horse and rider until they disappeared. ''How did Richard find us?''

''My brother is among the best trackers in the kingdom, if not the keenest. Whether man or beast, if there is some sign of passage, some mark of direction taken, Richard can follow.''

''Really?''

''I have seen him track prey with a less clear trail than his own destrier's hoofprint.''

''A good man to have on the hunt.''

''If one is not the hunted.'' On that ominous note, with a fluid swing, Gerard mounted the destrier. She took his

outstretched hand and then landed across his lap, expecting
another punishing ride. But the horse didn't move.

Gerard's eyes had darkened, glittering like emeralds. "I
know we must return to the manor, but we did not finish."

Pressed hard against him, Ardith couldn't mistake his
meaning. "Do you suffer, my lord?" she teased.

"If I thought that I could control my horse with you
astride, riding me, I would be willing to end my suffering
while we ride." He tilted his head, his smile devilish. "If
I told you to unleash my aching manroot, hike up your
skirts and take me inside you, right here, right now, would
you?"

A test, then, of her promise to obey. Would she agree to
a joining so utterly depraved? How erotically tempting! The
wretch. He deserved a show of obedience.

She reached for his lacings. His eyes darkened.

"Ardith?"

"Shall we finish before we are thrown, do you think?"

He grabbed hold of her hand. "Scamp. We would most
likely be thrown before we managed to join."

She gave him a long, aggrieved sigh. He laughed and
urged the horse forward.

They rode more slowly this time, back to the little boy
who wanted his father, back to an aunt who readied salves
for her niece.

During supper, Ardith marveled at the resemblance between Richard and Gerard. The half brothers *could* be mistaken as twins from a distance.

Though Gerard was taller and a bit broader in the shoulders than Richard, if they were armored and seated atop
horses, their faces obscured by the nose guard of a helmet,
friend and foe alike would be hard pressed to distinguish
one brother from the other. Because of the resemblance,
somewhere on Richard's body a fresh scar marred healthy
flesh from the near-mortal wound inflicted by Edward Siefeld.

Ardith liked Richard and wished him no ill, but she couldn't help being grateful that Siefeld had attacked the wrong man.

"The earl of Warwick sheltered at Wilmont on his way home from court," Richard said. "He told me that Henry will let Basil and Siefeld languish in the Tower for a while. Henry is again embroiled in church matters."

Gerard scowled. "Now what?"

"Nothing new. Henry still fights excommunication for his stand on royal investiture of bishops. However, Bishop Anselm has returned to England from exile. They... negotiate."

Intent on the men's conversation, Ardith absently picked up her goblet and took a sip of wine. She frowned at the faint, odd aftertaste—not of spice, but of herbs.

Elva had poured this goblet of wine.

Though Ardith wanted to remain near Gerard, hear the rest of Richard's tale, she slid from the bench to seek Elva.

All afternoon Elva had hovered, looking for signs of mistreatment. By deed and brightness of spirit, Ardith had tried to reassure her aunt, but apparently failed.

Why couldn't Elva believe her own eyes and ears? Hating the idea of a confrontation, but knowing it necessary, Ardith motioned Elva to a corner and held out the goblet. "You added a potion to my drink," she accused.

"A restorative," Elva admitted without apology.

Appalled at her aunt's temerity, Ardith's temper flared, though she kept her voice low. "I need no restorative. How dare you potion my drink without my knowledge?"

"Ardith, dear heart, I *know* these men of Wilmont, of how you must suffer. I sought only to ease—"

"Enough," Ardith said through clenched teeth. "I will hear no slander against Gerard."

"He holds you in thrall."

"He holds me by affection. Open your eyes to the truth, aunt. Gerard is no brute. Look." Ardith pushed up her sleeve. "I am unmarked." She upended the goblet, creating a puddle of wine on the earthen floor. "I need no restorative. Beware. Should you persist with this nonsense, *I* will send you back to Lenvil."

The sharp threat hit its mark. Elva's eyes widened in stunned comprehension. Ardith squelched the urge to apologize, to soothe the aunt she loved dearly, but she couldn't take back the threat of banishment. Before the desire to placate Elva overpowered the need for firmness, Ardith returned to her place at the table.

Though small mounds of snow dotted the hillsides, the winter winds had ceased to howl. Gerard welcomed the milder weather, but cursed the passage of days. A year had seemed an eternity when Henry had issued the betrothal decree. But three months had passed, and no child stirred within Ardith's womb.

Iron poker in hand, he stared at the banked coals of the pit while giving Ardith the privacy she craved to ready for sleep. Behind the drapery surrounding their pallet, Ardith was donning a night rail and the woman's rags needed to absorb her monthly courses.

He turned slightly when Ardith padded softly from behind the drapery. Her body veiled by a gown of white linen, feet bare, she drew the thick plait of auburn hair to lie gently over one shoulder. Her eyes glittered with tears she tried to stifle.

He searched for words of comfort. He gave the embers a poke, then another. Would every month end like this—Ardith in tears, he disappointed and tongue-tied?

"Gerard, I..." she began, then gasped, and stumbled, grabbing at her thigh.

Tossing the poker aside, he sped to scoop Ardith up before she could fall. With her secure in his arms, he sat on a stool and cradled Ardith in his lap.

Ardith squeezed her eyes shut against the sharp pain. She sensed the connection to her twin, the faint sensation that Corwin had reached out with his thoughts and touched her mind. He didn't, of course. As children they'd probed the link, learned they couldn't purposely read each other's mind or send silent messages.

Only in time of distress or injury did the link flare. And Corwin must be close by, for the pain belonged to Corwin.

"What hurts?" Gerard demanded.

"My leg. Here." Ardith rubbed her right thigh.

Gerard pulled up the night rail. The sharpness subsided to a dull ache, succumbing to the weakening of the link and the kneading circle of Gerard's hand.

"I see no bruise. Did you twist it wrongly?" he asked.

Gerard knew of the link, had known for months. But knowing of the link didn't mean he wouldn't recoil in horror if she told him the pain wasn't her own, but Corwin's.

His large, warm hands worked healing magic, though she noticed he was careful not to massage too widely, careful not to touch her woman's rags.

"You hurt, Ardith. Why?"

Why indeed? The pain had been sharp. She pulled slightly away from Gerard and closed her eyes, focusing on the moment the pain had hit. She sensed no fear, no alarm on Corwin's part. Other than the pain, he was all right.

"Ardith?"

She opened her eyes. His concern and worry touched her heart, banishing her fear of rejection. His love was as strong and sure as the hand that now lay still on her thigh.

"'Tis Corwin's pain. He must be near."

Confusion, then perception, flickered over his features. He looked down at the flesh under his hand and squeezed gently. "Corwin injured his leg and caused you pain," he said, a trace of anger sharpening his statement.

Compelled to defend Corwin against Gerard's unwarranted ire, Ardith said, "I am sure he did not injure his leg on purpose, Gerard."

"Is he badly injured?"

"I think not."

"And the others?"

Others? Of course, Stephen and the soldiers who'd accompanied Stephen and Corwin to inspect the Northbryre lands. For the first time in many years Ardith wished she could invade Corwin's mind and hear his thoughts.

"I cannot say with certainty. But I felt no alarm from Corwin, no sense of fear or danger."

"That does not ease my mind, Ardith."

"I can tell you no more. If I could, my love, I would."

Gerard sighed inwardly, letting loose the anger he'd summoned to mask the urge to recoil from Ardith's revelation.

So calmly, within the walls of Westminster, he'd listened to Corwin tell of a bond between brother and sister. Gerard had wanted to believe in the mysterious link, believe Corwin's statement that Ardith's body had healed completely from her long-ago injury. Yet doubt of the link's existence lingered.

Ardith's continued barrenness bolstered the doubt. But tonight she'd nearly fallen from pain she claimed to be Corwin's.

"How far away do you think they are?" he asked.

"Within half a day's ride, I would guess."

"Any idea in which direction?"

"Nay." She tilted her head, eyes narrowing. "Gerard, you are not contemplating riding about in the dead of night to search for them, are you?"

Aloud, the notion sounded foolhardy. Especially when he couldn't quite believe Ardith's claim.

"Not tonight. Morning is soon enough. Can you walk or must I carry you to our pallet?"

An impish smile tugged at the corners of her mouth. "I confess I *could* walk."

"Scamp," he accused. Charmed by her light laughter, he picked her up and strode the few feet to the far corner of the manor. He stopped just inside the hangings to look down at Daymon, sleeping peacefully in a tangle of furs at the foot of their pallet.

Gerard lowered Ardith to her feet, then bent to tuck a cover under his son's dimpled chin.

"He has your eyes, Gerard, and your golden hair," Ardith said softly. "And your chin, so proud even in the bud of his youth. I knew he was yours the first moment I saw him."

Gerard recalled another moment on the day of his son's arrival in Romsey—when he'd thrust Daymon at Ardith while questioning Richard. Ardith had taken the boy without hesitation, knowing Daymon a bastard but not holding the circumstances of birth against an innocent. She'd eased the child's uncertainty with soft words and gentle touches.

Afterward, Ardith had cared for Daymon, seen to his welfare with the attention of a natural mother. If only...

"Daymon is happy here, is he not?" He interrupted the disturbing direction of his thoughts.

"Aye. Daymon even likes the sheep."

"Then something is amiss with his nose."

"His nose is adorable and works perfectly well. He does not share your aversion to sheep."

Gerard took a long look at Daymon before joining Ardith under the furs. Not only had Ardith taken to the boy, but so had the tenants. Someday Daymon would need a place to call his own. Maybe this was the place.

Chapter Eighteen

Gerard paced the manor. Upon rising this morning, he'd realized he couldn't search for Corwin and Stephen. With only Ardith's word that Corwin might be near, he wouldn't spread his soldiers over the countryside to search for a man who could be leagues away, a man who might or might not have an injured leg, who might or might not have a mysterious bond with his twin.

Finally, desperate for a distraction, Gerard strode over to the table where his brother broke his fast and cuffed Richard on the shoulder. "How fares your sword arm? Have you regained your strength?"

"I wondered when you would ask. Care for some exercise?"

"Can you withstand me?"

"Is that not what you intend to find out?"

"Fetch the blades."

Minutes later, Gerard faced Richard in the yard. Sword sang upon sword as Gerard made the first probing strokes. Richard deflected each attack with ease.

Ardith watched from the doorway, standing next to Thomas, her bottom lip between her teeth. Neither brother wore a hauberk or helm, only tunics of thick, rough wool.

"Come, Gerard. Has this soft life left you timid? You fight like a woman," Richard taunted.

A feral grin spread across Gerard's face. "Save your breath, brother. You will need it."

Gerard pressed his assault, and Ardith's heartbeat sped to the cadence of the clashing swords. Richard defended with lightning reflexes.

"They are well matched," Thomas said without a hint of concern in his voice.

Ardith nodded. As though encircled by invisible boundaries, Gerard and Richard fought a battle for ground. Each foot given was quickly regained. They sweated, cursed and smiled like fools.

A crowd of peasants and men-at-arms gathered to watch the spectacle. Coins changed hands as wagers were placed. Shouts of encouragement split the air, but neither combatant noticed as they gamboled in a graceful, potentially lethal dance of power, poise and skill.

Richard's foot slipped slightly, yet he soon recovered and forced Gerard back. Just when Ardith thought she would scream, she first heard, then saw, an excuse to end the madness.

She turned to Thomas. "Can you stop them?"

"Aye, my lady, but they will not be pleased."

"Pleased or not, they must cease. We have guests."

Thomas glanced toward the road, then put two fingers in his mouth and blew a piercing whistle. Gerard and Richard halted instantly, both turning startled eyes toward the lad who dared interfere. Thomas pointed toward the road.

Without bothering to look, hearing the approaching horses, Gerard guessed the reason for Thomas's signal. The expression of pure joy on Ardith's face confirmed his deduction. Corwin had arrived. Then Ardith ran, heedless of flying skirts and veil, across the yard to greet the brother she adored.

Gerard stifled a reproach. Words born of jealousy soured in his mouth. Ardith loved him. He knew that with his whole heart and soul. But theirs was a bittersweet love, subject to uncertainty, plagued by the possibility of heartbreak.

Would there ever come a time when Ardith's face would shine for him as it now beamed for Corwin, with no taint of qualm over giving her love? Would there ever come a time when he could sweep Ardith off her feet in joyous greeting, knowing she was his for eternity?

"Stephen looks ready to tear something apart," Richard said thoughtfully.

Swords handed to Thomas, Gerard and Richard strode over to a dismounting and obviously disgruntled Stephen.

"Ye gods, Gerard. I have so much to tell you I do not know where to begin," Stephen said.

"Begin with the reason why Corwin limps," Gerard suggested, watching Corwin lean slightly against Ardith as the twins walked toward the manor.

"In my haste to reach you, I pushed the company too hard last night. We should have stopped before dark, but I thought if we pushed on..." Stephen took a long breath. "Corwin's horse stumbled in a rut and threw him. The horse is fine but Corwin landed on a sharp rock. His leg is badly bruised but he is otherwise all right. After the mishap, we camped until daylight."

"Where are your soldiers?"

"They should be here shortly. Corwin and I came ahead," Stephen explained. "I bring bad news, Gerard. Basil of Northbryre and Edward Siefeld have escaped from the Tower."

Rage and shock slammed into Gerard like a well-aimed fist to his gut. "When?"

"Several days ago. 'Tis generally believed the pair have already boarded a ship, bound for Normandy."

Vexation surged through Gerard. He'd allowed King Henry the privilege of punishing Basil and Siefeld. The king had given other matters precedence, allowing the pair to escape.

King Henry's court system and social justice be damned! Wilmont would seek its own justice, at the point of a sword.

"Gerard," Richard said in a calming voice. "Let us go into the manor. We can discuss plans over a goblet of ale."

Inside, trying to be careful of Corwin's stiffly held sore leg, Ardith helped her brother sit down on the bench.

"Felt it, did you?" Corwin asked.

"Like an arrow shot. I nearly fell." She touched her brother's thigh and sighed. "At least you did not break anything this time."

Corwin's fingers gently grazed her cheek. "And you, you are well, content. I can sense it."

Slightly embarrassed by Corwin's observation, Ardith quickly altered the course of the conversation. "Really, Corwin, how could you fall off a horse?" she scolded.

Corwin shrugged. "'Twas dark. The horse lost its footing and I lost my seat."

"And no wonder. 'Twas foolish to be riding about in the dead of night."

"Stephen's idea, though why he was in such a hurry to enrage Gerard, I fail to understand. Gerard should be roaring in here any moment."

"What has happened?"

"Basil of Northbryre and his mercenary captain, Edward Siefeld, have escaped from the Tower." To Ardith's gasp, Corwin nodded, then added, "But there is also trouble at Wilmont. Lady Ursula is—"

Gerard burst into the manor, followed by Richard and Stephen. Gerard dipped a goblet into the ale keg, quaffed the potent liquid in several deep swallows, then dipped the goblet again. He spared a greeting nod for Corwin before flopping down onto the bench, banging the goblet on the table.

"I will have the whoreson's head," Gerard vowed.

"Whose?" Richard asked. "Basil's? Siefeld's? Henry's?"

"Basil's first," Gerard snarled, then directed a glare at Stephen. "Well?"

"'Tis little consolation, I know, but Henry sends an apology and his vow to recapture Basil and Siefeld. He sent his own guard to track them down."

"I thought you said Basil had boarded ship?"

"So Henry believes. 'Twould be insane for Basil to remain in England when he could flee to his lands in Normandy."

"But Henry is not sure."

"That is why he ordered his guard to search the kingdom."

"Hellfire. The knave could be anywhere."

No one disagreed.

After a long silence, Gerard looked hard at Stephen. "The Conqueror's Tower is an impenetrable fortress, and impossible to escape from without help. Who would dare aid Basil?"

"'Tis believed Lady Diane furnished the swords to ease the escape."

Blond, beautiful, treacherous Diane de Varley had aided Wilmont's most dangerous enemy. Gerard vividly recalled rejecting Diane, her embarrassed anger and parting vow to avenge the insult. His hands tightened on the goblet, wishing the stem was Diane's lily-white neck.

"She is dead, Gerard," Stephen went on. "As reward for her help, Basil or Siefeld killed her, as well as two guards. Henry is livid. She may have aided a prisoner, but Diane was his ward, under royal protection. Henry wants Basil's head on a pike."

"He will have it, on *my* pike!"

In the ensuing silence, Gerard noticed Stephen run a hand through his raven-black hair, a nervous habit of Stephen's since childhood.

"There is more. Out with it, Stephen."

Stephen leaned forward, bracing his elbows on the trestle table. "After inspecting the Northbryre holdings, I stopped at Wilmont. I wanted to make sure that what I had seen of the holdings matched the charters and grants we sent to Walter from Westminster. But for minor details, all seems in order.'' He glanced at Richard. ''Some of our holdings need work.''

''But...?'' Gerard encouraged, knowing further bad news lurked within his brother's tale.

''Mother intends to banish every bastard and whore from Wilmont lands.''

Gerard closed his eyes, took a deep breath.

''I tried to reason with her, Gerard,'' Stephen added. ''I'm not sure if I convinced her to desist. I decided, with Walter's concurrence, that only direct intervention from you could stop her. Corwin and I set out at once. We stopped to overnight in London. That's when I learned of Basil's escape.''

Gerard's hands hit the table. He rose from the bench, shouting orders. ''We leave in the morning for Wilmont. Stephen, ready an escort. Richard, get a wagon loaded with supplies. Ardith, pack whatever you and Daymon will require for the journey.''

Ardith remained seated, her hands clasped in her lap, as everyone else in the manor jumped to do Gerard's bidding.

''You are not moving, Ardith,'' Gerard observed, a note of wariness in his tone.

Ardith marveled at his control. She'd expected him to bark a lecture on immediate obedience.

''I beg an indulgence, Gerard.''

He swung a leg over the bench, straddling the rough seat to face her. He leaned close, whispered gruffly, ''The only time you beg me for anything is in bed, when you wrap your legs around my thighs and cry out my name. Ah, look how you blush. Now, what silly notion has entered your head?''

She knew she had but one chance to sway Gerard. Ardith didn't want to go along. Though the weather had warmed with the promise of spring, too often cold blasts still sent man and beast scurrying for warm fires. The journey, at best, would be long and arduous. Nor did she wish to confront Lady Ursula, which would surely happen if Ardith went to Wilmont.

She mustered her arguments, hoped they sounded convincing. "You intend to return here after you deal with the situation at Wilmont."

His eyes narrowed. "Have you developed the ability to read my mind?"

"No. Your intent was rather clear. You ordered Stephen to choose an escort, which means you will leave most of your soldiers here. Richard is to gather a wagonload of supplies, again indicating a small party of travelers. Too, you have not yet named a steward for this manor, which you would do if you intended to remain at Wilmont. There are building projects you want to see completed, and trade contracts for fleece you will want to approve, before turning over affairs to a steward."

"I thought you no longer harbored notions of becoming steward here."

"You misunderstand. I do not seek the stewardship. But since you intend to return, I merely think it wise for Daymon and me to remain here." Ardith put a hand up, halting his objection. "Though Richard rightfully ignored the snow and cold to bring Daymon here, to escape your mother's rancor, the boy should not have to suffer the journey again."

Gerard's expression softened. He grasped her hand, raised it to his lips. "And you would stay here to care for my son. If I took only Stephen and Richard," he thought aloud, "we could travel swiftly. I could be back within a week, mayhap a bit longer if Mother proves stubborn. But I worry for your safety. With Basil on the loose..."

"Basil is running for his life. And did not Stephen say 'tis believed the man has already boarded ship? With Corwin here, and your men-at-arms, surely I will be safe."

"I would prefer having you close at hand."

"As I would prefer you not have to leave. But you must."

"Will you miss me?"

"With all my heart. Will you miss me?"

He leaned forward. As always, his kiss set Ardith reeling. "Already my mind rebels, my body feels the anguish. Why is it, woman, that I sometimes let you alter my plans?"

"Because, my love, even in your worst temper, you will usually listen to reason."

"Only from you."

Ardith smiled slightly. "I doubt that. I would wager you would hear an argument from Stephen or Richard, or someone else who holds your affection or esteem. You are just unaccustomed to being questioned by a mere woman."

"You could be right. The only other woman who dares is my mother, and I never let her win."

Ardith put her hand on his sleeve, asked haltingly, "May I ask one more favor?"

"What, then?"

"When you decide a punishment for Lady Ursula, try to be gentle. I know she has made life miserable for some of Wilmont's people, but please, think hard before you do something you will regret later, something that will haunt you."

He didn't answer, merely brought her palm to his lips before he left the manor to amend his orders.

A few days later, Ardith watched Meg feed little Gerard. There had been times seeing the two of them had pained her forcefully. Now, however, having set her mind on a course of action, Ardith merely enjoyed the sight.

"Meg, when you had problems giving birth, you told me about Sister Bernadette, from the abbey in Romsey. You said she had knowledge of the workings of a woman's body."

"'Tis said she is unrivaled as a midwife, has saved more than her share of babes and their mothers. How much of the tale is true?'' Meg shrugged. ''I only know what I hear.''

''They say every tale has at least a sliver of truth stuck into it, somewhere.''

''What tale?'' Corwin asked, coming up behind them.

''We need to talk, brother mine.''

''I do not like that tone, Ardith.''

Ardith grabbed Corwin's sleeve and pulled him out of the manor, toward the stables.

''Corwin, do you love me? Do you want me to be happy?''

''Now I know I am in trouble.''

''Not necessarily. Not if we can get to Romsey and back before Gerard returns from Wilmont.''

Corwin tossed up his hands. ''Sweet Jesu, Ardith! Romsey? Gerard would flay me alive! Do you know what he told me before he left? He was not pleased about leaving you and Daymon here, at all. He is not certain Basil and Siefeld have left the country. He said, and I repeat his words exactly, 'You will protect Ardith and Daymon with your life. Should any harm come to either, if they so much as suffer a bruise, I will hold you entirely responsible.' Now, I ask you, dear sister, what would he do to me if he found out I took you to Romsey? Why the devil would you want to go to Romsey, anyway?''

Ardith turned a deaf ear to Corwin's ranting, mulling over the distance to Romsey and the time required to make the journey. If they left early tomorrow morning, they could be back by late the day after, well before Gerard returned.

''I want to speak with Sister Bernadette at the abbey in Romsey,'' she finally answered.

''If you want so badly to meet this nun, I will send an escort to fetch her.''

''This is best done at the abbey.''

''What? Ardith, you are not making sense!''

Ardith looked into Corwin's azure eyes. The confusion marring those deep pools brought on a smile. ''I sometimes forget we cannot read each other's minds. Forgive me, Corwin. Please sit, and I will explain.''

Corwin ignored her gesture toward a crate. He stood, legs spread, arms crossed. ''I am not taking you to Romsey.''

Ardith sat on the crate. Corwin *must* have learned this stubbornness from Gerard.

''Meg told me of Sister Bernadette, said the nun knew more of the female body than any other in all of England. I must speak with her, and 'tis best done at the abbey. There is no privacy here, and for the questions I need to ask, I must have privacy.''

''What questions?''

Relieved that she'd at least roused Corwin's curiosity, she continued, ''About me. About the state of my womb. Corwin, I need to know if I can conceive. If anyone can tell me, I suspect 'twill be Sister Bernadette.''

Corwin looked away, his arms relaxed slightly. ''You still have several months with Gerard, as his betrothed. Surely, your ability to bear children will prove out.''

''Mayhap. But things have changed since Henry declared the betrothal. One of the reasons Gerard agreed to the decree was the threat of forced marriage to Lady Diane. With her death, so too died the bride the king intended for Gerard. Her death has freed Gerard to choose his own wife. If I cannot be his wife, then he should be looking for another, someone who will love him, care for Daymon as her own.''

''You want him to look for another?''

Fingers entwined, hands squeezed tightly together on her lap, Ardith said hoarsely, ''Of course not. Oh, Corwin, I love him so much. I *want* to be his wife. But he wastes time with me better spent choosing another woman before the king interferes again.''

''Not even you are this unselfish.''

''Nay. I think of myself, too. I want to know, Corwin. I *need* to know if there is any hope that I can marry Gerard, bear his children. Each time I have my monthly, Gerard looks at me differently. I see disappointment in his eyes, hear just the slightest reproach in his voice. I fear he will grow bitter, come to hate me for letting him down. I do not think I could bear his hatred, Corwin.''

''He could never hate you.''

''Never is a long time. He loves me now, but by year end, if he feels betrayed, who can say?''

Corwin put his hands on his hips, kicked at a piece of hay. ''If I took you to Romsey—'' he wagged a warning finger ''—mind you, I said *if*—what about Daymon?''

''Meg would look after him during the day and at night he could sleep in the armory. The soldiers would not object, and Daymon would think it a grand adventure.''

''You ask a lot of me, Ardith.''

Ardith stood and crossed her arms. ''I only ask you to help end that which you started.''

''Me?''

''Who was it that pleaded with Gerard to save me from Father's wrath? Who told Gerard he thought Elva wrong about my condition? If you had kept your peace, I would now be back at Lenvil, Gerard would be married to Diane, Basil would still be imprisoned—''

''All right! Enough. So maybe I deserve some blame, but not all. Had you said no to the betrothal, I would not be standing here listening to this insane proposal.''

Ardith knew Corwin had softened to the point of giving in. He needed but a final push. ''If you do not have the courage to take me to Romsey, then stay here. I will go alone.''

Corwin shook his head, moaned low in his throat. ''You know I cannot allow you to ride off on your own!''

Knowing full well she'd placed Corwin in an unfair position, because Gerard *would* learn of her journey, Ardith put a hand on Corwin's arm. ''Then come with me, Corwin. Please. If only to keep me from getting lost when I reach Romsey.''

Corwin's arms folded around her, pulling her close.

"Damn you, Ardith," he said softly, with no trace of rancor.

She returned the hug. "My thanks, Corwin."

"Too early for thanks. I may yet come to my senses and change my mind."

Several heartbeats later, Corwin pushed her away and looked her over. "You might fit into Thomas's clothes."

"Thomas's clothes? Whatever for?"

"If you are set on making this journey, then we do it *my* way. Understood?"

Chapter Nineteen

A young novice, whom Ardith thought too fair of face for a girl contemplating vows, waved Ardith and Corwin into a sparsely furnished, musty sitting room. Bristling under the disapproval in the girl's large, thickly-lashed brown eyes, Ardith whipped off the cap Corwin had insisted she wear and uncoiled the braid pinned to the top of her head.

"I will fetch Sister Bernadette. Who shall I say wishes to see her?"

"Corwin of Lenvil and his sister, Ardith," Corwin stated.

The novice again glanced over Ardith's attire: the rough tunic that stopped short of Ardith's knees, the hose held up by crisscrossed leather garters and barely covering her calves, the ankle-high felt shoes. Ardith's humiliation rose another notch when the girl said, "We are of a size, milady. Mayhap I can provide more appropriate attire before your audience with Sister Bernadette."

"My thanks," Ardith managed.

As the young woman closed the door behind her, Ardith spun, throwing the cap at Corwin. "I told you this was a foolish notion. Did you see the way she looked at me?"

Corwin circled, looking her up and down. "I think you look rather fetching in Thomas's clothes."

"The male clothes did not fool *her* for a moment."

"Up close, no. But from a distance the disguise works well. Have done, Ardith. You are here, about to speak with Sister Bernadette. Just get it done quickly so we can get back ahead of Gerard. If he rides in and finds you gone..." Corwin shuddered.

The novice returned, a dove-gray linen robe to match her own draped over an arm.

"I apologize for the delay, but Sister Bernadette is at prayer and cannot see you until after terce." She held out the robe and a rope belt. "'Tis not elegant, milady, but will be more comfortable, I think."

Noting the lessening of the girl's censure, Ardith took the robe. "Please, call me Ardith. You are?"

"Judith," she answered, smiling slightly.

"I thank you for the loan of your robe, Judith." Ardith glared at Corwin. "I do feel most uncomfortable in this garb."

Corwin followed Judith out into the passageway. Ardith quickly changed. She rolled the hose and laces in the tunic and put the bundle in the corner. Judith returned with a pitcher of water and goblets. Corwin carried bread and cheese. Judith left them to partake of the repast. As the minutes dragged on Ardith privately questioned the wisdom of talking Corwin into bringing her to an abbey filled with holy women.

Nonetheless, she was determined to see this through. She picked up the bread and took a healthy bite, washed the bread down with a swig of water. The lump sat hard in her stomach.

Ardith started when the door opened. A woman of middling years, richly gowned in silk, swished into the room. Corwin swiftly rose from his stool, smiling broadly. Ardith followed his lead.

Corwin took the woman's outstretched hand, bowed over it saying, "Your Majesty. How nice to see you again."

Queen Matilda! Ardith had heard that Matilda had retired to the abbey, but, caught in her own turmoil, hadn't given the royal presence a second thought. A plain-faced woman of noble Saxon birth, Henry's queen had fled London and the Norman nobility who held her in contempt. Her intelligence, lack of beauty, devotion to the church and a desire to minister to the poor and sick had made her an easy victim of the court's sharp tongues. Ardith empathized and liked the woman instantly.

Matilda smiled at Corwin, a gentle, sincere smile that lit her brown eyes. "Welcome, Corwin of Lenvil. Rise and let us look at you. Now we see why Judith is all aflutter. We believe you have made a conquest, Corwin."

His brow furrowed in question. "The little novice?"

"Judith is our niece, not destined for vows. But we digress. We came to meet your sister."

Corwin regained his poise and presented Ardith to the queen of England. Ardith dipped into a low curtsy.

"So you are the one," Matilda said, motioning Ardith to rise. "We have heard much about you."

"I fear to ask what you have heard, Your Majesty."

"We daresay more than you would wish. Henry and I correspond regularly. He wrote at length about your unusual betrothal to Gerard of Wilmont. He thought his decree a stroke of great statesmanship, until recently. Diane de Varley's betrayal and Basil of Northbryre's escape sits hard on Henry's mind." Matilda smiled wryly. "Lady Diane was always a strong-minded wench. Henry should have known she would do something foolish."

Matilda waved a dismissing hand. "But what intrigues us is the reason for your visit. Judith tells us you wish to see Sister Bernadette. We can think of only one reason a woman would ask to see a midwife. You do not, however, look ready to give birth."

Ardith put a trembling hand on her stomach.

"I hope, Your Majesty, that Sister Bernadette can determine whether or not I am truly barren."

Matilda cocked her head, studied Ardith for a moment. "Baron Gerard chose well. You are not only beautiful, but wise. Come, my dear. We will await the good sister in our chambers. Corwin, you may stay in the priest's hut, outside the walls. Ask one of my guards to point it out. We will send for you when we are finished.''

"I refuse to condone her immorality.''

Ardith's heart sank as Sister Bernadette pulled up to her full, dominating height and thrust out her ample chest. In black robes and veil, the nun looked like a dark angel.

"Now, Sister,'' Matilda cajoled. "How can you refuse this poor girl? Think of her anguish.''

"She ruts with a man not her husband. If she suffers anguish, 'tis God's punishment for her waywardness.''

"Wayward? This sweet child? None of this is of her doing. She only obeys her overlord and her king. Baron Gerard and King Henry bear the responsibility for her dilemma.''

Ardith turned away and walked across the stone floor of the chamber to the window shuttered with oak.

She noted the simple yet rich furnishings—an ornate bed with a thick mattress, a desk cluttered with parchment and quills, an oak table on which sat two gold goblets. Friendly, warm and inviting—as was the queen, who argued Ardith's case with the nun who refused to help the whore of Gerard, baron of Wilmont.

"I sense no remorse for her plight,'' Sister Bernadette countered. "She beds with a baron, a man of wealth and rank. She is no different from the other sluts who use their bodies to obtain worldly goods.''

"Sister Bernadette,'' the queen said in an exasperated tone. "Ardith seeks neither wealth nor rank, but a marriage she cannot have unless she proves fruitful. If she cannot conceive, the baron will have no choice but to cast her aside, take another as his wife.''

At the rustle of silk, Ardith turned from the window to see Queen Matilda rise from her chair and put a fragile hand on Sister Bernadette's arm.

Matilda smiled slyly. "And imagine, Sister, you would promote a love match."

Sister Bernadette harrumphed.

"'Tis true! Gerard of Wilmont asked for this marriage because he cares for Ardith—so Henry says. We also believe that Ardith cares for Gerard. Of the countless women you have attended at birthing, Sister, how many of those women loved the man whose child they bore?"

"'Tis a rare occurrence."

"Aye, rare indeed. Think, Sister, of the many women who suffer the marriage bed and the pain of childbirth out of duty. How many babes enter the world sickly or maimed because the father beat the mother? And but a few days ago, a man gave an infant girl to Abbess Christina to raise in the church because he suspected the child not of his loins. Ah, Sister, if more marriages occurred because of love than duty to family or state, would not this world be a happier place?"

Sister Bernadette fidgeted with the hem of her sleeve. "Nobles do not marry for affection. If the baron asked for the marriage, he does so for an alliance or wealth."

"He gets neither, only Ardith."

The nun's brow furrowed, and for the first time she spoke directly to Ardith. "Is this true, child?"

"Aye, Sister," Ardith answered.

"No alliance? No dowry?"

"My father offers no dowry. Wilmont holds Lenvil in vassalage, so Baron Gerard gains no lands or alliances."

"And you are Saxon?"

Ardith nodded, knowing if she spoke she'd betray her rising hope. Though concentrating on the nun, Ardith was aware the queen had resumed her seat by the table and raised a goblet to smiling lips.

"A most peculiar noble," Sister Bernadette observed. "Were he a peasant, would you regard him as highly?"

"His rank and wealth have helped shape the man," Ardith replied. "He is Norman, with a Norman's arrogance and pride. He wears his rank as naturally as a bear wears his fur. Were he not noble, he would not be Gerard. What you ask, Sister, is if all his possessions were taken from him on the morrow, would I still want the man as my husband? Aye, I would.''

"And he cares for you?"

Ardith couldn't help a small smile. "I fear he cares more than he thinks prudent. He has said as much."

"How often does he beat you?"

Ardith had to admit that her insolence might have brought on a beating from a lesser man. Gerard might shout till the beams shook, but she'd never feared the back of his hand.

"Never." At the nun's obvious disbelief, Ardith quickly added, "Gerard may be forceful, but he is never cruel. I have only seen him lay a hand to someone in anger but once. Truth be told, he need not. 'Tis sometimes a great aggravation, Sister, that when Gerard raises his voice to give an order, everyone jumps to do his bidding."

Ardith endured the nun's stare, tamped down the tension palpitating through the deepening silence.

In a quiet voice, the nun said, "Take off the robe, child, and lie down on the bed."

Startled by the nun's acquiescence, Ardith couldn't move. This was what she wanted, why she risked Gerard's wrath in coming to the abbey. She panicked. What if Sister Bernadette agreed with Elva? What if the twin link had led Corwin to believe falsely? Sweet Mother!

"Quickly, child, before I change my mind."

Ardith stared at the bed, the bed belonging to the queen of England! She swallowed hard.

"'Tis only a bed, Ardith," Matilda said, somehow understanding her reluctance.

After glancing from Matilda to Sister Bernadette, Ardith stepped out of her felt shoes, tugged off the robe and eased onto the coverlet.

Sister Bernadette loomed over her, ran an icy finger over the scar. Ardith shivered slightly.

"'Tis a thin mark," the nun said, frowning. "What do you remember of the mishap?"

"I will never forget the boar's charge, the sound of ripping cloth, the gouge of its tusk."

"And of after?"

"Very little. I fainted. I learned later that my brother killed the boar and carried me home. I woke to Elva hovering over me, to my mother sadly shaking her head. I thought I would die. Then the fever took hold and I slept for several days. 'Tis said I am fortunate to be alive."

The nun poked, prodded, and pressed on Ardith's midsection with a heavy hand.

"Who is Elva?"

"My father's sister, Lenvil's herbswoman and midwife."

Sister Bernadette nodded, staring at some spot on the wall as she repeated the manipulation. Then she rolled up a sleeve.

"Open your legs, child."

As the nun's intention became clear, Ardith wanted to die. Right here. Lying naked as the day of her birth on the queen's bed. Humiliation stiffened her spine and sent a heated flush through her body.

Only for Gerard would she suffer this degradation. No, she quickly admitted. Not for Gerard, but for herself, her peace of mind, her need to put behind the uncertainty. She closed her eyes and obeyed.

The intrusion came swiftly.

"Relax."

The nun pushed up with the offending hand, pushed down with the other.

"This Elva, 'twas she who declared you barren?"

"Aye," Ardith breathed.

The nun's hands came away. Ardith closed her legs.

Sister Bernadette rolled down her sleeve. "The woman is either inept or she lied to you deliberately. Your wound did not go deep enough to harm your female parts. Should God see fit to bless you with children, your body is quite capable of bearing the burden.''

Ardith sat beside Queen Matilda at the trestle table, surrounded by nuns, forcing down the evening meal.

...lied to you deliberately.

Inconceivable. But the phrase resisted attempts to push Sister Bernadette's words aside. Elva wasn't inept. Could Elva have erred, misjudged the depth of the wound?

"I had thought you would be pleased," Matilda said.

"I am, Majesty."

"Yet you frown and pick at your food."

Ardith abandoned all pretense of eating. "I have believed for so long in my barrenness, 'tis hard to accept otherwise."

"Take heart, Ardith. Sister Bernadette would not raise your hopes if there were doubts."

Elva hadn't doubted either. Elva had treated a girl's wound and fought the resulting fever. Then she'd declared Ardith unable to bear children, thus ruining the betrothal to Gerard—a Norman, the heir to Wilmont, Elva's hated enemy.

Judith's hasty entrance, the horrified look on her face, interrupted Ardith's disturbing thoughts. The girl dipped a quick curtsy to the queen.

"Auntie Maud," Judith said, nearly breathless. "The abbess requests your presence in her chambers when you have finished your meal. Lady Ardith, you are asked to come now."

"Surely the abbess will allow Ardith to finish—"

"'Tis not the abbess who requests Lady Ardith. A man has come to fetch her."

Ardith smiled slightly. "Corwin grows impatient."

Judith shook her head. "Not Corwin, milady. This man is huge, and he is—"

"*Arrr-dith!*" boomed down the passageway and bounced off the stone walls, startling the dining nuns.

"—most displeased."

"Gerard," Ardith whispered. She struggled briefly with the desire to stay seated, safely ensconced next to Queen Matilda. She swung her legs over the bench, intending to halt him in the passageway. She almost accomplished the feat.

Gerard burst into the refectory, his hard footsteps beating a cadence in rhythm to the sword clanging against chain mail. No helm covered his tawny mane of hair, nor did gauntlets cover the huge hands curled into fists. Anger radiated from the stern expression on his face, an anger so fierce Ardith pulled up short.

He, too, stopped, within a few steps inside the entrance. His green eyes glittered emerald as he looked her up and down, the novice's garment clearly offensive.

Ardith took a fortifying breath. She'd never cowered before Gerard's flash-fire temper. She wouldn't start now. She closed the distance between them with firm, unrushed steps.

"My lord, the queen," she whispered, hoping to divert the tirade she knew inevitable.

He tossed a curt nod in Matilda's direction. "Maud."

So much for diversion. "I can explain," Ardith said softly.

"I wish to leave here," he growled, putting his hands on her shoulders, his thumbs resting at the hollow of her throat. Gently, with a tenderness that belied his expression and stance, his thumbs stroked, evoking a familiar and welcome shiver of response to his touch.

"'Tis almost nightfall, Gerard. Surely 'tis not safe—"

"*Now* she worries over her safety."

Ardith curled her fingers in the rings of his hauberk. His expression had softened, the flaming anger nearly spent. Soon, she knew, the inferno would cool.

He wasn't so much angry that she'd come to the abbey as that she'd come without his permission and protection. At times, it seemed, Gerard's peace of mind depended upon knowing where she was, whether she stood within his sight or if they were leagues apart. At one time she'd thought he shielded her as one would guard a prized possession. Having come to know Gerard well, she now knew otherwise. When Gerard loved, he loved with his whole heart and took care of those he loved with equal passion.

He worried needlessly. She'd come to no harm. If ever he found her otherwise, hurt or endangered...Ardith suppressed a shudder. Gerard's fury would scorch all within his reach.

"Corwin brought me to the abbey. He would let no harm come to me," Ardith said, trying to ease his mind.

"Corwin," he huffed. "The lad has much to answer for. Imagine my surprise when I rode in and found Corwin sitting in the doorway of the priest's hut."

"Then he explained why we are here?"

"I did not speak to him. I had another matter to attend first. 'Twas the abbess who informed me you were also here."

"What other matter?" Ardith asked before hearing the swish of silk that signaled the queen's approach.

"Baron Gerard, you might wish to hear Ardith's news before you throttle her," Matilda admonished.

Gerard tilted his head, perplexed.

Ardith then noticed the silence. She turned her head slightly to see several pairs of worried eyes. The nuns thought...oh, dear. Ardith pressed lips together to stifle a giggle. The urge quelled, she squeezed Gerard's hand between her shoulder and cheek.

"They think you are about to commit mayhem, my lord."

He looked at his hands, so close to her throat, the thumbs that still stroked. "What makes you think I am not?"

"Gerard," she asked, "If you did not come to fetch me, then what brings you to Romsey?"

He took his hands from around her neck but didn't let her go. His arm circled her shoulders, pulling her tight against her side.

"Lady Ursula," he answered. "She is with the abbess."

"Ah. That explains the summons," Matilda said. "It seems every noblewoman who visits begs an audience. The abbess feels obliged to consent."

"Lady Ursula does not visit. She stays. My mother needs to learn the difference between devotion and fanaticism. Who better to teach her than Abbess Christina and Queen Matilda?" A hint of a smile touched Gerard's lips. "If you care to assume the task, Majesty, I would ask another boon. See if you can amend her attitude toward bastards."

Queen Matilda crossed her arms. "You ask a great deal, Gerard of Wilmont."

"Who better to uphold the innocence of noble bastards? What has Henry? Nine? Ten? Yet never have you held the children answerable to the self-indulgence of the father. To each you have shown kindness, even when Henry brought each in turn to court, to educate them and bestow rank and funds."

"We gather your mother still holds Richard responsible for Everart's wandering."

"Not only does she abhor Richard, but has taken to the notion of purging Wilmont of bastards."

Matilda shook her head sadly. "Such nonsense. We will do what we can." Then she smiled, the warm, sincere smile that had touched Ardith's heart. "Take good care of this young woman, Gerard of Wilmont. We like her."

Gerard heaved a long, aggrieved sigh. "I keep trying, Majesty, but Ardith insists on taking unwise risks."

"Your lady is both wise and brave." Queen Matilda's smile widened. "We believe you will find her efforts on your behalf most rewarding. You must visit me again, Ardith, soon."

The queen turned to leave. Ardith dared to stop her, putting fingertips on a royal arm without permission.

"I have not yet thanked you, Majesty, for your help."

Matilda leaned close and whispered, "You can thank me by making me a godmother."

Awed by the honor, Ardith watched Queen Matilda flounce out of the hall.

"A godmother? Ardith?"

Ardith looked up. The hope on Gerard's face was almost too much to bear. She grabbed his hand and led him to the sitting room where Thomas's clothes lay rolled in the corner.

The tale burst forth like water rushing down a stream. Throughout the telling, Gerard remained silent, sitting in a chair, his hands opening and closing.

Ardith unrolled the tunic, exposing the hose and leather lacings. "Corwin even made me wear male clothing, so I would not be recognized."

He took an audible breath. "Could you not have waited for me to return? Had you wanted to come to Romsey, see this nun, I would have brought you."

"'Twas impulsive, I know. But I did not expect you for several more days, and my need to see the nun grew so strong I could not wait." Ardith knelt before him, grasped his hands. "I did not intend to upset you, Gerard. Forgive me?"

"There is no harm done, I suppose."

"You worry overmuch, my love."

"Mayhap. I gather you have seen this nun." He squeezed her hands. "Ardith, the queen said...are you—?"

"Not yet, I think. But Sister Bernadette believes Elva may have...erred, that 'tis possible I can bear children."

Gerard swept her from the floor onto his lap, and into a smothering hug. She ignored the hard rings of the hauberk.

"Hellfire, Ardith. We could have wed years ago, if not for Elva's blunder. Damn her for keeping you from me, for putting us through this torment. Well, no longer."

Ardith guessed the direction of his thoughts and sat up straight. "Gerard, wait."

But he wasn't listening.

"We will have the banns read immediately," he continued. "I will find a priest. I can send for Father Dominic from Wilmont if need be. We can be wed by month's end."

"Gerard, the king, the betrothal decree."

"Henry can take his decree and—"

Her hand covered his mouth before he uttered words he would later regret. Sweet Mother, the man could be mulish. She understood his feelings, wanted the marriage to take place with all haste as much as, if not more than, Gerard. But ignoring the decree could only mean trouble.

She said pointedly, "You need King Henry's consent to marry, whether me or another. At the least, you must tell him of my visit here, petition him to set aside the decree."

He glared. She removed her hand from his mouth.

"It vexes me sorely to once again await Henry's *justice*, to take no action while Henry—"

"But you can take action."

"What?"

"You could double your efforts to satisfy the decree. Then no matter what Henry thinks...Gerard, what are you doing? Not now! We are in an abbey, for mercy's sake. Do not tear the robe—'tis not mine. Gerard!"

Chapter Twenty

Ardith sat on a boulder on the hillside, a letter from Queen Matilda in her hands. The queen wrote often, of Ursula, of Judith, of happenings at court. Matilda held hope for Ursula, but changing beliefs of a lifetime required time and patience. Always, before scrawling her name in closing, Matilda asked the same question.

This time, Ardith would answer. *Late, by two weeks.*

Gerard knew. His sidelong glances, his subtle steering of conversations, his gentleness, all indicated he knew. Yet he said nothing. His patience, however, was thinning.

Elva knew, too. Ardith couldn't mistake the anger and sorrow always present in her aunt's eyes.

Elva *had* lied. Since returning from the abbey, Ardith hadn't confronted her aunt, but suspecting continued treachery, refused all food and drink from her aunt's hand. Elva's stunned, nearly panicked reaction convinced Ardith of Elva's initial deceit, and her continuing endeavor to prevent conception by use of potions. The betrayal hurt.

If anyone else suspected, none dared jinx the possible pregnancy by saying the words aloud. She'd been late before, then bled.

But never this late.

Ardith looked up to watch Daymon chase the lambs that more often sidled up to their mothers than played with the tot. Spring had arrived with the birth of the lambs. Sunshine had signaled the flowers to bloom and the trees to leaf.

The season's promise of new life nettled.

Pip swung Daymon onto a ewe's back. The boy squealed with delight. The ewe bleated a protest. Of everyone, only Daymon seemed unaware of the swelling tension in the manor, some of it caused by speculation over her condition, some not.

King Henry hadn't answered Gerard's petition to set aside the betrothal decree, nor had Henry sent word on Basil's whereabouts. Stephen impatiently waited for Gerard to release him to oversee his new holdings. Corwin served the double stands of guard duty Gerard had assigned as punishment for taking Ardith to Romsey. Richard wore out the soldiers with constant bouts of swordplay, determined to regain all his strength—or at least enough to beat Gerard. Elva's surly mood had provoked Gerard beyond tolerance and he'd ordered her out of the manor, into a hovel.

As Pip, carrying Daymon, sauntered toward Ardith, she folded the queen's letter and slipped it into her boot.

"Here y'go, little one," Pip said, plopping Daymon onto Ardith's lap. "His eyes, milady, they droop."

"So they do," Ardith agreed, smiling down at Daymon. Dirt smudged his cheeks and sweat-dampened hair hung close to sleepy eyes. He reeked of sheep. His thumb found his mouth as he snuggled into a comfortable position, his head on her shoulder, his pudgy legs wrapped around her waist.

"Mayhap I should carry him down," Pip suggested.

"My thanks for the offer, Pip, but I can manage. Besides, you have a flock to tend."

"Aye, and a lamb to find. One of the little buggers has wandered off."

"Then find it, by all means. We both know how the baron prizes his sheep. We must not let one get away."

Pip rolled his eyes at the jest. Ardith laughed, then shifted Daymon and started down the hill toward the manor, where Wilmont's soldiers were again erecting buildings: a shed for shearing sheep and storing fleece, another privy, a smithy. Someday, Gerard had decided, this holding would belong to Daymon, under Pip's stewardship.

As she reached the bottom of the hill, she heard an odd sound coming from the woods. She stopped to listen. Birds sang, calling to mates as they hurried to build nests. A squirrel chattered at some intruder.

Then she heard the lamb. A plaintive cry for help. She looked up the hill but didn't see Pip.

"Shall we go lamb hunting?" she asked Daymon.

Daymon didn't answer, having fallen asleep. Ardith followed the lamb's call.

Daymon's deadweight strained her arms. Balancing him as she ducked under low hanging limbs proved taxing. She nearly tripped on the hem of her cloak. Yet she doggedly plodded on, directed by the lamb whose cry grew louder and more pitiful. It had to be trapped somewhere, entangled in the underbrush or down a hole.

"Hush!" Ardith heard Elva's command above the cries. "'Twill be only a moment now. Hush."

Elva? Had she also heard the lamb and gone to its rescue? Ardith opened her mouth to call out, then didn't, paying heed to the prickle of hair on the back of her neck. She looked around, spotted a patch of long grass and gently eased Daymon into nature's cradle, then quietly moved toward the clearing ahead, sure she would find Elva and the lamb.

At the edge of the clearing, Ardith stopped, momentarily confused by what she observed. Atop a flat-topped boulder lay the lamb, struggling against the rope binding its legs. Elva knelt before the rock, her head thrown back, her arms stretched skyward, muttering guttural words Ardith didn't understand. Flames shimmered on the candles on the forest floor, encircling woman and lamb.

A pagan ritual. A sacrifice. A requirement for asking a favor from the ancient gods. Ardith put a hand over her stomach, suddenly realizing why Elva intended to kill the lamb.

"Elva, stop." The words came out choked. Elva either didn't hear or purposely ignored the command. She reached down into the grass near her knees and pulled up a butchering knife.

Ardith screamed her aunt's name. Elva jerked and the chanting ceased, but she didn't turn.

"I will never forgive you," Ardith swore. "Do you hear me? If you persist, I will never forgive you, never speak to you again."

Elva resumed chanting, her voice now loud, the eerie words echoing in the woodland clearing. The knife rose higher.

Ardith ran toward her aunt, kicking over and snuffing out candles. "I have spoiled your circle. The gods will not hear. The sacrifice is in vain. Put down the knife."

Elva's face twisted in anguish, huge tears running down her cheeks. "Baron Wilmont would steal you from me again. I cannot let that happen!"

"I am here. No one steals me away."

"*He* did! Wilmont beast. Spawn of Satan. He took you from me at birth, said you were dead. Lies, all lies. 'Twas a miracle I got my baby back. Wilmont shall not have you again!"

Ardith tried to make sense of the prattle of beasts and the absurd notion that Elva could be her mother. True, Elva had been like a mother to her after her own had died, but Ardith had heard too many stories of the day she and Corwin had been born to doubt her parentage.

Those many years ago, when Elva had been a young woman serving as hostage to Wilmont, had she given birth to a girl child? What had happened to the baby? Had it died? Who had been the father? The first baron, Gerard's grandfather? Was this why Elva hated every male of Wilmont heritage with such passion?

Elva's upraised arm trembled. Relying only on instinct

and intuition, Ardith knelt beside her aunt and gently touched the shoulder of the knife-bearing arm.

"Elva, dearest, this lamb need not die. Listen as he calls to his mother. Can you not hear the ewe, calling out to her babe? Would you deprive the mother of her child?"

The upraised arm lowered slightly. Ardith deftly snatched the knife from Elva's grasp. With a quick flip of the wrist, Ardith cut the rope binding the lamb's legs. Shaking, the lamb stood on the flat-topped rock, then leaped off. Ardith put the knife on the ground.

Elva rocked slowly on her knees, keening.

Ardith wrapped her arms around Elva, making hushing noises as one would soothe a child. If everything she suspected was true, Elva's mind had taken a strange twist, confusing two parts of her life. And now Ardith was involved with a baron of Wilmont, and Elva feared a repeat of the past.

How sad. How horrible. And now that Ardith knew, what could she do? She couldn't change the past. She couldn't heal Elva's mind, but she might give Elva peace.

She pushed away gently. "Elva, you must make me a promise. You must help me bring my child into the world, a child of Wilmont and Lenvil."

Elva's eyes went wide.

Ardith hurriedly continued. "You knew I would bear this child. Has not fate decreed this child should be born?"

"The bones," Elva said softly.

"Aye, the bones," Ardith encouraged. "Do we, mere mortals, dare alter the will of the gods? What punishment will they inflict if we interfere? Who knows what they intend for this child of mixed blood, of Saxon and Norman?"

"Revenge?"

Ardith sighed at the hopeful look on Elva's face. "Your promise, Elva. If you wish to stay with me, you must promise to let fate run its course. You must not interfere."

Elva's head bobbed. Ardith settled for the vague agreement.

* * *

From a seat at the table, Gerard shouted at the king's messenger. "What the devil is Basil doing in Manchester?"

"By all reports, Basil of Northbryre is trying to raise an army, not only against you, but King Henry. His efforts met with little success, my lord."

Of course, Gerard inwardly scoffed. His fellow barons might shelter Basil, might listen to his plans, might wish the man well and neglect to inform Henry of Basil's treason. The Norman barons were a disgruntled lot, but they weren't fools, and wouldn't rally to a man as reckless as Basil.

"Is Basil still near Manchester?"

"We believe so, my lord. You are granted the privilege of capturing Basil. King Henry requires only that you bring Basil back to London. Alive."

"Alive?" Gerard roared.

The messenger took a step backward. "Aye, my lord."

"Do not bite the messenger, Gerard," Ardith said softly, placing a hand on his arm. "He only repeats Henry's command."

Gerard scowled, and dismissed the young man.

Then he grabbed Ardith's hand. "Walk with me," he said, and led Ardith out of the manor.

He sauntered up the hillside, deferring to Ardith's short stride—and her delicate condition. She hadn't confirmed his suspicions yet, but he could count weeks. She'd now missed a second monthly flow.

At the top of the hill, he eased onto the ground, settling his back against a tree. Ardith curled against him. As always, he could smell her unique scent—wildflowers and sunshine—sweet and alluring. The heat of her body penetrated his sherte, awakening the desire that lurked just under his skin, stirring whenever Ardith was close.

He wanted to make love to her; he wanted to shake her. Why hadn't she said the words that would seal their future?

"You surprise me, Gerard. I expected you to jump up from the table shouting orders."

"I have not yet decided what orders to give."

Eyes, pools of shimmering blue, narrowed in confusion. "You do intend to search for Basil," she stated, then cocked her head. "Yet you hesitate. Why so?"

"I have yet to decide what to do with you. If my mother were not at Romsey with the queen, I would take you there."

"There is no need for me to go anywhere. Really, Gerard you worry overmuch. I will be quite safe and content here. Go, catch Basil, deliver him to Henry, then return to me."

"So simple."

Her easy smile preceded soft laughter. "I have heard the stories your men-at-arms tell. If they speak true, you are a knight of unequaled skill, a cunning tactician, a leader they would follow into the most dire of battles. Even if they stretch the truth, you are still a man to be reckoned with. You can do whatever you set your mind to, Gerard."

"Can I?" He touched her cheek. So soft, Ardith's skin. "I set my mind and my body to siring a child, Ardith. Have I succeeded?"

Her smile faded. "I fear to say it aloud," she said.

Joy welled up, flowed, threatened to overwhelm his senses. If not for the anguish in Ardith's voice he might have shouted his happiness. Why wasn't she pleased? Why wasn't she dancing on air, singing with glee, planning a wedding?

Unless she wasn't sure, or something was very wrong.

"Ardith, are you well?"

"Too well."

"How can one be too well?"

"Look at my face, Gerard. Do you see a sallowness of skin or a darkening about the eyes? Nay, you do not." She removed her boots, pulled up her gown. "My ankles, they do not swell, not a mite. See?"

Gerard wrapped a hand around the dainty ankle she plopped onto his leg. "I see." He saw more—pretty feet, a shapely calf. His hand traveled the path.

"I am not ill of a morning. I do not tire easily. My breasts are not tender."

"Do you intend to bare those for me, too?"

"Gerard, be serious. I am frightened."

His roving hand stopped at her knee. "Of what?"

"That my body gives false signs. My monthly has stopped but no other changes happen."

"You are supposed to be dark eyed, and ill and tired?"

"Perhaps not all, but every woman has an ailment or two when carrying."

"So until some ailment appears, you are not sure if we have fulfilled the decree."

Her sigh eloquently answered.

"Damn Basil," he said. "He could have waited another week or two to surface. I dislike leaving you now, my love."

"But go you must."

Torn between the need to vanquish his enemy and the desire to remain with Ardith, Gerard gathered her onto his lap. He thought of taking her along, then dismissed the notion. The march to Manchester would be fast and hard, difficult for soldiers, hazardous for a woman with child.

"Go I must," he relented.

Two days after Gerard's departure, Ardith couldn't stand the thought of breaking fast, much less the smell or sight of food. She fell asleep at table at midday meal.

She wrote to the queen, pouring out her joy.

"Fire! Fire in the armory!"

Ardith tossed the coverlet aside and pulled on her boots. She checked Daymon, asleep in his nest of furs, then pushed aside the curtain that separated sleeping space from hall.

Stephen had risen, pulled on a tunic and boots. Yawning, he ran a hand through his hair. "Go back to sleep, Ardith. Some fool probably got drunk and dropped a torch."

"I should do something to help."

"I would rather you stay inside and keep Daymon from getting underfoot. Gerard would have my head if somebody stepped on him or doused him with a bucket of water."

A bit woozy from rising so fast, Ardith agreed.

Stephen flashed a smile. "You look a bit green, Ardith."

She smiled back. "Hush, or I will tell Gerard how you have mistreated me."

Laughing, he went out the door.

The sun wouldn't rise for an hour yet, but wide-awake, she wouldn't be able to sleep until Stephen returned with the story of the fire. And fires always meant burns, no matter how small the fire or how careful the men. They would need her salves.

Still smiling at Stephen's jest, she wished again that Gerard would hurry back.

Gerard had taken Richard with him, to track Basil, and Corwin, whom Gerard considered too easily swayed by Ardith's whims, and several of his soldiers. Stephen grumbled at being left behind, but Ardith was glad of his company. He slept in the manor on Thomas's usual pallet. He watched over her and Daymon with a doggedness that sometimes put her teeth on edge.

Ardith peeked out the door of the manor. Flame blazed skyward from the far end of the armory. Men shouted above the crackle of fire consuming wood, passing buckets of water along a human line from the well. The stabled horses, though not endangered, sensed the threat and voiced their fear. A warm breeze ruffled around her, carrying the tang of smoke to eyes and nose. She shut the door.

Intending to change from her night rail into a gown and dig out the salve, Ardith padded into the sleeping area. Next to the pallet she shared with Gerard, she knelt to open a chest.

The manor door opened, closed. Ardith grabbed the tin of salve and closed the lid. The drapery parted. Expecting Stephen, Ardith turned.

Before the fur coverlet came down over her head, knocking her off balance, she identified her assailant. Edward Siefeld. Basil's mercenary captain. The man who'd nearly killed Richard in Normandy, who'd stood before the king dressed all in black.

Her heart raced. She tried to scream, but even in her panic realized the effort useless. No one would hear. Her breathing became harsh and labored. *Fight!* She pushed at the fur. Strong arms came around her, pinning her arms to her sides, lifting. She kicked wildly. Her boot connected with something solid, a piece of Siefeld's body, she hoped.

"Be still or we kill the boy!" Siefeld's harshly spoken command pierced through the smothering fur, through the terror scrambling her senses.

Daymon! Oh, God. Ardith's body went limp.

"Do we take the boy?" a male voice asked.

"Aye. Wilmont's whore *and* bastard. A good day's loot."

"No!" Ardith yelled, twisting in Siefeld's arms.

"Handle him gently," Siefeld added. "If he remains asleep he won't cry out."

They moved out of the sleeping area. The manor door squealed on its hinges.

"Stephen!" she screamed.

There was a bloodcurdling cry of outrage, a crash.

"Damn. Here, watch her," Siefeld said, putting her on her feet. Ardith felt a second burly arm tighten around her. During the transfer, the fur slid off her face. She glanced around quickly. Hope died a swift death.

Two men stood in the center of the hall, swords drawn and pointing downward to where Stephen lay on the floor, propped on an elbow in a tangle of table and benches.

Siefeld drew his sword, loomed over Stephen. "Get a rope. Tie and gag him," he ordered one man, then told the other, "Close the door. See if anyone follows."

"Gerard won't let this go unpunished," Stephen rasped. "Be prepared to die a slow, painful death, Siefeld. You'll see your guts fall to the ground before you see the gates of hell.''

At a twist of Siefeld's wrist, the tip of his sword nicked Stephen's chin, drawing blood. Stephen smiled, an evil smile Ardith hadn't thought him capable of.

"Think of it, Siefeld. First your fingers, joint by joint, then your toes. He will save your eyes and ears for last, so you see each piece fall, hear yourself scream for mercy."

The sword took another bite, this one from Stephen's ear. Stephen never moved, never cried out, only smiled that feral smile. Ardith shuddered.

"He came alone, Captain. No one followed."

"Excellent. Help with the ropes."

With the speed of a striking snake, Stephen lunged for Siefeld's knees. Ardith watched in horror as the sword sliced into Stephen's shoulder. Momentum carried Stephen forward. He knocked Siefeld over. The sword flew from Siefeld's hand. Amid splintering wood and splattering blood the two men rolled in a vicious embrace.

Suddenly remembering the dagger hidden inside her boot, Ardith struggled against her captor. If Stephen could fight, so could she. If she could reach her dagger…

"Be still. Remember the boy," her captor said harshly.

Ardith bit her lower lip and obeyed. She silently prayed, urging Stephen onward, but the odds were against him.

Siefeld's men joined the fray, pinning Stephen to the ground, binding his hands and feet even as Stephen clawed and kicked. They rolled him off Siefeld, then trussed him like a boar readied for spit. Stephen panted, but so did Siefeld. Ardith silently approved of Siefeld's split lower lip, of the eye already turning dark and puffy, the sway in his step from an obviously injured leg.

"I will let you live, pup," Siefeld said as his underling stuffed a cloth in Stephen's mouth. "'Twill save me the trouble of sending a messenger. Tell your brother that Basil requires a ship, readied to sail for Normandy. Two weeks.

Portsmouth. If Gerard complies, he gets his whore and bastard back whole. If not..."

Siefeld didn't state the gruesome consequences, but Ardith understood. So, she guessed, did Stephen.

"Ardith! Ardith! I am coming, baby. I am coming!"

Recognizing Elva's voice, Ardith's heart sank to her toes.

The manor door banged open. Elva ran into the hall, a butchering knife raised above her head.

"Elva, no! Stop!"

But Elva didn't hear. She ran straight at Edward Siefeld. Siefeld raised his sword.

"She is but an old woman! Do not hurt her, please!" Ardith begged.

She saw the flicker of willingness on Siefeld's face, but Elva gave him no choice. Shrieking like a banshee, Elva raced to her doom.

Ardith closed her eyes tightly and turned her head. She heard the scrape of metal against bone, the gurgle of blood in Elva's throat, the thump of a body hitting the floor.

"Out. Now!" Siefeld commanded.

Ardith's captor pushed her forward. She forced her eyes open, blinking away tears. She merely glanced at Elva, crumpled at Siefeld's feet, refusing to look at the horror too closely.

But her gaze locked with Stephen's.

In his green, glittering eyes, she found what she looked for—a promise. A promise of rescue, and revenge.

Chapter Twenty-One

"Thought I might find you out here," Richard said smugly. "You are fond of watching the sun rise, of late."

Gerard almost smiled at his brother's attempt to explain an inability to sleep. For more than a week they'd searched for Basil, beginning in Manchester. They'd questioned peasants, serfs, merchants and nobles—two of the latter at sword point. South, all had directed.

The farther Gerard traveled, the closer he came to capturing Basil, the harder it became to sleep. The longer away from Ardith, from the warmth and comfort of her arms and voice, the more impossible to remain curled on a pallet.

"He is out there, Richard, but where? Who shelters him? Will he find someone willing to aid his revolt?"

"He has not thus far, nor will he, I think. From what we have heard, he is becoming desperate. He knows the king's men are after him, might even suspect we are, too. Desperate men make stupid mistakes, and Basil is not the smartest of men, nor is he the bravest. He will blunder, and then we will have him."

"We will ride into Oxford this morning. Mayhap Basil will be there."

Richard shrugged. "He has not yet left the roads. 'Tis likely he has, at least, passed through the city."

As rays of sun brightened the horizon, Gerard turned

toward the sound of someone crashing through the brush. Corwin burst through, his eyes wide, sweat trickling down his face.

"Hellfire, Corwin, what—"

Grabbing Gerard's sleeve, Corwin choked out, "I thought it a dream, a nightmare, but the terror clings like a shroud." Corwin raised his trembling hands, stared at them. "The distance, 'tis so far, but I cannot stop shaking. I cannot."

Corwin swallowed hard, struggling for composure. Gerard's gut twisted. He clamped on to Corwin's arms and shook him.

"Get hold of yourself, man! What frightens you?"

Just above a whisper, Corwin said, "Ardith. I can feel my twin's terror as though it were my own."

"Is Ardith hurt?"

"I feel no pain, only fright."

"Of what?"

"I know not. Gerard, please, I *must* return."

Gerard stared at Corwin, unsure of what to do, remembering the jolt of pain Ardith had felt when Corwin bruised his leg. She'd nearly fallen, yet Corwin's injury hadn't been serious. Was Corwin overreacting?

"Corwin, maybe she just—"

"Look at me!" Corwin snapped, wiping away sweat with unsteady hands. "We are leagues apart, yet the demons of hell snap at my heels. Damn it, Gerard, she is not frightened, she is *terrified!*"

If Ardith felt terror, she feared for the babe Gerard was sure she carried, not for herself. Only for Ardith, for their child, would he postpone a confrontation with Basil.

Gerard squeezed Corwin's arms. "Then saddle our horses. If we ride hard, we can reach Ardith by midday."

Corwin turned on his heel and ran toward the horses.

"Gerard?"

Confusion and questions flickered across Richard's face. Explanations would take too much time.

"Find Basil for me, Richard. Hold him until I return."

* * *

"Siefeld must have started the fire as a diversion," Stephen said. "It worked. While everyone strove to put out the flames, he and his men entered the manor. I am sorry, Gerard. I should not have left them alone."

Gerard picked up the goblet of ale, wanting to throw it across the room. Realizing the futility of the action, he took a long pull from the vessel, then put it down.

Corwin sat next to him, arms crossed on the table, chin resting on arms. He hadn't said a word since they'd met the messenger on the road whom Stephen had sent to find Gerard.

Stephen sat in a despondent slump, guilt etched in his face. Gerard saw the evidence of Stephen's fight to thwart the kidnapping—the sword cuts on chin and ear, the shoulder swathed in bandaging. Stephen had fought Siefeld, and failed. So had Elva. Three fresh graves dotted the burial grounds—Elva and two men-at-arms from the night watch.

Gerard's fury rose as he imagined the predawn scene. The fire that had almost destroyed the armory. People scurrying to douse the flames. Stephen taunting then attacking Siefeld. Elva flying at Ardith's kidnappers armed with only a knife.

He closed his eyes against the sight of Daymon, bundled in furs, whimpering and helpless in the arms of a mercenary. Gerard vowed that for whatever harm befell his son, Siefeld would suffer tenfold.

And Ardith. Ye gods, Ardith. Her terror had traveled leagues to affect Corwin. For daring to use Ardith in his scheme, Basil would die. For Ardith's pain and fright, the villain would die slowly.

Gerard placed the blame for Ardith's danger squarely upon his own shoulders. She'd placed her trust and love into his keeping, and he'd failed her.

"Gerard?" Stephen said softly. "When do we leave?"

Gerard didn't spare Stephen the edge of his tongue. "For

where? We assume Siefeld left in the same direction he
came from, but for where?"

"Portsmouth?"

"Not likely. Basil expects a ship waiting in the port in
a sennight, but he will not go there until he is ready to sail,
not if he values his skin. More likely he hides somewhere."

Corwin cleared his throat. "Gerard, if you were Basil,
sought for crimes against the crown, with no powerful
friends, with no funds, where would you go?"

The answer came instantly, stunning Gerard. "Home. I
would go to Wilmont, to gather whatever resources I could
to either fight or take with me into exile."

Bits of a plan raced through Gerard's head. Basil had
demanded a ship, readied to sail the Channel, not immediately, but in a sennight. Would Basil be obliging and do
the logical? Would he hold Ardith and Daymon at Northbryre while gathering mercenaries and funds?

"Stephen, when you and Corwin inspected Northbryre
for me, how did you find the people? Were they loyal to
Basil? Would they fight for him?"

"The people feared him. They were pleased to hear Wilmont now controlled the lands, especially the men-at-arms.
I assured those who had not already fled that Wilmont
would take them into service if they pledged loyalty."

"Then I think it time I accepted those pledges and inspected my Hampshire holdings.

"Get out," Siefeld ordered.

Ardith gladly complied, holding out a helping hand to
Daymon as she scrambled out of the hay wagon. After a
day and a half of travel, entertaining an increasingly restless
toddler, stopping only for hurried meals and to relieve bodily discomforts, she would happily burn the wagon to ashes.

She shuddered at the thought of fire. With fire, this nightmare had started.

"Where are we?" Ardith asked.

"Our last stop before Northbryre," Siefeld said, glancing

over his shoulder at the road just traveled. Two mercenaries stood a few feet off, hands near sword hilts, also staring at the dirt road.

"He will come, you know," Ardith taunted softly.

"Stephen? His wounds will prevent his sitting a saddle. Nor does he know where we are taking you," Siefeld scoffed.

"You do not watch for Stephen. You watch for Gerard, and well you should."

Siefeld's hand clamped on to her jaw and squeezed. Ardith refused to wince.

"Pray he does not. Pray he goes to Portsmouth and arranges for a ship. Now take care of your needs before we resume our journey."

With a shove, he let go. Ardith stumbled back a step. Until now, except during the kidnapping, neither Siefeld nor his men had touched her, roughly or otherwise. However, as they drew closer to Northbryre the men's stares became more bold, and Ardith became more aware of her state of undress, of the thin night rail she kept covered with the fur they'd wrapped her in during the kidnapping.

The fur had become both a shield and a comfort. The fur smelled of Gerard, who would come for her and Daymon as soon as he could. But would Gerard come in time?

Ardith stretched her hand toward Daymon.

Siefeld shook his head. "Nay. The boy stays here."

Her captors seemed to know she wouldn't try to escape without the boy. She'd watched for the opportunity, but the mercenaries guarded her closely.

Ardith turned and sought privacy, feeling the weight of the dagger in her boot, hearing Daymon screech her name as she disappeared from his sight. She hurried, returning quickly to Daymon and the confines of the hay wagon.

At sunset, the company reached what had to be Northbryre. Ardith grimaced at the disgraceful bailey and keep. Filth and decay met her eye everywhere, from the piles of waste near the stables to the crumbling stone of the keep.

Peasants and serfs, bodies thin and covered in rags, walked with slumped shoulders and heads bowed.

The earthen works surrounding the keep, however, were in good repair. Archers, arrows notched, walked the mounds.

Ardith reluctantly got out of the wagon with Daymon in her arms. Siefeld bowed mockingly, indicating the stairway that Ardith knew led to the keep's hall.

"Your host awaits, milady."

"He can wait till sheep roost in trees, for all I care."

"Guard your tongue. Basil is not as sweet-tempered as I."

With a sweep of haughtiness, Ardith turned and marched up the stairs. She might be a prisoner here, but she wouldn't cower. She had to be strong, for herself, for Daymon, for her unborn child.

Ardith nearly gagged as she entered the hall. Several mangy hunting dogs loped over rotting rushes to greet the new arrivals, nearly knocking Ardith to the floor in their enthusiasm. Daymon giggled and bent toward the dogs. Ardith quickly snatched him back.

From the raised dais beyond rickety trestle tables, came hoarse laughter. Sitting in a thronelike chair, flanked by two mercenaries, Basil of Northbryre raised a gold goblet to his lips. His eyes, beads of obsidian, narrowed and stared. A trickle of wine missed his mouth and dribbled down his chin to soak into rich robes of dark blue silk.

"Well done, Siefeld," Basil said in a soused slur. "Bring the baggage closer."

Ardith dodged Siefeld's hand, moving forward of her own accord. Basil's brow furrowed, indicating ire at her show of spirit. Ardith knew that the strong preyed on the weak and any sign of weakness invited disaster.

She disliked Siefeld, but she sensed little danger from the mercenary captain, if she followed orders. From Basil she sensed evil. Something about the man made the hair on the back of her neck itch in warning. Basil would harm her with minor provocation. Inside, she quaked with fear. Outside, she feigned bravado.

"Who is the child?" Basil asked.

"Gerard's whelp," Siefeld said. "I bring you two hostages, my lord. If Gerard does not care enough for his whore to meet your demands, he may do so for his son. I thought—"

"Thinking again, Siefeld? Dangerous."

Anger flashed across Siefeld's face, but he withheld further comment.

Basil pushed his ponderous body out of the chair. "In this case, I will allow, you may be right."

He wobbled across the dais and down the stairs, until he stood within arm's reach in front of her. He mockingly put a fist to his chest, bowed slightly.

"Welcome to Northbryre, whore of Wilmont. You will, of course, accept the hospitality of my hall."

"A stall in the stable would do us quite well, my lord," she answered, equally mocking.

His eyes widened. "You would reject a pallet in my hall?"

"Your hall is in dire need of cleaning. Surely the stables would smell sweeter."

Ardith ducked the suddenly flung backhand. The blow missed her head, and, deprived of a solid target, the force of the swing threw Basil slightly off balance.

"Shut your insolent mouth, slut, or your tongue will be the *first* piece of you I send to Gerard. Wish to bed down with animals, do you?" He motioned at Siefeld. "Chain her to the wall. She and the boy can sleep with the hounds."

Ardith cringed but kept silent. There were worse places to sleep, if sleep would come. If not, all the better to keep watch for a chance to escape, or for Gerard to come bursting through the door.

He would come. Ardith didn't believe Gerard would arrange for a ship and let Basil and Siefeld flee England and justice, no matter what her captors believed.

As Siefeld closed the hound's iron collar around her throat and thumbed shut the latch, he said in a low voice, "I will warn you a last time. Behave and you will not be hurt. If you give Basil reason to use the whip, I will not stay his hand, against you or the boy."

"Why do you serve such a master? He treats you no better than the rushes beneath his feet."

"Think you I have a choice? Since the day of our escape from the Tower, my fate rests with Basil's. I will do what I must to survive."

As will I.

Ardith wrapped her fur tightly around her. Daymon, considered too young to be any threat, had been allowed the freedom of the hall. To Ardith's relief, the boy didn't stray far from her side.

Slowly, using the fur to hide her movements, she fingered the latch on the iron collar. The latch slid easily, but she left the collar on, fearing the clank of the iron would attract attention. For now, she took comfort in knowing she could quickly remove the collar.

The blade in her boot also slid easily, ready to her hand should the need arise to defend herself or Daymon.

Though armed, with so many men about she couldn't hope to escape. Even if she did escape, where would she go? One of Gerard's holdings, a manor named Milhurst, bordered Northbryre, but in what direction?

As the evening wore on, emptying kegs of ale, the mercenaries who'd accompanied Siefeld told an embellished tale of the fire and kidnapping. Ardith tried not to listen, the horror too fresh to relive without feeling the panic.

Instead, she watched the serving wench who brought in platters of food and refilled the pitchers with ale. Like a wisp of wind, the young woman deftly dodged hands that reached out to grab bottom or breast. A stoic expression fixed firmly on her face, she fluttered about the table until, trenchers and cups full, the mercenaries returned to their revelry and seemed to forget her presence.

Ardith's brow furrowed, looking at the men, mercenaries all. Five of them sat with Basil and Siefeld, but others, in groups of three or four, had wandered in and out to offer their captain praise, have an ale or two and receive orders.

Where were the men-at-arms so necessary to defend a lord's keep? Were there no unlanded knights at Basil's command?

The wench picked up a bucket. As she crossed the room, her destination obvious, Siefeld called, "What do you, Nora?"

The wench halted and the men stilled at their captain's shout. Briefly, Nora closed her eyes and took an almost imperceptibly longer breath. She turned to face Siefeld.

"Why, I water and chain the hounds, as is done each night at this time."

Siefeld scowled. "Be quick about it," he ordered.

Nora hurried to do her chore. As the hounds finished drinking, she called them to their collars, except one—a large male who appeared wary of the female human wearing his collar and stealing his sleeping place. Ardith stared up into his brown eyes, hoping he wouldn't take issue. He sniffed at the fur coverlet, then circled and curled up at her feet.

"Milady."

Nora had said the word so softly that, for a moment, Ardith doubted her hearing. But like a soothing potion, the respectfully uttered title eased her distress.

Ardith stared at the dog, pondering Nora's intentions. At the edge of her vision she could see Nora's skirts swirl about bare feet and exposed ankles.

"Milady?" Nora said a bit louder.

"Nora," Ardith whispered.

"Are you who they say? The Baron Wilmont's lady?"

"Aye."

"Stephen said the baron would come, yet Basil reclaims the keep. Will Gerard of Wilmont come?"

Dare she truthfully answer Nora? Basil and Siefeld seemed to believe Gerard would arrange the means of their escape. If she again voiced the opinion that Gerard would come for her and Daymon, as she had once to Siefeld, would Nora repeat the words to Basil?

Ardith nearly decided not to answer, but the hope in Nora's question proved too strong to resist. The hope in her own heart nearly strangled her answer.

"Aye. Very soon now."

"Nora!"

The wench spun on callused heel to heed the male shout. On her way across the room, Nora grabbed hold of Daymon, who'd wandered to the middle of the hall. She spun Daymon around. "Out of my way, brat," she scolded, and with a swat on the behind sent him scurrying toward Ardith.

The men laughed at what Ardith recognized as an act of kindness, sending Daymon well out of harm's way. Though the men now ignored the boy, who knew what entertainment they would seek later. Tucking a crying Daymon against her side, Ardith's elbow bumped the bucket of fresh water that Nora had left by the hearth, seemingly forgotten.

As Ardith struggled to keep her eyes open, Basil finally succumbed. Two men carried him up the stairs. One by one the other men either passed out, sprawled across the table, or left the keep to seek pallets elsewhere, until only Siefeld and two sober men remained awake.

Guards. Two men to watch over an exhausted woman and a helpless child.

Oh, Gerard. Please hurry.

Chapter Twenty-Two

Gerard had hoped to overtake Siefeld on the road. But at sunset, riding into Milhurst, he knew Ardith and Daymon must now be within the castle at Northbryre—if, indeed, Siefeld had taken them to Northbryre.

Through the throng of Milhurst's people gathering to gawk at the newly arrived trio, a stooped, gray-haired man elbowed his way to Gerard's side.

"Gerard, my boy," Sir William said with a smile, clasping Gerard's outstretched hand. "I did not expect you so soon." The smile faded. "But then, you are no longer merely the son of my old friend. My lord Baron, welcome to Milhurst."

"My thanks, William. You expected me?"

"Of course. I sent a messenger to Wilmont the very day that Basil arrived and retook Northbryre." He sighed. "A matter in which I must take some responsibility, Gerard. Most of Northbryre's men-at-arms were here at the time, training."

Gerard's relief at having correctly guessed Basil's whereabouts nearly buckled his knees. Basil might still hold Ardith captive, but not for long. "And the other Northbryre men-at-arms?"

William shrugged. "Probably dead."

"Why did you not attack?" Stephen asked angrily.

Eyes narrowed, William explained, "My duty is to defend Milhurst. 'Tis not within my authority to order an attack without permission from the baron, even to retake Wilmont lands. The most I could do was notify the king's sheriff, but the man has not enough men to attack a keep as well fortified as Northbryre. Nor would he anyway. The sheriff is firmly in Basil's pocket."

Gerard then related the story of the kidnapping of Ardith and Daymon to William.

After a long moment of silence, William said, "Then laying siege to the keep is not an option. Basil would use torture of the hostages to force a retreat."

"Nor can we attack directly," Gerard said. "I fear Basil would kill Ardith and Daymon when he realized the battle lost."

"By sly means then," William said, a frown forming.

"As much as I prefer honorable battle, in this case we are not dealing with an honorable opponent. I wish to speak with the men-at-arms from Northbryre. I need to know how many mercenaries defend the keep, and their habits."

William left to gather the men.

"Do we wait for Richard?" Corwin asked. To Gerard's questioning look, he said, "By now, Richard knows what has happened and where we are. I imagine he is riding hard to join us. The prospect of a fight with Siefeld would appeal mightily to Richard."

Gerard rubbed his eyes. In his single-minded rush to reach Milhurst, he hadn't given Richard a thought. Richard deserved a chance at Siefeld—but not at Ardith or Daymon's expense. Gerard would delay, nonetheless, because he suddenly realized how tired and completely unfocused he'd become since he'd learned of the kidnapping. Men could die if he misdirected them. Ardith and Daymon could die if he made a mistake.

"I wait for no one. We move as soon as we are rested and have a sound plan." Gerard put a hand on Corwin's shoulder. "Corwin, do you feel anything from Ardith?"

"Nay. Her terror has vanished and I feel no pain."

"You will let me know if that changes."

"Immediately, my lord."

Ardith watched two of the mercenaries haul another trunk from the upper floor and carry it outside. All day the men had scurried about the keep and yard, loading the wagons she'd seen lined up in the bailey when allowed outside for bodily relief.

She'd learned much today, listening to the grumbles of fighting men forced to perform menial tasks. Northbryre's men-at-arms and peasants had fled, leaving only a few serfs and the mercenaries to empty the keep. Basil intended to leave on the morn, flee to an ally, until the day appointed to board ship. With each passing hour, with each crate removed, Ardith's confidence in a quick rescue dimmed.

Siefeld had been right about Stephen's weakened condition. Unable to come after her himself, Stephen would send someone to alert Gerard. Gerard would then need time to gather men and supplies. Then he must track Siefeld. All would take time, too many days.

Somehow, somewhere, Gerard would rescue her and Daymon. Her duty was to keep them safe until Gerard could get to them.

As the mercenaries devoured the last meal of the day and proceeded to drink themselves into a stupor, Ardith noticed that, unlike last night, an older woman served the men. Nora had seemed to disappear, hadn't come into the keep all day. Nor had Ardith seen Basil, who most likely hid in his chambers.

She gently ran her fingers through Daymon's hair as he slept, with his head on her lap, and thanked God for the serfs' care. Despite Ardith's efforts to keep him close, Daymon had gotten underfoot and now sported a bruise on his cheek from a mercenary's rough shove. Afterward, the serfs glanced at Daymon whenever they passed through the hall, shooing him toward Ardith if he wandered into busy pathways.

A shadow fell over her. Ardith looked up to see Siefeld looming, a scowl on his face.

"Upstairs," he commanded, pointing to the stairway.

"Why?" Ardith blurted.

"Basil wishes to speak with you."

Wary, Ardith slowly removed the iron collar. She reached for Daymon.

"Leave the boy."

Foreboding coiled in her stomach. Ardith bit back the urge to protest, fought the desire to grab Daymon and run. Neither would do any good. With as much dignity as she could muster, she preceded Siefeld up the stairs. "The open door," he directed with a push at her shoulder.

Knowing Basil planned to leave the following morn, Ardith had expected the lord's chambers to be cleared of furnishings. Not so. Tapestries hung on the outer wall. Carpeting hadn't been rolled. Trunks remained in the chamber, as did a heavy oak table and two chairs. In the middle of the room stood the bed, the coverings in place. In each corner candles burned brightly.

Basil stood near the foot of the bed, a slight frown on his face, studying the dregs of whatever liquid he swirled in a bejeweled goblet. He looked up when she entered the room. His frown turned to a smug smile as he waved a dismissing hand. She heard the door shut as Siefeld left her to Basil's whims.

"Come, my dear, sit," he said.

"I prefer to stand."

"Close to the door? Do not be foolish. If you run from me, Siefeld would bring you back."

Ardith clutched her fur, steeled her courage and chose the far chair, keeping the table between her and Basil. "Siefeld said you wanted to speak with me."

"A few words only, to let you know the way of things." He put the goblet down, put his palms on the table and leaned forward. "I have decided that a woman of your kind would serve me better in my bed than chained with the dogs."

The words, confirming her suspicions, sent a chill down her spine. She pulled her right foot back and close in. Leaning slightly, she snaked a trembling hand toward her boot.

"You would find me an unwilling bedmate," she warned, amazed at the steadiness of her voice.

"You will please me. You see, how long the child lives depends on how well you perform your new duties."

Ardith flipped open the leather flap, touched cold metal. With sudden insight, she accused, "You never intended to hand us over to Gerard, but to kill both Daymon and me. How do you plan to board ship in Portsmouth without hostages to release?"

"'Tis but a ploy to lead him astray. Can you not imagine Gerard of Wilmont, scouring the area around Portsmouth, looking for a whore and bastard to rescue? Already a ship awaits me in Dover. By the time Gerard realizes he follows a false trail, I will be well on my way to Normandy."

Ardith wrapped her fingers around the dagger's hilt, feeling the metal warm to her hand.

Gerard stood next to Richard, who'd arrived at Milhurst an hour ago, inspecting the earthen berm surrounding Northbryre.

Chained with the dogs.

Nora's words thrummed in rhythm with his heartbeat. He tried to erase the pitiful picture the wench had drawn with breathless words, having run the leagues between Northbryre and Milhurst. He failed.

"All are ready," Richard whispered. "We await your order."

"After the next guard passes," Gerard whispered back.

Through the long afternoon, the plans for tonight's attack had been finally set. Only a misstep, an alarm sounded by a guard not disposed of, could upset the rescue.

William put a hand on Gerard's sleeve. "Though it pains me to do so, I feel it my duty to remind you that Henry wants Basil brought to London."

Gerard opened his mouth to protest, but William quickly continued. "Basil killed Diane, Henry's ward, during the escape from the Tower. Can you blame Henry for reserving the right to punish Basil? Take care, Gerard. God go with you."

Chained with the dogs.

Henry be damned. Given the slightest excuse, Gerard would ensure that Basil didn't live to see sunrise.

A mercenary strolled into view, walking the perimeter. He paused to look around, then continued his assigned rounds. Gerard glanced over his shoulder. Richard and Corwin stood near several men-at-arms who'd served at Northbryre and knew the keep well.

Corwin put a hand to his forehead. In a shaky voice, he said, "Gerard, I think we had best hurry."

Ardith's resolve faltered. Could she do it? Could she turn the situation around at the point of a dagger, take Basil as *her* prisoner?

She had no choice. To prevent rape, and eventually death for both herself and Daymon, she must take advantage of the opportunity presented.

Basil tilted his head, his obsidian eyes flashing. "But mayhap I have been too hasty. Mayhap I should let you live. Would it not be more satisfying to let Gerard have you back, knowing when he touches you that I have also touched you? How will he feel, I wonder, when he thrusts within you, to know that I have rutted in the same pathway?"

Ardith pulled out the dagger and pushed aside the fur.

Basil's eyes went wide, then he threw back his head and laughed. "So the kitten has a claw and means to scratch."

As she rose from the chair, the hours of lessons came flooding back—every move Gerard had demonstrated, every word he uttered in instruction. "I am prepared to do more than scratch. Shall we see how many pieces I must carve out of your hide before you realize that you are now *my* hostage?"

"Your hostage? Never!" he roared, and upended the table.

Ardith scooted out of the way as the pitcher and goblets flew toward her, the table landing on its top.

"My hostage," she repeated, circling, mindful of her footing and stance. She watched him closely, noting the position of his hands, his feet. She saw the lunge coming in the quick shift of his eyes.

Sidestep. Slash upward.

The blade sliced across Basil's upper arm, through layers of silk and linen, drawing blood. The coppery scent turned her stomach, but she stood her ground.

Basil looked down at his arm, disbelieving. "Bitch. I will see you in hell for this."

"Mayhap, but you will be there long before me."

Now what? Ardith wondered. Gerard had taught her how to wound, even kill, but not what to do with a prisoner. She needed a rope, something to tie him up with, but how did one truss up the goose while holding the carving knife?

Ardith pointed to the chair. "Sit," she ordered. "Wait. Remove your girdle first and drop it."

Favoring his wounded arm, Basil unwound the silk from his waist and dropped it to the floor.

"Well done, Basil. Now sit."

"You will not get away with this."

"Pray I do. Pray Siefeld is willing to follow orders for the sake of your life. Put your hands behind the chair."

"I cannot. My arm."

"Shall I cut it off?"

Sweet Mother, had she really threatened to slice off his arm? Damn Gerard. He hadn't warned her how this sense of power could loosen one's tongue. She picked up Basil's girdle and circled the chair.

On one end of the girdle she made a loop and a half-knot. She slipped it over his hand and pulled tight. As she prepared to complete the knot, Basil pulled forward and shot out of the chair. Jerked forward, Ardith grabbed the chair, but it didn't support her weight. She fell to the floor.

Basil loomed, grinning menacingly. He picked up the chair and tossed it into the corner. The crash echoed through the room. He stepped toward her. Ardith rolled away, but not fast enough to avoid a vicious kick that connected with her hip. She stifled a groan, unwilling to give Basil the satisfaction.

"Whore! She-demon!"

Ardith scrambled to hands and knees. Trapped between Basil and the bed, she squelched the panic to look for an escape route. She tried to crawl toward the door, but couldn't move quickly enough.

He grabbed hold of her plait, snapping her neck backward. She lashed out with the dagger, striking his leather boot, doing no damage. His hold tightened on her hair, bringing tears to her eyes.

"Not so haughty, now, are we?" he jeered. "Drop the dagger, whore."

Ardith tightened her grip. To let go of the dagger meant surrender, a price too high.

"Nay? Still want to fight? I will take the fight out of you. I will show you who is lord here." He released her hair and kicked her buttocks, sending her sprawling. She reached forward to brace against the fall, but her head hit the floor. Her vision blurred, bright points of light swarming before her eyes.

"The boy. The little bastard," Basil hissed and turned toward the door. "Siefeld!"

"Nay!" she screamed, and managed to stand.

"Then drop the dagger," he ordered.

"Come and take it, coward," she shouted. "Does your lackey fight all your battles? Can you not take a dagger from a woman? Did Siefeld kill Lady Diane because you could not?''

His face reddened. His fists curled. She should be quaking, but she remained poised in a defensive stance, her mind now amazingly clear, despite the lump forming on her head.

Basil's sudden, furious lunge came as no surprise.

Her hand wielded the dagger with no conscious command. The Lion's Tooth bit through fabric and flesh, scraped bone, until the blade sank well within Basil's body.

On an inward gasp of air, he swayed forward and caught hold of her sleeve, knocking them both to the floor.

A quick inspection of the hall told Gerard everything he needed to know. The mercenaries who sat at the table scrambled for weapons. Siefeld stood on the third stair, drawing his sword. Daymon's small head peeked up over one of the hounds.

No Basil. No Ardith.

Richard and the soldiers rushed the mercenaries. Corwin shot past Gerard toward Daymon.

Gerard turned on Siefeld. "Where is she?"

Siefeld looked about the hall. "What difference? You bring so few against so many. Surely, you did not hope—"

Stephen's shout cut short Siefeld's words as the second wave of soldiers flooded into the hall.

"Where is she?" Gerard shouted over the echoing ring of sword striking sword, the cries of attackers and defenders.

"Enjoying my lord Basil," Siefeld spit out.

Gerard moved toward the stairs, sword at the ready.

Richard appeared at his side, an arm shooting out to block Gerard's progress.

"He is mine, Gerard," Richard said in a deadly voice, staring upward at Siefeld.

With a fury Richard advanced, stair by stair, his sword flashing in such quick strokes that one strike blurred into the next. Gerard climbed the stairs behind the combatants as Siefeld retreated under Richard's onslaught. After they'd passed by it, Gerard opened the door to the lord's chamber.

On the floor lay Basil, sprawled on his belly, blood pooling around his body. Ardith knelt beside Basil, her white night rail smeared red, staring at her blood-covered hands.

Evidence of a hard-fought battle met his gaze: an overturned table, a broken chair in the corner, a toppled candle stand. The candles had scattered across the floor, the tiny flames licking at the edge of the carpet.

"Ardith?" he whispered.

She looked up, her body trembling. A drop of blood eased down her upper lip from her nose amid a bruised face. Tears streamed down her cheeks. "Oh, Gerard," she wailed before her eyes rolled upward.

Gerard dropped his sword and caught her. As much as he wanted to rest for a moment, hold Ardith close until his pulse ceased racing, he couldn't. Smoke had begun to curl from where the candle flame consumed carpet.

He ripped away the tattered, bloodied night rail. He ran his hand over her face, touching a lump on her forehead. Her nose had begun to swell, but wasn't broken. Around her throat circled a red ring—chafing from the iron collar. A large bruise marred her hip. He found no wound to account for the blood on her night rail. The blood must all be Basil's.

Gently, he picked her up, put her on the bed and wrapped her in a coverlet. He bent to retrieve his sword. Basil groaned, his head turning.

Basil's eyes locked on to Gerard's. "Mercy," he begged, choking on the thickening smoke.

Gerard looked down at the man who'd caused so much pain to so many people, who'd dared to treat Ardith as a bitch and chained her to a wall.

With the swipe of his hand, Gerard toppled another candle stand, flinging another dozen lit candles across the carpet.

Chapter Twenty-Three

Ardith screamed.

Gerard sat down on the bed, flipped back the coverlet and enfolded her into a sheltering embrace. "Hush, love," he soothed. "'Tis a dream, only a dream."

She clutched at his sherte and hid her face against his chest. Helpless to strip away her memories or control her dreams, he merely held her until the sobs subsided.

He brushed aside a wisp of hair, uncovering the lump turned purple. The head injury had scared him witless, especially when she'd lain still for so many hours. Though she woke to a nightmare, he rejoiced that she woke at all.

"Where are we?" Ardith asked.

"Milhurst. In the sleeping chamber."

"Daymon?"

"Sleeping in the hall between Stephen and Richard."

She fingered the clean night rail. "Not mine," she said.

"William's daughter's. Yours was…ruined."

Ardith's body stiffened, her hand trembled.

He tightened his hold. "Do not think about it, love. 'Tis over. You are safe here."

"About time you woke," Corwin grumbled from the arch between the hall and sleeping chamber.

Gerard resented the intrusion, but motioned Corwin to enter as Ardith turned to the sound of her twin's voice. He let go of her, swallowing the lump in his throat when she reached out to invite Corwin to her.

Corwin pulled her to her knees and hugged her hard. "Damn, but you gave me a scare. Not nice, Ardith."

"Really? When?"

"Four days ago, just before dawn, I woke up shaking and sweating so much I thought I was dying. Then you did so again, just before we entered Northbryre."

"Four days ago? That was when...where were you?"

"Camped north of Oxford."

"Oxford? So far?"

"Aye." Corwin tilted her head back and frowned. "The lump on your head is purple, your eyes have turned black. Your nose looks like a squash." He touched her nose. "Can you breathe through that thing?"

Outraged, Gerard got up, meaning to throw Corwin out of the room for making light of Ardith's injuries. Then Ardith gave a short laugh. Gerard stood still as her fist hit Corwin lightly on the arm.

"Only you would be so blunt," she complained.

"Have I ever been otherwise?"

"Nay, never."

"Hungry?"

Ardith sat back on her heels, rubbed her stomach. "I could eat a piece of bread, and a little water."

The change in her mood slammed into Gerard's gullet. Ardith preferred Corwin's company. And why not? Corwin wasn't responsible for her pain, the horror of her kidnapping, the humiliation she'd endured. With Corwin, she could smile.

"I will have food sent," Gerard said, moving to leave.

"Gerard," she said softly.

He stopped, looked back at the sorely abused woman he loved, but couldn't help.

"My thanks," she said.

For what? he wondered. For fetching food? For carrying her out of Northbryre before the flames consumed the keep?

Better she should scold him for coming too late, for allowing the kidnapping, for placing her life in jeopardy.

Without a word, he left the room.

"Get under the covers," Corwin ordered. "If you catch a chill, Gerard will have my head for my neglect."

Propped by bolsters, covers drawn up over her legs, Ardith wondered at Gerard's curtness. From experience, she knew he hated tears, yet he'd held her while she wept, offered the safe haven of his arms while she struggled with the vision of plunging into a river of blood.

"He is angry," she concluded.

"Gerard? Nay, merely tired, I would think. He sat in here all night watching over you. I doubt he slept, as he has not slept for more than moments since you were taken."

Ardith shook her head. "Something else eats at him."

Corwin shrugged. "He still has much to deal with, not the least of which is the message he must send to Henry about Basil's death. Then there is putting Northbryre back to rights. The fire destroyed the upper floor and Basil with it. Ah, Ardith. You are shaking. I should not be reminding you of your ordeal."

Ardith leaned back against the bolster and closed her eyes. Forever she would remember Basil's look of utter disbelief as he keeled over. And the blood, all the blood. But a fire?

"I remember no fire."

"'Tis no wonder. Gerard said that when he entered Basil's chamber, he found you both lying on the floor, the carpet aflame from a toppled candle stand, the room filling with smoke. He had time to rescue only you."

Ardith put fingertips to temples, trying to remember.

A serving wench walked in with the bread and water.

"Why not try to eat then go back to sleep," Corwin coaxed. "We can sort all this out for you later."

* * *

"What are you doing out of bed?"

Ardith turned, carefully, to face Gerard as he entered the sleeping chamber. "Walking," she said with a smile.

"You should rest."

"I rested all day. Do not make me get back in bed yet."

"How do you feel?"

"Wonderful," she lied. Her head ached, her nose hurt, her legs shook. "I know I must look a fright—"

"Not as bad as Corwin suggested."

"He tends to be honest with me, sometimes painfully so. I need not see my face to know the bruises have colored."

Gerard strode across the floor. With a gentleness she thrilled to whenever he touched her thus, he cupped her face so tenderly the bruises seemed to heal.

"To me, you will always be beautiful," he said, then brushed his lips across hers in a kiss that fluttered against her mouth like butterfly wings.

He stepped back, an odd, almost sad smile on his face. "But come, I forget my purpose. I came in to see if you wished your evening meal now."

She wanted another kiss, a fervent mesh of mouths. She wanted his arms around her in a firm and loving embrace. But Gerard held himself aloof.

He wanted her to eat.

There was so much she wanted to tell him, *had* to tell him. Maybe Gerard had the right of it, that some things were better said after she'd regained her strength, when she could speak of Basil without horror rising to choke off the words.

Resigned, but unwilling to relinquish his company, she asked, "Could I take my meal in the hall? I really do not care to lay abed any longer, and I have not seen Daymon."

"He asked to see you. I kept him out, so as not to disturb your sleep."

"Daymon has been through much these past days. He needs to see me, to make sure I am well. 'Twould ease his mind if I came into the hall."

Gerard's gaze flickered downward. "I did not think to bring any of your gowns."

Ardith fingered the sleeve of the borrowed night rail. "Mayhap William's daughter would let me use one of her gowns."

"Nay. Much too short."

"Oh," she said softly, her spirit sinking.

Gerard looked about the room, then strode over to a trunk and flipped open the lid. He dug through the clothing. "This will do," he said, pulling out a woolen cloak.

Ardith glanced about the floor. "My boots?"

"Being cleaned. They are still wet. These probably won't fit well, but will keep your feet warm."

Ardith slid her feet into the felt slippers he pulled from the trunk, stood immobile as Gerard wrapped the cloak around her shoulders. The strangest sensation of repeating the past washed over her, brought unwanted moisture to her eyes as he whisked her from her feet in strong arms.

"Ardith?"

"Oh, Gerard." She gulped.

She wrapped her arms around his neck and clung tightly as he walked over to the bed and sat down.

"Why do you cry?"

"You will think me silly," she said, wiping away the tear.

"Mayhap, but tell me anyway."

"I had this sudden vision of the day we first met, me hiding behind a tapestry in night rail and mantle, you carrying me from the hall to my pallet."

"You were hurting then, too."

"Not so much from my injury as from a broken heart." She sighed, remembering the forlorn little girl, curled on her pallet, crying her eyes out. "When you found me, I had just overheard our fathers talking. Baron Everart had offered a betrothal and my father refused, saying I was damaged. While I mulled over his meaning, you came along, swept me from my feet and carried me away. After

you left the chamber, I asked Elva about the betrothal. She
said I should be happy to escape the clutches of the young
lion—you. I was not happy. I think I cried half the night.
I could not even eat the piece of boar Corwin brought to
me. Young as I was, I am sure I loved you even then.''

"Why did Elva lie? Did she hate me so much?"

"Not you, but the first Baron Wilmont," she said, then
told him of the incident in the woods when Elva had tried
to sacrifice a lamb. "Something snapped in her mind. She
confused me with herself and her lost child, and you became Wilmont, yourself and yet your grandfather. She saw
her past repeating and tried to change the outcome."

His hold tightened slightly. "Ardith, about Elva..."

"I know she is dead, and I will mourn, later. She tried
to stop Siefeld, Gerard. Though her love was selfish, she
did love me as her own, enough to give her life in my
defense."

After securing his hold, Gerard rose from the bed to carry
her from the chamber. "I think it time we ended this talk
before we ruin your appetite."

"I doubt that, Gerard. I could eat an entire boar. I am,
after all, eating for two."

That stopped him in his tracks.

"Are you sure?"

"Two days after you left for Manchester, my disposition
turned surly and my stomach shunned food until midday.
Aye, Gerard, I am sure."

He kissed her forehead. "Food, then. Enough for two."

That was all he had to say? Food for two? After so many
months of hoping and anguish, did he feel no joy, no sense
of completion? Blessed Mother, at this point, she would
even welcome his declaration of arrogant male pride in having proved his virility!

Milhurst shared so many similarities with Lenvil that Ardith felt at home. The central fire pit glowed, surrounded
by rocks. A small dais graced the far end. Even a tapestry
hung in the corner.

"Where is everyone?" Ardith asked, noting the lack of people she'd expected to see.

"William and Richard herded the captured mercenaries over to the sheriff of Hampshire's keep. They should return soon. Corwin and Stephen are preparing the wagons taken from Northbryre for a trip to Portsmouth. Daymon is with them."

"Stephen is here? I worried about him. He was badly wounded when—"

"His pride keeps him on his feet," Gerard cut off her words, signaling a servant. "He insists on going along to sell Basil's belongings. The funds will be used to repair Northbryre."

"Corwin told me about the fire. I do not remember it."

"You need not remember. Eat."

Hot meat, turnips and carrots, enfolded in gravy, steamed from a trencher of thick, almost white bread. The heavenly aroma tickled her nose and stirred her stomach. Goodness, she *was* hungry. She looked up to thank the servant who'd placed the ambrosia on the table.

"Nora!" Ardith said, delighted.

"Milady," Nora answered, smiling, dipping into a curtsy.

"I wondered where you had gone. I missed you. Gerard, we must reward this girl in some way. She risked Siefeld's wrath to bring me water, and she watched over Daymon."

"You did not tell me that," Gerard scolded Nora, then told Ardith, "She also ran the leagues between Northbryre and Milhurst, hoping to stir Sir William into action. Her news helped us plan our attack."

"And I have my reward, milady," Nora injected. "The baron has released my family from serfdom, given my father a hide of land. 'Tis more than I ever dared hope."

After Nora left, Ardith put her hand over Gerard's. "You are a generous overlord, Gerard. My thanks."

"I reward loyalty where deserved," he said, then scowled. "Are you about to cry again?"

"Nay, Gerard," she said, blinking back the moisture he'd seen in her eyes. "I am about to eat."

And she did, with vigor, calling for a second trencher as Richard came into the manor. "You have a visitor, Gerard. The sheriff wishes a moment of your time."

Gerard raised a questioning eyebrow.

A wry smile spread across Richard's face. "A matter of recompense. It seems Basil convinced the sheriff that King Henry had granted Basil a pardon, but Basil felt it prudent to leave England and visit his lands in Normandy. He then promised the sheriff a handsome sum to arrange for a ship out of Dover. The sheriff insists on repayment of the funds he gave to the ship's captain to stand ready."

Gerard looked about to explode. "Did you tell the sheriff what he could do with this absurd claim?"

"Aye. But he felt you might be more sympathetic to his plight than I."

"Like hell."

"I tried to tell him, Gerard, but he would not listen. He begs the indulgence of an audience, my lord baron."

Gerard grumbled under his breath all the way out the door.

"How fare you, my lady?" Richard asked, seeming totally unconcerned about the storm about to break outside. He tilted his head and teased, "Corwin was right. Can you breathe?"

"Not only can I breathe, I can smell, thank you."

The shouting began. Gerard's voice boomed, though Ardith couldn't understand the words. Then rose another voice, high and shrill, threatening.

"You are not to fret, Ardith," Richard ordered gently. "Gerard will chew on the miscreant for a while, then spit him out. The sheriff is supposed to serve the interests of the crown, not any one baron. He should have verified Basil's claim of pardon before doing his bidding. By the time Gerard is through, the sheriff of Hampshire will understand his duty."

The lesson didn't last long. Gerard strode into the manor as though nothing untoward had occurred. William followed, smiling and shaking his head.

"I am suddenly quite ravenous," Gerard said, sliding onto the bench. "Is there any stew left?"

"You did not invite the sheriff to dine?" Richard asked with mock incredulity.

William responded, "Gerard invited the sheriff to seek his payment from Basil, if he could find anything but bones left—"

"William," Gerard said in a soft, very low voice, the admonishment clear.

William bowed to Ardith. "My apology, my lady. We will not speak of it again."

Gerard pulled the covers up as Ardith curled into his side, laying her head on his shoulder, tossing an arm over his chest. Within moments, she slept.

Milhurst's healer had proclaimed Ardith's injuries mild. After his anger at Corwin for teasing Ardith had subsided, Gerard realized Corwin's lack of concern confirmed the healer's opinion. If Ardith were in any danger, Corwin would fret.

Even Ardith had tried to ease his mind. He suspected her head ached, that her legs weren't as steady as she pretended, yet she'd put on a brave face for his benefit.

Her face would heal. She'd suffered no injury to threaten the babe she carried, at least no visible injury. The thought still gnawed at him that Basil might have raped Ardith, but he knew he would never ask, would never say a word that might force Ardith to relive the horror.

Ardith had tried to kill Basil for whatever offense he might have committed.

No one else knew. He hadn't really realized himself until he'd removed her boots and found the dagger missing. He'd been so intent on removing Ardith from Northbryre he hadn't given thought to the weapon used to cause Basil's blood to pool around his body.

Basil's chamber had burned, the flames hot and bright. Surely, nothing remained of Basil but ashes, nothing remained of the dagger but a puddle of metal.

Everyone accepted the story that Basil had died in the flames. They had no reason not to, for it was, for the most part, the truth.

Ardith woke as Gerard got out of the bed. She stretched in the languorous movement of a body well rested, having slept soundly for long hours. She opened her eyes to see Gerard pull on his boots. He still looked tired, as though he hadn't slept at all.

From out in the yard, she heard men shouting, the jangle of harnesses and the impatient pounding of hooves. She tossed aside the coverlet.

"I had hoped you would sleep a while yet," Gerard said.

"I would like to say farewell to Corwin."

"I will send him in."

"Nay, Gerard. I would rather go out."

"You feel strong enough?"

"I feel quite well," she answered honestly.

"Then I will send Nora in to help you dress. The women were supposed to find you a suitable gown."

Nora burst into the chamber almost the instant Gerard had left, carrying a work gown. "'Tis not fancy, milady. The linen is a bit rough."

Ardith smiled. She changed quickly, accepting the help Nora seemed to think necessary. The gown fitted loosely, but Ardith paid it no heed. The felt slippers, however, flopped on her feet, making walking difficult.

"Nora, do you know where my boots are?"

"They dry by the fire. Shall I fetch them?"

"Please."

The boots were warm, and cleaner than they'd been in weeks. She stood and wiggled her toes in the soft hide. But as she headed for the archway, she stopped. An odd feeling of dread urged Ardith to privacy.

"Nora, would you go out and tell Gerard not to let Corwin leave until I get there?"

After Nora scooted out, Ardith pulled the gown up above the boot top. She lifted the flap and put her hand on the hilt of the dagger. From the moment her fingers touched metal, Ardith knew the Lion's Tooth wasn't her own.

Though nearly identical to the dagger Gerard had given her those many months ago, Ardith knew this dagger wasn't the blade she kept in her boot. This wasn't the dagger she'd pulled on Basil to keep him at bay, used to slash his arm, plunged into his body.

This dagger belonged to Gerard. It boasted a slightly thicker hilt and added weight.

So where was her dagger?

Ardith sat very still as the answer formed. If Gerard had retrieved her Lion's Tooth, he'd have returned it to her boot. But she'd driven the dagger deep into Basil, and there it still must be, at Northbryre, amid the smoldering ruins.

Gerard knew she'd killed Basil, yet he'd told everyone Basil perished in the fire. As hard as she tried, Ardith couldn't remember a candle stand toppling, or flames or smoke.

Had Gerard started a fire in Basil's chamber to cover the murder? The thought chilled her but made sense. King Henry had ordered Gerard to return Basil to London, alive, for punishment. Without intending to, by killing Basil she'd disobeyed a direct order of the king of England—and put Gerard in the awkward position of explaining Basil's death.

Since only she and Gerard knew how Basil had died, the false tale might be believed, even by the king.

Ardith slid the dagger into her boot. For now, she would let Gerard have his way in this. She wouldn't breathe a word of the truth to another soul.

Chapter Twenty-Four

Ardith focused on Meg's welcoming wave, though she noted the changes about the manor. In the two weeks since her kidnapping, the soldiers had repaired the armory. The only outward signs that anything untoward had happened here were the three fresh graves, one of them Elva's.

Gerard planned only to stay the night, to gather personal belongings and officially make Pip the steward. Tomorrow they would begin the journey to Wilmont, but if Gerard continued at the pace he'd set for the past few days, Ardith wondered if she would see Wilmont by first snowfall.

His coddling and continued remoteness were becoming irksome in the extreme.

She'd accepted his preoccupation as necessary while he toured the Northbryre lands, taking pledges from the men-at-arms and accepting into his protection those peasants who chose to remain under his lordship.

She'd buried her disappointment in Gerard's lack of desire for intimacy, understanding his reluctance to do anything that might irritate her injuries or endanger their child. But she'd healed well. So said Milhurst's herbswoman. So said the fading bruises on her face. And so said the nagging voice of the inner woman who longed for her mate to give over his brooding for an overdue coupling.

Ardith reined in and waited for Gerard to dismount and

assist her descent. As he reached up to grasp her waist, Ardith smiled down. She ran her fingertips over his arms, leaning forward slightly, deliberately arching her back. Her breasts, swollen from pregnancy, tips hardened for want of his touch, protruded nicely, she thought.

The deepening green of his eyes, the direct stare at her shamelessly thrust bosom, confirmed his interest and solidified her purpose. Farther, she leaned, wrapping her fingers around his neck as he pulled her against the wide expanse of his chest. Ever so slowly she slid along the length of him. As the aching female part of her rubbed against the growing male part of him, she wiggled. He held her there, suspended for several delightful moments before lowering her to her feet.

His mouth a mere breath from her ear, he whispered, "What are you about, scamp?"

"Indulging a...whim, my lord."

A slow, definitely indulgent smile spread across Gerard's face, until a male voice hailed the baron. Ardith turned to see who dared interfere. A man, liveried in the colors of the king's guard, approached from the direction of the stables.

The guard bowed to Gerard. "My lord baron, by authority of Henry, king of England and duke of Normandy, I am ordered to bring you to London forthwith, to explain the death of Basil of Northbryre. We will strike out at once."

Very aware of the slight tremor of Ardith's body, Gerard said flatly, "We will do no such thing."

"I have orders to place you under arrest if I must. I would prefer you come peaceably," the guard warned.

"And I will, given another day," Gerard countered. "I have no quarrel with Henry's order to appear at court. Surely, you can grant me what remains of today to set my affairs in order, to see my lady and son properly settled."

Gerard waited for capitulation as the guard assessed the odds of successfully arresting a baron, glancing first at

Richard, who stood with hand on sword hilt beside Gerard, to the armory filled with men-at-arms.

The guard bowed. "Until the morrow, Baron Gerard," he relented, and strode off.

"What the devil does Henry want?" Richard asked.

"A report."

"I thought you sent him one from Milhurst."

"One that apparently did not appease his curiosity." Gerard waved a hand to silence Richard's next comment. "I expected a summons. Henry will want to hear every gruesome detail."

Gerard tucked Ardith under his arm and headed for the manor. His wish to see her safely ensconced at Wilmont before dealing with Henry had proved short-lived. That Henry wasn't satisfied with the written report came as no surprise, but the urgency of the demand for an audience suggested that Henry was suspicious of the accuracy of the report. A suspicious Henry was a dangerous Henry.

"Gerard?" Worry lines flanked her eyes. Her mouth was turned downward in a grim, tight line.

"You are not to fret, Ardith. This jaunt to London merely delays our plans a bit."

She suddenly stopped and slipped away from his side. "Jaunt," she said tersely. "Gerard, riding into London under the threat of arrest by the king's guard, commanded to an audience with Henry is not a jaunt. As for our plans, this surely changes them."

He shrugged in what he hoped appeared a gesture of a man at ease. "Granted, I had planned to continue on to Wilmont, summon Father Dominic, get married, then watch my wife grow fat with child."

The hard set of her mouth eased. "And now?"

"Now, I must take time to appease Henry."

"So we leave on the morn for London."

"We leave on the morn for the abbey in Romsey, where you and Daymon will stay under the watchful eyes of Queen Matilda, while I go to London. Do you think we might hit a streak of good fortune and find a priest visiting the abbey? We could get married—''

"I would rather go with you."

"Nay, there is no reason for you to come. Henry will ask a few questions. I will give him the answers he wants to hear. Henry glories in this kind of tale and merely wants to hear the tale from me."

Ardith took a long breath. The tale was so bloody and repellent. She would forever remember Basil's threats, see his body lunge forward and his disbelieving eyes widen, as the dagger slid into his body. But to tell the tale aloud, even to Gerard, had proved impossible. The words had stuck in her throat every time she tried.

"Ardith, do not think about Basil. He died in the fire, an unfortunate incident neither of us could have prevented."

Ardith nodded her understanding. Gerard would perpetuate the story he'd invented. And maybe the king would believe it. And maybe, by the grace of God, both she and Gerard would escape whatever punishment Henry thought to mete out for disobeying a direct royal order.

Gerard's finger nudged her chin. "If I remember rightly, my scamp was about to make a lewd suggestion before the guard interrupted."

The scamp had fled, the playful mood banished by this latest threat to their happiness, their very lives if Henry decided to...no, not their lives, not if all the stories she'd heard were true. Henry preferred torture, and maiming, and dismemberment—and wasn't above using innocents when meting out punishment.

"Make love to me, Gerard," she said softly, with no attempt to hide the plea in her voice.

He was silent for a moment. "We will not harm the child?"

Ever the protector! "Nay, nor the mother. You have held yourself from me these past days, Gerard. Do so no longer. I need you."

"As I need you," he whispered. Gently, he lifted her into the cradle of his arms and carried her into the manor.

Several days later, Gerard crossed his arms in an effort to contain his impatience as King Henry thrummed his fingers on the chair's arm. Henry's urgent summons hadn't guaranteed an immediate audience, or, when finally granted, a brief one.

Gerard wanted an end to this inquisition, to forever put behind him the frustration and fears that had churned his innards while dealing with Basil.

He wanted peace. He wanted to return to the abbey, fetch Ardith and Daymon and take them home to Wilmont. He wanted to get married and get on with his life.

"Surely, Gerard, you have more to offer us," Henry finally stated.

"What more would you like to know, sire?" Gerard held his temper in check. "We have spent the greater portion of the morning discussing the events leading to the deaths of Basil of Northbryre and Edward Siefeld. You have a written statement from Sir William at Milhurst. You have questioned Richard. I know you are disappointed in being robbed of Basil's punishment, but given the choice of saving Ardith or saving Basil, I chose Ardith, and by God, sire, would do so again."

Henry sighed, a foreboding sound. "We had hoped our vassal still loyal. We would hear the truth, Baron Gerard."

Gerard knew his only course in this battle of wills was to stay the one he'd set upon. Any other endangered Wilmont, his brothers, or Daymon. Or Ardith.

Gerard's eyes narrowed. "My king knows me the most loyal of his barons. Indeed, Wilmont has served the kingdom well and full when others have rebelled."

"Yea, and we listen and want to believe. But you lie to us, Gerard, and that we cannot forgive."

Henry waved a hand at the door. A guard opened it. Into the audience room stepped the sheriff of Hampshire, a smug look on his face. At the king's feet the sheriff placed a small pillow, upon which rested a Lion's Tooth—blackened, the jewels missing, but one of the famous pair nonetheless.

Ardith's dagger.

"Do you, Gerard, deny this blade?"

He would be utterly foolish to deny the dagger, even suspecting what was to come. "To what purpose, sire? We both recognize the dagger as a Lion's Tooth, one of the pair your father gifted my grandsire."

The king rose from his chair. "Our sheriff brings us this blade, having taken it from Basil of Northbryre's charred remains. One would wonder how it got there."

"Not by my hand."

"Then Richard or Stephen, perhaps."

"Nay, sire. Neither Richard nor Stephen entered Basil's chamber, and there are witnesses aplenty to confirm their whereabouts during the rescue. This blade did not take Basil's life. He was breathing and awake when I left him. He died in the fire."

"*Someone* put this dagger into Basil. And you, Gerard, are the most likely."

Gerard didn't need to close his eyes to see Ardith kneeling over the body, staring at the blood covering her hands, or to remember the anguish on her face when she'd looked up as he entered the chamber.

Ardith hadn't killed Basil, merely wounded him. And if Ardith had drawn the blade, she'd believed her life, or maybe Daymon's, endangered. To tell Henry the truth meant subjecting Ardith to a royal audience and inquisition at the very least, and to Henry's sadistic brand of justice. Not even if facing all the rings of hell would Gerard breathe Ardith's name in connection with Basil's death.

Henry picked up the dagger, studied it. "We have seen this blade many times, have marveled at your skill. Give us reason to doubt our eyes. Reach into your boot and pull out a Lion's Tooth."

He couldn't, of course. He'd put it in Ardith's boot while at Milhurst.

After an eternal silence, Henry demanded, "We would have your confession, Gerard."

Gerard said nothing.

"Then we will let our baron ponder this mysterious appearance of his dagger in the body of Basil of Northbryre. And he may do so while under guard in White Tower."

At the queen's soft touch on her shoulder, Ardith turned from the unshuttered window in Matilda's chamber. "Watching the road will not help," Matilda said. "Gerard will arrive when he arrives. Patience, my dear."

"I have been patient for three weeks, Majesty. He promised to return for Daymon and me in two."

Matilda smiled. "Do you tire of my company?"

"Nay, never, Majesty! 'Tis just that—"

"You begrudge the separation." With a wink, Matilda added, "I understand."

Ardith glanced at Lady Ursula, who sat at the loom, half expecting a negating comment. But Gerard's mother never missed a beat in her weaving, until Daymon, who played on the rug near his grandmother's feet, let out a squeal when his block tower toppled over. Ursula looked down at the tot and a hint of a smile touched her lips before she resumed her chore.

Ardith longed to tell Gerard of the drastic change in his mother, due to Matilda's perseverance. But as the weeks passed, and Ardith's gravid condition with an as yet illegitimate child became more obvious, she couldn't help fear Lady Ursula's budding tolerance would end.

"Come sit," Matilda commanded with a gentle push on Ardith's shoulder. "You must not hold Gerard responsible for neglecting you. 'Tis Henry who prolongs the separation."

Ardith sank into a chair. "Have you had no word from the king?"

"Nay. Henry is yet upset with me for my last letter. I implored him to give Bishop Anselm another hearing. He punishes me by withholding his letters."

Through the open window drifted the unmistakable sounds of a mounted group of men approaching the abbey. Ardith bolted to the window, leaning out to see a large knight at the head of the column, helmed and armored, on a black destrier, turn the corner around the building and disappear from sight.

"At last," she declared, and headed for the door, but stopped when the queen cleared her throat. With a quick curtsy, Ardith asked permission to leave the royal presence with a terse, "By your leave, Majesty."

Matilda chuckled and waved a dismissing hand. "Go, but have a care. You carry my godchild."

Ardith placed a hand on her stomach, a slow smile spreading across her face. "I will, Majesty," she promised, and managed to check her steps down the hallways and stairways leading to the abbey door.

As she stepped outside, her smile faded. Dismounted, removing his helmet, stood Richard. Beside him, taking the helmet from Richard's hand, Thomas nodded in her direction. From the grim set of Richard's face, and Thomas's mere presence, Ardith knew something horrible had happened to Gerard.

"Have the men fed and rested and ready to leave on the morrow," Richard said to Thomas, then turned to address Ardith. "That is, if Ardith can be ready on such short notice."

"I can be ready to leave within the hour if you wish."

As Thomas and the soldiers moved off, Richard shook his head. "There is no need for such haste." He paused, then said, "I am sorry, Ardith. I wish I brought better news."

"What has happened?" she asked urgently.

"The audience with King Henry did not go well. Henry has ordered Gerard imprisoned in White Tower."

"The Tower!"

"Do you remember, at Milhurst, when the sheriff of Hampshire sought restitution from Gerard, and Gerard told the sheriff to seek payment at Northbryre?"

Ardith nodded.

"The sheriff took Gerard at his word and searched the rubble for anything of value. He found little treasure, but came across the means of revenging Gerard's harsh words. The sheriff found Basil, and stuck in the body, a dagger easily recognizable as belonging to Wilmont. The sheriff took the dagger to Henry, who accused Gerard of lying about Basil's death. My stubborn brother would neither produce the dagger from his boot nor change his tale of Basil's death."

Her heart sinking, she commented, "So Henry locked Gerard in the Tower."

"Nay, not locked. Not even Henry would dare that. Gerard stays in an upper chamber sometimes used by the king as a residence and lacks for no bodily comfort."

"You have spoken to him, seen him?"

"I have. He wants me to take you and Daymon to Wilmont, where we can protect you, if necessary. He wants you two far from Henry's reach if the trial goes badly."

Ardith placed a trembling hand on Richard's arm. "When is the trial?"

"In two days."

Two days. Only two days in which to reach White Tower in London and somehow convince Gerard to tell Henry the truth—or do so herself.

"Richard, Gerard did not kill Basil."

With a sad smile and gentle voice Richard said, "So I surmised. If Gerard had killed Basil, he would confess the deed, give Henry a full account. Since he stands fast on his tale, that means he protects someone, and there was only one other person in that bedchamber, someone who might have had access to a Lion's Tooth."

Ardith took a deep breath to keep steady under the rush

of relief. Richard knew the truth, but didn't condemn. Maybe the king wouldn't either, once he heard why she'd drawn the blade.

"You must take me to London," she said with more conviction than she felt.

Richard shook his head. "'Twould do no good, Ardith. You could stand in the middle of Westminster Hall and shout a confession and no one would listen because they would choose not to hear, much less believe. You see, this is no longer a matter of one man's death. The Norman barons are gathering in London, all of them prepared to stand witness to Gerard. If Henry does not yield, if he chooses to punish Gerard, the barons will rebel. Indeed, Henry could face an armed challenge to the throne."

Ardith's fingers tightened on Richard's sleeve. "They would declare war against Henry?"

Richard nodded. "They would welcome the excuse."

She struggled to understand the Norman barons' reasoning. Failing, she asked, "If they wanted war, why did they not stand witness for Basil at his trial? And after, when Basil tried to unite them, why did they refuse?"

"Basil had neither the resources nor leadership ability to wage a war against Henry. Gerard does."

Ardith released Richard's sleeve and walked a few steps away, her head whirling with visions of men dying on a battlefield, their senseless deaths her fault. If she hadn't killed Basil...but what was done was done. Now, she had to thwart the barons. Somehow, she had to get someone to listen to reason. Starting with Gerard.

She turned to face the first challenge to accomplishing the impossible—convincing Richard to take her to London.

Chapter Twenty-Five

Ardith held her head high and followed Richard, who elbowed his way through the throng. The nearer they came to the doors of Westminster Hall, the thicker the crowd.

She hadn't had time to change her travel clothes and mantle, dust-coated and deeply creased from the ride from Romsey. As soon as they'd arrived, they'd heard about the trial taking place. The king had sent for Gerard and was about to pass judgment.

They entered the hall to the echo of a war cry, the Lion of Wilmont's roar. "Enough!"

Into the sudden, chilling silence, King Henry chided, "We are pleased you have decided to break your silence, Gerard. Is there aught you wish to confide?"

Ardith could see the king on his throne at the far end of the hall. Kester stood near him. She couldn't see Gerard, but found Corwin among the crowd, looking harried.

Desperate to reach Gerard, she put her hand on Richard's back. He understood her silent message, for he again shoved people aside. Some thought to take exception, until realizing his identity and allowing him to pass.

As they neared the front of the hall, she bumped against Sir Percival. He nodded a greeting before she swept by. Several men whom Ardith recognized as barons milled about the stairs, many clad in chain mail, among them Charles, earl of Warwick.

Only a fool would not realize the barons' intent. Only the ignorant would not feel the tension pulsing through the hall. King Henry was neither ignorant nor a fool.

Gerard's voice rang angrily. "I have listened for as long as I can bear to this vainglorious sheriff! Think you he brings you this tale out of loyalty or sense of justice? Bah! And you, sire, to whom I am pledged, to whom I have given both my loyalty and friendship, have chosen to believe him. Well, despite his pretty phrases, and despite your wish for revenge, I tell you, sire, Basil died as a result of the fire in his bedchamber."

Richard broke through the crowd, stopping at the edge of the small circle of space surrounding Gerard.

Obviously, Gerard had decided to flaunt his position, and did so with customary flare. A wide band of highly polished gold kept his shoulder-length hair in place. He'd donned a courtly dalmatica of red silk shot through with gold, trimmed with wide strips of intricate embroidery at neck, cuff, and hem. A thick gold chain twice circled his waist.

In the full regalia of his Norman heritage, and at the height of his fury, Gerard looked utterly magnificent, without doubt a man of considerable wealth, and considerable physical strength.

He flung a bejeweled hand into the air. "Twenty good men of my own rank have spoken for me. By the rules of your court, sire, I have done all I must to prove my innocence."

"And the dagger, Gerard, the Lion's Tooth of Wilmont?"

Ardith held her breath as Gerard answered, "If, indeed, its point found itself within Basil's flesh—a fact that carries some doubt, I might add, brought to us by a corrupted sheriff—it did not kill Basil. He was alive when I left him on the chamber floor. That he could not crawl out before either the smoke or flame got to him is no fault of mine."

Stunned, oblivious to all but Gerard's statements, Ardith moved toward him. He must have heard because he turned and stared, the anger leaving his face, his arms opening.

She glided into his embrace. Gerard's arms, strong and comforting, wrapped around her like a cocoon. With his chin resting atop her head, she knew he was glaring at Richard, but his revelation still whirled in her head.

She hadn't killed Basil, only wounded him. He'd died, but not at her hand. No mortal sin stained her soul, no punishable offense hung over her head.

Gerard whispered harshly, "What the devil are you doing here? I told Richard to take you to Wilmont."

"Do not be angry with Richard. I gave him little choice."

"Threatened to come alone, did you? To what end?"

Ardith suddenly realized how inappropriate were her actions before the court. She tried to back away, but Gerard held tight. Not, she was certain, from affection but to keep their words private.

"I came to confess, if I had to," she whispered back. "I thought I killed Basil, Gerard. I truly did."

"But I told you how Basil died. Did you not believe me?"

"I remember no fire, Gerard. All I remember is the look on Basil's face—and the blood, so much blood. I thought you started the fire in an effort to protect me from Henry's retribution. You *can* be overbearingly protective, my love."

"And so my little warrior planned to stand before the king and admit her misdeed. A truly noble gesture, scamp, but not necessary. I do not need to be rescued."

From the dais came the sound of a loudly cleared throat. "Baron Gerard, if you are nearly done coddling this woman, might we proceed?" King Henry chastised.

Gerard's spine stiffened at the rebuke, yet he kept his voice hushed. "Go back to Richard."

Reluctantly, Ardith released him and obeyed.

Gerard watched her walk back to stand between Richard

and Corwin, who'd somehow made his way to the front, then turned back to face the king, wishing he could have eased Ardith's fears. But Henry stubbornly focused on the dagger, and unless the king let go of the fixation, the possibility of bodily harm existed within Gerard's remaining options. War he did not want, though many were willing to take up arms for his cause. But war against Henry had been Basil's hope, and even in death Basil's wishes must not be granted.

The last option also involved a fight, a fight Gerard hoped to avoid but would instigate if necessary.

Ardith's appearance had made the task of ending this trial more urgent. She'd drawn Henry's attention, if only briefly, an attention that must be quickly diverted. "If I coddle her, sire, 'tis because she carries my heir. Surely, of all the men in this kingdom, *you* would know how irrational a woman in gravid condition can be."

Snickers erupted among the crowd. King Henry, however, was not amused.

"Filled her belly, did you?" Henry snapped. "Have you married the chit yet?"

"Your summons to court forestalled the nuptials, sire. I would like nothing better than your permission to return to Wilmont and legitimize my child."

"We would be lax in our duty to the good citizens of England should we turn loose a murderer."

"For the last time I tell you, with God as my witness, I did not kill Basil of Northbryre."

"The dagger, Gerard. Who—"

"What matter! Is this not *my* trial? Do *I* not stand accused of Basil's murder? Do you, sire, or do you not take my word as good and true?"

The king rose from his throne. "Nay, we do not!"

Silence prevailed for the space of several heartbeats.

Quietly, but clearly, Gerard risked more than he cared to think about as he announced, "Then you leave me no choice. As is my right, I place my fate in God's hands and demand ordeal by combat."

The king's eyes narrowed. "You dare challenge your king?"

"I would not presume, sire. Choose your champion."

Men shifted from foot to foot. Swords scrapped against chain mail. Low murmurs underscored the unease.

The king glanced about the hall. "Choose. Hah! Those on whom we might bestow the honor have stood as your witnesses!"

A circumstance Gerard hoped would work in his favor. If no one of equal rank and skill would accept the challenge, Henry would be forced to accept the opinion of the court and dismiss the murder charge.

The king's gaze shifted from baron to chain mail-clad baron, then outward toward the crowd. He shouted, "Baron Gerard has demanded ordeal by combat. The prize is Wilmont! Who among you will champion your king for such a holding?"

Silence hung like a suffocating shroud. Not a sound, not a breath stirred the air. Gerard risked a glance at Charles of Warwick. A slight twitch of his ally's mouth, a suppressed urge to smile, raised Gerard's hopes of a peaceful and successful end. Just as Gerard thought he'd won, a low voice pierced the bubble of silence.

"I might consider it, sire, if Ardith of Lenvil is part of the bargain."

Gerard instantly recognized Sir Percival's voice. He spun around to watch that bear of a man come forward. "I had planned to bargain with her father before I knew of Gerard's interest. I would still have her."

"But she carries Gerard's brat!"

Percival shrugged a massive shoulder. "Along with a sack of coins the church will have it."

Charles stepped forward. "Unacceptable, sire. Though Percival is Gerard's equal in arms, he is not in rank. Ordeal by combat demands—"

Henry waved him to silence. "We know the law, Charles."

From a fold in his royal robes, the king produced a rolled parchment, tied with a red ribbon. Gerard suddenly realized what the king was about to do, and how well the monarch had been prepared for all circumstances.

Henry held up the scroll. "Behold. These lands, taken by the crown from Basil of Northbryre for acts of treason, we do hereby give to our champion, Percival, for his good service this day. There are, we assure you, sufficient hides of land within this bequest to qualify him for full rank of tenant-in-chief—a baron."

Henry tossed the scroll toward Percival, who nearly tripped on the stair to catch it. "As for the wench, we declare Ardith of Lenvil a royal ward, her fate to be decided by the outcome of the ordeal. Arm yourselves and seek peace with God. The ordeal begins at the last bell of none."

Ardith started to follow Gerard out of the hall, but was quickly stopped by Richard on one side and Corwin on the other.

"He has no time for you, Ardith," Corwin said. "He has but an hour to confess his sins and don his armor."

"He will need help donning his hauberk," she argued.

"Warwick went with him. Damn it, haven't you caused enough trouble without distracting him now?"

Ardith stopped straining against the men's hold. Corwin had the right of it. 'Twas her fault Gerard faced ordeal by combat. Had she not come to Westminster, had Percival not seen her, he might not have had the foolish notion to challenge Gerard and the trial would have ended as Gerard had obviously planned.

Richard tugged on her arm. "The crowd leaves for the yard. Come, let us find a place to watch unhindered."

As they left the hall, two of the palace guards fell into step behind them, bringing a lump of dread to Ardith's throat as the full impact of the events to come hit her. If

Gerard should lose this contest, she would go to Percival. Wilmont would go to Percival. And knowing Gerard, he would fight till his dying breath to prevent both.

"Richard," she choked out. "The earl of Warwick said Percival was Gerard's equal in arms. Is he?"

"'Twas Percival who gave Gerard the scar he wears on his neck. Not deliberately, of course, but aye, they are well matched."

The hour until midafternoon seemed to Ardith the longest of her life. After only a few minutes the tension caused her feet to move, and with her moved Corwin and Richard and the guards. She gave up her pacing.

Shortly before the appointed hour, the combatants came out of the palace, both fully armored in chain mail, coif and helm. Both carried broadswords. Neither man paid heed to the crowd as they made their way to the center of the yard.

Still as statues they stood, facing each other, the tips of the broadswords pointed downward. Ardith jumped when the abbey bell pealed, calling the monks to prayer. Gerard shifted his grip on the pommel of his sword. The last note of the bell's call had not yet faded when the first clang of sword on sword pierced the air.

Ardith forgot to breathe. Mantle crushed in her hands, she watched the contest with rising dread. She'd observed Gerard practice his skills many times. She'd seen him instruct his men. She'd even become accustomed to the hard-fought contests between Richard and Gerard. Unlike those friendly battles, these men fought in earnest.

His face set in grim determination, Gerard circled Percival, who only turned his body to keep Gerard in sight. Swords clashed once, twice, each man testing the other for arm length and strength. At times Gerard met Percival's slicing blows with an upraised blocking sword, at other times he danced out of reach.

Then Percival turned once more, his face coming within clear sight. Though slightly obscured by the surrounding mail coif and the nose guard of his helm, his expression made Ardith gasp. His eyes shone with the wildness of a trapped beast, whose only chance for survival was to tear apart whoever stood in the way of escape.

The sword strikes came faster, heavier, louder, Gerard taking the offensive, pressing Percival back. Both hands wrapped around the pommel, Percival hauled back and swung around up over his head, then down, as though to slice Gerard down the middle from head to toe. Gerard sidestepped, ducked under and rammed Percival's midsection with his shoulder. Percival landed on his rump in a cloud of dust. Gerard stepped back several paces, his chest heaving.

"Damn you, Gerard," Richard harshly muttered his thoughts aloud. "Not now, you fool. It won't work."

Ardith tore her attention from the field to look up at Richard. Anger glinted from his eyes, anger at Gerard.

"Richard?"

Without taking his focus from his brother, Richard said, "Gerard will lose if he persists."

She grabbed Richard's sleeve. "How so?"

Richard flung a hand toward where Gerard stood, still panting, waiting for Percival to gain his feet. "He thinks to spare Percival a wounding blow. He purposely gave quarter when he should have used the opening Percival allowed. Should Gerard make such a mistake, Percival will not hesitate to take advantage."

The sound of steel striking steel snapped Ardith's attention back to the field of combat. Percival had not only regained his footing, but pressed Gerard hard with a chain of sweeping, punishing strokes.

Gerard retreated under the onslaught, blocking each blow but not regaining the upper hand. Then blade scraped along blade, a flash of sparks running the edges until hilt met hilt. Chest to chest, swords pressed between chain mail–covered bodies, they pushed and shoved until, with a twist and bend, Gerard spun away.

Again, Percival swept his great broadsword over his head. But this time Gerard met the downward blow, deflecting the stroke with an answering force of power. Then, with the finesse and grace Ardith had seen so many times before, he attacked with a flurry of quick, powerful blows so typical of his style.

Percival lost his grip, his sword flying from his hand toward the onlookers. The crowd roared. Was it over? Had Gerard won? The hope vanished as Percival charged like a man obsessed, slamming into Gerard like a battering ram.

Gerard dropped his sword, stumbling backward. The men tumbled to the ground and rolled in the dirt, each trying to pin the other to the earth without success, each keeping the other from within fingertip's reach of the swords. Percival lost his helm. Gerard lost a gauntlet. Both dripped with sweat from the exertion.

Again, Richard muttered instructions to a man who couldn't possibly hear. "Get off, man, get off."

Percival seemingly took the advice, and as he swayed on his feet he reached toward his girdle—and withdrew a dagger.

Horrified, Ardith said aloud, "Percival has a dagger."

"Of course he has a dagger," Richard said sarcastically. "So does Gerard. He has but to draw it, which he had best do right quickly."

Ardith bit her bottom lip, watching Percival advance on Gerard, who didn't reach for his dagger because he didn't have his dagger. His Lion's Tooth rested against her ankle, sitting useless to Gerard within the pocket of her boot.

She quickly scanned the crowd. All watched Percival take step after menacing step toward Gerard, dagger poised for a downward jab. With her mantle concealing her actions, Ardith bent and withdrew the blade. She must, somehow, return the weapon to its rightful owner.

But how? Dare she call Gerard's name and toss the weapon onto the field? Or would the distraction herald his doom?

Percival lunged. Gerard grabbed Percival's upraised wrist with both hands, twisting and bending, flinging Percival around and down. But he didn't stay down.

Then Ardith spotted the rock, a mere arm's span away from Gerard's foot. Of all the silly visions to have, the rock suddenly looked like a turnip, resting on a mound of hay, ready for slicing. Ardith shifted her grip, prayed for a true aim, and quickly brought the weapon from under her mantle to over her shoulder and let fly. It flew true. To the astonished gasp of the crowd, to Corwin's spat profanity—and quite to her own amazement—the dagger landed point down within inches of her target, closer to Gerard than aimed.

The dagger's sudden appearance didn't seem to surprise Gerard. He never looked away from Percival as he reached down and snatched up the weapon.

Gerard moved like lightning, catching Percival off guard. Within moments, Percival lay on his back, dazed, the point of Gerard's dagger indenting the vulnerable underside of an up-tilted chin. The crowd erupted into cheers.

In a voice strong enough to be heard above the throng, Gerard commanded, "Yield or die."

Though Ardith didn't hear it, Percival must have yielded, for those nearest the combatants cheered louder as Gerard rose and shoved the dagger into its rightful sheath.

It was over. Gerard had won. No one, not even the king, dared question the outcome.

Wiping the sweat from his brow, Gerard turned to where he now knew Ardith must be standing. And there she stood, between Richard and Corwin, her fingertips touching her mouth as she stared at him. Apprehensive. Vulnerable. The lady who'd just thrown a dagger halfway across a yard, at the precise moment he'd needed it, in the most convenient spot imaginable, had the temerity to look vulnerable.

Hellfire, he didn't know whether to give her a tongue thrashing for her mere presence in Westminster, beat her

soundly for interfering in the contest or get down on bent
knee to thank her for, just possibly, saving his life.

Gerard shook his head. He'd already scolded, would cut
off his own hand before touching her harshly, and as for
getting down on bent knee, he'd be a fool to do such a
thing. Already she could bend his will to her own. To let
her know she held that power would invite disaster. He'd
have no peace.

Peace. He could have it now. He was free. Free of Basil
and the murder charge. Free to marry Ardith. Free to go
home and spend his days listening to her laughter and spend
his nights in her loving embrace.

He started toward her, but only made three steps before
King Henry called his name. Gerard turned to look at
Henry, who stared pointedly at Ardith.

"As we recall, Gerard, you have not as yet done us
knight's service this year. Our sheriff informs us of poach-
ers in New Forest. Forty days should be plenty of time in
which to clear them out, should it not?"

Clearly, Henry had guessed who'd wounded Basil. Hellfire, anyone who'd seen Ardith throw the dagger had
guessed.

Gerard decided not to contest Henry's last effort to ex-
tract a measure of punishment. "Are you requesting all of
Wilmont's duty, sire, or just mine?"

"Only your services are required. You *will* leave within
the hour, will you not?"

Gerard nodded his agreement, then resumed his course
toward Ardith. She inspected him from head to toe, and
only when she'd determined nothing broken or bleeding or
askew did she hold out her hands.

"You are unharmed?" she asked with deceptive calm.

"Nary a scratch," he lied, resisting the urge to rub his
hip where Percival's knee had driven chain mail into skin.
There would be a nasty bruise, but Ardith needn't know.

"'Tis my fault the king sends you away."

"His pettiness sends me away." Gerard brought her right hand to his lips. "That was quite a throw, Ardith."

"I saw Percival draw his dagger...and I had yours...I was not sure if I could, or if I should..."

"I am very glad you did."

She finally smiled.

He tasted that smile, briefly. A longer kiss would lead to more and he couldn't afford the time. He would *not* give Henry any excuse to extend the service.

"Richard, take her to Wilmont. I will return as soon as I dare."

Her head snapped up. "Gerard, first we must go back to the abbey. I left Daymon with the queen and your mother."

Gerard shook his head, emphatically. "You may send someone to fetch Daymon, but you are not to go yourself."

"Gerard, I...oh, very well, if you insist."

"I do." He looked pointedly at Richard, then Corwin, then back to Richard. "You are to take her straight to Wilmont. And damn it, Richard, she had best be there when I arrive."

Forty days.

Forty days of chasing a poacher who would soon be replaced by another peasant who couldn't understand why he couldn't hunt in the king's forest. Forty long days of mud, and bad food, and a sheriff who was either incompetent or had been ordered by Henry to assure Gerard served the full service. Forty endless days and nights of missing Ardith—and wondering what mischief she'd been up to.

On a hunch, he'd stopped at Lenvil. According to Corwin, who now rode at Gerard's side, Ardith had left Wilmont only once, to visit Harold during a particularly bad spell. Richard had accompanied her along with half the castle guard.

She'd sent for Daymon. Lady Ursula had returned with the boy and Ardith hadn't sent her back. Gerard had trouble believing his mother had become protective of Daymon, but he would wait to see for himself before passing judgment.

As the castle came into view, Gerard caught sight of a flash of yellow on the battlements. Ardith.

"Care to race?" Corwin asked as they passed over the bridge that marked the starting point of many such races.

The spark of yellow moved to the corner stairway, then disappeared from sight. Knowing what was bound to happen, having witnessed Ardith's greeting for Corwin too many times for comfort, Gerard slowed to nearly stopped.

"Nay, not today."

As soon as the heavy gates began to open, Ardith squeezed through, and as he knew she would, she started to run.

Corwin chuckled. "My God, look how she has swollen! You had best marry her soon, Gerard."

She tore off the veil that insisted on flying into her face, sending fabric and circlet to the ground. Her heavy braid bounced, coming apart. She had most definitely swelled, leaving no doubt that she was well and truly with child.

And still she ran.

Gerard growled, "Get up there, man. Slow her down before she falls. That is my heir she is leading with."

Corwin gave him a puzzled look, then sped off. Gerard pulled to a halt and dismounted. He would let Ardith have her greeting with Corwin, but this time he wouldn't watch. He turned to inspect a perfectly good girth strap.

He heard Corwin's horse slow, heard the twins' voices, then the sound of hoofbeats again. Confused, he looked up to see Corwin galloping toward the castle, leaving Ardith standing in the road.

A brilliant smile spread across her lovely face. She took a step forward, and then another, before breaking into a run.

For me. My God, for me.

Every wish he'd ever hoped to have granted paled to

insignificance when compared to the sight of Ardith scampering up the road. To him.

She runs to me!

Love and tears glistened in her azure eyes. Awed beyond imagining, Gerard dropped the reins and opened his arms. She hit him hard, throwing her arms around his neck, covering his face with wet, warm kisses.

"Welcome home, my lord. What took you so long? I have watched for you for days and days. Are you well? Have you—"

He swept her off her feet and silenced her with a kiss. He'd come home, as he'd never come home before, and might never come home again.

* * * * *

Four Bright New Stars!
Harlequin Historical™ launches its *March Madness* celebration with these four exciting historical romance debuts:

THE MAIDEN AND THE WARRIOR
By Jacqueline Navin
A fierce warrior is saved by the love of a spirited
maiden bride.

LAST CHANCE BRIDE
By Jillian Hart
A lonely spinster finds hope in the arms of an embittered
widower.

GABRIEL'S HEART
By Madeline George
An ex-sheriff must choose between revenge or the feisty
socialite who has stolen his heart.

A DUKE DECEIVED
By Cheryl Bolen
A handsome duke falls for a penniless noblewoman
whom he must marry in haste.

Look for all four books from four fabulous new authors
wherever Harlequin Historicals are sold.

Harlequin®
Historical

Coming in August 1997!

THE BETTY NEELS
RUBY COLLECTION

August 1997—Stars Through the Mist

September 1997—The Doubtful Marriage

October 1997—The End of the Rainbow

November 1997—Three for a Wedding

December 1997—Roses for Christmas

January 1998—The Hasty Marriage

COLLECTOR'S EDITION

This August start assembling the
Betty Neels Ruby Collection. Six of the
most requested and best-loved titles have
been especially chosen for this collection.
From August 1997 until January 1998,
one title per month will be available to avid
fans. Spot the collection by the lush ruby red
cover with the gold Collector's Edition banner
and your favorite author's name—Betty Neels!

Available in August at your favorite retail outlet.

HARLEQUIN®

Look us up on-line at: http://www.romance.net   BNRUBY

DEBBIE MACOMBER

invites you to the

HEART OF TEXAS

Join Debbie Macomber as she brings you the lives
and loves of the folks in the ranching community
of Promise, Texas.

If you loved Midnight Sons—don't miss
Heart of Texas! A brand-new six-book series
from Debbie Macomber.

Available in February 1998
at your favorite retail store.

Heart of Texas by Debbie Macomber

Lonesome Cowboy	February '98
Texas Two-Step	March '98
Caroline's Child	April '98
Dr. Texas	May '98
Nell's Cowboy	June '98
Lone Star Baby	July '98

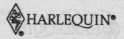

HARLEQUIN®

HPHRT1

KEY TO MY HEART

Unlock the secrets of romance just in time for the most romantic day of the year— Valentine's Day!

Key to My Heart
features three of your favorite authors,

Kasey Michaels,
Rebecca York
and Muriel Jensen,

to bring you wonderful tales of romance and Valentine's Day dreams come true.

As an added bonus you can receive Harlequin's special Valentine's Day necklace. FREE with the purchase of every *Key to My Heart* collection.

Available in January,
wherever Harlequin books are sold.

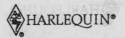

PHKEY349

**Make a Valentine's date
for the premiere of
◆ HARLEQUIN® Movies
starting February 14, 1998 with**

Debbie Macomber's
This Matter of
Marriage

on **the movie channel** tmc

Just tune in to **The Movie Channel** the **second Saturday night** of every month at 9:00 p.m. EST to join us, and be swept away by the sheer thrill of romance brought to life. Watch for details of upcoming movies—in books, in your television viewing guide and in stores.

If you are not currently a subscriber to The Movie Channel, simply call your local cable or satellite provider for more details. Call today, and don't miss out on the romance!

*100% pure movies.
100% pure fun.*

◆ HARLEQUIN™
Makes any time special.™